W9-CKH-206

HOUSE
of
ECHOES

HOUSE
of
ECHOES

Barbara Erskine

G.K. Hall & Co. • Chivers Press
Thorndike, Maine USA   Bath, Avon, England

This Large Print edition is published by G.K. Hall & Co., USA and by Chivers Press, England.

Published in 1996 in the U.S. by arrangement with Dutton Signet, a division of Penguin Books USA Inc.

Published in 1997 in the U.K. by arrangement with HarperCollins Publishers Ltd.

U.S.	Hardcover	0-7838-1851-3	(Core Collection Edition)
U.K.	Hardcover	0-7451-5393-3	(Windsor Large Print)
U.K.	Softcover	0-7451-3850-0	(Paragon Large Print)

The text of this Large Print edition is unabridged.
Other aspects of the book may vary from the original edition.

Set in 16 pt. News Plantin by Juanita Macdonald.

Printed in the United States on permanent paper.

British Library Cataloguing in Publication Data available

Library of Congress Cataloging in Publication Data

Erskine, Barbara.
    House of echoes / Barbara Erskine.
        p.   cm.
    ISBN 0-7838-1851-3 (lg. print : hc)
    1. Large type books.
    2. Inheritance and succession — England — Essex — Fiction.
    3. Married women — England — Essex — Fiction.
    4. Family — England — Essex — Fiction. I. Title.
[PR6055.R7H6   1996b]
823'.914—dc20   96-31680

JOSS GRANT'S FAMILY TREE

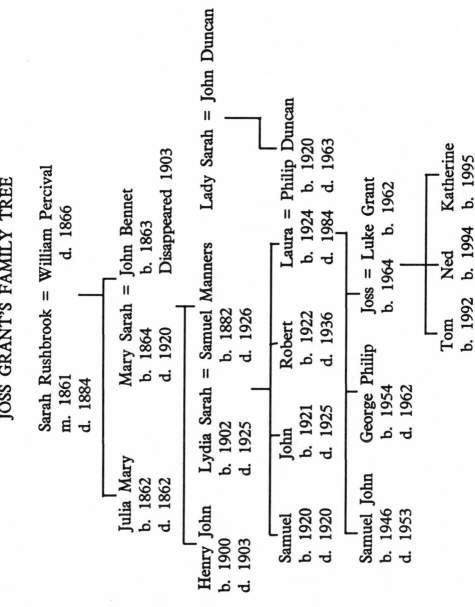

PROLOGUE

A beam of cold sunshine finds its way through a knothole in the wood of the shutters and strays across the dusty boards. Laserlike, it creeps from right to left until it reaches the flower lying in its path. One by one, in the spotlight, the petals fall open, their thin creamy whiteness already edged with brown.

In the silence the skirt skimming over the boards makes no sound; the footsteps from the past are quiet.

With no ear there to hear them the echoes in the house are silent.

CHAPTER 1

Had she really not wanted to know?

Joss put her foot down and accelerated into a bend.

Or had she been afraid of the truth?

"Are you sure you don't want me to come with you?" Before she left home, her husband, Luke, reached in through the open window and put his hand over hers as it rested on the wheel. On the seat beside her was the gazetteer and the file with the copy of her birth and adoption certificates and the note of the address. Belheddon Hall. She had glanced up at him and shaken her head. "I must do this alone, Luke. Just this first time."

The gate, hidden behind the yews and laurels, had not been opened for a long while. The wood was damp and swollen and slimy with lichen. It caught on the untrimmed grass as she pushed it back, and it hung open behind her as she stepped out onto an overgrown path that appeared to lead into an area of woodland. Pushing her hands down into her pockets, she walked cautiously forward, feeling half guilty, half exhilarated as the wind whipped her hair into her eyes. The woods around her smelled of rotting leaves and beech mast, bitter and sharp with early autumn.

Somewhere near her a pheasant crashed out of the undergrowth with an explosion of alarm calls and she stopped, her heart thundering under her ribs, staring around. As the frightened bird flew low through the trees and out of sight, the silence returned. Even the cheerful rustling of the leaves overhead died away as the wind dropped. She stared around, straining her ears for some kind of sound. Ahead, the path curved out of sight around a stand of holly trees, their glossy leaves almost black in the dull afternoon light, their berries shocking in their abundant redness.

The holly bears a berry as red as any blood.

The line from the carol floated through her head. She gazed at the trees for a moment, strangely reluctant to walk any farther, the hairs on the back of her neck prickling as she became aware suddenly that eyes were watching her from the thicket on her left. Holding her breath, she turned her head.

For several seconds she and the fox stared at each other, then he was gone. He made no sound, but the space he had filled beneath the old hawthorn bush was empty. She was so relieved she almost laughed out loud. Whatever thoughts had raced through her head at that moment, they had not included a fox.

With a lighter heart she stepped forward, aware that the wind was once more blowing strongly in her face, and two minutes later she rounded the corner near the holly bushes to find herself on the edge of an overgrown lawn. In front of her stood the house.

It was an old gray building with gabled roofs and mullioned windows, the plastered walls covered in ivy and wisteria and scarlet Virginia creeper. She stood quite still, staring. Belheddon Hall. Her birthplace.

Almost on tiptoe, she crept forward. Internal shutters gave the windows that faced her an oddly blind aspect, but for a moment she had the strangest feeling that she was being watched from somewhere behind those shutters. She shivered and turned her attention firmly to the porticoed front door that looked up the long tree-lined drive leading out of sight, presumably to the front gates. Where once there had been gravel there were now knee-high thistles and ragwort and windblown rose bay.

She sniffed. Emotions she didn't know she had been harboring seemed to be welling up inside her: loss, grief, loneliness, disappointment, even anger. Abruptly, she turned her back on the house and gazed down the drive, rubbing her eyes with the back of her hand.

She spent a long time wandering around the overgrown gardens and lawns, exploring the lake with its perimeter of reeds and bulrushes and weeds, and the stable yard and coach houses that lay through the archway at the side of the house.

Her shoulders hunched against the wind, she tried the front door and the back, both locked and bolted as she had known they would be, and she stood at last on the terrace at the back of the house looking down toward the lake. It was a wonderful house, wild, deserted, locked in its dreams of yesterday. With a sigh, she turned and stared up at the blind windows. It had been her home if only for a few months, and presumably the scene of whatever unhappiness had made her mother give her away. It was in her blood and it had rejected her.

It was for Tom she was doing this, she had reflected wryly as she drove through the network of quiet North Essex lanes. Tom. Her baby son. Until she had held him in her arms and gazed into that small, crumpled red face, so like his father's, she had been content to leave her origins a mystery.

She had been happy and secure with her adoptive parents. She was special after all, a chosen child. Her daydreams about her real parents had been vague and stereotypical, her mother in turn princess, parlor maid, poet, painter, prostitute. The choices and permutations were endless, harmless fun. One day she would search for the truth, but if she were honest she knew she had put off looking for fear that the truth might be dull. It was not until she had looked down at Tom and known what it was like to hold her own baby in her arms that she realized she had to find out not just who her own real mother was, but how and why she had been able to give away her daughter. Between one minute and the next, vague curiosity had become burning obsession.

At first it was too easy. Her mother, it appeared from the records, was Laura Catherine Duncan, née Manners, her father, Philip George Henry Duncan, deceased. He had died seven months before she was born. She was born at Belheddon Hall, in Essex, on June 21, 1964.

Alice and Joe, her adoptive parents, long prepared for this moment, had tried to persuade her to go to one of the agencies that track down families for adopted children but she had said no, this was something she wanted to do for herself. Even if her mother no longer lived at Belheddon Hall, she wanted to see it, to explore the village where she was born, to see if she could feel her roots.

On the map, Belheddon appeared as a small village on the coast of East Anglia on the border between Suffolk and Essex. Surprisingly remote, it looked north across the broad expanse of water where the Stour Estuary met the North Sea, some five miles from the small town of Manningtree.

She had hoped for something more romantic than Essex, the West Country perhaps, or Scotland, but her brief to herself had been strict. She was not going to prejudge anything or anyone. She was keeping an open mind.

Her mouth was dry with nerves as at last she drove into Belheddon and pulled up outside the single small shop, its window anesthetically lined with yellowing cellophane. Belheddon Post Office and Stores. She closed her eyes as she put on

13

the hand brake and turned off the engine, surprised to find that her hands were shaking.

On the cold pavement a scatter of dead leaves
cartwheeled past the car. The sign above the door
swung violently backward and forward in the
wind as, climbing stiffly out, Joss glanced round.
It had been a long journey. If she had pictured
the whole of Essex as a suburban wasteland ir-
revocably merged into North East London, she
couldn't have been more wrong. The drive had
taken more than two and a half hours from Kensington, where she and Luke lived, and for at
least the last hour it had been through deep country.

Ahead of her the street was empty of both cars
and people. Straight at this point, it ran between
two lines of pretty cottages before curving away
across the village green toward the estuary. It
was only a small village — no more perhaps than
a couple of dozen houses, a few thatched, two
or three timber-framed, the last spires of wind-
swept hollyhocks standing sentinel in their gardens. There was no sign of a church.

Taking a deep breath, she pushed open the
door of the shop, which was to her surprise a
great deal more sophisticated than she had expected. To her left the window of the small post
office was enclosed behind piles of postcards and
stationery and racks of sweets; to her right she
found herself facing an attractive and well stocked
delicatessen counter. The woman serving behind
it was small, plump, perhaps some sixty years
old, with wispy white hair and piercing gray eyes.
Reaching with a plastic-gloved hand into the dis-

play for a lump of green cheese, she glanced up at Joss and smiled. "I won't keep you a moment, my dear."

The woman in front of Joss in the queue succumbed to her curiosity and turned around. Tall, with dark hair escaping from a knotted head scarf, and with a weather-beaten face that spoke of years living within reach of the cold east wind, she gave Joss a friendly grin. "Sorry, I've been buying up the shop. Won't be two ticks now."

"That's all right." Joss smiled. "I actually came in to ask if you can direct me to Belheddon Hall."

Both women looked surprised. "It's up by the church." The woman in front of her had narrowed her eyes. "It's all closed up, you know. There's no one there."

Joss bit her lip, trying to master her disappointment. "So the Duncans don't live there anymore?"

Both women shook their heads. "It's been empty five years at least." The woman behind the counter shivered theatrically. "Spooky old place." Wrapping the cheese deftly in some plastic wrap, she slipped the parcel into a paper bag. She glanced up at her customer. "There you are, my dear. That will be four pounds ten pence altogether. My husband and I have only had the shop since eighty-nine." She smiled back at Joss. "I never knew the people up at the hall."

The other woman shook her head. "Nor I. I believe old Mrs. Duncan who used to live at the schoolhouse was a relation. But she died a couple of years back."

Joss pushed her hands down into her pockets.

Her sense of letdown was acute. "Is there anyone who might know what happened to the family?"

The postmistress shook her head. "I always heard they kept to themselves at the end. Mary Sutton, though. She would remember. She used to work up at the Hall. She sometimes acts a bit ga-ga, but I'm sure she could tell you something."

"Where could I find her?"

"Apple Cottage. On the corner of the green. With the blue gate."

The gate was stiff and warped. Joss pushed it open and made her way up the narrow path, dodging between overhanging thistles, downy with blown silk. There was no bell or knocker on the door, so she rapped with her knuckles. Five minutes later she gave up. There was obviously no one at home.

Standing at the gate, she stared around. Now that she had walked a little way out of the village street she could see the church tower partially concealed by trees on the far side of the green. And the Hall was somewhere beside it.

Leaving the car where it was, she began to walk across the grass.

"So, do you like our little church? It's thirteenth century, you know." The voice behind her made her jump as she leaned thoughtfully on the lych-gate, staring up the path, which disappeared around the church.

Behind her a tall, thin man in a dog collar was propping his bicycle against the hedge. He saw her glance at it and shrugged. "My car's

16

in dock. Something wrong with the brakes. Anyway, I enjoy cycling on these lovely autumn afternoons." He had seen the pensive woman as he turned out of New Barn Road. Coming to a stop, he had watched her for several minutes, impressed by her stillness. As she turned now and smiled at him he saw that she was youngish — late twenties or early thirties perhaps — and attractive in a quirky sort of way. Her hair was dark and heavy, cut in a bob with a fringe across her eyes — eyes that were a vivid Siamese-cat blue. He watched as his bicycle subsided into the nettles and gave a humorous shrug. "I was just coming to collect some books I left in the vestry. Would you like to see around before I lock up?"

She nodded. "I was actually looking for the Hall. But I'd love to see the church."

"You can reach the Hall through the gate over there, behind the yews." He led the way up the path. "It's empty, alas. Has been for many years."

"Did you know the people who lived there?" The intensity of the gaze she fixed on him disarmed him slightly.

"I'm afraid not. It was empty when I came to the parish. It's a shame. We need a family there."

"Is it for sale then?" She was dismayed.

"No. No, that's the problem. It still belongs to the Duncan family. I believe Mrs. Duncan lives in France now."

Mrs. Duncan. Laura Catherine. Her mother.

"You don't have her address, do you?" Joss could hear her voice shaking slightly. "I'm a sort of relative. That's why I came."

"I see." He gave her another quick glance as they had reached the church. Taking out a key, he unlocked the door in the porch and, ushering her into the dim interior, reached for the light switches. "I'm afraid I don't know where she is, but my predecessor might. He was in the parish for twenty-five years and I think he kept in touch with her when she left. I can give you his address at least."

"Thank you." Joss stared around. It was a beautiful small church, plain, with a whitewashed interior that showed off the carved stone of the thirteenth-century windows and the arched doorways and the brasses and plaques with which it was lined. On the south side there was a side aisle where the oak pews gave way to rows of rush-seated chairs. The church had been decorated for Harvest Festival and every window sill and shelf and pew end was piled with fruit and vegetables and flowers. "It's lovely."

"Isn't it." He surveyed it with fond pride. "I'm lucky to have such a charming church. I have three others, of course, with three other parishes, but none is as nice as this."

"Is my —" Joss was looking around. My father, she had been going to say. "Is Philip Duncan buried here?"

"Indeed he is. Out by the oak tree. You'll see his grave if you walk through to the Hall."

"Is it all right if I go and look at the house? Is there a caretaker or something?" Joss called after him as he disappeared to collect his books.

"No. I'm sure it will be all right if you go

18

and wander around. There's no one to mind any-more, sadly. The gardens used to be beautiful, but they're a wilderness now." He reappeared from the shadows and closed the vestry door behind him. "Here, I've scribbled down Edgar Gower's address. I don't know his phone number offhand, I'm afraid. He lives near Aldeburgh." He pushed a piece of paper into her hand.

She watched from the churchyard as he strode back to his bike, vaulted onto it, and rode away, his pile of books heaped in the bicycle basket. Suddenly she felt very lonely.

The gravestone by the oak tree was simple and unadorned.

PHILIP DUNCAN
BORN 31ST JANUARY 1920
DIED 14TH NOVEMBER 1963
+

Nothing else. No mention of his grieving widow. Or his child. She looked down at it for several minutes. When at last she turned away, pulling the collar of her coat up with a shiver against the strengthening wind, she found there were tears in her eyes.

It was a long time before she could drag herself away from the old house and walk, thoughtfully, back to the car. Climbing in, savoring the familiar atmosphere of home, she leaned back in her seat and looked around. On the shelf lay one of Tom's socks, pulled off as he sat in his car seat behind her as a prelude to sucking his toes.

19

She stayed slumped for several minutes, lost in thought, then suddenly she sat upright and gripped the steering wheel.

In her pocket she had the address of someone who knew her mother, who remembered her, who would know where she was now.

Leaning across the seat, she reached for the road atlas. Aldeburgh was not all that far away. She glanced up. The sky was a patchwork of scudding black clouds and brilliant sunshine. Evening was still a long way off.

CHAPTER 2

Pulling into the long broad main street in Aldeburgh, she sat still for a moment peering through
the windshield at the shops and houses. It was
an attractive place, bright, neat, and at the moment very quiet.

Clutching her piece of paper, she climbed out
of the car and approached a man who was standing
staring into the window of an antique shop. At
his feet a Jack Russell terrier strained at the leash,
anxious to get to the beach. He glanced at her
piece of paper. "Crag Path? Through there. Overlooking the sea." He smiled. "A friend of Edgar
Gower's are you? Delightful man. Delightful."
Unexpectedly, he gave a shout of laughter as he
strode away.

Joss found she was smiling herself as, intrigued,
she followed the direction of his pointing finger
and threaded her way down the side of a
fisherman's cottage, crossed a narrow road, and
found herself on a promenade, on one side of
which stood a line of east-facing houses, on the
other, beyond the seawall, a shingle beach and
then a gray, turbulent sea. The wind was very

cold here, and she shivered as she walked down the road looking for house numbers. Edgar Gower's house was tall and narrow, white-painted with a high balcony overlooking the sea. To her relief she could see lights on in the downstairs room and there was a plume of pale wood smoke coming from the chimney.

He opened the door to her himself, a tall, angular man with a ruddy complexion and a startling halo of white hair. His eyes were a brilliant blue.

"Mr. Gower?"

Under his piercing gaze Joss suddenly felt extraordinarily self-conscious. He did not appear to be gentle or reassuring as his successor at Belheddon had been; this man of the cloth was a complete contrast.

"Who wants me?" The eyes did not appear to have blinked. Although his gaze was fierce, his voice was comparatively soft, scarcely audible as behind her the waves, crashing successively onto the beach, rattled the shingle in a shifting deafening background roar.

"I was given your address by the rector at Belheddon. I'm so sorry to come without telephoning —"

"Why have you come?" He cut short her floundering. He had made no move to ask her in and she realized suddenly that he had a coat on over a thick rough-knit sweater. He had obviously been on the point of going out.

"I'm sorry. This is obviously not a good time —"

"Perhaps you will allow me to be the judge of that, my dear." He spoke with ill-concealed though mild irritation. "Once you have told me the purpose of your visit."

"I think you knew my mother." She blurted it out without preamble, transfixed by the unblinking eyes.

"Indeed?"

"Laura Duncan."

For a moment he stared at her in complete silence and she saw that at last she had succeeded in disconcerting him. She held her breath, returning his gaze with difficulty.

"So," he said at last. "You are little Lydia."

Suddenly Joss found it difficult to speak. "Jocelyn," she whispered. "Jocelyn Grant."

"Jocelyn Grant. I see." He nodded slowly. "You and I should walk, I think. Come." Stepping out onto the path, he slammed his door behind him and turned right, striding purposefully along the road behind the seawall without a backward glance to see if she were following.

"How did you find out about your mother?" He spoke loudly against the noise of the wind. His hair was streaming behind him, reminding Joss irresistibly of an Old Testament prophet in full cry.

"I went to St. Catherine's House to find my birth certificate. My name is Jocelyn, not Lydia." She was growing short of breath, trying to keep up with him. "Jocelyn Mary."

"Mary was your great grandmother, Lydia your grandmother."

"Please, is my mother still alive?" She had had to run a few steps to stay beside him.

He stopped. His expression, beaten by the wind

into fiery aggressiveness, suddenly softened with compassion. Joss's heart sank. "She's dead?" she whispered.

"I'm afraid so, my dear. Some years ago. In France."

Joss bit her lip. "I had so hoped —"

"It is as well there is no chance of your meeting, my dear. I doubt if your mother would have wanted it," he said. The kindness and sympathy in his voice were palpable; she was beginning to suspect that he must have been a very good pastor.

"Why did she give me away?" Her voice was trembling and she felt her tears on her cheeks. Embarrassed, she tried to wipe them away.

"Because she loved you. Because she wanted to save your life."

"Save my life?" Shocked, Joss echoed him numbly.

He looked down at her for a moment, then he reached into his pocket and drew out a handkerchief. Carefully he wiped her cheeks. He smiled, but there was unhappiness in his eyes as he shook his head. "I prayed you would never come to find me, Jocelyn Grant."

He turned away from her and took several steps back along the path, then he stopped and swung back to face her. "Are you able to forget that you ever went to Belheddon? Are you able to put it out of your mind forever?"

Joss gasped. Confused, she shook her head. "How can I?"

His shoulders slumped. "How indeed." He sighed. "Come."

Abruptly, he turned and retraced his steps and she followed him in silence, her stomach churning uncomfortably.

His narrow front hall, as he closed the door against the roar of wind and sea, was uncannily quiet. Shrugging off his own coat, he helped her with her jacket and slung both onto a many-branched Victorian hat stand, then he headed for the staircase.

The room into which he showed her was a large comfortable study overlooking the seawall and the white-topped waves. It smelled strongly of pipe smoke and the huge vase of scented viburnum and tobacco flowers mixed with Michaelmas daisies, which stood on a table amid piles of books. Gesturing her to a deep shabby armchair, he went back to the door and bellowed down the stairs. "Dot! Tea and sympathy. My study. Twenty minutes!"

"Sympathy?" Joss tried to smile.

He hauled himself onto the edge of his large untidy kneehole desk and looked at her thoughtfully. "Are you strong, Jocelyn Grant?"

She took a deep breath. "I think so."

"Are you married?" His eyes had traveled thoughtfully to her hands and his gaze rested on her wedding ring.

"As you see."

"And do you have children?"

She glanced up. His gaze was steady. She tried to read it and failed. "I have a little boy, yes. He's eighteen months old."

He sighed. Standing up, he walked around his desk and went to stand at the window, staring

25

down at the sea. There was a long silence.

"It was after I had Tom that I realized I wanted to find out about my real parents," she said at last.

"Of course." He did not turn around.

"Is that my father — the Philip who is buried in the churchyard at Belheddon?" she went on after another silence.

"It is."

"Did you bury him?"

He nodded slowly.

"What did he die of?"

"He had a riding accident." He turned. "I liked Philip very much. He was a kind and courageous man. He adored your mother."

"Was it because of the accident she gave me away?"

He hesitated. "Yes, I think that was part of it, certainly." Sitting down behind his desk, he leaned forward on his elbows and rubbed his face wearily. "Your mother was never very strong physically, although emotionally she was the strongest of us all. After Philip's death she gave up. There had been two other children before you. They both died before they reached their teens. Then there was a long gap and then you came along. She had already planned to leave. I don't think she and Philip wanted any more children . . ." His voice died away thoughtfully. "I'm sorry, my dear, but you must have been expecting some tale of woe; why else would a woman of Laura's background give away her child?"

"I . . ." Joss cleared her throat and tried again.

26

"I didn't know anything about her background. Only the address."

He nodded. "Jocelyn. Once more, can I beg you to forget about all this? For your own sake and the sake of your family, don't embroil yourself in the affairs of the Duncans. You have your own life, your own child. Look forward, not backward. There is too much unhappiness attached to that house." His face lightened as a quiet tap sounded at his door. "Come in, Dot!"

The door opened and the corner of a tray emerged, pushing it back. Mr. Gower did not stand up. He was frowning. "Come in, my love and join us for tea. Meet Jocelyn Grant."

Joss half turned in her chair and smiled at the small, slim woman who had appeared, bent beneath the weight of the tray. Leaping to her feet, she reached out to help her. "It's all right, my dear. I'm stronger than I look!" Dot Gower's voice was not only strong but melodious. "Sit down, sit down." She plonked the tray down in front of her husband where, balanced on top of his papers, it sloped alarmingly toward the window. "So, shall I pour?"

"Dot," Edgar Gower said slowly, "Jocelyn is Laura Duncan's child."

Dot Gower's eyes were, Joss suddenly discovered, as piercing as her husband's. Disconcerted by the woman's stare, she subsided back into her chair.

"Poor Laura." Dot turned after a moment back to her teapot. "She would have been so proud of you, my dear. You are very beautiful."

Joss felt suddenly very uncomfortable. "Thank

27

you. What was she like?"

"Middle height, slim, gray hair, even when she was comparatively young, gray eyes." Edgar Gower appraised Joss once more. "You don't have her eyes — or Philip's. But you do have her build, and I should imagine her hair was like yours once. She was kind, intelligent, humorous — but the deaths of the boys — she never got over that, and once Philip had gone . . ." He sighed as he reached out to take his teacup. "Thank you, my dear. Jocelyn, please. For your own sake, forget Belheddon. They have all gone. There is nothing there for you."

"Edgar!" Dot straightened from the tray and turned on her husband, her face sharp. "You promised!"

"Dot. No!"

They were locked for a moment in some intense silent conflict that Joss didn't understand. The atmosphere in the room had become tense. Abruptly Edgar slammed down his cup, slopping tea into the saucer and stood up. He strode over to the fireplace. "Think, Dot. Think what you are saying —"

"Excuse me," Joss said at last. "Please. What are you talking about? If this is something to do with me, I think I should know about it."

"Yes, it is." Dot's voice was very firm. "Edgar made your mother a solemn promise before she left England and he has to keep it."

Edgar's face was working furiously, reflecting some inner battle as yet unresolved. "I promised, but nothing but unhappiness will come of it."

"Come of what?" Joss stood up. "Please. I obviously have a right to know." She was growing afraid. Suddenly she didn't want to know, but it was too late.

Edgar took a deep breath. "Very well. You are right. I have to abide by Laura's wishes." He sighed again and, straightening his shoulders, walked back to his desk. "In fact, there is nothing very much that I can tell you myself, but I promised her that should you ever come back to Belheddon I would see to it that you were given the address of her solicitors in London. I suspect she has left you something in her will; I know she wrote you a letter the day you were legally adopted. She gave it to John Cornish, her lawyer." He reached into a bottom drawer of his desk and, after a moment or two riffling through the papers, produced a card. He pushed it across the desk toward her.

"But why didn't you want me to know about it?" Joss looked at him in confusion. "Why did you feel I shouldn't know?" A jolt of excitement had shot through her. She clutched the card tightly. A glance had shown her it was a large firm of solicitors in Lincoln's Inn Fields.

"Belheddon Hall is an unhappy house, my dear, that's why. The past is the past. I feel it should be allowed to rest. Your mother felt that way too. That is why she wanted you to have a fresh start."

"Then why did she write to me?"

"I suspect to comfort herself."

Joss looked down at the card. "Can I come and see you again after I have seen the solicitors?"

For a moment she thought he was going to shake his head. A shadow had crossed his face, and something else. Fear. She stared at him aghast, but as quickly as it had appeared the expression had gone. He gave her a grave smile. "You may come whenever you wish, my dear. Dot and I will help you in every way we can."

It was not until she was out in the rapidly falling dusk and retracing her steps toward the car that she thought again about that remark and wondered what exactly he had meant. Why should she need help — help was the word he had used — and why was he afraid?

CHAPTER 3

It was very late before she drove at last into the narrow mews in Kensington and backed the car into an impossibly small space near the house. Wearily, she climbed out and reached for her front door keys.

The light was still on in the kitchen at the back. Luke was sitting wedged into the corner behind the small table, staring down at a cup of cold coffee. His tall frame and broad shoulders dwarfed the narrow room; his elbows, spread over a scattering of papers, supported his chin as though he could scarcely lift his head. His normally ruddy complexion was pale.

"Hi, darling!" She bent and kissed him on the top of the ruffled dark hair. "I'm sorry it's so late. I had to go all the way up to Aldeburgh. Is Tom asleep?" She was aching to go up and cuddle the little boy.

He nodded. "Hours ago. How did it go?"

At last she noticed his drawn, tired face and her bubbling excitement died. "Luke? What is it? What's wrong?" She slid onto the stool next to him and reached out to touch his hand.

31

He shook his head slowly. "Joss, I don't know how to tell you. Henderson and Grant is no more."

She stared at him in shock. "But Barry said —"

"Barry has disappeared, Joss. And he's taken all the money. I thought he was my friend. I thought our partnership was secure. I was wrong. Wrong!" He slammed the table suddenly with his fist. "I went to the bank and the account had been emptied. I've been with accountants all day and the police. Your sister came and looked after Tom. I didn't know what to do." He ran his fingers through his disheveled hair and it dawned on Joss that he was near to tears.

"Oh, Luke —"

"We're going to lose the house, Joss." He blundered to his feet, sending the stool on which he was sitting sliding back across the tiles. Wrenching open the back door that led into their pocket-handkerchief-size garden, he stepped out onto the dark terrace and stared upward toward the sky.

Joss hadn't moved. All thoughts of her day had vanished. She was staring at the pale terracotta tiles on the wall above the worktop. It had taken her eighteen months to save up for those tiles, to find them at last and get someone to put them up for her. It had at long last finished the kitchen, the dream kitchen of their first home.

"Joss." Luke was standing in the doorway. "I'm sorry."

She rose to her feet and went to him, resting her head on his chest as he folded his arms around her. He smelled comfortably of Luke, a mixture of engine oil and aftershave and old wool and — Luke. She snuggled against him, drawing strength from just being near him. "We'll think of something," she murmured into his jersey. "We'll manage."

He clutched her even tighter. "Will we?"

"I'll go back to teaching. That will tide us over. Especially if Lyn will look after Tom. I'm lucky to have a sister who likes babies. She gets on with him so well . . ." Her voice trailed away.

She had hated teaching toward the end; loathed it, feeling frustrated and confined by the syllabus, not enjoying the challenge of the kids anymore. She had been in the wrong job; she knew that, though she was good at it, very good. She was not a born teacher, she was an academic and a romantic. The two did not go well together. Her pregnancy had been a godsend — unplanned, unexpected, and, unbelievably, a joy. One of its best points had been that she could finish with teaching forever. She had resigned at the end of the spring term, resisted the blandishments of David Tregarron, the head of department, to change her mind, and thrown herself into the joys of approaching motherhood. She sighed. There was a chance the school could have her back. She had only recently heard that her replacement was already leaving. But even if that didn't happen they would certainly give her a good reference. The trouble was she didn't want to teach anymore. She wanted to look after Tom.

Taking a deep breath, she stood back. The comforting normality of filling the kettle and plugging

33

it in gave her time to gather her wits a little. "Hot drink and then bed. Neither of us is any good at thinking when we're tired," she said firmly. "Tomorrow we will make a plan."

"Bless you, Joss." He hugged her quickly. Then guiltily he remembered where she had been. "So, tell me what happened. How did you get on? Did you find your mother?"

She shook her head, spooning the coffee into the mugs. "She died several years ago. The house is empty. I don't think there are any family left."

"Oh, Joss —"

"It doesn't matter, Luke. I've found out about them. She was unhappy and ill and her husband had died. That was why she gave me away. And" — suddenly she brightened — "apparently she left me a letter. There is a firm of solicitors I've got to contact. Who knows," she laughed suddenly, "perhaps she has left me a fortune."

"Mrs. Grant?" John Cornish appeared at the door of his office and ushered her inside. "Forgive me for keeping you waiting." He waved her toward a chair and sat down himself at his desk. A slim plastic file lay on the blotter in front of him. He drew it toward him and then glanced up at her. A man in his early sixties, his dark suit and austere manner belied the kindness in his gentle face. "You brought your birth and adoption certificates and your wedding certificate? I'm sorry. It's a formality —"

She nodded and pulled them out of her shoulder bag.

"And you got my name from Edgar Gower?"

Joss nodded again.

Cornish shook his head. "I must say, I have always wondered if you would get in touch. There were only two years to go, you know."

"Two years?" Joss sat tensely on the edge of the chair, her fingers knotted into the soft leather of her bag.

He nodded. "It's a strange story. May I give you some coffee before I start?" He gestured toward a tray already standing on the table by the wall.

"Please." She needed coffee. Her mouth was very dry.

When they were both served, John Cornish resumed his seat and sat back in his chair. He did not touch either the file on his desk or the envelope of certificates she had given him.

"Your mother, Laura Catherine Duncan, died on February 15, 1989. She moved to France from Belheddon Hall in Essex in the spring of 1984 and since then the house has remained empty. Her husband, your father, Philip Duncan, died in November 1963. His mother, who lived in the village of Belheddon, died three years ago, and the two sons of Laura and Philip, your brothers, died in 1953 and 1962, respectively. I am afraid to my knowledge there is no close family extant."

Joss bit her lip. Dragging her eyes away from his face, she stared down into her cup.

"Your mother left two letters for you," Cornish went on. "One, I understand, was written at the time of your adoption. The other was entrusted to me before she left the country. It had some

35

rather strange conditions attached to it."

"Conditions?" Joss cleared her throat nervously.

He smiled. "I was instructed to give it to you only if you appeared within seven years of her death. I was not to seek you out in any way. It had to be your decision to look for your roots."

"And if I hadn't contacted you?"

"Then you would not have inherited Belheddon Hall."

Joss's mouth fell open. "What did you say?" Her hands had started to shake.

He smiled at her, clearly delighted at the effect of his words. "The house and its grounds, which I believe extend to about ten acres, are yours, my dear. It has been waiting for you. I understand a lot of the contents are still there as well, although some things were sold before Laura left England."

"What would have happened to it if I hadn't contacted you?" Stunned, Joss frowned. She was still trying to make sense of his words.

"Then the house was to be sold at auction with its contents and the proceeds were to go to charity." He paused. "My dear, I should warn you that although enough provision was made for the payment of any inheritance taxes, there is no money to go with the bequest. It is possible that you have been left an appallingly large white elephant, and there are conditions and covenants attached to the bequest. You may not turn it down, even though of course you cannot be forced to live there, and you may not sell the property for a period of seven years starting from the first day you set foot inside the house." He turned to the file before him and stood up. "I shall give you her letters and leave you alone for a moment while you read them." He handed her two envelopes with a smile. "I shall be in my secretary's office if you need me."

She sat looking down at the two envelopes for several minutes without moving. One was addressed: "To my daughter, Lydia." The other had her name — the name she had taken from her stepparents, Jocelyn Davies, and the date April 1984.

She picked up the one addressed to Lydia and slowly ran her finger under the flap.

The single page was embossed with the address: Belheddon Hall, Belheddon, Essex. "My darling Lydia, One day, I hope you will understand why I have done as I have done. I had no choice. I love you. I shall always love you. Please God you will be happy and safe with your new mother and father. My blessings go with you, my darling baby. God bless you always."

There was no signature. Joss felt her eyes flood with tears. She sniffed frantically, dropping the letter onto the desk. It was several seconds before she tore open the second envelope. It too was headed Belheddon Hall. This letter was longer.

My dearest Jocelyn. I am not supposed to know your name but there are people who find out these things and once in a while I have had news of you. I hope you have been happy. I have been so proud of you, my darling. Forgive me, Jocelyn, but I can no longer fight your father's wishes, I have no strength left. I am leaving Belheddon with all its blessings and its curses, but he will only let me escape if I give in. He wants Belheddon to be yours and I have to obey. If you read this letter, he will have got his way. God bless you, Jocelyn, and keep you safe. Laura Duncan.

Joss read the letter again, puzzled. So it was her father's wish that she inherit the house. She thought of the lone grave beneath the oak tree and shook her head slowly.

It was five minutes later that John Cornish put his head around the door. "All right?"

She nodded numbly. "I'm finding it hard to assimilate all this."

He resumed his chair and gave her a kind smile. "I can imagine."

"What happens now?"

He shrugged eloquently. "I give you a box of keys and you go away and, as our American cousins say, enjoy."

"And that is all?"

"Bar a few small formalities — papers to sign and so forth — that is all."

She hesitated. "My husband's engineering company has just folded. He's been swindled by his partner. There is a chance he is going to be made bankrupt. We've lost our house — I won't lose Belheddon?"

He shook his head. "I'm so sorry. But this house is yours, not your husband's. Unless you yourself are being made bankrupt, it is safe."

"And we could go and live there?"

He laughed. "Indeed you can. Though you should remember it has been closed up a long time. I have no idea what condition it is in."

"I don't care what condition it's in. It is going to save our lives!" Joss could hardly contain herself. "Mr. Cornish, I don't know how to thank you!"

He beamed at her. "It is your mother you should thank, Mrs. Grant, not me."

"And my father." Joss bit her lip. "I gather it was my father who wanted me to have the house."

It was several minutes before John Cornish's secretary, on his instructions, appeared in his office carrying a small tin box, which she laid reverently on the desk.

"The keys, if I remember, are all neatly labeled." John Cornish pushed it toward Joss. "If you have any problems, let me know."

She stared down at it. "You mean, that's it?"

He smiled happily. "That's it."

"It's my house?"

"It's your house, to do with as you wish, provided you abide by the conditions." He stood up again and extended his hand. "Congratulations, Mrs. Grant. I wish you and your husband every happiness with your inheritance."

CHAPTER 4

"I don't believe it. Things like that don't happen in real life." Lyn Davies was sitting opposite her adoptive sister at the small kitchen table, her eyes round with envy.

Joss reached down to Tom, sitting playing by her feet, and hoisted him onto her knee. "I can't believe it's true either. I have to keep pinching myself. It makes up for losing this." She glanced around her at the little kitchen.

"I'll say. Talk about falling on your feet!" Lyn scowled. "Have you told Mum and Dad about all this?" Two years younger than Joss, she had been conceived after Joss's adoption, five years after Alice had been told she could never have a child of her own. Totally unlike Joss to look at, she had short, curly blond hair, was squarely built, and had deep gray eyes. Nobody had ever taken them for sisters.

Joss nodded. "I rang last night. They think it's like a fairy story. You know, Mum was so worried I'd be disappointed when I wanted to look for my real parents; but she was so good about it." She glanced at Lyn. "She didn't mind."

"Of course she minded!" Lyn reached for the pot and poured herself another mug of thick black coffee. "She was desperately unhappy about it. She was frightened you might find another family and forget her and Dad."

Joss was shocked. "She wasn't! She can't have believed that." She narrowed her eyes. "She didn't feel that at all. You're stirring again, Lyn. I wish you wouldn't." She took a deep breath. "Look, are you sure you want Tom tomorrow?" She hugged the little boy close. "Luke and I can take him with us —"

Lyn shook her head. "No. I'll have him. He'll only get in your way while you're measuring for curtains or whatever." Catching sight of Joss's face, she scowled again. "All right, sorry. I didn't mean it. I know you can't afford curtains. Go on, you and Luke go and enjoy your day out. It will do him good to get away from all this mess with H&G. Mum and I will love having Tom!"

Luke drove, his handsome square face haggard with worry and loss of sleep. For a second Joss reached over and touched his hand. "Cheer up. You're going to love it."

"Am I?" He turned to her and finally he grinned. "Yes, you're right, I am. If the roof keeps most of the rain out and there is a garden big enough to grow vegetables in, I'm going to love it. I don't care what it looks like."

The last weeks had been a nightmare of solicitors, bank managers, and police investigators. Meetings with them and with creditors and ac-

41

countants had filled Luke's every waking hour as he watched the small engineering company which had been his whole life taken apart and put under the microscope. They were not to be bankrupted at least. But it was no comfort to know that Barry Henderson was being sought by Interpol. The sour taste Barry's betrayal had left in his mouth and the inevitable loss of the mews cottage had detracted badly from his pleasure in Joss's windfall. And from the relief he felt when he realized that for the time at least they would have a roof, however leaky, over their heads while they decided what to do with the rest of their lives.

They pulled up at last outside the village shop. "Are you going to introduce yourself?" Luke smiled at her. "The new lady of the manor."

Joss shrugged. "What do I say?"

"Tell them the truth. You've got to tell them, Joss. They are the post office. They'll be delivering mail pretty soon. Go on. Give the village something to gossip about." He swung himself out of the car.

The wind was icy, worrying the branches of the ash tree which grew at the road junction opposite like an angry dog, tearing off the remaining leaves. Joss followed him, turning up the collar of her jacket with a shudder as the wind tore at her hair and whipped it into her eyes.

The shop was empty. They stood looking around, savoring the mixed smells of cheese and ham and exotic smoked sausages and the silence after the wind. Moments later the postmistress appeared from a doorway at the back of the counter. She was carrying a cup of coffee. "Hello, my dears. How can I help you?" She set the cup down. Then she peered at Joss. "Of course, you were in here the other day, asking about the Hall. Did you manage to find Mary Sutton?"

Joss shook her head. "There was no one there when I knocked, but I met the vicar up at the church and he gave me the address of his predecessor, who knew the Duncans."

"I see." The woman put her head on one side. "You've some special interest in the Hall, have you?" Her eyes were bright with curiosity.

Joss heard Luke chuckle. She trod heavily on his toe. Smiling, she held out her hand. "Perhaps I should introduce myself. I am Joss Grant — this is my husband, Luke. It looks as though we are going to be living there, at least for a while. Laura and Philip Duncan were my parents. They gave me up for adoption when I was a baby, but it appears that they left the house to me."

The woman's mouth dropped open. "Well I never! Oh, my dear! That great place!" Far from being pleased as Joss expected, she appeared to be horrified. "You're never going to live there! You couldn't possibly."

Taken aback, Joss frowned. "Why on earth not? It didn't look to me as though it was in too bad condition."

"Oh, I didn't mean that." The woman was immediately embarrassed. "Take no notice of me! It's a lovely place. You are very lucky. The village will be pleased. The Hall has been empty too long. Much too long." She shook her head.

43

"There's me forgetting my manners. I'm Sally Fairchild. My husband, Alan, is the postmaster here; I'm the deli counter." She laughed. "Alan retired from his accountancy five years back and we thought we'd take over a village shop in our declining years. Thought it would be a nice restful job. Haven't had time to sit down since . . ."

Luke looked across at Joss as they settled themselves back into the car. On the backseat there was a box of supplies — enough for an army for three days at least, Luke had said with a smile, as they selected a picnic for themselves from Sally Fairchild's luxurious counter. "So. What do you make of all that?"

Joss reached for her seat belt. "Nice woman. I had the feeling though that, whatever she said about the village being pleased, they wouldn't be."

Glancing into the mirror, Luke pulled the car away from the curb. "Up here? She certainly had reservations, didn't she. Do you still want to stop off and see this Mary Sutton?"

Joss shook her head. "Let's go to the house first. I can't wait to see what it's like." She reached into the glove compartment and brought out the box of keys, hugging it against her chest. "We can't expect the locals to accept us just like that. When I rang David Tregarron to tell him our plans he said it would take twenty years for anyone around here to accept a stranger. As I was a blood relation, probably nineteen years eight months."

Luke laughed.

"Up there now, around the green," Joss went

on. "I think the drive must lead off the lane beyond the church. He said he would come and see us." David had been more than just her boss. He was a confidant, friend, sparring partner. His warmth and genuine regret when she had phoned him a couple of days earlier had touched her deeply. "There. That must be it."

The wrought iron gate, standing between two stone gateposts, topped with moss-covered pineapples, was standing half open in the tall hedge. Luke drew the car to a halt. Climbing out, he peered up the drive as he tried to force the gate back over the muddy gravel. There was no notice to say this was Belheddon Hall, no sign of the house as the overgrown driveway curved out of sight between the high laurel hedges.

He climbed back into the car. "OK?" Her excitement was tangible. He reached across and squeezed her hand. "The return of the prodigal daughter. Let's go."

The drive was not very long. One sweep past the hedges and they were there, drawing up on the grassy gravel in front of the house. Luke pulled up and cut the engine.

"Joss!" It was all he said. For several seconds they sat in silence, staring through the windshield.

It was Joss who moved first, opening the door and stepping out into the freezing wind. Silently, she stood staring up at the house. It was her birthplace. Her inheritance. Her home.

Behind her, Luke stood for a moment watching her. He was intensely proud of his wife — she was beautiful, intelligent, hard working, sexy — sternly he cut short that train of thought — and now an heiress as well! Silently, he stepped up behind her and put his hands on her shoulders. "So, how does it feel to be home?" he said softly. He had read her thoughts exactly.

She smiled, brushing her cheek against his hand. "Strange. A little frightening."

"It's a big house, Joss."

"And we have no money." She turned and looked up at him. "You have always liked challenges." Her eyes were sparkling.

"If we're seriously going to live here for any length of time, we'll need cash from somewhere for taxes, heat, electricity, and food. On top of that there will be endless ongoing repairs. Shouldn't be a problem." He grinned. "Your mother did leave you a magic lamp, a bag of gold coins, and six live-in servants?"

"Of course."

"Then, as I said, no problem. Come on. Where's the key? Let's go in."

The keyhole in the front door was two inches high. Joss already knew the contents of the key box by heart; there was nothing in there which would fit. She reached for a couple of Yale keys. Both were labeled "back door."

They walked along the front of the house, passing the shuttered lower windows, and turned through the stone archway. There a square range of coach houses, garages, and stables surrounded a cobbled courtyard one side of which was the east wall of the house. By the back door stood a black iron pump.

"Joss!" Luke stared around. "You realize what I could do here, don't you! I've had the most brilliant idea! Looking for jobs in London will probably be a dead loss, but I could work here!" In three steps he had reached one of the doors. Pulling it open, he peered into an empty garage. "Cars! I can restore cars. I can start again. My God, there would be room to do it, too. It would give us a living of sorts." Excitedly, he peered into stable after stable.

Behind him, Joss was smiling. The house was working its spell. She could see his depression lifting as she watched. She stood there for a few minutes more, then, unable to resist it any longer, she turned alone to the back door.

The door was swollen with damp and grated against the York stone flags of a narrow dark hallway. "Wait for me!" Coming up behind her, Luke caught her hand. "I think this is somewhere I should carry you over the threshold, don't you?"

Giggling, Joss clung to his neck as he swept her off her feet and walked with her into the darkness of the first room down the passage. There he set her down, panting. "My God, woman. What have you been eating? Bricks?"

They stared around in silence. The huge room was shadowy, a pale, reluctant light filtering around the edge of the shutters. "It's the kitchen," Joss whispered. A huge fireplace took up the whole of one wall. In it a double-size cooking range slumbered like some great black engine. On it stood an iron kettle. In the center of the room stood a scrubbed oak table and around it six bentwood chairs. One was pulled out, as though the person seated on it had only a moment before stood up and left the room. To the left a glass-fronted dresser, dusty and hung with spiderwebs, showed the gleam of china.

Silently, hand in hand like two trespassing children, Joss and Luke moved toward the door in the far wall. Over it a board hung with a line of fifteen bells, each controlled by a wire, which showed how in days gone by the servants had been summoned from the kitchen quarters to other parts of the house.

Beyond the kitchen they found a bewildering range of small pantries and sculleries, and at the end of the passage a baize-lined door. They stopped.

"Upstairs and downstairs." Luke smiled, running his hands over the green door lining. "Are you ready to go above stairs?"

Joss nodded. She was trembling. Luke pushed the door open and they peered out into a broad corridor. Again it was shadowy, bisected by fine lines of dusty sunlight. Here the scrubbed flags finished and they found themselves walking on broad oak boards which once had carried gleaming polish. Instead of an array of exotic carpets, a drift of dried leaves had blown in under the front door and lay scattered over it.

To the right on one side of the front door they found the dining room. A long table stood there in the shuttered darkness, surrounded by — awed, Luke counted out loud — twelve chairs. To the left a large door, much older than anything they had seen so far, Gothic, churchlike, led into an enormous, high-ceilinged room. Amazed, they stood staring up. The room had soaring arched beams and at the far end there was a minstrel's gallery, screened from the room by oak paneling carved into intricate arches. "My God." Joss took a few steps into the room. "It's a time warp." She stared around with a shiver. "Oh, Luke."

There was very little furniture in the room. Two heavy oak coffer chests stood against the walls, and there was a small refectory table in the middle of the floor. The fireplace still held the remains of the last fire that had been lit there.

On the far side of the room an archway, hung with a dusty curtain, led into a further hallway from which a broad oak staircase curved up out of sight into the darkness. They stood peering up.

"I think we should open some shutters," Luke said softly. "What this house needs is some sunlight." He felt vaguely uneasy. He glanced at Joss. Her face was pale in the gloomy darkness and she looked unhappy. "Come on, Joss, let's let in the sun."

He strode toward the window and spent several minutes wrestling with the bars which held the shutters closed. Finally he managed to lift them out of their sockets and he threw open the shutters. Sunshine poured in across the dusty boards. "Better?" He hadn't been imagining it. She was deathly pale.

She nodded. "I'm stunned."

"Me too." He looked around. "What this room needs is a suit of armor or two. You know, we could run this place as a hotel! Fill it with tourists. Make our fortune." He strode across the floor to a door beyond the hall and threw it open. "The library!" he called. "Come and look! There are enough books here even for you!" He disappeared from sight and she heard the rattle of iron on wood as once again he fought with a set of shutters.

She did not follow him for a moment. Turning around slowly, she stared about her at the empty room. The silence of the house was beginning to oppress her. It was as if it were listening, watching, holding its breath.

"Joss! Come and see." Luke was in the doorway. He was beaming. "It's wonderful."

Joss gave herself a small shake. With a shiver, she followed him through the doorway and immediately she felt better. "Luke!" It was, as he had said, wonderful. A small, bright room, full of mellow autumn light, looking down across the back lawns toward the small lake. The walls were lined to the ceiling with books except where an old rolltop desk stood, in front of it a shabby leather chair. Around the fire stood a cluster of three armchairs, a side table, an overflowing magazine rack, and a sewing basket, still with its silks and needles witness to the last hours of Laura Duncan's occupancy.

Joss stared around, a lump in her throat. "It is as if she just stood up and walked out. She didn't even take her sewing things." She ran her hand over the contents of the basket. There were tears in her eyes.

"Come on." Luke put his arm around her again. "Everything was planned. She didn't need her sewing things, that's all. She was looking forward to a life of leisure in France. I bet in her shoes, you wouldn't take your darning needles either."

50

He squeezed her shoulder. "The desk is locked. Is the key there, in the box?"

It wasn't. They tried a succession before they gave up and resumed their tour of the house. The only other room on the ground floor was a small sitting room which looked out across the drive. The squeaking shutters opened reluctantly to show their car, already dusted with crisp brown leaves from the chestnut tree on the edge of the front lawn. On the grass a trio of rabbits grazed unconcerned within a few feet of its wheels.

At the foot of the stairs Joss paused. Above them a gracious sweep of oak treads curved around out of sight into the darkness. Aware that Luke was immediately behind her, she still hesitated a moment, her hand on the carved newel post.

"What's the matter?"

She shrugged. "I don't know. I just had the feeling — as if there was someone up there. Waiting."

Luke rumpled her hair affectionately. "Perhaps there is. The skeleton in the cupboard. Come on, let Uncle Luke go first." He took the stairs two at a time, disappearing around the corner.

Joss did not move. She heard his footsteps echoing across the floor, the now familiar rattle of shutters, and suddenly the stairs above her head were flooded with light. "Come on. No skeletons." His footsteps crossed the floor again, growing fainter until she could hear them no more.

"Luke!" Suddenly, she was frightened. "Luke, where are you?" Slowly she began to climb.

51

The stairs creaked slightly beneath her weight. The polished handrail was smooth and cold under her palm. She looked up, her concentration focused on the upper landing as she rounded the curve toward it. A broad corridor ran crossways in front of her with three doors opening off it. "Luke?"

There was no reply.

She stepped onto a faded Persian rug and glanced quickly into the doorway on her right. It led into a large bedroom which looked out across the back garden and beyond it, over the hedge, toward a huge stubble field and then the estuary. The room was sparsely furnished. A bed, covered by a dust sheet, a Victorian chest of drawers, a mahogany cupboard. There was no sign of Luke. The doorway halfway down the landing led into a large, beautiful bedroom dominated by an ornate four-poster bed. Joss gasped. In spite of the dust sheets which covered the furniture she could see how exquisite it all was. Stepping forward, she pulled at the sheet that lay over the bed to reveal an embroidered bedcover, matching the hangings and tester.

"So, Mrs. Grant. What do you think of your bedroom, eh?" Luke appeared behind her so suddenly she let out a little cry of fright. He put his arms around her. "This is the kind of style to which you would like to become accustomed, I suspect?" He was laughing.

Her fear forgotten, Joss smiled. "I can't believe it. It's like Sleeping Beauty's palace."

"And Sleeping Beauty needs a kiss from a prince to wake her up and show her she's not dreaming!"

"Luke —" Her squeal of protest as he pulled her onto the high bed and began to kiss her was muffled as he climbed up beside her. "I think we need to stake our claim on this bed, don't you, Mrs. Grant?" He was fumbling for the buttons on her jersey under her jacket.

"Luke, we can't —"

"Why not? It's your house, your bed!"

She gasped as his hands, ice cold from the chill in the house, met the warm flesh of her breasts and pulled away her bra. Her excitement was rising to match his. "Luke —"

"Shut up." He dropped his mouth, teasing her with his tongue, his hands busy with her skirt and tights. "Concentrate on your husband, my love." He smiled down at her.

"I am." She reached up, pulling away his sweater and shirt and pushing them back so that she could kiss his chest, his shoulders, pulling him down toward her, oblivious to everything now but the urgency which was building between them.

In the corner of the room a shadowy figure stood motionless, watching them.

"Yes!" Luke's cry of triumph was muffled by the hangings of the bed. In the ceiling beams the stray sunlight from the garden wavered and died as dark clouds raced in from the east.

Clinging to Luke, Joss opened her eyes, staring up at the embroidered tester above her head. A rosette of pale cream silk, threadbare, cobwebbed, nestled in the center of the fabric. Stretching, contented as a cat, Joss gazed around, not wanting to move, enjoying Luke's weight, his warmth, his closeness. It was a moment before her eyes registered something in the corner, another fraction of a second before her brain reacted. She blinked, suddenly frightened, but there was nothing there. Just a trick of the light.

Luke raised his head at last and looked down. Joss was crying.

"Sweetheart, what is it?" Contrite, he wiped the tears with a gentle hand. "Did I hurt you?"

She shook her head. "Take no notice. I'm all right. I don't know why I'm crying." Sniffing, she wriggled away from him and slid off the bed.

Pulling down her skirt she went to retrieve her tights from the dusty boards. It was as she was putting them on that the sound of a bell pealed through the house.

Luke stood up. Pulling his sweater on over his head, he padded across to the front window and looked out. "There's someone at the front door!" He smothered a laugh. "How embarrassing! Our first visitor and we're caught in delicto!"

"Not caught!" She pushed her feet into her shoes and smoothed her hair. "Go on, then. Let them in."

They couldn't. There was no sign of the front door key. By dint of shouting through the two-inch keyhole, Luke directed their visitor to the back door and it was in the shadowy kitchen that they received their first guest, a tall distinguished-looking woman, dressed in a heavy woollen coat, swathed in a tartan scarf.

"Janet Goodyear. Next door neighbor." She extended a hand to them both in turn. "Sally Fairchild told me you were here. My dears, I can't tell you how excited the village will be when they hear you've arrived. Are you seriously going to live here? It's such a godforsaken pile." Pulling off her gloves and throwing them on the table, she walked over to the range and pulled open the door of one of the ovens. She wrinkled her nose cheerfully. "This kitchen is going to need at least twenty thou spent on it! I know a brilliant designer if you need one. He would make a really good job of all this."

Luke and Joss exchanged glances. "Actually, I want to leave the kitchen as it is," Joss said. Luke frowned. Her voice was ominously quiet. "The range will refurbish beautifully."

Their visitor looked surprised. "I suppose so. But you'd do much better, you know, to swop it for a decent Aga. And God help you when it comes to the roof. Laura and Philip were always having trouble with the roof." She turned back from her poking around, her smile all warmth. "Oh, my dears, I can't tell you how lovely it will be to have neighbors here. I can't wait for you to move in. Now, what I've actually come for is to ask if you'd like to pop over for lunch. We live just across the garden there, in the farmhouse." She waved a vaguely expansive hand. "My husband owns most of the land around here."

Joss opened her mouth to reply, but Luke was ahead of her. "It's kind of you, Mrs. Goodyear, but we've brought our own food. I think on this occasion we'll take a rain check, if you don't mind. We've got a lot of measurements and notes to take while we're here."

"Twenty thou!" he exploded with laughter when at last they had managed to get rid of her. "If she knew that we are going to move in here without a penny to our name she would probably have us struck off her Christmas card list before we were ever on it!"

"I don't think she meant to sound so frightening. I quite liked her." Joss had pulled open one of the tall cupboards. "She's right in one way, though, Luke. There is a lot to do. The roof — presumably — water, electricity; we don't know if it all works. And the stove. I suppose we could get it going" — she stared at it doubtfully — "but it is going to gobble fuel."

"We'll cope." He put his arms around her again and gave her a hug. He was, she noticed, looking happy for the first time since he had found out about Barry's treachery. Really happy. "For a start there was a massive amount of coal in one of the sheds in the courtyard, did you notice?" he said, "and there will be logs. We'll manage, Joss. Somehow. You'll see."

CHAPTER 5

An empty beer glass had left a wet ring on the pub table which Joss was busy transforming into a figure eight with variations when David Tregarron fought his way back toward her from the bar carrying two spritzers and a bag of nuts.

The head of the History Department at Dame Felicia's School in Kensington, David was thirty-eight years old, two years divorced, and, as housemaster and second head, lived above the job, over four dormitories of unruly little boys, in a Victorian flat with minimal mod cons. His divorce had been an unpleasant messy business, and Joss had been one of his anchor points at the time. She and he might not agree over teaching methods, but her loyalty to him as his marriage had unraveled had been unswerving. She had comforted him as his wife took off into the sunset with her new man, propped him up in the staff room with coffee and Alka-Seltzer, and cheerfully agreed with all his maudlin lamentations over a woman she had never actually met.

When once, some time after the divorce was made absolute, he had grabbed her hand and said,

"Joss, divorce Luke and marry me," he had realized as soon as he had said it that he was only half joking. He had seen the danger in time and pulled himself together. Being fond of Joss was permissible. Anything more was totally beyond the pale.

"So, how is Luke taking all this newfound wealth?" He lowered himself cautiously onto a plush-covered stool and passed her one of the glasses.

Joss gave a wry grin. "Amazement. Relief. Disbelief. Not necessarily in that order."

"And you?"

She sighed. "Roughly the same. I'm still pinching myself. So much has happened to us in the last few weeks, David! I don't think even in my wildest dreams I ever imagined anything like this happening to us!" She sipped thoughtfully from her glass for a moment. "It was nice of you to call and ask me out. Do you know, this is the first break I've had away from the house in days. There has been so much to do. The firm going under has been a complete nightmare."

David grimaced. "I was so sorry to hear about it." He glanced at her. "Are they making Luke bankrupt?"

Joss shook her head. "No, thank God! The mews cottage has saved us. Luke's grandfather bought it after the war when it was worth a few hundred pounds. When Luke's father gave it to us as a wedding present he handed us a fortune, bless him." She gave a sad, fond smile. "It's going on the market for a lot of money. If I ever get my hands on Barry I'll throttle him personally if Luke or the police don't get to him first. Our lovely little house!"

"That's really tough. But now you have your stately roof in East Anglia to fall back on."

She gave a wry grin. "I know. It sounds like a fairy tale. It is a fairy tale! Oh, David, it was so beautiful! And Luke is full of plans. He's going to turn his hand to restoring old cars again. He is a trained engineer after all, and it's what he always loved doing best. I think he was pretty sick of spending all his time on management and paperwork. And they've let him keep some of the machinery and tools from H&G — it's outdated by other people's standards apparently and the buyer didn't want them. He's retrieved lathes and boring and gear-cutting equipment and all sorts of stuff. I hope he's right in thinking he can make us some money that way, because we're going to be awfully short of cash. Next summer we can live off the garden, but it's a lousy time of year to be starting out as gardeners! Do you realize we'll be moving in only a few weeks before Christmas!"

"Joss, I've had an idea." David edged himself out of the way of a crowd of noisy drinkers who were settling around the table next to theirs. "That's why I persuaded you to come and have this drink." He paused and gave a theatrical sigh. "I know you and I didn't always see eye to eye over history and its teaching!"

Joss laughed. "Always the master of understatement!"

"And we've had the odd tiff."

"Ditto." She raised her eyes to his fondly.

"What is this leading to, David? You are not usually so deferential in your suggestions."

"First, tell me, are you intending to go back to teaching up there in your new home?"

Joss shook her head. "I doubt it. I expect there's a village school — I don't even know that yet — but I shouldn't think there's any scope locally for the kind of teaching I do. Anyway, I think I've had it with teaching, David, to be honest."

"You weren't sorry when you handed in your resignation before Tom was born. Even I could see that."

"And you were probably relieved to see the back of me." She looked down at her glass.

"You know that's not true." He hesitated. "You're a good teacher, Joss. I was desperately sorry to lose you." He paused. "In more ways than one." There was an uncomfortable silence. Pulling himself together with a visible effort, he went on. "You care about the kids, and you inspire them. Something not all history teachers manage, by any means. I know we sometimes rowed about your methods, but I was only worried about your ability to stick to the curriculum." He stopped and shook his head. "I'm making a mess of this. What I'm trying to say is, that I've a suggestion to make and I don't want you to get hold of the wrong end of the stick. This is not an insult or a sinister plot to undermine your intellectual integrity. And above all I am not criticizing your knowledge or interpretation of history, but I think you should give some serious consideration to the idea of turning your hand to writing. Fiction."

He waited, his eyes fixed on her face.

"Which is more my line than serious history, you mean." Joss hid a smile.

"I knew you would say that!" He smacked the table with the palm of his hand. "No, it is not what I mean. All right. You told the kids stories. They loved it. I don't think it was good history but it was good teaching. They wanted more and they missed you like hell when you left. Joss, what I'm saying is that you are a born storyteller. You could make money out of it. I'm sure you could. I've read some of your short stories. You even won that competition. I'm being serious. I have a feeling that you could do it. I know one or two people in the publishing business, and if you like, I will show them some of your writing. I don't want to get your hopes up too much because it's a chancy business, but I have a feeling about you." He smiled at her again. "A good feeling, Joss."

She returned his smile. "You're a nice man, David." She reached out her hand to his.

"I know." He left his fingers lying there beneath hers on the table for just a moment too long, then reluctantly he withdrew them. "So, I have your permission to show some stories around?"

"You have my permission. Thanks."

"And I can come and see you as soon as you're settled?"

"Of course you can. I shall miss you, David."

He picked up his glass. "And I you, Joss. And I you."

Joss was kneeling on the floor packing china

when she told Luke of David's idea that evening.

He considered it for a minute, his head on one side, then thoughtfully he nodded. "You can write and you did win that competition. Joss, it's a brilliant scheme!"

"Winning a competition with a short story is not the same as making a living out of writing, Luke."

"No, but you could give it a go. And we are going to need money, Joss. Make no mistake about it."

She frowned, wrapping her arms around her knees as she sat on the floor. "It's going to be tough at Belheddon, isn't it."

He nodded. "Just pray the roof doesn't leak. Your mother and father meant well, leaving the place to you, I'm sure they did, but it's going to take some looking after."

"We'll manage though. Or you will. I'm glad I married a practical man! And who knows, once we're settled, maybe I'll even write a best-seller, too." She glanced up at him through the dark fringe of her hair. "It's a dream come true, Luke."

He slid from his chair and sat down next to her among the debris of boxes and partly packed cups and plates. "I know it is, Joss." Putting his arm around her shoulders he pulled her to him and kissed her. "Just remember, we have to keep a tight grip on reality. We are going to have to work our socks off to keep that place going, and it's not going to be easy."

CHAPTER 6

As the moving van drove slowly out of the drive and turned out of sight, Joss turned to Luke. She caught his hand. "That's it. Bridges burned. No going back. No regrets?" She looked up at him.

He smiled. "No, Joss, no regrets. This is the start of a big adventure."

Slowly they walked back into the kitchen. The room had in many ways not changed at all since the first day they had seen it. The stove was still there, and to their joy had been found to be fully functional after an overhaul; the dresser was still there, the plates and cups washed and sparkling. The heavy table, decorated now with a scarlet poinsettia, a gift from John Cornish, had been scrubbed almost white by Joss's mother, Alice. The crates of their own china and glass stood piled along the wall. Tom's high chair was pulled up at the head of the table.

Alice was bending over the pan on the stove, stirring something which smelled extremely appetizing as they walked in.

"Moving men gone?" Her husband, Joe, was

unwrapping saucepans with his small grandson's help, making a huge pile of newspaper in the middle of the room.

"Gone at last, thank God." Luke threw himself down in one of the chairs. "That smells wonderful, Alice."

His mother-in-law smiled. "You know, I'm really enjoying cooking on this range. I think I'm getting the hang of it at last. This is real cooking!" The range had been one of the urgent things they had had repaired before the move. She glanced at Joss. "Why don't we all have a glass of wine, while I finish this. Let Lyn take Tom, Joe. She can give him his tea." Comfortably, she stood away from the stove, wiping her hands on the front of her apron.

There were two bottles of wine in a Sainsburys carrier on the table and a six-pack of beer. "Corkscrew?" Joss extricated the bottles and stood them in line with the poinsettia. After the weeks of worry and packing and organizing the move, she was so exhausted she could hardly stand.

"On my Boy Scout knife." Luke grinned at her. "Do you remember the moving foreman telling us: Leave out the kettle and the corkscrew or you'll never find them again after." He fished around in the pocket of his jacket and produced a corkscrew which had obviously been nowhere near a Boy Scout in its life. "Beer for you, Joe? And I think I'll join you. It's thirsty work, moving house!"

Sitting at the table, watching her sister cut up an apple and put the pieces in front of Tom, Joss felt a sudden wave of total contentment. It would probably take them years to sort out the house, months to unpack, but at least they were here properly now. No more London, no more office for Luke as he tried to sort out the last minute details of his former life. And here they had enough room to put up Joe and Alice and Lyn and anyone else who wanted to come and stay for as long as they wanted.

Helping herself to a glass, Alice sat down next to her. "I'll leave that to simmer for a couple of hours. Then we can eat. You look done in, love." She put her hand over Joss's.

"Done in, but happy." Joss smiled. "It's going to work. I know it is."

" 'Course it is." Joe had gone back to pushing the crumpled newspaper into a black plastic sack, considerably hampered by Tom, who was pulling out the pieces as fast as Joe was putting them in, and tossing them around the room. "You're all going to be very happy here." He reached for his beer. "So, let's drink a toast. To Belheddon Hall and all who sail in her!"

The sound of the back doorbell was almost drowned by their raised voices. It was Luke who, with a groan, levered himself to his feet and went to answer it.

They had seen Janet Goodyear several times since she had introduced herself on their first visit to the house almost three months before, and Joss was beginning to like her more and more. Her first impression of an interfering and nosy neighbor had been replaced by one of a good-hearted and genuinely kind, if not always tactful, woman, who, far from being pushy, was in fact diffident about intruding on her new neighbors. In her basket this time was a bottle of Scotch ("For emergencies, but I can see you've thought of the alcohol bit already") and what turned out to be a corn dolly. Accepting a glass of wine from Luke, she pulled up a chair next to Joss. "You'll probably think I'm dotty," she said cheerfully, "but I want you to hang this up somewhere in the kitchen here. For luck."

Joss reached over and picked up the intricately plaited figure. "It's beautiful. I've seen them, of course —"

"This isn't a souvenir shop piece of tweeness," Janet interrupted. "Please don't think it is. It was made specially for you. There's an old chap who used to work on the farm — he does some odd gardening jobs for us now — and he made it for you. He asked me to bring it. It's to ward off evil."

Joss raised her eyes from the plaited straw. "Evil?"

"Well" — Janet shrugged — "you have probably gathered by now that the locals are a bit funny about this house." She laughed uncomfortably. "I don't believe it. I've always loved it here. It has such a nice atmosphere."

"What do they say exactly?" Joss pushed a plate of chopped food in front of Tom and put a spoon into his hand.

"I don't know that we want to know, dear," Alice put in quietly. "You look at the range, Mrs. Goodyear. What do you think of it now?" Joss had told her mother about the estimate of twenty thousand.

66

"I think it's wonderful." Still cheerfully un-aware of the consternation her initial comments on the state of the house had caused, Janet swung around to inspect it. "It's so clever of you to get it fixed quickly."

"You could join us for supper later," Joss in-terrupted. "Mum has made enough for an army, as usual."

"Thank you but no." Janet drained her glass and stood up. "I only came to bring you the dolly. The last thing you all want is a visitor on your first evening. Later, though, I'd love to come. And in the meantime if you need any-thing at all we are very close. Please, please don't hesitate to ask." She smiled around at them, then, pulling her scarf back over her head, she was gone.

"Nice woman, Janet Goodyear," Luke said to Joss when they were alone in the great hall later. They had made no attempt to introduce any of their furniture there. The room was too big, too stately, and, they both agreed, needed no more than was there already.

The meal had been eaten and the beds made up and Luke's first job, a rusty, shabby 1929 Bentley, had been ushered into the yard on the back of a low loader. It hadn't even required an advertisement in the paper. A card in the shop, and a few words in the pub, and the phone had rung three days later. Colonel Maxim, from the next village, had owned the car for twelve years and had never got around to working on it himself. Luke could start on it as soon as possible, and when that was done, there was a 1930 Alvis belonging to a friend.

Tom, exhausted by the excitement of the day, had gone to bed in his own room without a murmur. The old nurseries led off the main bedroom, which was to be Joss and Luke's, and, with the doors open into the short passage which separated the two rooms, they would easily be able to hear him if he cried. The nursery complex consisted of three rooms, one of which had been converted into a bathroom. It was a cold, north-facing room, and even the string bag full of Tom's colorful bath toys did nothing to cheer it up. "Curtains, bright rug, wall heater, and lots of vivid, warm towels," Joss dictated as she took the little boy on her knee after his bath and cuddled him dry. Lyn was making a shopping list, sitting on the closed lid of the lavatory. "Tom's bathroom and bedroom are a priority." She shivered in spite of the heat from the gas-cylinder heater Luke had put into the room. "I want him to love this place."

"At least your four-poster will keep the draft out," Lyn commented. The bedroom she had been allocated off the main staircase, although facing south across the garden, was bitterly cold. In the past it was obvious a fire had been lit in the grate in there. There was a rudimentary central heating system, working off the range, but the heat didn't seem to reach the bedrooms, and they had already decided that they would just have to stay cold. A thousand blankets, hot water bottles, and thermal pajamas were going to be the order of the day from now on.

"How long do you think Joe and Alice will

stay?" Joss pulled the fleece-lined pajama top over Tom's curls.

"As long as you like." Lyn was adding soap, toilet paper, and cleaning materials to her list. "Mum doesn't want to get in the way, but she'd really love to stay right up to Christmas. She'd help you get the place straight."

"I know she would, bless her. And I'd like her to. In fact I'd love you all to stay, if you'd like to."

"So, what do you think of it all?" Luke put his arm round Joss's shoulders. They had lit a small fire and were standing looking down at it as the dry logs cracked and spat. Lyn and Alice and Joe had all gone to bed, exhausted by their day.

"I suppose it's like a dream come true." Joss leaned her elbow against the heavy oak bressummer beam that spanned the huge fireplace, looking down into the flames. "I think we should have the tree in here. A huge one, covered in fairy lights."

"Sounds good."

"Tom will be thrilled. He was too young to know what was going on last year." Joss smiled to herself. "Did you hear him talking to Dad? 'Tom put paper there.' He was getting really cross, taking it out of the bag as fast as Dad put it in."

"Luckily your father loved it." Luke frowned. "It must be very strange for them, knowing this house belonged to your real parents."

"Strange for them!" Joss shook her head hard,

as if trying to clear her brain. "Think what it's like for me. I don't even like to call Dad, Dad. It's as if I feel my other father might be listening."

Luke nodded. "I rang my parents while you were upstairs. Just to say we're here."

Joss smiled fondly. "How are they? How is life in Chicago?" She knew how much Luke was missing them, especially his father. Geoffrey Grant's sabbatical year in the States seemed to have dragged on for a long, long time.

"They're great. And they're coming home early next summer." He paused. He and Joss had been planning a trip out to see them. That was not going to happen now, of course. "They can't wait to see the house, Joss. It's hard to know how to explain all this over the phone." He gave a snort of laughter.

Joss smiled. "I suppose it is!" She lapsed into thoughtful silence.

"Have you had another look for the key to the desk in the study yet?" Luke nudged the logs with the toe of his sneaker and watched with satisfaction as a curtain of sparks spread out over the sooty bricks at the back of the hearth.

"I haven't been in the study since we arrived this morning." She stood up straight. "I'm going to have a tot of Janet Goodyear's present and then I think I might go and have a poke around while you have your bath."

The room was cold, the windows were black reflections of the night. With a shiver Joss set her glass down on one of the little tables and went to close the shutters and pull the heavy brocade curtains. The table lamp threw a subdued light across the rugs on the floor, illuminating the abandoned workbasket beside it. Joss stood looking down at it for a long time. There was a lump in her throat at the thought that her mother had used those small, filigree scissors and that the silver thimble must have fit her finger. Hesitantly, Joss reached for it and slipped it on her own finger. It fit.

There was a key in the bottom of the workbasket, lost under the silks and cotton threads — a small ornate key which Joss knew instinctively would fit the keyhole in the desk.

Reaching up, she switched on the lamp which rested on top of the desk and stared at the array of small pigeonholes which the opened lid revealed. It was tidy but not empty and it was immediately obvious that the desk had been her mother's, not her father's. Taking a sip from her glass, Joss reached for a bundle of letters. With a strange feeling half of guilt, half excitement, she pulled off the ribbon which bound them together.

They were all addressed to her mother and they came from someone called Nancy. She glanced through them, wondering who Nancy was. A close friend and a gossip, by the look of it, who had lived in Eastbourne. They told her nothing at all about her mother, but quite a lot about the unknown Nancy. With a tolerant smile she retied the ribbon and tucked them back in their place.

There were pens and a bottle of ink, paper clips, tags, envelopes, all the paraphernalia of a busy person; a drawer of unused headed note paper, and there, in another drawer by itself, a leather-bound notebook. Curious, Joss pulled it out and opened it. On the flyleaf, in her mother's hand, was written "For my daughter, Lydia." Joss shivered. Had her mother been so sure then that she would come to Belheddon, that one day she would sit down on this chair at this desk and pull open the drawers one by one until she found — she flicked it open — not a diary, as she had half expected, just empty pages, undated.

And one short scrawled paragraph, toward the middle of the book. "He came again today, without warning and without mercy. My fear makes him stronger —"

"Joss?" Luke's voice in the doorway made her jump out of her skin. He was dressed in his bathrobe and from where she sat she could smell the musky drift of his aftershave.

She slammed the book shut and took a deep breath.

"What is it? Is something wrong?"

"No. Nothing." Slotting the notebook back into its drawer, she pulled down the flap on the desk, turning the key. "The desk was my mother's. It seems so strange to read her letters and things —"

my fear makes him stronger . . .

Who, for God's sake? Who was her mother so frightened of and why had she written about him in an otherwise empty notebook which she had left especially for Joss to read?

As she lay in the four-poster bed, staring up at the silk decoration in the darkness over her head, Joss found it hard to close her eyes. Beside her, Luke had fallen into a restless sleep almost as soon as his head had touched the pillow. They were both worn out. After all, the day had started at five in London and now, at midnight, they were at Belheddon, and for better or for worse this was now their home.

Moving her head slightly to left or right, Joss could see the squares of starlight which showed the two windows on opposite sides of the room. Divided by stone mullions in the old plaster, one looked over the front of the house and down the drive toward the village, the other across the back garden and down toward the lake and beyond it, over the hedge to the river estuary and beyond it the distant North Sea. Initially Luke had closed the curtains when he came upstairs. They were heavy with woollen embroidery, double-lined against the cold, luxurious. Looking at them, Joss was grateful for their weight against the drafts, but even so she pulled them open before she climbed into the high bed. "Too claustrophobic," she explained to Luke as he lay back beside her. His only answer, minutes later, was a gentle snore. Outside the moon shone onto a garden as bright as day as the frosty sparkle hardened into a skim of ice. Shivering, Joss huddled down under the duvet — a modern concession, the embroidered bedcover carefully folded away for safety — glad of the solid warmth of her sleeping husband. Surreptitiously her hand strayed to his shoulder. As she snuggled up against him in the darkness she did not see the slight movement in the corner of the room.

73

CHAPTER 7

It was still dark when Joss slipped from the bed, tiptoeing across the icy floor in bare feet. Behind her Luke gave a quiet murmur and, punching the pillow, turned over and went back to sleep. Switching on the light in the bathroom, Joss reached for her clothes left piled on the chair. Thick trousers, shirt, two sweaters, heavy thermal socks. In the ice-cold room her breath came in small clouds. On the window pane, as she held back the curtain and peered out into the darkness, she was enchanted and horrified to find the beautiful, lacy designs of Jack Frost on the inside of the glass. With a rueful smile she padded across the floor and glanced through Tom's door. Worn out by the excitement of the day before, he was sleeping flat on his back, his arms above his head on the pillow, his cheeks pink with sleep. Tiptoeing to the chest where his night-light burned, she glanced at the thermometer that Alice had suggested they keep in the room. The temperature was steady. With a fond smile, she tiptoed out of the room and left the door slightly ajar. If he woke, Luke would hear him.

74

Putting the kettle on the stove, Joss went to the back door and pulled it open. The morning blackness was totally silent. No birdsong. No traffic murmur in the distance as there would have been in London, no cheerful clink of milk bottles. Pulling on her heavy coat, she stepped out into the courtyard. The bulk of the old Bentley had been pulled into the coach house and the doors closed. There was nothing here now but their own Citroën, covered in a thick white frost. The gate out into the garden was painfully cold even beneath her gloved hands as she pushed it back and let herself out onto the matted lawn. Above her head the stars were still blazing as though it were full night. Glancing up, she saw a faint light shining from behind the curtains in Lyn's room. Was she too unable to sleep then in a strange bed?

The grass was spiky, brittle beneath her boots. She could almost hear the tinkle of broken glass as she walked across it, skirting the skeletal branches of a blackly silhouetted tree, down toward the gleam of water. In the east now, she realized, the stars were dimming. Soon it would begin to grow light.

She stood for several moments, gloved hands in pockets, staring down at the ice as around her the garden began imperceptibly to brighten. She was numb with cold, but through the chill she could feel something else. Apprehension — fear even — of what they had done. They had had no real choice. Even if Luke had found a job working for someone else she doubted they could have afforded the rent on a flat of a decent size and certainly they couldn't have bought a place of their own. They could no longer live in London. But this, this was so different. Another world from the one they had planned together when they had first got married. She frowned, stamping her feet, reluctant as yet to go back inside. A new world, new people, new memories — no, memories wasn't the right word. A history to be learned and assimilated and in some way lived.

Sammy!

The voice, a boy's voice, called suddenly out of the darkness behind her. Joss spun around.

Sammy!

It came again, more distant now.

Across the lawn, in the house, a light had appeared in her and Luke's bedroom. The curtains weren't quite closed and a broad vee of light flooded out across the frosted grass.

"Hello?" Joss's voice was a husky intrusion into the intense silence. "Who's there?" She glanced around. The stars were disappearing fast now. A dull grayness was drifting in among the bushes in the shrubbery near her. She frowned. "Is there someone there?" She called again, more loudly this time, her voice seeming to echo across the water. In the distance a bird called loudly. Then the silence returned.

Turning sharply back to the house, she found she was shivering violently as she hurried back

76

in the direction of the kitchen. Pulling off her boots and gloves, she ran inside, blowing on her fingers, to find the kettle cheerfully filling the room with steam. When Luke appeared, some ten minutes later, she was sitting at the table, still in her heavy coat, her hands cupped around a mug of tea.

"So, Joss, how is it?" He smiled at her as he found himself a mug on the draining board.

She reached up to kiss him on the mouth. "Wonderful, strange. Terrifying."

He laughed, briefly resting his hand over hers. "We'll cope, Joss." His face became serious for a moment. "Are you happy about Alice and Joe staying? You don't want to establish your own territory a bit before they muscle in?" He searched her face seriously. "I know how much this house means to you, love. I do understand how you must feel about it all. If there is any conflict —"

"There isn't." She shook her head adamantly. "I need them here, Luke. I can't explain it, but I need them. It's as though they represent something solid, something to hang onto — a life belt — from my old life. Besides, I love them. They are my parents. Whatever, whoever Laura was, I never knew her." Pushing back the chair, she stood up abruptly. "I don't want her taking over my life. I don't want her to think she can buy my affection — my love — with all this." She gestured at the kitchen around them.

"I don't think that's what she intended, Joss." Luke was watching her, puzzled. Her dark hair had fallen in a curtain across her eyes and she

77

hadn't tossed it back, a habitual gesture of hers which he loved. Instead, it hung there, hiding her face, concealing her expression.

"Luke." She still hadn't looked at him. "I walked down to the lake while it was still dark. There was someone out there."

"Out in the garden?" He pulled up a chair and sat opposite her. "Who?"

"They were calling. For someone called Sammy."

He laughed. "Probably a cat. You know how sound travels. On a cold, still night, and near water. It was probably someone in the village."

At last she had pushed back her hair. She gave him a small lopsided grin, blowing on her tea. "Of course. Why didn't I think of that."

"Because you are an idiot and I love you." He smiled, still watching her face. She was white with exhaustion. The stress of the last two months had told heavily on her. Preoccupied with the business, he had had to leave the organization of the sale of the house, the packing, and the move to her as well as the frequent trips to East Anglia to supervise the opening up of the house and to check the plumbing and electricity. Although Lyn had from time to time taken Tom off her hands for a few hours to help her, he knew the strain had been enormous. She had lost about a stone, and the dark rings under her eyes were gaunt reminders of night after night tossing, sleepless, beside him as they lay staring up at the ceiling locked in silent thought in the dark before the move.

"First day of the rest of our lives, Joss." He

raised his mug to clink against hers. "Cheers."

"Cheers." She smiled.

Alice and Joe appeared a half hour later as Joss was strapping Tom into his high chair. "Good morning, sweetheart." Alice stopped and kissed the little boy on the head. "Joss, my love, your father and I have been talking and we've decided to go back to town today."

"But Mum —" Joss stared at her aghast. "Why? I thought you liked it here —"

"We do, Jossie." Joe sat down and pulled the teapot toward him. "And we'll be back. We've things to do at home, and shopping." He wiggled his eyebrows at Tom, who giggled and banged his spoon on the table in front of him. "Shopping to do with Father Christmas. We'll be back, love, before you know it. Your mum needs to rest a bit, Joss. She's not really up to doing much at the moment." He shook his head. "And I know her. She won't be able to sit still as long as she knows there's work to be done and besides, I think, and your mother agrees with me, that you and Luke need a few days to settle in on your own."

"But we don't. We've already discussed this, and I want you here." She knew she sounded like a spoiled child. With a miserable sniff, Joss turned toward the stove and reached for the kettle. "You can't go. Mum needn't do anything heavy. She can rest here —"

"I think maybe they're right, Joss," Luke said quietly. He glanced over her head at his father-in-law.

"Well, at least Lyn can stay." Joss took a deep

breath. Picking up a jug of milk, she reached for Tom's beaker.

"No, love. Lyn is coming with us." Joe hooked the toast rack toward him. Selecting a piece, he buttered it and cut it into strips, putting them down in front of his grandson. "We've talked it over with her too. She can come back next week if you want her, if she hasn't got another temporary job by then." He sighed. Uninterested in anything academic, Lyn had left school at sixteen and drifted from one unsatisfactory temporary job to another. While Joss had stayed on to do her A levels and followed that with a brilliant career at Bristol University and then a teaching post, Lyn, at the age of thirty, with two failed relationships and an aborted attempt at running her own catering business behind her, had moved back in with her parents and resumed her halfhearted trawl through the agencies. Joe shook his head. "Then your mum and I will return on the Wednesday after that in plenty of time for Christmas. And we'll all stay as long as you like to help you get straight."

"They had it all planned!" Standing in the coach house later, with Tom's gloved hand clutched in her own, Joss stared at her husband's back as he leaned over the huge rusting engine of the Bentley. "Why? Was it your idea?"

Luke straightened. "No, it wasn't. But I had the same feeling they did. You need to be here on your own, Joss. It's important. You need to explore. To get the feel of the place. They know you as well as I do — better, for God's sake. We all know how special places are to you." He walked over to the bench by the wall where already he had laid out a selection of his tools.

She shook her head. "Am I so predictable? You can all tell how I feel before I feel it?"

" 'Fraid so!" he chuckled.

"And what about you? What are you going to feel about this place?"

"Cold, mostly." And uneasy, he was going to say, though he wasn't quite sure why. The same way Joe and Alice had felt. They hadn't said anything, but he could see it in their eyes. No wonder they had wanted to get away. "So, if you could arrange to have the kettle on in say half an hour, I can come in and thaw out. I want to keep to my plan if I can. Work on the old bus for George Maxim in the mornings, and on the house and garden in the afternoon. That way I can divide my time. Joss —" He looked suddenly concerned. "We weren't all ganging up on you, love. I promise. Listen, if you think you are going to feel a bit lonely, why don't you ask that Goodyear woman and her husband over for a meal. They are obviously dying to find out about us, and we can do some reciprocal pumping about the house."

"Right, Tom Tom, let's start at the top today for a change." Two days of unrelenting unpacking and sorting and cleaning later, her phone call made, and her invitation for supper at the end of the week ecstatically accepted by the Goodyears and the Fairchilds at the post office, Joss picked up a duster and broom and made for the stairs, the little boy running purposefully behind her.

In the attic a series of small rooms led out of one another, all empty, all wallpapered in small faded flowers and leaves, all with sloping roofs and dark, dusty beams. Those facing south were full of bright winter sunshine warm behind the glass of the windows, those which looked out over the front of the house were cold and shadowed. Joss glanced at the little boy. He was staying very close to her, his thumb firmly held in his mouth. "Nice house, Tom?" She smiled at him encouragingly. They were looking at a pile of old books.

"Tom go down." He reached out for her long sweater and wound his fingers into it.

"We'll go down in a minute, to make Daddy some coffee —" She broke off. Somewhere nearby she heard a child's laugh. There was a scuffle of feet, running, then silence.

"Boy," Tom informed her hopefully. He peered around her shyly.

Joss swallowed. "There aren't any boys here, Tom Tom." But of course, there must be. Boys from the village. The house had been empty so long it would have been very strange if no one had found their way in to explore the old place.

"Hello?" she called. "Who's there?"

There was silence.

"Sammy?" She remembered the name out of nowhere, out of the dark. "Sammy, are you there?" The silence was intense. It no longer seemed to be the silence of emptiness; it was a listening, inquiring silence.

"Mummy, look." Tom tugged at her sweater. "Flutterby!" A ragged peacock butterfly, woken by the heat of the sun on the glass, was fluttering feebly against the window, its wings shushing faintly, shedding red-blue dust.

"Poor thing, it's trapped." Joss looked at it sadly. To let it go out into the cold would mean certain death.

The laughter came from the other end of the attic this time; pealing, joyous, followed again by the sound of feet. Tom laughed. "See boys," he cried. "Me wants to see boys."

"Mummy wants to see boys too," Joss agreed. She stooped and picked him up, abandoning the butterfly as she pulled open the door which separated this room from the next. "They shouldn't be here. We're going to have to tell them to go home for their lunch —" She broke off. The next room, larger than the rest, was the last. Beyond it, out of the high windows, she could look down on the stable yard, seeing the doors pulled wide where Luke was standing in the coach house entrance talking to a strange man. Joss swung around. "Where have those naughty boys gone?"

"Naughty boys gone," Tom echoed sadly. He too was staring around, tears welling in his eyes. This was where the sound of the children had come from without a doubt, but the room was empty even of the clutter which had stood in some of the others. The boards, sloping with age, were dusty. They showed no footmarks.

"Tom. I think we'll go downstairs." She was uneasy. "Let's go and make Daddy his coffee, then you can go and call him for me." She backed toward the door. Suddenly she didn't want to meet these hidden children after all.

The morning of their first informal supper party three days later Luke pulled open the cellar door and switched on the lights. Tom was asleep upstairs when he had dragged Joss away from her polishing. "Let's have a real look at that wine. We'll see if we can find something decent to drink tonight."

Running down the creaking staircase ahead of her, he stared around. The cellar was cold and smelled strongly of damp. A preliminary glance a few days earlier had, to their excitement, told them the cellar contained a great deal of wine, racks of bottles, bins and cases stretched away into the darkness of a second cellar beyond the first. "Joss?" He turned and looked for her.

Joss was standing at the top of the stairs.

"Joss, come on. Help me choose."

She shook her head. "I'm sorry, Luke. No." She took a step backward. She couldn't explain her sudden revulsion. "I'll go and put on the coffee or something."

He stared up at the doorway. "Joss? What's wrong?" But she had gone. He shrugged. Turning, he stood in front of the first wine rack and stared at it. Joss's father had obviously had a good eye. He recognized some of the vintages, but this would need an expert to go over it one day. Perhaps David Tregarron would help him look over it when he came down to see them. David's passion for wine, even greater than his love of history, had been legendary in Joss's staff room. Luke shivered. It was cold down here —

good for the wine, of course, but not for people. Reaching out toward the rack, he stopped suddenly and, turning, looked behind him. He thought he had heard something in the corner of the cellar out of sight behind the racks. He listened, his eyes searching the shadows where the light from the single strip light failed to reach. There was no other sound.

Uncomfortably, he moved slightly. "Joss? Are you still up there?" His voice sounded very hollow. There was no reply.

He turned back to the wine rack, trying to concentrate on the bottles, but in spite of himself he was listening, glancing toward the darker corners. Grabbing two bottles at last, more or less at random, he looked around with a shiver and then, turning for the stairs, raced up them two at a time. Slamming the cellar door behind him, he turned the key with relief. Then he laughed out loud. "Clot! What did you think was down there!" By the time he had reached the kitchen and put the bottles on the table he had recovered himself completely.

Roy and Janet Goodyear and the Fairchilds arrived together for their first dinner party at exactly eight o'clock, trooping in through the back door and standing staring around in the kitchen with evident delight.

"Well, you've certainly made a fine job of everything," Roy Goodyear commented thoughtfully when they had all returned to the kitchen after a tour of the house. "It all looks so nice and lived in, now." Joss followed his gaze. It did look good. Their china and glass unpacked, the dresser decorated with pretty plates and flowers, the long table laid, and the range warming the room to a satisfactory glow. Luke had strung their Christmas cards from the bell wires, and a huge bunch of mistletoe hung over the door out into the pantry.

"I'm sorry we're eating in the kitchen," Joss said while filling Janet's glass.

"My dear, we wouldn't want to be anywhere else. You've got it really lovely and cosy here." Sally Fairchild had seated herself at the table, her elbows spread among the knives and forks. Joss could see her gaze going now and then to the corn dolly, which Luke had suspended from a length of fishing twine over the table.

"I expect the Duncans were very formal when they lived here." Luke lifted the heavy casserole from the oven and carried it to the table. "Sit down, Roy. And you, Alan."

"They were when Philip was alive." Roy Goodyear levered his heavy frame into a chair next to his wife. In his late fifties, he was taller by a head than Janet, his face weather-beaten to the color of raw steak, his eyes a strangely light amber under the bushy gray brows. "Your father was a very formal man, Joss." Both couples now knew the full story of Joss's parentage. "But in the sixties people from his background still did observe all the formalities. They wouldn't have known anything else. They kept a staff here, of course. Cook and housemaid and two gardeners. When we came to dinner here we always dressed. Philip had a magnificent cellar." He cocked an eye at Luke. "I suppose it's too much to hope that it's still there."

"It is, as a matter of fact." He glanced at Joss. He had not mentioned his hasty exit from the cellar to her, nor asked her why she had refused to go down there with him. "We've got a friend in London — Joss's ex-boss, in fact — who is a bit of a wine buff. I thought we might ask him to come down and have a look down there."

Roy had already glanced at the bottle and nodded contentedly. "Well, if he needs any help or encouragement, don't forget your neighbors across the fields. I would very much like to see what you've got."

"Apart from the ghost, of course," Janet put in quietly.

There was a moment's silence. Joss glanced at her sharply. "I suppose there had to be a ghost."

"And not just any old ghost, either. The villagers say it is the devil himself who lives here." Alan Fairchild raised his glass and squinted through it critically. "Isn't that right, Janet? You are the expert on these matters." He grinned broadly. Silent until now, he was obviously enjoying the sensation his words had caused.

"Alan!" Sally Fairchild blushed pink in the candlelight. "I told you not to say anything about all that. These poor people! They've got to live here."

"Well, if he lives in the cellar, I didn't see him." With a glance at Joss, Luke lifted the lid off the casserole for her and handed her the serving ladle, his face veiled in fragrant steam.

Joss was frowning. "If we're sharing the house, I'd like to know who with," she said. She smiled at Alan. "Come on. Spill the beans. Who else lives here? I know we have visits from time to time by village children. I'd quite like that to stop. I don't know how they get in."

"Kids are the end these days." Janet reached for a piece of bread. "No discipline at all. It shouldn't surprise me if they do come here because the house has been empty for so long, but with the legend —" she paused. "I'd have thought they'd be too scared."

"The devil you mean?" Joss's voice was light, but Luke could hear the edge to it.

He reached for a plate. "You're not serious about the devil, I hope."

"Of course he's not serious." It was Joss who answered. "All old houses have legends, and we should be pleased this one is no exception."

"It's a very old site, of course," Janet said thoughtfully. "I believe it goes back to Roman times. Houses with a history as long as that always seem very glamorous. They collect legends. It doesn't mean there is anything to be frightened of. After all, Laura lived here for years practically on her own, and I believe her mother did before that, when she was widowed."

My fear makes him stronger . . .

The words in Joss's head for a moment blotted out all other conversation. Her mother, alone in the house, had been terrified.

"Have the family owned the house for a long time then?" Luke was carrying around the dish of sprouts.

"I should think a hundred years, certainly. Maybe more than that. If you look in the church

88

you'll see memorials to people who have lived at the Hall. But I don't think the same name crops up again and again the way it does in some parishes." Roy shrugged. "You want to talk to one of the local history buffs. They'll know all about it. Someone like Gerald Andrews. He lives in Ipswich now, but he had a house in the village here for years, and I think he wrote a booklet about this place. I'll give you his phone number."

"You said my mother lived here practically on her own," Joss said thoughtfully. Everyone served at last, she sat down and reached for her napkin. "Did she not have a companion, then?"

He came again today without warning and without mercy . . .

The words had etched themselves into her brain. They conjured for her a picture of a woman alone, victimized. Terrified, in the large, empty house.

"She had several, I believe. I don't think any of them stayed very long and at the end she lived here quite alone, although of course Mary Sutton always stayed in close touch with her. I don't think Laura minded being alone though, do you Janet? She used to walk down to the village every day with her dog, and she had lots of visitors. She wasn't in any sense a recluse. People used to come down from London. And of course there was the Frenchman."

"The Frenchman?" Luke's eyebrows shot up. "That sounds definitely intriguing."

"It was." Janet smiled. "My dear, I don't know if it's true. It was just village gossip, but everyone thought, in the end, that that was where she had gone. She went to live in France and we guessed she'd gone to be with him. She was a very attractive woman."

"As is her daughter!" Gallantly, Roy raised his glass.

Joss smiled at him. "And the house stayed empty after she left?"

"Completely. The village was devastated. It was — is — after all the heart and soul of the place, together with the church. Have you made contact with Mary Sutton yet?"

Joss shook her head. "I've tried every time I've been into the village, but there is never any answer. I wonder if she's gone away or something?"

The four guests glanced at each other. Sally Fairchild shrugged. "That's strange. She's there. She's not ill or anything. She was in the shop yesterday." She shook her head. "Perhaps she's nervous of answering the door to a stranger. I'll have a word next time she comes in. Tell her who you are. You must speak to her. She worked here for years. She would remember your mother as a child."

"And she would presumably remember the devil if she'd met him face to face." Joss's words, spoken with a seriousness which she hadn't perhaps intended, were followed by a moment of silence.

"Joss —" Luke warned.

"My dear, I've upset you." Alan was looking contrite. "Take no notice of me. It's a silly tale. Suitable for around-the-fire, late-at-night, well-

90

into-your-third-brandy sessions. Not to be taken seriously."

"I know." Joss forced a smile. "I'm sorry. I didn't intend to sound so portentous." She reached for her wineglass and twisted it between her fingers. "You knew Edgar Gower, presumably, when he was here?" She turned to Roy.

He nodded. "Great fun, Edgar. What a character! Now, he knew your mother very well indeed."

Joss nodded. "It was he who put me in touch with the solicitor; it was through him I found out about Belheddon." She glanced at Luke and then turned back to the Goodyears. "He tried to dissuade me from following it up. He felt the house was an unhappy place."

"He was a superstitious old duffer." Janet snorted fondly. "He used to encourage Laura to think the house was haunted. It upset her a lot. I got very cross with him."

"So you didn't believe in the ghosts?"

"No." The hesitation had been infinitesimal. "And don't let him get to you, either, Joss. I'm sure the bishop thought he was going a bit dotty at the end and that's why he retired him. Keep away from him, my dear."

"I wrote to him to say we'd inherited the house. I wanted to thank him, but he never replied." She had also phoned twice but there had been no answer.

"That's hardly surprising. He's probably too busy having apocalyptic visions!" Roy put in.

"No, that's unfair!" Janet turned on her husband. "They go off to South Africa every winter

91

since his retirement to spend several months with their daughter. That's why he's not been in touch, Joss."

"I see." Joss was astonished for a moment at her disappointment. She had seen Edgar as a strength, there in the background to advise them if ever they should need it. His words returned to her suddenly — words she tried to push to the back of her mind whenever she remembered them, words she had never repeated to Luke. "I prayed you would never come to find me, Jocelyn Grant."

The conversation had moved on without her. Vaguely, she heard Alan talking about village cricket, then Sally laughing at some anecdote about a neighbor. She missed it. Edgar's voice was still there in her ears: "There is too much unhappiness attached to that house. The past is the past. It should be allowed to rest." She shook her head abruptly. He had asked her if she had children and when she had told him, he had said nothing; and he had sighed.

Pushing her chair back with a shiver, she stood up suddenly. "Luke, give everyone second helpings. I'm just going to pop upstairs and make sure Tom is all right."

The hall was silent, lit by the table lamp in the corner. She paused for a moment, shivering in the draft which swept in under the front door. The kitchen was the only room in the house they had so far managed to heat up to modern standards, thanks to the range.

She needed to think. Staring at the lamp, she found her mind whirling. Edgar Gower, the house, her mother's fear — there had to be some basis for all the stories. And the devil. Why should people think the devil lived at Belheddon?

Pushing open the heavy door into the great hall, she stopped in horror. Tom's piercing screams filled the room, echoing down the stairs from his bedroom.

"Tom!" She took the stairs two at a time. The little boy was standing up in his crib, tears streaming down his face, his hands locked onto the bars. The room was ice cold. In the near darkness of the teddy bear night-light in the corner she could see his small face beetroot red in the shadows. Swooping on him, she scooped him up into her arms. His pajamas were soaking wet.

"Tom, what is it, darling." She nuzzled his hair. He was dripping with sweat.

"Tom go home." His sobs were heartrending. "Tom go to Tom's house."

Joss bit her lip. "This is Tom's house, darling. Tom's new house." She cradled his head against her shoulder. "What happened? Did you have a bad dream?"

She held him away from her on her knee, studying his face. "Tom Tom? What is it?"

"Tom go home." He was staring over her shoulder toward the window, snuffling pathetically, taking comfort from her arms.

"I tell you what." She reached to turn on the main light, flooding the room with brightness. "Let's change your jym-jams, and make you a nice clean, dry bed, then you can come downstairs for a few minutes to Mummy and Daddy's party before going back to sleep. How would that be?"

Holding him on her hip she went through the familiar routine, extracting clean dry clothes and bedding from his chest of drawers, changing him, sponging his face and hands, brushing his hair with the soft baby hairbrush, aware that every few minutes he kept glancing back toward the window. His thumb had been firmly plugged into his mouth as she sat him on the rug and turned to make his bed, stripping off the wet covers, wiping over the rubber sheet.

"Man go away." He took his thumb out long enough to speak and then plugged it in again.

Joss turned. "What man?" Her voice was sharper than she intended, and she saw the little boy's eyes fill with tears. Desperately, he held out his arms to her. Stooping, she hauled him off the ground. "What man, Tom Tom? Did you dream about a nasty man?" In spite of herself she followed his gaze to the corner of the room. She had found some pretty ready-made curtains for his window. They showed clowns somersaulting through hoops and balloons and ribbons. Those and the soft colorful rugs had turned the nursery into one of the brightest rooms in the house. But in the shadows of the little night-light, had there been anything there to cast a shadow and frighten him? She bit her lip.

"Tell me about the man, Tom," she said gently.

"Tin man." Tom reached for the locket on a chain around her neck and pulled it experimentally. She smiled, firmly extricating it from his grasp. "A tin man? From one of your books?" That explained it. She sighed with relief. Lyn must have been reading him *The Wizard of Oz* before she left. With a glance around the room she hugged him close. "Come on, Tom Tom, let's take you down to meet the neighbors."

She knew from experience that within ten minutes, sitting on Luke's knee in a warm kitchen, the little boy would be fast asleep and tomorrow, before anything else, she would buy a baby alarm so that never again would the little boy scream unheard in his distant bedroom. With a final glance around she carried him out into the darkened main bedroom. It was very cold in there. The undrawn curtains allowed frosty moonlight to spill across the floor, reflecting a soft gleam on the polished oak boards, throwing the shadow from the four-poster bed as thick bars over the rug in front of her feet. She stopped, cradling Tom's head against her shoulder, staring suddenly into the far corner. It was deep in shadow. Her jacket, hanging from the wardrobe handle, was a wedge of blackness against the black. Her arms tightened around the little boy protectively.

Katherine.

It was a whisper in the silence. Tom raised his head. "Daddy?" he said. He craned around her shoulder to see.

Joss shook her head slightly. It was nothing. Her imagination. Luke was in the kitchen. "No, darling. There's no one there." She kissed his head. "Daddy's downstairs. Let's go and find him."

"Tin man." The thumb was drawn out of the mouth long enough for Tom to point over her

95

shoulder into the darkness of the corner. "Tin man there." His face crumpled and a small sob escaped him before he buried his face in her shoulder again.

"No, darling. No tin man. Just shadows." Joss made for the door. She almost ran along the corridor and down the stairs.

"Hey, who is this?" Roy stood up and held out his arms to Tom. "How come you've been missing the party, old chap?"

"Joss?" Luke had spotted Joss's white face. "What is it? What was wrong?"

She shook her head. "Nothing. He was crying and we didn't hear him. I expect he had had a bad dream."

A dream about a tin man who skulked in dark corners.

CHAPTER 8

The drawers of the desk were full of papers and letters, the general detritus of a lifetime, dealt with, filed, and forgotten. Sitting on the floor with them spread out around her a couple of evenings later, Joss could find nothing to explain or even relate to her mother's mysterious notebook. She had studied it again and again. No pages had been torn out. No entries eradicated in any way. It was as if, having carefully inscribed the flyleaf for Joss, her mother had once, and once only, grabbed the empty notebook in desperation and scribbled those two lone sentences in it. They haunted Joss. They were a plea for help, a despairing scream. What had happened? Who could have upset her so much? Could it have been the Frenchman who the village thought had come to woo her?

She had said nothing to Luke about the notebook. It was as if her mother had whispered a secret to her and she did not want to betray the confidence. This was something she had to find out on her own. Putting down the notebook, she reached for the coffee mug standing on the carpet next to her and sipped thoughtfully, staring out of the French doors across the lawn. There had been another heavy frost in the night and the grass was still white in the shelter of the tall hedge beyond the stables. Above it the sky was a clear brilliant blue. In the silence, through the window, she could hear the clear ring of metal on metal. Luke was well into his work on the Bentley.

A robin hopped across the York stone terrace outside the window and stood head to one side staring down at the ground. Joss smiled. Earlier she had thrown out the breakfast crumbs, but there was little left now after the flock of sparrows and blackbirds had descended on them from the trees.

The house was very silent. Tom was asleep and for now at least she had the place to herself. Lightly she touched the back of the notebook with her finger. "Mother." The word hovered in the air. The room was very cold. Joss shivered. She had two thick sweaters on over her jeans and a long silk scarf wound round and round her neck against the insidious drafts which permeated the house, but even so her hands were frozen. In a moment she would go back to the kitchen to warm up and replenish her coffee. In a moment. She sat still, staring around, trying to feel her mother's presence. The room had been Laura's special, favorite place, of that she had no doubt. Her mother's books, her sewing, her desk, her letters — and yet nothing remained. There was no scent in the cushions, no warmth of contact as her hand brushed the place where her mother's hand had been, no vibrations which still held the vital essence of the woman who had borne her.

The envelope with the French stamp had slipped between some old bills in a faded green cardboard wallet. Joss stared down at it for a moment, registering the slanted handwriting, the faded violet ink. The postmark, she noted, was Paris and the year it was posted 1979. Inside was one flimsy sheet of paper.

Ma chère Laura — As you see I did not reach home yesterday as I intended. My appointment was postponed until tomorrow. I shall ring you afterwards. Take care of yourself, my dear lady. My prayers are with you.

Joss squinted at the paper more closely. The signature was an indecipherable squiggle. Screwing up her eyes she tried to make out the first letter. P? B? Sighing, she laid the paper down. There was no address.

"So, what are you up to?" Luke had come into the room so quietly she had not heard him.

Startled, she looked up. "Sorting through the desk."

He was dressed like her in several old sweaters; over them, the stained overalls and the woollen scarf did nothing to hide how cold he was. He rubbed his oily hands together. "Feel like some coffee? I need to thaw out."

"Yes, please." She was pushing the papers together in a heap on the carpet in front of her when the telephone rang. "Mrs. Grant?" The voice was unfamiliar, female, elderly. "I understand you have been trying to reach me. My name is Mary Sutton."

Joss felt a leap of excitement. "That's right, Mrs. Sutton —"

"Miss, dear. Miss Sutton." The voice at the other end was suddenly prim. "I do not answer my door to strangers, you understand. But now I know who you are you may come and see me. I have something which may interest you."

"Now?" Joss was taken aback.

"That's right. It is here. Now."

"Right. I'll come over now." Joss shrugged as she hung up. "A somewhat peremptory Miss Sutton wishes to see me now. I'll take a rain check on the coffee, Luke, and go before she changes her mind. She says she has something for me. Will you watch Tom Tom?"

"OK." Luke leaned across and kissed her cheek. "See you later then."

This time when Joss knocked at the cottage door on the green it opened almost immediately. Mary Sutton was a small wizened woman with wispy white hair, caught back in a knot on the top of her head. Her narrow, birdlike face was framed by heavy tortoiseshell spectacles.

Joss was shown into a small neat front room which smelled strongly of old baking and long-dead flowers. A heavy brown oilcloth covered the table, on which was a small notebook. It was identical to the one Joss had found in her mother's desk. Her eyes were glued to it as she took the proffered seat on an upright chair near the window.

After several long seconds of silent scrutiny the

solemn face before her broke suddenly into a huge beam. "You may call me Mary, my dear, as your mother did." Mary turned away and began to pour out tea which had been laid ready on a tray on the sideboard. "I looked after you when you were very small. It was I who gave you to the adoption people when they came to collect you." She blinked hard through her pebble lenses. "Your mother could not bring herself to be there. She walked in the fields down by the river until you had gone."

Joss stared at her aghast, trapped into silence by the lump in her throat. Behind the glasses, the old lady's eyes, magnified into huge half globes, were brimming with tears.

"Why did she give me away?" It was several minutes before Joss could bring herself to ask. She accepted the teacup with shaking hands and put it down hastily on the edge of the table. Her eyes had returned from Mary's face to the notebook.

"It was not because she didn't love you, my dear. On the contrary, she did it because she loved you so much." Mary sat down and pulled her skirt tightly over her knees, tucking the voluminous fabric under her bony legs. "The others had died, you see. She thought if you stayed at Belheddon, you would die too."

"The others?" Joss's mouth was dry.

"Sammy and George. Your brothers."

"Sammy?" Joss stared at her. She had gone cold all over.

"What, dear?" Mary frowned. "What did you say?"

101

"You looked after them? My brothers?" Joss whispered.

Mary nodded. "Since they were born." She gave a wistful little smile. "Little rascals they were, both of them. So like their father. Your mother adored them. It nearly broke her when she lost them. First Sammy, then Georgie. It was too much for any woman to bear."

"How old were they when they died?" Joss's fingers were clenched in her lap.

"Sammy was seven, near as makes no difference. Georgie was born a year after that, in 1954, and he died on his eighth birthday, bless him."

"How?" Joss's whisper was almost inaudible.

"Terrible. Both of them. Sammy had been collecting tadpoles. They found him in the lake." There was a long silence. "When Georgie died it was nearly the end of your mother."

Joss stared at her speechlessly as, shaking her head, Mary sipped at her tea. "They found him at the bottom of the cellar steps, you see. He knew he was never allowed down there, and Mr. Philip, he had the cellar keys. They were still there, locked in his desk." She sighed. "Sorrows long gone, my dear. You must not grieve over them. Your mother would not have wanted that." She reached for the notebook and took it off the table, holding it on her lap with little gentle stroking movements of her fingers. "I've kept this all these years. It's right you should have them. Your mother's poems." Still she didn't release the volume, holding it close as if she could not bear to part with it.

"You must have loved her very much," Joss

said at last. She found there were tears in her eyes.

Mary made no response, continuing to stroke the notebook quietly.

"Did you — did you know the French gentleman who came here?" She studied the old lady's face. There was a slight pursing of the lips, no more.

"I knew him."

"What was he like?"

"Your mother was fond of him."

"I don't even know his name."

Mary looked up at last. This at least was something she seemed able to divulge without reservation. "Paul Deauville. He was an art dealer. He traveled the world, I understand."

"Did he live in Paris?"

"He did."

"And my mother went to live with him?"

A definite frisson — almost a shudder. "He took your mother away from Belheddon."

"Do you think he made her happy?"

Mary met Joss's eye and held it steady through the grotesquely magnifying lenses of her glasses. "I hope so, my dear. I never heard from her again after she left."

As if she were afraid she had said too much, Mary clamped her lips shut, and after several more perfunctory attempts at questioning her Joss rose to leave. It was only as she turned to walk through the front door into the blinding frosty sunlight that Mary at last relinquished the notebook.

"Take care of it. There is so little of her left."

The old lady caught her arm.

"I will." Joss hesitated. "Mary, will you come and see us? I should like you to meet my little boy, Tom."

"No." Mary shook her head. "No, my dear. I'll not come to the house, if you don't mind. Best not." With that she stepped back into the shadows of her narrow front hall and closed the door almost in Joss's face.

The graves were there, beyond her father's. Quite overgrown now, she hadn't seen the two small white cross headstones side by side in the nettles under the tree. She stood looking down at them for a long time. Samuel John and George Philip. Someone had left a small bowl of white chrysanthemums on each. Joss smiled through her tears. Mary at least had never forgotten them.

Luke and Tom were busy in the coach house when she got home. With one look at their happy oily faces, she left them to their mechanical endeavors and, clutching the notebook, retreated to the study. The sunshine through the window had warmed the room, and she smiled a little to herself as she stooped and, throwing on some logs, coaxed the fire back into life. In a few moments it would be almost bearable. Curling up on the armchair in the corner, she opened the notebook at the first page. *Laura Manners — Commonplace Book.* The inscription in the flyleaf of this notebook was in the same flamboyant hand as that in the other. She glanced at the first few pages and felt a sharp pang of disappointment. She had assumed her mother would have written the poems herself, but these were bits and pieces copied out from many authors — a collection, obviously, of her favorite poems and pieces of prose. There was Keats's ode "To Autumn," a couple of Shakespeare sonnets, some Byron, Gray's "Elegy."

Slowly, page after page she leafed through, reading a few lines here and there, trying to form a picture of her mother's taste and education from the words on the page. Romantic, eclectic, occasionally obscure. There were lines from Racine and Dante in the original French and Italian, a small verse from Schiller. She was something of a linguist then. There were even Latin epigrams. Then suddenly the mood of the book changed. Taped between two pages was a single sheet, old and torn, very frail, held in place by tape that had discolored badly. It was an India paper page, torn, Joss guessed, from a Roman missal. On it, in English and in Latin, was a prayer for the blessing of holy water.

> . . . *I do this that the evil spirit may be driven away from thee, and that thou mayest banish the enemy's power entirely, uprooting and casting out the enemy himself with all his rebel angels . . .*
>
> *. . . so that whatsoever in the homes of the faithful or elsewhere shall have been sprinkled with it may be delivered from everything unclean and hurtful. Let no breath of contagion hover there, no taint of corruption. May all the wiles of the lurking enemy come to nothing, and may anything that threatens the safety or peace of*

those who dwell there be put to flight by the
sprinkling of this water . . .

Joss stared around, letting the book fall into her lap, realizing she had been reading the words out loud. The house was very silent.

Exorcizo te, in nomine Dei + Patris om-
nipotentis, et in nomine Jesu + Christi Filii
ejus, Domine nostri, et in virtute Spiritus +
Sancti . . .

The devil himself lives here . . .
Alan Fairchild's words echoed through her head.

For several minutes she sat staring into space, then, closing the notebook, she stood up and, going to the desk, she reached for the phone.

David Tregarron was in the staff room marking test papers when they put her call through.

"So, how is life in the outback, Jocelyn?" His booming voice seemed to echo around the room.

"Quite a strain, actually." She frowned. The words had come spontaneously, accurately, instead of the easier platitude she had framed in her head. "I hope you can come and see us soon." She sounded so much more desperate than she had intended. "David, would you do me a favor? When you are next in the British Library Reading Room, would you look up Belheddon for me and see if you can find anything about its history?"

There was a slight pause as he tried to interpret her tone. "Of course I will. From what you said

106

before, it sounds like a wonderful old place. I'm looking forward to my first visit."

"So am I." She heard the fervor in her voice with surprise. "I'd like to know what the name means."

"Belheddon? That sounds fairly straightforward. *Bel* — beautiful, of course. Or if the name is much older, it might come from a Celtic derivation, like the Irish, which, if I remember rightly, has much the same meaning as *aber* in Wales or Scotland — the mouth of a river. Or it could come from the old gods Bel, you remember Beltane, or Baal from the Bible, who came to represent the devil himself. Then I think *heddon* means heather — or a temple on a heathery hill or some such —"

"What did you say?" Joss's voice was sharp.

"A temple —"

"No, before that. About the devil."

"Well, it's just a possibility, I suppose. Rather romantic, really. Perhaps the original site housed a temple."

"There's a local legend, David, that the devil lives here." Her voice was strangely thin and harsh.

"And you sound afraid rather than amused. Oh, come on, Joss. You're not letting the credulous yokels get to you, are you?" The jovial manner had dropped away abruptly. "You don't believe in any of this, surely?"

"Of course not." She laughed. "I'd just like to know why the house has this reputation. It is sort of dramatic!"

"Well, I suppose it is on dark nights with the

wind howling around. I must say, I can't wait to come and see it." There was a pause. "I don't suppose I could look in this weekend, could I? I know it's getting awfully near Christmas, but term's practically over. I can look a few things up for you, find a few books, perhaps?"

She laughed, extraordinarily pleased. "Of course you can come! That would be wonderful. One thing we are not short of is space, providing you pack enough warm clothes. It's like the Arctic here."

When Luke came in, carrying a filthy small boy, both of them cold and terribly pleased with themselves, Joss was smiling to herself as she stirred a huge pan of soup. "David's coming up the day after tomorrow."

"Great." Luke held Tom under one arm over the sink and reached for the hand cleaner. "It will be nice to see him. He'll bring news no doubt of dear old London and civilization." He chuckled, smearing green goo all over his small son's hands as Tom crowed with delight. Luke glanced at her over the sticky curls. "He's not going to make you feel you're missing out, is he? Rural stagnation instead of academia?"

She shook her head. "Nope. If I want to get back into it, I can always start some kind of research project with the prospect of a book in about a thousand years' time. Or something less academic and more lucrative. The book David suggested I have a go at, perhaps. I might just have to chat with him about that." The idea had in fact been growing on her.

Reaching for the pepper mill, she ground it

over the soup, stirred, put down the wooden spoon, and sat down at the kitchen table. "You haven't asked how I got on with Mary Sutton."

Luke raised an eyebrow. "I could see it was good and bad when you came back. Want to tell me now?"

"Both my little brothers died here, Luke. In accidents."

She was looking at Tom, suddenly aching to hold him. How could her mother have borne to lose two boys?

"Nothing will happen to Tom Tom, Joss." Luke could always read her mind. He changed the subject adroitly. "Listen, talking about Tom Tom and your writing, what do you think of the idea of asking Lyn if she'd like to come and help you look after him. As a sort of proper job." Drying Tom's hands, he posted the little boy in Joss's direction with a gentle slap on the behind.

Joss held out her arms. "While she's out of work, you mean? She's certainly good with Tom, and we could do with some help, though we could only pay her pocket money. It would give me time to get on with the house." She smiled. "And write my best-seller."

"No joking, Joss. We need the money. You've had stuff published in the past. I'm sure you could do it."

"In the past it was in academic journals, Luke. They don't exactly pay megabucks. And just those few short stories."

He smiled. "Minibucks would do, love. I do think you should give it a go. Anything to help.

Keep us in bread and spuds until next year when we start our own vegetable patch, vineyard, bed and breakfast business, vintage car restoration workshop — with small business grant" — he had all the papers spread out over the dining room table — "herb nursery, play group, and counterfeit-money press."

She laughed. "I'm glad we're not contemplating anything too ambitious. Pour me a glass of wine to celebrate and we'll drink to Grant, Grant and Davies Industries." She hauled Tom onto her lap and dropped a kiss onto his hair, screwing up her face at the smell of oil and hand cleaner and dirt. "You need a bath, young man."

Tom wriggled around to smile dazzlingly up at her. "Tom go swim in the water outside," he said.

Joss froze. Her arms tightened around him as suddenly the image of another small boy rose before her eyes, a small boy collecting tadpoles from the lake.

"No, Tom," she whispered. "Not outside. You don't swim outside. Not ever."

CHAPTER 9

"Luke?"

"Mmm."

Luke was poring over some papers, sitting at her mother's desk in the study. They had had supper and had brought the last of the bottle of wine, eked out from lunch, to drink by the fire. Joss was sitting on the rug, feeding twigs to the hungry, crackling flames. Outside the curtains, a deep penetrating frost had settled over the silent garden.

"I suppose with a cellar full of wine, we could afford to open another bottle, couldn't we?" Beside her sat a box of letters and papers, extricated from beneath some old silk curtains in the bottom drawer of the chest in her bedroom. It was still tied with a piece of string. The label on the box said Bourne and Hollingsworth. It was postmarked September 23, 1937, and addressed to John Duncan Esq., Belheddon Hall, Essex.

"We could. But one of us would have to fetch it."

"Bags you do."

He laughed. "Bags we both do. It means we'd

have to go down there."

"Ah." She bit her lip.

"It's not so scary, Joss. There's electric light and hundreds and hundreds of wonderful bottles. No rats."

"I'm not scared of rats!" She was scornful.

"Right, then." He threw down his pen and stood up. "Come on."

"Why don't I fetch the corkscrew from the kitchen?"

"Joss."

She gave an awkward shrug. "It's just — Luke, one of my brothers died falling down the cellar stairs."

He sat down again abruptly. "Oh, Joss. Why didn't you tell me?"

"I only found out this morning from Mary Sutton. But last time, when you went down — I felt it. Something strange — something frightening."

"Only the smell of cold and damp, Joss." His voice was very gentle. "Surely there would be nothing frightening about a little boy's death. Sad, yes. Very sad. But a long time ago. We are here now, to bring happiness to the house."

"Do you think so?"

"Why else did your mother give it to you?"

"I'm not sure." She hugged her knees, gazing into the flames. "She gave it to me because my father wanted me to have it." She shook her head. "It's strange. He seems such a shadowy figure. No one talks about him. No one seems to remember him."

"He died a long time before your mother, didn't

he? That's probably why." He stood up again. "Come on." Stooping, he caught her hand and hauled her to her feet. "We'll find a bottle of Philip's best and get gloriously uninhibited, while Tom's asleep and we've still got the house to ourselves. Sound good?"

"Sounds good." She reached up and kissed him.

The key was in the door. Turning it, Luke reached around into the dark for the light switch and clicked it on, looking down the wooden stairs toward the small underground vaults and the wine racks. Dust lay over the bottles. The cellar was very cold. Cautiously, he padded down the steps ahead of Joss and waited for her at the bottom. "OK?"

She nodded. The air was a curious combination of stale and fresh — the stillness and silence of a tomb and yet, through the mustiness, the clear freshness of the frosted garden outside.

"See." Luke pointed to the top of the wall. "Gratings lead out to the flower beds outside the front walls of the house. The air gets in, but for some reason the temperature never varies much. Perfect for wine." He turned his attention to the rack nearest them. "Some of these newer ones are probably best. I'd hate to drink something worth hundreds, just in order to seduce my wife!"

"Thanks very much!"

There was nothing frightening down here now. Just stillness and, perhaps, memories. She tried not to think of an eight-year-old boy, excited, happy, on his birthday, opening the door and peering down into the dark . . . The thought could not be tolerated. Angrily, she pushed it away. "Just grab something and let's go. It's cold down here."

"OK. Here goes. We don't tell David, right? We'll dispose of the evidence in the bottle bank before he gets here." He pulled two bottles from the rack. "Come on then."

The cellar door safely locked, the corkscrew retrieved from the kitchen, Tom Tom checked — the baby alarm switched on — they settled back by the fire. "So, let's see what we've got." Luke scrutinized the label. "Doudet Naudin 1945. Joss, this is old after all! I suspect this ought to breathe before we drink it."

"Draw the cork and put it by the fire for a bit." Joss reached for the box of letters. Anything to take her mind off the child, peering through the door into forbidden territory, full of excitement, on his birthday . . .

Belheddon Hall,
Belheddon,
Essex
29th September, 1920
Dear John,
Samuel and I were so pleased to see you here yesterday, and to hear that you are once more to settle at Pilgrim Hall. And so you are to marry! Lady Sarah is a lovely and gentle person. I know she will make you so very happy. As we told you, my confinement is expected within a few weeks but as soon as possible after that I hope we may entertain you both at Belheddon. My Samuel is hoping next year to

resume tennis parties here at the Hall. It would be such fun if you could both come. Your ever affectionate cousin, Lydia Manners.

Lydia Manners. Joss turned the sheet of paper over in her hand. The grandmother after whom her mother had named her when she was born. She pulled another small bundle of letters out of the Bourne and Hollingsworth box. Tied with pale blue ribbon, they were labeled "Father's Letters." It was not Laura's writing. Joss frowned as she leafed through them. Different handwriting, different dates, different addresses, addresses that meant nothing to her. Then another, from Belheddon Hall. It was short and to the point.

Our son little Samuel was born safely on 30th November. Please thank Lady Sarah for her note. I will write more soon. Yr affectionate Cousin, Lydia.

The envelope was addressed to John Duncan at Pilgrim Hall. So John was John Duncan, a relative of Philip's. Perhaps his father and so her own grandfather? Putting down the letters, Joss stared into the fire thoughtfully, listening to the voices echoing in her head, voices from her unknown past.

"How about some wine now?" Luke had been watching her for some time as she sorted through the box. Pushing aside his invoices with relief, he flung himself down beside her on the floor and put his arm around her. "You are looking too serious."

She smiled, nestling up against him. "Not at all. Just learning some more about the past. My father's family this time." She watched as Luke poured two glasses. The wine was delicious. It was dark brown and smoky, like a wood in November. She could feel the rich warmth of it running through her veins. After only a few sips she was feeling extraordinarily sexy. "Is it the wine, or just the suggestion," she whispered.

"What suggestion?" Luke tightened his arm around her, leaning back against the arm chair. His hand drooped lazily over her shoulder and fondled her breast through the heavy wool of her sweater.

"That one." She pushed the box of papers aside with her foot and took another sip. "This wine seems very strong."

Luke chuckled. "I suspect it was worth a fortune, but who cares, if we get our money's worth? Shall we go upstairs?" He was nuzzling her ear, gently nibbling the lobe.

"Not yet. Another glass first. Luke —" She turned to him, suddenly serious. "I wouldn't dare ask you this if I were entirely sober. You don't regret coming here, do you?"

"Regret it! Certainly not." He inserted his hand under the collar of her sweater.

"You are sure. We've no income to speak of —"

"Then we won't speak of it." As he would never speak to her of his nightmares about the business, the creditors lurking in the woodwork, the waves of depression which sometimes swept over him when he thought about Barry and what

116

he had done to them. What was the point? That was all in the past. Putting his glass down, he leaned across, pressing his lips against hers. "Come on. It's time we went upstairs."

Sammy! Sammy, where are you?

The snow had melted; already snowdrops were pushing up through the frozen ground. The little boy ducked under the graceful boughs of the old fir tree and disappeared out of sight. When he reappeared, he was running down the lawn toward the lake.

"Stop!" Joss screamed. "Stop! Don't go down there! Please —"

Someone was in her way. Pushing against him she struggled to get past —

"Hey! Stop it!" Luke wriggled out of reach of her flailing fists. "Joss, stop it! What's the matter?"

"Sammy!" She was battling up out of a fog of sleep, her mouth sour, her head thudding like a jackhammer. "Sammy!"

"Wake up, Joss. You're dreaming." Luke caught her hand as it struggled free of the entangling duvet. "Joss! Wake up!"

She was naked, her clothes trailed across the floor; her shoulders, bare above the duvet, ached with cold. The moonlight, streaming across the floor, showed the overturned glass on the floor beside the bed, the empty bottle on the table by the lamp. Dragging herself back to the present, she turned her head on the pillow, still disorientated. "Sammy —"

"No Sammy. No such person, Joss. It's Luke, your husband. Remember?" He stroked her shoulder, wincing at the ice-cold feel of her skin, and drew the duvet higher to cover her.

"Tom —"

"Tom's OK. Not a peep out of him. Go back to sleep. It will soon be morning." He tucked her up tenderly and remained, propped on his elbow, looking at her for a few moments, studying her face in the strangely ethereal moonlight. Her eyes had closed. She had never really awoken. It had all been some frightening dream. "Too much wine." He glanced ruefully at the bottle. He already had the beginnings of a headache. By morning it would have turned into something approaching a hangover. Stupid. He threw himself back on the pillow, staring up at the embroidered bed hangings while beside him Joss's breathing slowed and she settled back into deep sleep.

The shadow in the corner, ever watchful, stirred slightly, scarcely more than a flicker of the moonlight on the curtains, and a shiver of lust curled into the darkness.

CHAPTER 10

David had leaped at the idea of a weekend in East Anglia before he sat down and thought out the consequences. Peering now through the windshield of his eight-year-old Vauxhall at the ancient, creeper-covered facade of Belheddon Hall, he felt a pang of something near terminal jealousy. Then his better nature asserted itself firmly. If anyone deserved the fairy tale romance which had handed her this pile on a plate, it was Joss. He thought again of the few rough notes he had scribbled down for her and he smiled to himself. The house was far, far older even than the architecture visible from where he sat implied, and it had an enviably romantic history.

Climbing stiffly out of the car, he straightened to stretch the exquisite agony of cramp out of his bones before diving headfirst back in to withdraw suitcase, box of goodies from Harrod's food hall, and briefcase.

"See here." He tapped a page of notes with his finger as they sat an hour later at the lunch table. "The church was built in 1249. I don't know for sure, but I would think the foundations of this house go back that far at least. I'm no expert, of course, but that glorious room of yours with the gallery looks fifteenth century if not earlier. Why haven't you contacted this local historian chappy yet?"

"We haven't had time." Joss whisked off Tom's bib and wiped his face with it while David watched with horrified disgust. "Wait while I put this young man down for his rest, then we'll talk some more. Put the coffee on, Luke." She hauled the child out of his high chair and straddled him across her hip. "You don't know how glad I am to see you, David." She rested a hand lightly on his shoulder as she passed. "I need to know about the house."

David frowned as she disappeared through the door. "Need to know is rather a strong term."

"It's weird for her, living here." Luke filled the kettle and put it on the hot plate. "Imagine it. Generations of her ancestors and yet she knows almost nothing even about her mother." Sitting down, he leaned forward and cut himself a generous lump of cheese. "She's been having a lot of nightmares. Some tactless old biddy who lives locally told her that both her elder brothers died here in accidents. She's got a bit obsessed by the thought."

David raised an eyebrow. "I can hardly blame her for that." He shivered. "How dreadful. Well, the more distant past seems to have been more cheerful. A junior branch of the De Vere family lived here for a couple of hundred years. One of them got his head chopped off in the Tower."

Luke laughed, reaching for the wine. "And you

find that more cheerful?"

"I'm a historian; it fills me with morbid delight." David chuckled contentedly. "History is a moving staircase. Characters step onto the bottom, rise slowly. They get to the top, they descend. Occasionally something goes wrong and they fall off or get a foot trapped. They face forward, looking up at the heights, or they face backward, looking down." He smiled, pleased with his metaphor. "In the end it makes no difference. One disappears, one leaves no trace, and already another queue of figures crowds behind one, all rising and falling in just the same way."

"Chateau bottled philosophy." Luke topped up Joss's glass as she reappeared. She had combed her hair and removed from her cheek the imprint of Tom's gravy-covered fingers. "This has been a house of substance for hundreds of years, my love. You should be very proud to be its chatelaine."

"I am." Switching on the baby alarm which stood on the dresser, Joss sat down contentedly. "I'll take you over to the church later, David. It's very beautiful. They were doing the Christmas decorations and flowers earlier." She smiled. "Janet said I would be let off helping this year, as we've only just arrived."

"Imagine!" Luke shook his head in wonder. "Joss, do you remember the old joke about the flower ladies hanging in the porch? Another few weeks and you'll be a pillar of the church."

David was scrutinizing Joss's face. She had lost a lot of weight since he had seen her last; there were dark rings under her eyes, and in spite of

121

the laughter he sensed a tenseness about her which worried him. It was two hours before he had the chance to talk to her alone, when she put Tom in his buggy and they pushed him across the drive and down the narrow overgrown path toward the churchyard gate.

"That's my father's grave." She pointed down at the headstone.

"Poor Joss." David pushed his hands deep into his pockets against the cold. "It must have been disappointing to find neither he nor your mother was still alive."

"To put it mildly." She pushed Tom on a few feet and stopped as the little boy pointed at a robin which had alighted on a headstone only a few feet from them. "Did you find out anything else about the name?"

"Belheddon." He chewed his lip. "The name goes back a very long way. Multitudes of spellings, of course, like most old English place-names, but basically the same in the Domesday Book. That takes you back to 1087. How far did you want me to go?" He grinned at her, blowing out a cloud of condensed air to make Tom laugh.

"You mentioned Celtic. Iron Age? Bronze Age?"

"That was guesswork, Joss, and I'm afraid I haven't made any more progress on the definitions. There was a possibility of it coming from *belwe,* which means bellow in Middle English. *Heddon* does seem most likely to mean heather hill. Perhaps they grazed noisy cattle up here once! But we're really talking archaeology here. There are recognized sites around here — I noticed in

122

one of the county histories that there are several very close to the house — but who knows when it comes to names? I don't know yet if there is anything Roman."

"Why would the devil live here, David?"

She had her back to him, watching the robin. He frowned. There was a strange tone to her voice — a forced jocularity.

"I very much doubt if he does." She turned and he met her eye. "What is frightening you, Joss?"

She shrugged, fussing with Tom's harness. The little boy had started to whine. "I don't know. I'm usually quite sane. And I adore the house. It's just that somehow, something is not right here."

"But not the devil." It was his most school-masterly tone, stern with just a hint of mocking reproach.

"No. No, of course not." Comforting the child, she sounded far from sure.

"Joss. If the devil chose anywhere to live on Earth, I doubt that, even as his country residence, he would chose Belheddon." He smiled, the corners of his eyes creasing deeply. "For one thing, it's far too cold."

She laughed. "And I'm keeping you hanging around. Let's go into the church."

The iron latch was icy, even through her gloves. Turning the ring handle with an effort, she humped the buggy through the doors and down into the shadowy aisle.

"It's a lovely old church." David stared around him.

She nodded. "I've even been to one or two services. I've always loved evensong." She led the way toward the far wall. "Look, there are several memorials and brass plaques to people from the Hall. None with the same names, though. It's as if a dozen families have lived here. It's so frustrating. I don't know who, if any, are my relations." She stood staring up at a worn stone memorial by the pulpit. "Look. Sarah, beloved wife of William Percival, late of Belheddon Hall, died the 4th day of December, 1884. Then, much later, there was Lydia Manners, my grandmother, then my parents' name was Duncan. All different families."

"Have you found the family Bible?" He had wandered up into the chancel. "Ah, here are some De Veres. 1456 and 1453, both of Belheddon Hall. Perhaps they were your ancestors too."

Joss pushed the buggy after him. "I hadn't thought to look for a Bible. What a good idea!"

"Well, if there is one and it is sufficiently huge, you ought to be able to find it quite easily. I'll help you look when we get back to the house. But Joss" — He put his arm round her gravely — "I very much doubt if you are descended from the devil!"

"It would be an interesting thought, wouldn't it." She stood in front of the altar rail and stared up at the stained glass window. "I suspect if I was there would have been a smell of scorching by now, if not whirling winds and screaming demons flocking round my head."

Katherine.

The sound in the echoing chancel arch above her was no more than a whisper of the wind. Neither of them heard it.

David sat down in one of the pews. "Joss, about the writing. I gave your short story, 'Son of the Sword,' to my friend Robert Cassie at Hibberds. It intrigued me so much when I read it. That mystery thriller angle set in the past: I thought it worked really well, and I was always sad it was a short story. I thought it would make a good novel then, and I still do." He glanced up at her under his eyelashes. "Bob agreed with me. I don't know if that particular idea appeals, but if you thought you could expand it into a full-length novel, he would be interested to hear your ideas on how to do it; perhaps write some character sketches, a few chapters, that sort of thing."

She stood stock-still, looking down at him. "Was he serious?"

David nodded. "I told you you could do it, Joss. He liked the characters; he loved the mystery — and of course, in the story, it's never solved." He raised an eyebrow. "Do you know what happened at the end yourself?"

Joss laughed. "Of course I do."

"Well, then. All you have to do is tell the story."

They found the family Bible that evening. The huge, leather-covered tome was stored sideways in the bottom of the bookshelf behind her mother's chair in the study. "Bookworm." David fingered the crumbling edges to the pages. "And probably mice. And there you are. Dozens of entries written on the endpapers. Fascinating!

125

Let's take it through to the kitchen and we can put it on the table under the bright light."

Luke was scrubbing oil off his hands at the sink when they carried in their find in triumph and laid it reverently down. "Now what have you found." He grinned at them tolerantly. "You are like a couple of school kids, you two. Such excitement!"

David opened the book with careful fingers. "Here we are. The first entry is dated 1694."

"And the last?" Joss craned over his shoulder.

He turned the heavy handmade page. "Samuel Philip John Duncan, born 10th September, 1946."

"Sammy." Joss swallowed hard. Neither Georgie nor she, the rejected member of the Duncan family, were there.

David stood back from the table, half diffident, half reluctant to relinquish his treasure. "Go on, have a look."

Joss sat down, leaning forward, her finger on the page. "There she is," she said, "the Sarah in the church. Sarah Rushbrook married William Percival 1st May, 1861. Then Julia Mary born 10th April, 1862, died 17th June, 1862 — she only lived two months."

"It was a cruel time. Infant mortality was appalling, Joss. Remember your statistics," David put in sternly. He was suddenly strangely uncomfortable with this close encounter with the past.

Joss went on. "Mary Sarah, born 2nd July, 1864. Married John Bennet Spring 1893. Our firstborn, Henry John was born the 12th October 1900 — she must have written that. Our daughter

126

Lydia — I suppose that's my grandmother — was born in 1902 and then, oh no —" She stopped for a moment. "Little Henry John died in 1903. He was only three years old. That entry is in a different handwriting. The next entry is dated 24th June, 1919. In the year 1903, three months after the death of our son Henry, my husband John Bennet disappeared. I no longer expect his return. This day my daughter, Lydia Sarah, married Samuel Manners, who has come to Belheddon in his turn."

"That sounds a bit cryptic." Luke was sitting opposite her, his attention suddenly caught. "What's next?"

"Our son, Samuel, was born on 30th November, 1920. Three days later my mother, Mary Sarah Bennet, died of the influenza."

"Incredible." David shook his head. "It's a social history in miniature. I wonder if she caught the tail end of the great flu epidemic which spread around the world after the First World War. Poor woman. So she probably never saw her grandson."

"I wonder what happened to poor old John Bennet?" Thoughtfully, Luke sat back in his chair.

"There is a letter in the study," Joss said slowly, her mind suddenly on another track. "A note from Lydia to her cousin John Duncan, telling him about her son's birth. She must have written it straight away, before she realized her mother was dying." She glanced back at the page. She had three more children, John, Robert, and Laura, my mother, each born two years apart and then

127

—" She paused. "Look, she herself died the year after Laura's birth. She was only twenty-three years old!"

"How sad." Luke reached out and touched her hand. "It was all a long time ago, Joss. You mustn't get depressed about it, you know."

She smiled. "I'm not really. It's just so strange. Reading her letter, holding it in my hand. It brings her so close."

"I expect the house is full of letters and documents about the family," David put in. "The fact that your mother obviously left everything just as it was is wonderful from the historian's point of view. Just wonderful. There must be pictures of these people. Portraits, photos, daguerreotypes." He rocked back on his chair, balancing against the table with his fingertips. "You must draw up a family tree."

Joss smiled. "It would be interesting. Especially for Tom Tom when he's big." She shook her head slowly, turning back to the endpapers where the scrawled inscriptions, faded to brown, raced across the page. The first four generations, she realized, had been filled in by the same hand — a catching-up job in the front of the new Bible, perhaps. After that, year after year, generation after generation, each new branch of the family was recorded by a different pen, a different name. "If I copy these out, I can take the list over to the church and find out how many of them were buried there," she said. "I wonder what did happen to John Bennet. There is no further mention of him. It would be interesting to see if he was buried here. Do you think he

128

had an accident?"

"Perhaps he was murdered." Luke chuckled. "Not every name in this book can have died a gentle natural death —"

"Luke —" Joss's protest was interrupted by a sudden indignant wail from the baby alarm.

"I'll go." Luke was already on his feet. "You two put away that Bible and start to think about supper."

Joss stood up and closed the heavy book, frowning at the echoing crescendo of sobs. "I should go —"

"Luke can deal with it." David put his hand on her arm. He left it there just a moment too long and moved it hastily. "Joss. Don't push Luke out with all this, will you. The family. The history. The house. It's a lot for him to take on board."

"It's a lot for me to take on board!" She thumped the heavy book down on the dresser as over the intercom they heard the sound of a door opening, and then Luke's voice, sharp with fear. "Tom! What have you done?"

Joss glanced at David, then she turned and ran for the door. When she arrived in the nursery, with David close on her heels, Tom was in Luke's arms. The crib was over by the window.

"It's OK. He's all right." He surrendered the screaming child. "He must have rocked the cot across the floor. It is a bit sloping up here. Then he woke up in a different place and had a bit of a fright, didn't you, old son?" He ruffled the little boy's hair.

Joss clutched Tom close, feeling the small body

trembling violently against her own. "Silly sausage. What happened? Did you rock the cot so much it moved?"

Tom snuffled. Already his eyes were closing. "It might have been a dream," Luke whispered. "For all that noise, he's barely awake, you know."

Joss nodded. She waited while he pushed the cot back into the corner and turned back the coverings. "Tom Tom go back to bed now," she murmured gently. The little boy said nothing, the long honey-blond eyelashes already heavy against his cheeks.

"Clever invention, that alarm," David commented when they were once more back in the kitchen. "Does he often do that?"

Joss shook her head. "Not very. Moving has unsettled him a bit, that's all. And he's excited about Christmas. Alice and Joe and Lyn will soon be back. Lyn has agreed to come and help me look after him as a part-time nanny. And on top of all that Luke has promised him we will do the tree tomorrow." She was laying the table, her careless movements quick and imprecise. David leaned across and neatened the knives and forks, meticulously uncrossing two knife blades with a shake of his head. "The devil apart, do you think this house is haunted?" he asked suddenly, squaring the cutlery with neat precision.

"Why?" Luke turned from the stove, wooden spoon in hand, and stared at him. "Have you seen something?"

"Seen, no." David sat down slowly.

"Heard then?" Joss met his eye. The voices.

The little boys' voices. Had he too heard them?

David shrugged. "No. Nothing precise. Just a feeling."

The feeling had been in Tom's bedroom, but he was not going to say so. It was strange. A coldness which was not physical cold — the electric heater had seen to that. More a cold of — he caught himself up with something like a suppressed laugh. He was going to describe it to himself as a cold of the soul.

CHAPTER 11

"Presents, food, blankets, hot water bottles. I'm like a Red Cross relief van!" Lyn had driven into the courtyard next morning, her old blue mini groaning under the weight of luggage and parcels. "Mum and Dad are coming back on Wednesday, but I thought I'd give you a hand." She smiled shyly at David. "I'm going to be Tom's nanny so Joss can write world-shaking best-sellers!"

"I'm glad to hear it." David grinned. He had only met Joss's younger sister on a couple of occasions, and had thought her hard and, he had to admit, a little boring. For sisters, the two had had little in common. Now, of course, he knew why. They weren't sisters at all.

It was eleven before he managed to cajole Joss away from the house on the pretext of hunting up some of the names from the Bible in the church. They started in front of Sarah Percival. "I noticed her because the memorial was so ornate. There must be older ones," she whispered. She wandered away from him down the aisle. "Here we are. Mary Sarah Bennet died in 1920. It just says of Belheddon Hall. No mention of her disappearing husband."

"Perhaps she didn't want him buried with her." David was staring absently up into the shadows near the north door. "There's a lovely little brass here. To the memory of Katherine —" He screwed up his eyes. "It's been polished so often I can't make out the second name. We need more light." He stepped closer, reaching up the wall to trace the letters with his finger. "She died in fourteen something."

Katherine.

In the silence of the old church, Joss flinched as though she had been hit. She was standing on the chancel steps, staring at a small plaque on the wall behind the lectern. At David's words she turned, to see him stroking his fingers lightly over the small, highly polished brass. "Don't touch it, David —" she cried out before she had time to think.

He stepped back guiltily. "Why on earth not? It's not like walking on them —"

"Did you hear?" She pressed her fingers against her temples.

"Hear what?" He stepped away from the pulpit and came to stand next to her. "Joss? What is it?"

"Katherine," she whispered.

he had been riding — riding through the summer heat, trying to reach her . . .

"That was me, Joss. I read out her name. Look.

Up there on the wall. A little brass. There are some dead flowers on the shelf in front of it."

riding — riding — the messenger had taken two days to reach him — already it might be too late —

In the cut-glass bowl the water was green and slimy. Joss stared down at it. "We must renew the flowers. Poor things, they've been dead so long. Nobody cares — "

foam flew from his horse's mouth, flecking his mantle with white . . .

"There aren't any flowers at this time of year unless you go to a shop," David commented. He wandered away toward the choir stalls once more. "Did you bring a notebook? Let's copy some of these names down."

Joss had picked up the vase. She stared at it vacantly. "There are always flowers in the country, if you know where to look," she said slowly. "I'll bring some over later."

He glanced at her over his shoulder. She seemed strangely preoccupied. "Shouldn't you leave it to the flower ladies?" he said after a moment.

She shrugged. "They don't seem to have bothered. No one has noticed. The vase was hidden there, in the shadows. Poor Katherine —"

Katherine!
Furiously he bent lower over the animal's neck, urging it even faster, conscious of the thud

of hooves on the sunbaked ground, knowing in some reasoning part of himself that his best mount would be lamed for life if he kept up the pace any longer.

"David!"

The pounding in Joss's skull was like the thud of a horse's hooves, on and on and on, one two three, one two three, over the hard, unrelenting ground. Everything was spinning —

"Joss?" As she collapsed onto the narrow oak pew, David was beside her. "Joss? What is it?" He took her hand and rubbed it. It was ice cold. "Joss, you're white as a sheet! Can you stand? Come on, let's take you home."

behind him, far behind, a scattering of men, the messenger among them, tried to keep up with him; soon they would have fallen out of sight.

In the silent bedroom Joss lay on the bed. Sitting beside her was their new doctor, Simon Fraser, summoned by Luke. His hand was cool and firm as he held her wrist, his eyes on his watch. At last he put her hand down. He had already listened to her chest and pressed her stomach experimentally. "Mrs. Grant." He looked up at last, his eyes a pale clear blue beneath his gold-rimmed glasses. "When did you last have a period?"

Joss sat up, relieved to find her head had stopped spinning. She opened her mouth to answer and then hesitated. "What with the move and everything, I've sort of lost track —" Her smile faded. "You don't mean —"

He nodded. "My guess is you are about three months pregnant." He tucked his stethoscope into his case and clicked the locks shut. "Let's get you down to the hospital for a scan and we'll find out just how far along you are." He stood up and smiled down at her. "Was it planned?"

Katherine.

It was there again, the sound in her head. She strained to hear the words, but they were too far away.

Katherine, my love, wait for me . . .

"Mrs. Grant? Joss?" Simon Fraser was staring at her intently. "Are you all right?"

Joss focused on him, frowning.

"I asked if the baby was planned," he repeated patiently.

She shrugged. "No. Yes. I suppose so. We wanted another to keep Tom company. Perhaps not quite so soon. There's so much to do —"

It had gone. The voice had faded.

"Well, you are not going to be the one doing it." He lifted his case. "I'm going to be stern, Mrs. Grant. That turn you had this morning is probably quite normal — hormones leaping about and rearranging themselves — but, I've seen too many women wear themselves out in the early months of pregnancy and then regret it later. Just take it easy. The house, the boxes, the unpacking — none of it will go away by itself, but at the same time, none of it is so urgent you need to

136

risk yourself or your baby. Understood?" He grinned, a sudden boyish smile which lit his face. "I've always wanted to come and see this house — it's so beautiful — but I don't want to be coming up here at all hours because the new lady squire is overtaxing herself. Right?"

Joss sat up and swung her legs over the side of the bed. "It sounds to me as though you've been got at. Luke must have talked to you before you came up here, Doctor."

He laughed. "Maybe. Maybe not, but I'm a fairly good judge of human nature."

Luke's hug, in the kitchen later, swept her off her feet. "Clever, clever darling! Let's have some champagne! David — are you prepared to brave the cellar? There is some there."

"Luke —" Protesting, Joss subsided into a chair. "I shouldn't have champagne. Besides, shouldn't we wait until I've had the proper tests?" She still felt a little odd — disoriented, as though she had woken too suddenly from a dream.

"No chance." Luke was glowing with excitement. "We'll have another bottle then. Besides, there's no doubt, is there? He said he could feel it! I'm sure, and you are too, aren't you —" He paused for a moment on his way to collect four glasses and looked at her shrewdly. "A woman always knows."

Raising her fingers to her forehead, Joss pressed distractedly against her brow. "I don't know. I suppose there have been signs." Queasiness in the mornings for the last few days, for one. In the rush to get Tom up and dressed she hadn't taken much notice. Her tiredness she had put

137

down to the fact that she was doing much too much. "So nanny" — she looked at Lyn — "you'll have another charge soon, it seems."

Lyn's eyes were sparkling. "You'll have to pay me more to look after two."

"Oh great. Thanks!"

"At least writing your book will keep you sitting still. You've got no excuse not to start, now," Luke said firmly. He put the glasses down on the table and then dropped a kiss on the top of her head. "I'll go and help David find a bottle."

David was standing in the cellar in front of the wine racks as Luke walked slowly down the steps. "It's bloody cold down here. This is all vintage, you know. And some of it is still in really good condition." He glanced at Luke and lowered his voice. "If you need money you could do worse than sell some of this. There are some very valuable wines here. Look at this! Haut-Brion '49 — and look, Chateau d'Yquem!"

"What sort of money are we talking about?" Luke reached for a bottle and extracted it carefully from the rack. "This is" — he squinted — "1948."

"Don't shake it whatever you do! That's about three hundred fifty quids' worth you've got in your hand. You are looking at thousands, Luke. Ten. Twenty. Maybe more."

"You know, I did wonder. That's why I wanted you to have a look at them."

David nodded. "I can give you the name of someone at the wine auction house at Sotheby's who would come and value it and catalog it. It would be a tragedy in a way to get rid of it,

138

but I know you're strapped for cash, and with another kid on the way, you could do worse than raise some this way. Besides, you're just as happy with plonk, aren't you, you ignoramus!" He chuckled.

"I think I'd better put this back —" Luke glanced at the bottle in his hand.

"You'd better! Come on. Let's find some champagne for the baby." David selected a bottle from the rack and studied the label, "Pommery Brut 1945. Not bad!"

"Just twenty or thirty quid a bottle, I suppose?" Luke groaned.

"More like fifty! It's a strange life you lead here, isn't it." David shook his head slowly. "All the trappings of grandeur, yet a bit short of cash."

"A bit!" Luke grinned. He was not going to let himself think about Barry and G&H's money. "We were planning to live off the land here. Literally. The money I can make from doing up cars is peanuts — it's a mug's game — so slow. But at least it will bring in enough hopefully for electricity bills and taxes, that sort of thing. Joss would never hear of selling anything out of the house — she is so obsessed with the history of it all, but wine is a different matter. I'm sure she would feel differently about that. It could make the difference between hell and a hard place for us, David." He cradled the bottle in his arms. "Tell me something. Do you think Joss really could make any money out of writing?"

David grimaced. "She can write. She has a wonderful imagination. I've told her that I've taken the liberty of showing some of her stuff to a publisher friend of mine. He particularly liked one of her short stories. He's keen to see more, and he wouldn't say that unless he meant it. But beyond that it's in the lap of the gods." He gave a sudden shiver. "Come on, old chap. Let's get out of here. It's so bloody cold. A hot meal is what we all need, I think!"

It wasn't until quite a bit later that Joss managed to go back to the church alone. She had in her hand a small bunch of holly mixed with red dead nettle, and winter jasmine and shiny green sprigs of ivy covered in flowers.

The church was almost dark when she found the key in its hiding place and pushed open the heavy door to make her way up the dim nave. The vase was clean and full of fresh water as she stood it gently on the shelf in front of the little brass. "There you are, Katherine," she whispered. "New flowers for Christmas. Katherine?" She paused, almost expecting there to be a response, a repeat of the strange reverberation in her head, but there was none. The church was silent. With a wry smile she turned away.

The kitchen was empty. For a moment she stood in front of the stove, warming her hands. The others were all out, all occupied. She should be unpacking boxes or packing presents; there was no time to stand and do nothing. On the other hand, now would be the perfect time, alone and undisturbed, to turn once more to the box of letters in her mother's study. And the doctor did tell her to rest . . .

The great hall was already taking on the look of Christmas. Luke and David had brought in the seven-foot tree they had cut in the copse behind the lake that morning, and the whole room smelled of the fresh spicy boughs. It was standing near the window, firmly wedged into a huge urn filled with earth. Lyn had found the boxes of decorations, and they stood on the floor near the tree. They had promised Tom that he could help decorate the tree after his supper and before he went to bed. She smiled. The little boy's face as the tree was dragged in had been a sight to behold.

She had filled a huge silver bowl with holly and ivy and yellow jasmine and it stood in the center of the table, a blaze of color in the dark of the room.

Katherine.

Joss frowned. There was a strange electric tingle in the air, a crackle of static as though a storm were about to break. It was there again: the echo at the back of her head — the voice she could not quite hear.

As he thundered into the courtyard the house lay quiet under the blazing sun. His horse's breath was whistling in its throat as he dragged it to a halt. There was no sign of servants, even the dogs were silent . . .

Puzzled, Joss shook her head. She was staring hard at the bowl of flowers. The silver, still dull

141

where her quick rub with a duster had failed to remove the years of tarnish, shone softly in the dull light from the lamp near the table. As she watched, a yellow petal from the jasmine fell onto the gleaming black oak.

Throwing himself from the saddle, he left the sweating trembling horse and ran inside. The great hall, dim after the sunlight, was equally empty. In five strides he was across it and on the stairs which led up to her solar . . .

The smell of resin from the newly cut fir tree was overpowering. Joss could feel the pain tightening in a band around her forehead.

"Katherine!" His voice was hoarse with dust and fear. "Katherine!"

"Joss!" The cry echoed through the open doorway. "Joss, where are you?"

Luke was carrying a great bunch of mistletoe. "Joss. Come here. Look what I've found!" In quick strides he crossed the room to her side and held the huge pale-green silvery bouquet above her head. "A kiss, my love. Now!" His eyes narrowed with laughter. "Come on, before we decide where to put it!"

Katherine!

Joss stared at Luke sightlessly, her mind focused inward, trying to catch the sounds as they came, seemingly from endless distances away.

"Joss?" Luke stared at her. He lowered the mistletoe. "Joss? What's wrong?" His voice grew sharp. "Joss, can you hear me?"

Katherine!

It was growing fainter, muffled, distant.
"Joss!"
She smiled suddenly, reaching out to touch the mistletoe berries. They were cold and waxy from the old orchard where lichen-covered apple trees tangled with greengage and plum.

In the end they put one bunch in the kitchen and one in the great hall hanging from the gallery. Before he left to return home, David gave Joss a lingering kiss under the bunch in the kitchen. "If I find out any more about the house I'll stick it in the post. And in the meantime, you get a couple of chapters under your belt to send to my friend Bob Cassie. I have a good feeling about your writing."

"And so do I, Joss." After he had gone, Luke and Joss were discussing it in the study. "It makes perfect sense. Lyn is here to help you with Tom and the baby when it's born. You can write, we all know that. And we do need the money."

"I know."

"Have you got any ideas?" He glanced at her sideways.

She laughed. "You know I have, you idiot! And you know I've already made some notes on how to expand that story. I'm going to take it back to when my hero is a boy living in a house a bit like this one. He's a page, learning to be a

143

gentleman, and then he gets mixed up in the wars between the white rose and the red."

"Great stuff." Luke dropped a kiss on her head. "Perhaps they'll televise it and make us million-aires!"

Laughing, she pushed him away. "It's got to be written and published first, so why don't you go out and play cars while I make a start right now."

She had found an empty notebook of her mother's in one of the drawers. Sitting down at the desk, she opened it at the first page and picked up a felt-tipped pen. The rest of the story was there, hovering at the edge of her mind. She could see her hero so clearly as a boy. He would be about fourteen at the beginning of the novel. He was tall, with sandy hair and a spattering of freck-les across his nose. He wore a velvet cap with a jaunty feather and he worked for the lord of Belheddon.

She stared out of the window. She could see a robin sitting on the bare branches of the climbing rose outside. It seemed to be staring in, its bright eyes black and intent. He was called Richard, her hero, and the daughter of the house, the her-oine of her short story, his age exactly, was called Anne.

Georgie!

She shook her head slightly. The robin had hopped onto the window sill. It was pecking at something in the soft moss which grew around the stone of the mullions.

144

Georgie!

The voice was calling in the distance. The robin heard it. She saw it stand suddenly still, then with a bob of its head it turned and flew off. Joss's fingers tightened around her pen. Richard was of course in love with Anne, even at the beginning, but it was a sweet innocent adolescent love that only later was to be dragged into adventure and war as opposing sides brought tension and dissent and murder to the house.

She wrote tentatively, sketching in the first scene, twice glancing at the window, and once at the door as she thought she heard the scuffle of feet. In the fireplace the logs shifted and spat companionably, once filling the room with sweet-smelling smoke as a gust of wind outside blew back down the chimney.

Georgie! Where are you?

The voice this time was exasperated. It was right outside the door. Joss stood up, her heart pounding as she went to pull it open. The hallway outside was empty, the cellar door closed and locked.

Shutting the study door, she leaned with her back against it, biting her lip. It was her imagination, of course. Nothing more. Stupid. Idiot. The silence of the empty house was getting to her. Wearily, she pushed herself away from the door and went back to the desk.

On her notebook lay a rose.

She stared at it in astonishment. "Luke?" She

glanced around the room, puzzled. "Luke, where are you?"

A log fell with a crackle in the fire basket and a shower of sparks illuminated the soot-stained brickwork of the chimney.

"Luke, where are you, you idiot?" She picked up the flower and held it to her nose. The white petals were ice cold and without scent. She shivered and laid it down. "Luke?" Her voice was sharper. "I know you're there." She strode across to the window and pulled the curtain away from the wall. There was no sign of him.

"Luke!" She ran to the door and tugged it open. "Luke, where are you?"

There was no answering shout.

"Luke!" The scent of resinous pine was stronger than ever as she ran toward the kitchen.

Luke was standing over the sink scrubbing his hands. "Hello. I wondered where you were —" He broke off as she threw her arms around his neck. Reaching for the towel on the draining board, he dried his hands and then gently he pushed her away. "Joss? What is it? What's happened?"

"Nothing." She clung to him again. "I'm being neurotic and hormonal. It's allowed, remember?"

"You're not going to let me forget, love." He guided her to the table and pushed her into the armchair at the end of it. "Now. Tell me."

"The rose. You put a rose on my desk . . ." Her voice trailed away. "You did, didn't you?"

Luke frowned, puzzled. With a quick glance at her, he sat down next to her. "I've been out working on that car, Joss. It seemed a good idea before it got too dark. The lights in that coach house are not good and it's freezing out there. Lyn is still out with Tom. They went to collect some fir cones but they'll be back at any moment, unless they came past me without my noticing. Now what's this about a rose?"

"It appeared on my desk."

"And that frightened you? You cuckoo, David must have left it."

"I suppose so." She sniffed sheepishly. "I thought I heard —" She broke off. She had been about to say "someone calling Georgie" but she stopped herself in time. If she had, she was going mad. It was her imagination, working overtime in a shadowy too-silent house.

"Where is this rose? Let's fetch it in." Luke suddenly stood up. "Come on, then I'll help you put the supper on for the infant prodigy. He's going to refuse to go to bed until he's had his money's worth of the Christmas tree this evening."

The fire in the study had died to ashes. Stooping, Luke threw on a couple more logs as Joss walked over to the desk. Her pen lay on the page, a long dash of ink witness to the haste with which she had thrown it down. Next to it lay a dried rosebud, the petals curled and brown, thin and crackly as paper. She picked it up and stared at it. "It was fresh — cold —" She touched it with the tip of her finger. The petals felt like tissue, a crisped curled margin of the leaf crumbling to nothing as she touched it.

Luke glanced at her. "Imagination, old thing. I expect it fell out of one of those pigeonholes.

You said they were full of your mother's rubbish."
Gently he took the rose out of her hand. Walking
over to the fire he tossed it into the flames and
in a fraction of a second it had blazed up and
disappeared.

CHAPTER 12

Lydia's book fell open at the marker, a large dried leaf which smelled faintly and softly of peppermint.

16th March, 1925. He has returned. My fear grows hourly. I have sent Polly to the rectory for Simms and I have despatched the children with Nanny to Pilgrim Hall with a note to Lady Sarah beseeching her to keep them all overnight. Apart from the servants I am alone.

Joss looked up, her eyes drawn to the dusty attic window. The sun was slanting directly into the room, lighting the beige daisies which were still visible on a wallpaper faded by the years. In spite of the warmth of the sun behind the glass she found she was shivering, conscious of the echoing rooms of the empty house below her.

The rest of the page was empty. She turned it and then the next and the next after that. All were blank. The next entry was dated April 12, nearly a month after the first.

And now it is Easter. The garden is full of daffodils and I have gathered baskets of them to decorate every room. The slime from their stems stained my gown — a reprimand perhaps for my attempts to climb from the pit of despair. The best of the flowers I have saved for my little one's grave.

April 14th. Samuel has taken the children to his mama. Without Nanny I cannot look after them.

April 15th. Polly has left. She was the last. Now I am truly alone. Except for it.

April 16th. Simms came again. He begged me to leave the house empty. He brought more holy water to sprinkle, but I suspect like all the perfumes of Arabia, even jugs full of the miraculous liquid cannot wipe away the blood. I cannot go to the rectory. In the end I sent him away . . .

"Joss!"

Luke's voice at the foot of the attic stairs was loud and sudden. "Tom's crying."

"I'm coming." She put the diary back in the drawer of the dressing table and turned the key. There were only two more entries in the book and suddenly she was afraid to read them. She could hear Tom's voice now, quite clearly. How could she not have heard it before?

Which of Lydia's children had died? Who among her lively, much-loved brood occupied the grave in the churchyard which she had decorated with Easter daffodils?

Two at a time she fled down the steep stairs

150

and along the corridor to the nursery. At every step the fretful wails grew louder.

He was standing up in his crib, his face screwed up, wet with anger and misery. As he saw her, he stretched out his little arms.

"Tom!" She scooped him up and cuddled him close. "What is it, darling?" Her face was in his soft hair. It smelled of raspberries from his jelly at lunch.

How could Lydia have borne to lose a child, one of her beloved family?

She hugged Tom closer, aware that his bottom was damp. Already the sobs were turning to snuffles as he snuggled against her.

"Is he OK?" Luke put his head around the door.

Joss nodded. For a moment she couldn't speak for the lump in her throat. "I'll change him and bring him down. It's almost time for his tea. Where's Lyn?"

Luke shrugged. Striding into the room he threw the little boy a pretend punch. "You OK, soldier?" He glanced at Joss. "You too?" He raised a finger to her cheek. "Still feeling bad?"

Joss forced a smile. "Just a bit tired, that's all."

Tom changed and smart in a new pair of dungarees and a striped sweater his grandmother had knitted him, Joss carried him into the study. Putting him down on the floor, she gave him the pot of pencils off her desk to play with, then she sat down at the desk and reached for her notebook. On the table nearby sat Luke's PC. The file headed "Son of the Sword" already con-

151

tained several pages of character studies and the beginning of her synopsis. She looked at her notebook, staring down sightlessly at the pages, then back at the blank screen of the computer. She wanted to get on with her story, but her eye had been caught by the family Bible, lying on its shelf in the corner. With a sigh of resignation, she closed the notebook. She knew she could not concentrate on it until she had spent just a bit longer on the story unfolding on the flyleaves of that huge old tome. Heaving it up off its shelf, she laid it on the desk and opened it.

Lydia Sarah Bennet married Samuel Manners in 1919. They had four children. Baby Samuel, who died three months after his birth in 1920, John, who was born the following year and died aged four in 1925, Robert, born in 1922, who died at the age of fourteen, and Laura, her mother, who was born in 1924 and died in 1984, aged sixty. Lydia herself had died in 1925. Joss bit her lip. The diary entries must have been written only a few months before she herself was dead.

She swallowed, looking down at the page in front of her. The faded ink was blurred and in places the pen that had made the entries had blotted the page with a smattering of little stains. Slowly she closed the book.

"Mummy. Tom's tea." The anxious voice from the carpet caught her attention. He was sitting on the hearth rug looking up at her. His face was covered in purple ink.

"Oh, Tom!" Exasperated, she bent to pick him up. "You dreadful child. Where did you find the pen?"

"Tom's colors," he said firmly. "Me draw pictures." His fist was clamped around a narrow fountain pen that Joss could see at once was very old. It couldn't still have had ink in it, so the lubrication for the nib had appeared when the little boy had sucked it. Shaking her head, she slung him onto her hip. "Except for it . . ." The phrase was running around and around in her head. "Except for it . . ." "My fear makes him stronger . . ." Words written by two women in their diaries more than half a century apart, two women driven to extreme fear by something which came to them in the house. Two women who had resorted to the church and to holy water to try to protect themselves, but to no avail.

As she carried Tom through the great hall she glanced at the Christmas tree. Covered now in silver balls and long glittering swaths of silver cobwebs and decorated with dozens of small colored lights, it stood in the corner of the room like a talisman. Already she and Luke had placed a pile of parcels under it, including one for each of them from David. Tomorrow Alice and Joe would arrive and with them lots more presents. "Me see tree." At the sight of it, Tom began to struggle in her arms. "Me walk." As she set him on his feet he was already running toward the corner, his chubby hand pointing at the top of the tree. "Tom's angel!"

"Tom's angel, to keep us safe," Joss agreed. Luke had lifted the little boy up so he could put on the finishing touch, the beautiful little doll, made by Lyn, with its sparkling feathered wings. "Please," she murmured under her breath as she watched the little boy standing open-mouthed below the sweeping branches, "let it keep us safe."

They were halfway through an early supper when the front doorbell pealed through the house and almost at once they heard the raised voices from the front drive.

"Carol singers!" Lyn was first on her feet.

The group stayed twenty minutes, standing around the tree while they had a glass of wine each and sang carols. Joss watched from the oak high-backed chair in the corner. For how many hundreds of years had just such groups of singers brought wassail to the house? Through narrowed eyes she could picture them as Anne and Richard in her story would have seen them, clustered in front of the huge fireplace, muffled against the cold, in boots and scarves, with red noses and chapped hands. Their lanterns were standing in a semicircle on the table, and Lyn had lit the candles in the old sconces and turned out the lights, so there was no electric light save for the little colored balls of glass upon the tree. Even the carols would have been the same — from "This Endris Night" they had launched into "Adam Lay Ybounden." She let the words sweep over her, filling the room, resonating around the walls. Katherine might have heard these songs five hundred years ago on just such an icy night. She shivered. She could picture her so easily — long dark hair, hidden by the neat headdress, her deep sapphire eyes sparkling with happiness, her gown sweeping across the floor as she raised a goblet of wine in toast to her lord —

Sweetheart! He had first met her at the Yule-tide feast, his eyes following the graceful figure as she danced and played with her cousins. The music had brought a sparkle to her eyes, her cheeks glowed from the heat of the fire.

Joss shuddered so violently that Lyn noticed. "Joss, are you all right?" She was there beside her, putting her arm around her shoulders. "What's wrong?"

Joss shook her head, staring down at her feet, shadowy in the candlelight. "Nothing. Just a bit cold." The singers hadn't noticed. They sang on, reaching effortlessly for the high notes, their voices curling into the beams. But it was their last carol. They had to move on to the Goodyears' farm and then to the rectory itself. Scarves were rewound, gloves pulled on, change found for their collecting bag.

The silence when they had gone was strangely profound. As if reluctant to lose the mood, they sat on by the fire staring into the embers.

Katherine, my love, wait for me!

They were so nearly audible, the words, like a half-remembered dream, slipping away before it is grasped. With a sigh Joss shook her head.

"The carols were beautiful. You know, it's strange, but you would expect there to be a feeling of evil in this house if the devil lived here. But there isn't."

"Of course there isn't." Luke dropped a kiss on her head. "I wish you would forget about the devil. This is a fabulous, happy house, full of good memories." He ruffled her hair affectionately. "The devil would hate it!"

He was asleep when Joss climbed up into the high bed later. She had lain for a long time in the bath, trying to soak the chill out of her bones in water that was not quite hot enough to do the trick, and she had found herself pressing against the warm enamel, trying to extricate the last hint of heat from the rapidly cooling bath. When she finally dragged herself out onto the mat and wrapped herself in the towel, she realized that the heating system, such as it was, fired from the range in the kitchen, had long ago turned itself off for the night with its usual ticking and groaning. There would be no more hot water and no more barely warm radiators until next morning, when, with more ticking and groaning, the system would, God willing, drag itself once more back into life. Shivering, she looked in on Tom. He was pink and warm, tucked securely under his cellular blankets and fast asleep. Leaving his door a fraction ajar, she crept into her room and, reluctantly taking off her dressing gown, slid in beside Luke.

Outside, the moon was a hard sliver against a star-flecked sky. Frost had whitened the garden and it was almost as bright as day. Luke hadn't quite drawn the curtains over the back window and she could see the brilliance of the night through the crack. Moonlight spilled across the floor and onto the quilt.

They were all there, in the shadowy room:

156

the servants, the family, the priest. White faces turned toward him as he burst in, his spurs ringing on the boards and catching in the soft sweet hay which had been spread everywhere to muffle the noise.

"Katherine?" He stopped a few feet from the high bed, his breath rasping in his throat, his heart thudding with fear. Her face was beautiful and completely calm.

There was no sign of pain. Her glorious dark hair, free of its coif, lay spread across the pillow; her eyelashes were thick upon the alabaster cheeks.

"Katherine!" He heard his own voice as a scream and at last someone moved. The woman who had so often shown him up to this very room and brought him wine, stepped forward, a small bundle in her arms.

"You have a son, my lord. At least you have a son!"

Uneasily Joss turned to Luke and snuggled against his back. The moonlight disturbed her. It was relentless, hard, accentuating the cold. Shivering, she pulled the covers higher, burying her head in the pillow beside that of her husband, feeling his warmth, his solidity, reassuring beside her.

Frozen with horror he stared down at the woman on the bed.

"Katherine."

This time the word was a sob, a prayer.

Throwing himself across the body he took her

in his arms and wept.

With a sigh Joss slept at last, uneasily, her dreams uncomfortable and unremembered, unaware of the shadow which drifted across the moon throwing a dark swath across the bed. She did not feel the chill in the room deepen, nor the brush of cold fingers across her hair.

Katherine, Katherine, Katherine!
The name rose into the darkest corners of the room and was lost in the shadows of the roof beyond the beams, weaving, writhing with pain, sinking into the fabric of the house.
His face wet with tears he looked up. "Leave me," he cried. "Leave me with her."
He turned to the servant, and his mouth was twisted with hate. "Take that child away. He killed her. He killed my love, God curse him. He killed the sweetest, gentlest woman in the world!"

When she woke it was with a splitting headache, and only seconds later the realization that she was going to be sick. Not pausing to grab her dressing gown, she threw herself out of bed and ran for the bathroom, falling on her knees in front of the lavatory. It was Luke, gently stroking her head while she vomited, who wrapped something around her shoulders and later brought her a cup of tea.

CHAPTER 13

Dr. Robert Simms was rector of the church at Belheddon from 1902 until 1926. Standing in front of the stained glass window which had been erected in his memory in the church, Joss wondered just how much he had been able to comfort Lydia in her last months. Had he sprinkled holy water around the house? Had he buried her son? Presumably he had buried her. The grave out in the churchyard was overgrown now with nettles and covered in ivy but, scraping away the moss, she had found the inscription. Samuel Manners, born 1882, died 1926, Lydia Sarah Manners, born 1902, died 1925, their baby son, Samuel, born and died in 1920, and their second son, John, born 1921, died 1925, and Robert, their third son, born 1922 and died 1936.

What happened to the sons of this house that they died so young? Walking back slowly up the path from the church toward the gate into the garden, Joss stopped for a minute beside her brothers' graves. Luke had cut the nettles now, and she had scraped away some of the moss and planted bulbs in the cold earth between them.

She shivered. Edgar Gower's words kept returning to her: "Don't embroil yourself in the affairs of the Duncans; Belheddon Hall is an unhappy house, my dear. The past is the past; it should be allowed to rest." Was there something terribly wrong at Belheddon? And if there was, why did she feel so happy here? Why did Luke love it so much? Why had they not felt the evil which had so terrified Lydia and Laura?

Luke was lying under the Bentley, a spanner in his hand, when she walked into the courtyard. "Hi there!" His voice came from the shadows beneath the chassis. "Lyn has taken Tom into Colchester. Are you feeling better after your walk?"

"A bit." She leaned against the coach house wall, hands in pockets, staring down at his feet. "Luke, do you want a coffee? There's something I want to ask you."

"Why not." He scooted himself out from beneath the car and grinned. There was a patch of oil on his forehead, and his hands, as always now, were ingrained with black.

"So?" Blowing on the hot mug, he sat at the kitchen table. "What's the problem?"

"There's something wrong, Luke. Terribly wrong. Can't you feel it?" She sat opposite him. The smell of the coffee was making her feel sick again.

His face sobered. "In what way wrong? Not the baby?"

"No, not the baby. Luke, I've found letters and diaries and things, written by my mother and grandmother."

"I know. I've seen you engrossed in them." He reached for the biscuit tin and levered off the lid. "I thought they interested you." He poured some more coffee into his mug.

"They both talk about something dreadful, something terrifying in the house."

"Oh, Joss." He shook his head. "Not that again. Not the devil himself, living in the cellar? For goodness' sake!" He heaved himself to his feet, grabbing another biscuit. "Listen, love, I've got to go back to work. I need to try and sort out that carburetor by lunchtime if I can." He bent over her and kissed the top of her head. "Don't look for problems where there aren't any. We are damn lucky to have this place. We're happy here. It's given us the chance of a new start, and it's given you a second family to research and get to know. But keep your imagination for your book, Joss. This was real life. Real people living in real times. It wasn't fiction. Maybe your grandmother and your mother were neurotic. You don't know. Maybe they were both incipient novelists — perhaps that's where you get it from. We don't know. All we know is that this is a fabulous, happy house. Alice and Joe will be here tomorrow, it's Christmas in three days, and our own family is the one that you should be thinking about."

He had been right, of course. Every time over Christmas that her thoughts returned to the tragedy of her brothers' deaths, or her mother's or her grandmother's fears, Joss firmly brought them back to the realities of running a house full of people, cooking on an antiquated stove, thinking about the book and scribbling notes on the pad she kept in the pocket of her jeans, and keeping Tom's excitement within bounds, all while hiding as much as possible her morning sickness and exhaustion. Alice was not fooled for a moment, but she went along with the deception in spite of Joe's protests that she must not do too much herself, calmly and firmly taking as much as possible out of Joss's hands, and slowly, to her surprise, Joss found that she was indeed beginning to relax. With people in it, the house did not seem so large. The silences had gone; every room was full of family whispering, wrapping presents, hiding parcels. The silver glitter on the tree was the only thing that moved in the shadows and the voices were silent. Twice she went out onto the lawn late at night to look up at the stars alone. Awed by their frosty beauty, she stood quite still, her hands pushed down into the pockets of her jacket, imagining the ethereal beauty of the music of the spheres ringing through the silence of the garden. But in reality she could hear nothing but the distant piping of the peewits under the moon on the fields and the quick urgent hunting calls of the little owl as it quartered the old gardens beyond the lake.

"Sammy? Georgie?" Her call was tentative, making her feel a little foolish. She knew there was no one there. Probably she had imagined it all.

She smiled to herself as she turned back toward the courtyard. It was going to be a good Christmas and they were all going to enjoy Belheddon and be very very happy there.

Three weeks after Christmas, Joe came and found Joss dozing by the fire in the study, her notebooks on her knee, a pen lying slack between her fingers. "Your mother's not well, Joss. The doctor said she mustn't tire herself out and that's just what she's been doing these last few weeks. I'm taking her home so she can rest. And Lyn will still be here to help. She's a good girl, and she's loving the country life." His face creased into a network of deep wrinkles as he smiled at her fondly.

"Dad." Joss reached out for his hand. She had been dreaming, she realized, about Richard, happily living inside the plot of her book, walking around an earlier, more primitive but sun-filled Belheddon. "I had no idea Mum was ill! Why didn't she tell me?"

"She didn't want anyone to know. And there's nothing rest and a bit of TLC from her old husband can't put right. Don't you go worrying yourself now. Just let us go home quietly."

Sitting in her bedroom later, Joss looked up at Lyn, who was standing by the window. "She wouldn't tell me what was wrong."

"Nor me." Lyn bit her lip. "You know what she's like. She never makes a fuss." There were tears brimming in her eyes. She turned to Joss. "If she gets worse I'll have to go back. I can't leave them on their own."

"Of course you can't. Lyn, why won't they stay here? We could both look after them."

Lyn shook her head. "Come on, Joss. This is

your home. Your real parents' home. However lovely it is here, this is not Mum and Dad's scene. It's not really mine, though I'm prepared to make a big sacrifice." She gave a wan smile. "They're not really happy out of London, you know that. All their friends are there. The rest of the family is there. This is fantasy land. They are pleased for you — really pleased — but they don't belong."

"I suppose so." Joss leaned back on the bed with a sigh. "Why do things have to change, Lyn? Why do people get old and ill. It seems so unfair."

"It's life." Lyn headed for the door. "Some people get old, others have babies. I'm not a philosopher like you, but even I can see that's the way it works. I expect every new generation puts up a fight as it sees old age coming, then it gives up and accepts the inevitable. You rest now. You look washed out, too. You know the doctor told you not to do too much. I'll take Tom for a walk and we'll have a cup of tea later, OK? Once it gets dark and Luke's indoors."

Shivering, Joss pulled the counterpane up over herself. Outside, the garden was very still. A sprinkling of snow that morning had melted and everything was dank and dripping. She smiled as she heard Tom's voice, shrill and excited, outside the window, then it faded as Lyn took him down the drive toward the village and the room sank back into silence. After a while she dozed, drifting in and out of sleep. The room grew darker. Shivering, she wriggled down farther into the bed, her eyes shut.

The hand on her forehead was cool, gentle. It seemed to soothe her.

Katherine, my clever love.

"Luke?" she murmured, barely awake. His hand had moved down to her breast and languidly, still half asleep, she stirred beneath the gentle fingers. "I'll come down, soon." She slept again.

When she woke it was dark. She lay still for a moment, still wrapped in her dream, her body glowing, sleepily aware of the hands which had caressed her breasts as she slept. Groping for the light switch, she looked at her watch. It was nearly five. With a groan she heaved herself off the bed and stood up. The house was still silent. Probably Lyn had put the television on in the kitchen to keep Tom quiet while she made his tea, the routine they had fallen into so Joss could keep the afternoons for writing. She had almost two complete chapters finished now as well as a sheaf of notes and a chronology of the Wars of the Roses. Luke would be in by now. The house downstairs would be warm and busy and welcoming. She shivered, reaching for a thick sweater and pulling it over her head. All she had to do was go downstairs.

The last two entries in the diary had been short. Her grandmother had written: "I feel strangely weak. The doctor came again this morning and said it was the result of being tired. I shall get up when the rain stops and the sun returns. How I crave the sun."

Four days later she wrote: "The loneliness becomes worse. I do not let them know I am alone. The effort of going downstairs for some beef tea is too much. Perhaps tomorrow." That was all. The rest of the book was empty. Four days later she was dead.

Shivering, Joss put the diary back into the bedside drawer. She wished she had not read that. The thought of the woman alone in the house, completely alone and dying, was intolerable. She stood up, conscious of a slight cramp in her leg, and went to look down into the garden. It was nearly dark. Rain slanted down across the grass, dissolving the last remaining patches of snow.

"Joss!"

It was Lyn calling up the staircase. "Phone call for you."

Shaking herself, Joss turned away from the darkness and ran downstairs. In the study Lyn had thrown several logs onto the fire and the room was almost hot. "David." She nodded toward the phone which lay on the desk. "He sounds excited."

"David?" Joss put the receiver to her ear.

"Joss. Only a week until school starts. Can I come up and see you?" He sounded almost breathless.

"Of course. You know we've got room." Joss sat down at the desk, pressing the phone to her ear, unaware that her voice was seductively husky with sleep. Her hands were, she realized suddenly, shaking. "Any special reason?"

"Wait and see. I'll be down tomorrow if that's all right. And you will never guess who I met at a dinner yesterday. A chap called Gerald Andrews, who is your friendly local historian. He and I belong to the same club, it seems. Listen, we had quite a talk about Belheddon. I gave him your phone number and he is going to get in touch. And Joss, I am having lunch next week with Robert Cassie. If you have got some stuff ready for your book I could deliver it in person and if that's not an incentive, I don't know what is! See you tomorrow."

"He's coming down." Joss put the phone down and came to join Lyn by the fire. "He seems to have found out some more about the house."

"You and your bloody house!" Lyn shook her head. "Can't you think of anything else?"

Joss flinched. "I'm sorry. Am I being boring?"

"You certainly are." Lyn reached for the poker and stabbed ferociously at the fire. "Still, I'm glad David is coming down. He seems to be our only remaining link with civilization."

"The country is getting to you." Joss smiled, determined not to be goaded.

"Well, even you can't like it in this bloody weather. No doubt it will improve when spring comes." Lyn relented a little. "The vicar came while you were asleep. He brought the parish magazine, a piece of paper asking for jumble, and a packet for you from someone called Mary Sutton."

Joss stared at her. "Why didn't you tell me that before? Where is it?"

"In the kitchen. Joss —"

As Joss scrambled to her feet she was brought up short by the anguish in Lyn's voice. "You do realize Ma might be dying, don't you."

Joss froze. "She's not dying, Lyn. She's tired. Not very well —"

"She's got to have lots of tests, Joss. Dad told me on the phone. She doesn't want you to know. She thinks it might upset you." Lyn's voice was suddenly harsh. "Apparently they don't mind upsetting me."

"Oh Lyn." Joss knelt and put her arm around her sister's shoulders. "You know Mum and Dad. It's because of the baby. They come from a generation who thought any old thing could upset a baby on the way. They've told you because they want your comfort."

"I wanted to go to be with them. They don't want me. They want me to stay here."

"Then stay here." Joss's arms tightened around her. "When they need you they will tell you."

"You think so?" Lyn's eyes were full of tears.

"Of course."

For a while they sat together in front of the fire, lost in thought, then at last Joss climbed stiffly to her feet. "Come on. Let's make a cup of tea."

Lyn nodded. She sniffed. "I'll get the young lord and master up from his rest. You go and put the kettle on."

The packet from Mary Sutton was a large envelope. Lyn had left it on the kitchen table with the parish magazine, a flimsy pamphlet with a lurid purple cover. Eyeing the package, Joss filled the kettle and put it on the hot plate. Only then did she allow herself to open it. It contained another notebook — by now Joss was familiar with her mother's jottings; she must have bought a

168

whole stack of notebooks in a job lot somewhere — and a few more letters and some photographs. She glanced at the photos. Sammy and Georgie. She didn't need the penciled names on the back to identify them. They were black-and-white school photos, she guessed, both wearing the same school uniform in spite of the ten-year gap between them. Sammy was very dark — she could see the resemblance to herself, with a thin, intense face and round light-colored eyes, perhaps blue like her own. Georgie was fairer, chubbier, more mischievous. Both had been about six when the photos were taken. She stared down at them for a long time before she saw the note scribbled by Mary. "I thought you should have the photos of my boys. The other things I found the other day. You may as well have them too."

The notebook was full of loosely scribbled writing. Poems, recipes, and again diary entries, seemingly carelessly and unchronologically scattered. Her mother, she was beginning to think, had a butterfly mind, leaping from here to there, from thought to thought, idea to idea, and from self-conscious musing to the need to confide somewhere, if only to an inanimate diary.

The two letters were addressed to Mary. Joss picked them up, touched that Mary should part with them. One was dated 1956. "Take care of my little one, Mary dear. Remember the doctor's advice about his tummy aches. Kiss him for me and look after him. I'm so much happier to know he is there with you in your mother's cottage —" Joss looked up. The letter was headed Belheddon Hall. Why had Laura thought it necessary for Georgie to go and stay with Mary in the village?

She smiled at Lyn and Tom as they appeared in the doorway. "Tea is nearly ready."

Next morning, almost before they were up, David appeared with an extra belated Christmas present for Tom — a furry, hideously green hippopotamus with which the little boy fell instantly in love and christened, for some obscure reason, Joseph. "Arimathea or Carpenter?" David asked mischievously, and the little boy answered solemnly, "Hittopomatus."

In the laughter which followed, David glanced at Joss. Pregnancy seemed to be agreeing with her. She was growing more attractive every time he saw her. Sternly he reined in his thoughts. "So, have you written enough for me to take to Bob?"

She nodded. "Two chapters, like you said. I printed them up yesterday."

He grinned. "Great. Well, here's your reward. More stuff about the house." He put a folder down on the table in front of her. "I've found out who Katherine is. Or was." He smiled. "Katherine de Vere was the eldest daughter of the Robert de Vere who lived here in the mid-fifteenth century. She was betrothed to the son of a local earl."

Handsome and lighthearted, the young man rode to Belheddon daily and Katherine's father laughed out loud in delight.

"We have a love match here," he guffawed

170

to all who would listen, and when he saw the debonair Richard tuck his daughter's favor in his cap he slapped him on the back and planned the wedding.

She had eyes for no one but this young neighbor. While she curtseyed to the king and served him with wine, she did not look up and see his face.

To her he was old.

David turned the page in his folder and went on:

"I'm not sure whether or not she actually married him. The records are a bit cryptic about that, I thought. Anyway, only a year later, in 1482, poor Katherine died, and she's in the church as Katherine de Vere. She was only seventeen or eighteen. When her father died, Belheddon Hall passed to an Edward, presumably her younger brother. He too died at the age of eighteen, but he had time to marry and have a daughter. By that time we are in the reign of Henry VII. The strange thing is —" He paused and looked around — "that already, by the end of the sixteenth century, the house had a reputation for being haunted." He grinned at Joss. "Do you want to know this?"

"No!" "Yes!" Luke and Joss spoke simultaneously.

David shrugged. He reached for a page out of the file. " 'The beauteous house of Belheddon Hall, though well-favored, did not boast many tenants. Men and dogs alike fled in terror from the wails of an apparition that inhabited its lofty

171

chambers.' That was written in the late seventeenth century by a diarist called James Cope who stayed here — only once. 'For more than a hundred years the house has been inhabited by this creature whose unhappiness is distressing to the ear and frightening to the eye.' " He laughed. "He then adds: 'Though I stayed three nights it did not, to my sorrow, appear and has not been seen these last forty years.' "

"He doesn't mention the devil, though, does he," Luke put in tartly. "That's interesting. An old gossip like that would have put that snippet in if he had heard it."

David nodded. "Interestingly though, there is a mention of the devil in an account written only fifty years later by James Fosset, an antiquarian who spent several months collecting stories and history in the district. His theory seems to me to be on the right lines. Listen. 'Belheddon Hall, one of the most beautiful of the local houses, was built on a much earlier site. Some say it goes back to the dawn of time. The name derives from the old English *bealu,* meaning evil or calamity, and *heddon,* meaning a heather-covered hill and would appear to point to the site having been used in pagan times as a site of worship and perhaps of sacrifice. Superstition and fear cling to the site and as little as a hundred years ago a witch was taken and hanged after having concourse with the devil in the grounds of the house.' Do you see a pattern beginning to form? The hauntings, the pagan site, some poor old woman taken as a witch. Slowly the pieces are falling into place. Somehow over the ages the two have got amalgamated and the result is a wonderful legend that it is the devil who haunts, or inhabits, the house. There. Your problem is solved. Andrews was a fascinating man. He knew most of this, I suspect, though he hadn't come across the Fosset references. He says Edward IV actually came to the house on several occasions. That was when the De Vere family lived here. In fact he may have given them the house as at an earlier date the manor was in royal domain. After their day he thinks a whole host of different families lived here — none seem to have stayed more than a few generations, if that, although he thinks on several occasions the house passed down through the female line, so of course the surnames would have been different, just as it has now, of course, with you." He looked up at Joss and smiled. "I hope you are pleased with my humble efforts?"

Joss nodded slowly. Her head was buzzing.

"The king! The king is coming!"
The excitement in the house was reaching fever pitch.
Katherine scowled as her mother reached for the brush and dragged it through her tangled curls.
"Be sweet to him, child." The cold lips were very close to Katherine's ear.
The earl's son was a good catch, but the king was better.
"Be loving. Whatever your king desires, remember, it is his to command!"

"There is so much to take in." Joss gave a

little half laugh. "It's fascinating. I especially like the link with Edward IV. As my book is set during the Wars of the Roses, I can do my research right here." She shook her head again. Briefly she wondered if David too had heard the strange echo that seemed to fill the spaces of the house.

CHAPTER 14

In the kitchen Tom was whining crossly, pulling at Lyn's long checked skirt. "Pick me up!" When she ignored him, he stamped his small foot and wailed even louder.

Joss frowned. Her arms full of dirty washing, she had pushed open the kitchen door and come in to find Lyn on the phone. "Lyn?"

Tom's wails grew louder.

Lyn turned away from him in irritation, clapping her free hand over the ear that was not pressed to the receiver. "Listen, I can come up any time," she said into the phone, "you know I can. I want to." She pushed Tom none too gently toward his toys and his wails doubled in volume.

Joss dropped the clothes she was carrying onto the floor in front of the washing machine and went to Tom, squatting down to give him a hug. "Leave Aunty Lyn while she's on the phone." She looked up at Lyn. "Is that Mum you're talking to?" she whispered.

Lyn nodded.

"How is she? Can I speak to her?"

But Lyn was already hanging up. "She's OK."

"But she's not! I wanted to speak to her."

"Then ring her back." Lyn scowled. "Tom was making such a racket I couldn't hear myself think."

Joss shook her head. "You know he doesn't like us talking on the phone. He just wants attention and hates us being distracted from him. It's a phase they all go through."

"Well, I hope it's not a long one!" Lyn stared at the washing in distaste. "I suppose you want me to put that lot in the machine."

Joss narrowed her eyes. Lyn's voice was full of resentment.

"No, I can do it. What's wrong, Lyn?"

"You don't care about Mum at all, do you. You haven't given her a thought. When did you last ring her? She said she hadn't spoken to you in days!"

"Lyn —"

"No. You don't care anymore, do you. You're just going to forget them. Your new family is so much more exciting. We were never good enough for you, were we!" Lyn stormed across to the window and stood, arms folded, staring out.

"That's not true! For goodness' sake, what's the matter with you?" Joss had to raise her voice as, upset by Lyn's tone, Tom started to scream in earnest. Stooping, Joss picked him up and swung him onto her hip. "Lyn, what is it? Did Mum say something? Does she know what's wrong with her?"

Lyn shook her head without speaking.

176

"Is it cancer, Lyn?" Joss put her hand on her sister's shoulder.

Lyn shrugged miserably.

"You must go, if you want to." Joss's voice was gentler. "You don't have to stay here, you know."

Lyn sniffed. "You need me."

"I know I do. And Luke and I love having you here, Lyn. But if you're not happy —"

"I love Tom."

Joss smiled. "I know that too. And I love Mum and Dad. I always have and I always will. You mustn't believe for a minute that I don't. If I didn't ring Mum yesterday, it was only that I was too busy —"

"Too busy to pick up the phone for two minutes?" Lyn was still staring out of the window.

"It didn't mean I stopped loving her, Lyn."

"That's what she thinks."

"She does not!" Joss was angry suddenly. "And you know it." She turned away and unceremoniously dumped Tom on the floor in front of a pile of colored blocks. Scooping up the heap of clothes, she pushed them into the machine and reached for the detergent.

"She's going into hospital tomorrow, Joss." Lyn's gaze was fixed unseeing on the window catch as she scratched at the flaking paint with her nail. Her voice was leaden.

Joss sat down at the kitchen table. "Why didn't you say so?"

"She's going to die."

"Lyn —"

"I can't bear it if she dies." There were tears

running down Lyn's cheeks.

"She won't die." Joss put her head in her hands and took a deep unsteady breath. "She won't, Lyn. She's going to be all right. I'm sure she is." She had to be. She couldn't cope, she realized suddenly, if her mum, the woman who had been her mother all her remembered life, was not there in the background to support her. She looked down at Tom. Suddenly engrossed in his toys, he had ceased to wail as he examined a large yellow beaker and she was overwhelmed by a sudden rush of love for him. It was love that made everyone so vulnerable, in the end. She sighed again. That was what made families such a joy and such a heartbreak.

Gerald Andrews drew his cup toward him and raised it with difficulty in arthritic fingers. He beamed at Joss, however, as he got it at last to his lips. "My dear, it was good of you to ask me to tea. You don't know how much I have longed to come to see this house. It seems extraordinary that I should have written a history of it and yet never set foot across the threshold."

The history in question, a slim booklet in pale buff cardboard covers, lay between them on the kitchen table. On the front an eighteenth-century woodcut showed the front of the house with the beech tree perhaps half as big as it now was.

"I couldn't believe my luck when I found myself talking to David Tregarron and he said he knew you!" He picked up a biscuit.

"It's lucky for me too." Joss was dying to look through the book. "I have so much catching up to do. I know so little of my family."

He nodded. "I wrote to your mother several times asking if I might come and see her when I was writing that, but I understand she had not been well. Miss Sutton wrote back and each time said it was not convenient. Then your mother left and it was too late."

"You lived in the area a long time?" Unable to resist it any longer, Joss picked up the pamphlet and opened it. The first chapter was called "Early Days."

"About ten years. I compiled some half dozen of these little books. All on the notable houses of the district. The Old Rectory, Pilgrim Hall, Pickersticks House . . ."

"Pilgrim Hall?" Joss looked up. "My father's home?"

"Your grandfather's home. John Duncan was appointed guardian to your mother and her brother Robert when their mother and father died. I suppose it was inevitable that his son should fall in love with Laura. He kept both houses going for awhile, then after Robert died he took Laura back to live at Pilgrim Hall with them. This place was practically derelict for a bit, but of course it was Laura's inheritance and they couldn't sell. John Duncan came into a lot of money, late in life — an inheritance as far as I remember from some relative who had lived in the Far East. He was a strange man, John. He hated Belheddon and Pilgrim Hall with equal loathing. He settled money on the two children, Philip and his ward, Laura, and went to live abroad. His wife, Lady Sarah, stayed on for several years, until the children got married, then she sold Pilgrim Hall, which is much smaller than this, and went off to join him. He never came back, not even for the wedding. It was a frightful scandal at the time. People locally thought he'd gone off with a dusky lady." He gave a delighted chuckle. "I don't somehow think Lady Sarah would have stood for that. She would have beaten any rivals to death with her umbrella. Powerful lady, your grandmother on the Duncan side."

Joss smiled. "They died abroad, did they?"

"John did, I believe. He had vowed never to come back to England. I never found out why. Some kind of quarrel with the family, I suppose. After he died, Lady Sarah came home. She even tried to buy back Pilgrim Hall. That must have been in the sixties, but by then they had built a huge annex and turned it into a country house hotel. I met her once, because I had already published the booklet on Pilgrim Hall. She wanted a copy for herself. It must have been the mid to late sixties because your father, Philip, was already dead — that dreadful accident with the horse, so sad, but I expect you know all about that. She suggested that I write about Belheddon. She was very scathing about the place. Thought it was cursed. She thought Laura was mad to stay here, but Laura seemed to be unable to tear herself away. I can remember her telling me that she was fixated on the house. She would walk about on her own, even at night, for hours, sometimes talking to herself." He glanced at Joss. "She thought Laura had finally lost her mind when she gave you up for adoption. The whole village took it very badly. Your mother was virtually ostracized afterward. Lady Sarah said she would never speak to her again, and not long after that she moved somewhere up north." He hesitated. "It was her theory that the house was cursed which attracted my attention. I don't normally believe in these things" — he smiled almost apologetically — "but this place had had more than its share of tragedy by any standards."

"So many of the children die." Unconsciously Joss put her hands protectively over her stomach.

He frowned. "You shouldn't perhaps read too much into infants' deaths. Such high mortality is profoundly shocking, but remember, in every age but our own such things were normal."

"I suppose so." She was staring at the booklet in her hands.

" 'Four major rivers find their sources in Belheddon Ridge, a sandy, gravel escarpment which cuts across the clays of East Anglia in an east-west slash through the landscape, visible for miles'," she read. " 'Such a place was an obvious candidate for early settlement, and indeed there is archaeological evidence of an iron age camp under what is now the west lawn of the house . . .' " She turned the pages eagerly. "There never seems to have been one family in the house for any length of time," she said at last. She glanced up at him. "From the letters and diaries I've been studying and the family Bible, there seem to be so many names, although they are related."

"Female descent." Andrews reached for another biscuit. "It happens. If you look you will find the house was nearly always inherited by daughters, so of course the surname changes generation after generation. Not always. There were times when it stood empty and when it had tenants, but it seems always to have come back in the end to some relation or other. It's had a longer history in one family than you might think."

"Really?" She looked up at him eagerly. "We're not descended from the De Veres?"

"Oh, almost certainly. That was something which intrigued me, as I was telling Dr. Tregarron. The trouble is, I didn't have enough time to follow it through in detail — you could get a genealogist to do it, I suppose, if you were interested. Matrilineal descent is an interesting phenomenon. Strange to us, but a matter of course to some peoples. In this case, obviously, it wasn't a policy decision, it just worked out that way. No sons." He stuffed his biscuit into his mouth and glanced at his watch. "I hate to seem too eager, Mrs. Grant, but you said I might glance at some of the main rooms."

"Of course." Reluctantly, Joss put down the book. "I'll show you around."

In the course of the next hour Joss was given a potted, breathless, and ecstatic history of the English manor house, taking in pargeting, chamfering, stopping, plasterwork, the art of the fresco ("almost certainly, under this paneling. The paneling would protect it, you know"), staircases, solars, bedchambers, and the great hall as center of the house. Her head reeling, Joss followed in his wake, wishing again and again she had a tape recorder with her to take down this man's encyclopedic knowledge. He laughed when she told

182

him as much. "I'll come again, if you let me. We can make notes. Now, the cellar." They were standing at the foot of the main staircase and his nose was quivering like a dog scenting a rabbit. "There we may see traces of early vaulting."

Joss pointed at the door. "Down there. Do you mind if I don't come down? I get claustrophobia." She laughed deprecatingly, aware of his sudden shrewd gaze.

"Am I tiring you, Mrs. Grant? I know I go on and on. I used to drive my wife mad. The trouble is I get so excited about things." Already he had fumbled awkwardly with the key, swung open the door, and found the light switch. She watched as he disappeared, hampered by his stiffness, down the steep stairs, then she turned away into the study. She waited by the window, staring out across the lawn. Hours seemed to pass. Frowning, she glanced at her watch. Wafting across the great hall from the kitchen came the odor of onions and garlic. Lyn must be putting on the lunch while Tom would be watching *Sesame Street* on the TV. There was no sound from the cellar. She walked across to the door and peered down the stairs anxiously. "Mr. Andrews?" There was no answer. "Mr. Andrews?" There was a sudden tightness in her chest. "Are you all right?"

She could feel the cold air rising. It smelled musty and damp and somehow very old. With a shiver she put her hand on the splintery banister and leaned forward, trying to see into the first cellar. "Mr. Andrews?" The stairs were very steep, the old worn wood split and pitted. Reluctantly, she put her foot on the first step. "Mr. Andrews, are you all right?" The unshaded bulb was very bright. It threw the shadows of the wine bins, black wedges, across the floor. "Mr. Andrews?" Her voice was shaking now, threaded with panic. Clutching the rail, she crept down another two steps. This was where Georgie had fallen, his small body hurtling down the steps to lie in a crumpled heap at the bottom. Shaking the thought out of her head, she stepped down again, forcing herself down the steps one by one. There was a sudden movement on the wall near her. She froze with terror, staring, and her eyes focused at last on a small brown lizard, clinging to the stone. It stared back at her and then with a flick of its tail it ran up the wall and disappeared through a crack into the darkness behind the wall.

"Mrs. Grant, look at this!" The voice, so loud and excited, right behind her, made Joss jump around with a small cry. "Oh, my dear, I'm sorry. Did I startle you?" Gerald Andrews appeared through the arch which led into the next cellar. "Come and see. There is the most perfect medieval vaulting through here. Very early. Oh, I wish I'd known about this when I wrote the book. It takes the date of the original house back I should say to the thirteenth or fourteenth century . . ." Already he had disappeared through the arch again, beckoning her to follow.

Taking a deep breath, Joss made her way past the gleaming racks of bottles, awaiting the visit and tasting next week from the wine expert from Sotheby's, and found herself staring up at the stone arches of the second cellar.

"You see, under the great hall. A flint undercroft, built of the same stuff as the church." He was spluttering with excitement. "And the carving, here, on the keystone and the corbels, see?" He beamed at her. "You have a treasure here, Mrs. Grant, a real treasure. This vault has been here, if I'm right, for six or seven hundred years."

"Seven hundred?" Joss stared at him, her fear subsiding as his enthusiasm increased. She hugged herself against the chill.

He nodded, patting the wall. "May I bring a colleague to see this? And someone from the Historic Buildings Department? It is quite wonderful. And here, all along!"

She smiled. "Of course you may. How exciting. You may have to bring out a new edition of your book."

He laughed. "How accurately you read my thoughts, my dear. I'm a silly old fool, I know. I get so carried away, but it is so exciting. It's suddenly seeing history before you — the bones of history — the actual fabric within which events took place."

"Would this have been a cellar then?" Joss glanced over her shoulder.

"Maybe. An undercroft, a storeroom, even a well chamber." He laughed, staring around. "But no well."

"The well is in the courtyard." She was edging back toward the stairs, trying to draw him away from his wall. "Why don't we go back up, Mr. Andrews. It's so cold down here. You can always come back."

185

He was stricken. "How selfish of me. I'm sorry, my dear. You do look cold. Of course we must go." He cast one last longing glance back at his vaulting and followed her to the staircase.

Luke had driven into Colchester after lunch to collect some parts, taking Lyn and Tom with him, and they hadn't returned when at last she waved Gerald Andrews down the drive. Reaching for her coat, Joss opened the back door and went out into the garden. Beyond the lake, a small gate in the hedge led out into the lane. A few hundred yards' walk led up to the back of the field from where she could look down on the estuary and out to sea. She stood for several minutes, her hands in her pockets, looking down at the water, then with a shiver she turned back into the lane, which with its thickly tangled hedges was more sheltered. Slowly she walked back, savoring the sweetness of the smell of spring flowers and wet earth and sodden bark after the sharp salt tang nearer the sea. From here she could see the church tower, and now and then, from a higher point on the bank, the roofs of the Hall. In the deep shade between the hedge banks it was cold and damp and she shivered again, hurrying to get back.

As she let herself in through the wicket gate by the rowan tree she saw a boy standing by the lake. He had his back to her and he seemed to be standing staring down into the water. "Sammy?" Her whisper was choked with fear. "Sammy!" This time it was a shout. The boy did not turn. He did not seem to hear her. Running now, she crossed the lawn, around thickets of elder and winter dead hawthorn shrouded in ivy, and burst out on the bank of the lake near the little landing stage.

There was no one to be seen.

"Sammy!" Her cry put up a heron which had been standing motionless in the shallows on the far side of the water. With an angry harsh cry it lifted laboriously into the sky and skimmed the hedge out of sight.

"Sammy," she whispered again. But he was gone. If a real child had been playing by the water the heron would have flown away long before she arrived on the scene.

She put her hand to her side with a small grimace. Her desperate run across the grass had given her a stitch. Frowning with pain, she doubled over for a minute, then slowly she began to walk back toward the house.

Lyn and Tom were in the kitchen. Tom's face, covered in cake mixture, betrayed the fact that they had been back long enough to start cooking.

"You OK?" Lyn glanced at Joss as Tom ran to her and gave her knees a sticky hug.

Joss grimaced. "A bit of a stitch. Silly."

"Go and sit down by the fire. I'll bring you a cup of tea." Lyn slid her baking tins into the oven. "Go on. Off with you."

The fire in the study was almost out. Bending down wearily, Joss threw on some logs and a shovel of coal, then she picked up David's notes and sat down in the old armchair. Her back was aching now too and she felt inordinately tired.

When Lyn came in half an hour later with a cup of tea she was fast asleep. For a minute Lyn stood staring down at her, then with a shrug she turned away. She did not leave the tea.

"Luke!" Joss's cry turned into a gasp as a violent cramp tore her out of her sleep. "Luke, the baby! Something's wrong." Miserably hugging her stomach, she slipped to her knees on the carpet. "Luke!"

There was a hand on her shoulder. Gentle, caressing, he was there. Sobbing, she reached up to grip his knuckles. The lightest touch across her back, fingers rubbing her shoulders. She could smell roses. Where had Luke found roses at this time of year? Her hand groped for his. There was no one there. Shocked, she stared around, another kind of fear flooding icily through her as she realized the room was empty. "Luke!" Her voice rose to a shriek.

"Joss? Were you calling?" The door was pushed open and Lyn put her head around it. "Joss? Oh God! What's the matter?"

Luke drove her to the hospital. His face was white, and Joss kept noticing the smear of oil across his left cheek. She smiled fondly. Poor Luke. He was always being dragged away from his precious car.

The pains had stopped now. All she felt was a strangely overwhelming tiredness. She could hardly move. She couldn't keep her eyes open. Even her fear for the baby couldn't keep her awake.

She was vaguely aware of being wheeled in a chair from the car to an elevator, and of being put into bed. Then she was lost in velvety black-

188

ness. Twice she woke up. The first time Simon Fraser was there, sitting at her bedside, holding her wrist. He smiled, his sandy hair flopping around his face, his glasses reflecting distorted images of the side ward where they had put her. "Hello there." He leaned forward. "Welcome back to planet Earth. How are you feeling?"

"My baby — ?"

"Still there." He grinned. "You're going up for a scan a bit later, just to make sure all is well. Rest now, Joss."

When she woke again Luke was there. The smear was gone from his face and he was wearing a clean shirt, but he was as pale and strained as before. "Joss, darling. How are you feeling?"

"Is the baby all right?" Her mouth felt like sandpaper. Her voice was husky.

"Yes, it's fine." He leaned forward and kissed her on the lips. "What happened? Did you fall?"

She shook her head slowly, feeling the coarse cotton of the pillow slip abrading her hair. "No. I was asleep." She had run across the lawn, she remembered that. It had given her a stitch. Then someone had been there, in the study with her. Someone had touched her. Not Luke. Not Lyn. The touch had not been frightening; it was as if someone had been trying to comfort her, to help. She drew her brows together, trying desperately to remember, but already she was feeling sleepy again. "I can't stay awake." Her mouth refused to form the words properly.

Luke's face was swimming, suddenly huge, close to hers. "I'll leave you now. You must sleep. I'll come back later." She felt the touch of his lips, but already she was slipping back into the dark.

Later they took her to another ward. Someone smeared her stomach with jelly and ran something cold and hard across it.

"There you are. Can you see the screen, dear? There. The little mite is all safe, curled up out of harm's way. See?"

Joss peered obediently at the flickering blurred screen beside the bed. She could not make out anything, but her relief at the radiographer's words was enormous. "Is it all right? Can you tell?"

"It's fine. Absolutely fine." The woman was wiping her stomach with tissues and pulling down her gown. "You're going to have a beautiful June baby."

Already they were pulling back the curtains, wheeling her away, bringing in the next patient.

Simon Fraser was waiting for her when they brought her back to her bed. "I had to visit another couple of patients, so I thought I'd look in on you again. How are you feeling?"

"Better." Joss eased herself up on her pillows.

"Good." He put his head on one side. "Home, then rest for a couple of weeks. I've spoken to your sister. She says she can cope with everything. Is that right?"

Joss laughed weakly. "She's very good at coping."

"Good. You've got to make up your mind to rest, Joss. I mean that."

When she got home she found that the whole family had been suborned. She was firmly escorted to bed and there, she discovered, she had to stay even when they came to collect the wine from the cellar for the auction.

They told her about it that evening. "You should have seen the care they took packing it all up. It was treated like gold dust. They said the labels and capsules had to be kept in as good condition as possible. I hardly dared breathe as I watched them." Luke sat down on the bed after he and Lyn and Tom came up when the van had finally left. "It could be our bail money, Joss. When he tasted it, the man from Sotheby's said it looked good. The cellar conditions are perfect. So, here's hoping the auction goes well."

It was something to distract her. And so was the return of David a few days later.

"Books. Articles. A letter from your new publisher!" He tipped an armful of things onto the bed and then hauled himself up onto the counterpane next to her.

"My new publisher?" She stared at him, hardly daring to hope.

He nodded, clearly delighted. "He liked your outline and the chapters you sent him. I think he's given you a few suggestions in the letter and made one or two notes which he thinks will be helpful. And he's prepared to give you a contract and a small advance. No —" He raised his hand to forestall her excitement. "It won't be enough to retile the roof, but it is a start. And it means you have a perfect excuse to lie here in bed composing wonderful prose and be waited on hand and foot by Luke and Lyn while that baby of yours gets bigger."

Joss laughed. "Well, I hope he gets bigger soon. At the moment I'm flat as a pancake. If I hadn't seen that scan I might have wondered if he was still there."

"He is a *he*, is he?"

"I don't know. That was a figure of speech. And a dreadfully sexist one at that." She smiled. "The nurse thought it would be a boy, though. She said boys always give more trouble than girls, the way they mean to go on."

"And that's not sexist, I suppose?"

"No. That's observation." She was opening the letter David had dropped on the bed. The one with the Hibberds colophon.

"It's from Robert Cassie himself," David put in, watching her face. "He was enormously intrigued to hear you were going to set it in this house."

"Three thousand pounds, David! He's going to pay me three thousand pounds!" She waved the letter at him. "You say that's not much? It's a fortune! Lyn! Look at this!" Her sister had just appeared in the doorway with a tea tray.

Tom had scrambled after her. He ran across the room and tried to climb up onto the high bed. "Mummy carry Tom," he announced, wriggling down among her books and papers, and bouncing on the duvet.

"You mind your little brother, old son," David said. He picked up the child and sat him on his knee. "Or sister, though heaven forbid that a girl should be so unprincipled as to threaten to arrive early." He laughed as Joss leaned forward to smack him.

Joss lay back on the pillows after they had all gone downstairs, Robert Cassie's letter in her hand and reread for the tenth time. A contract. An advance against royalties, and an option on her next book; her next book, when she had hardly started this one!

Her eyes strayed to the PC, which Luke had carried upstairs for her and set up on the table by the window. She had made a lot of progress on the book, her enforced bed rest giving her all the time she needed to get the story down. It was galloping through her brain so fast she couldn't keep up with it, the adventures coming thick and fast. Later she would get up and put on her dressing gown and sit at the table in the window watching the dusk creep in across the garden while beneath her fingers Richard hid in the newly built haystack beneath a huge summer moon.

When Luke looked in, half an hour later, she was asleep, the letter still in her hand. He took it gently and read it with a smile, then quietly he sat down next to the bed, looking at her. Her face, still thin and tired, but rested by sleep, was extraordinarily beautiful, even sexy, in the shaded lamplight. He bent forward and kissed her lightly, so as not to wake her.

Behind him, outside the window, a bird flapped suddenly against the glass, tossed by the wind, and as suddenly it had gone. The curtain blew inward and he shivered as he felt the cold draft penetrating deep into the room. Standing up, he went and peered out. It was black outside and all he could see was the reflection of the lamp behind him. With a shudder he pulled the curtains across.

He stood for a moment looking down at Joss. There was a slight smile on her face now and her cheeks had flushed with a little color. On the pillow beside her lay a rosebud. It was white, the petals slightly tinged with pink. He stared at it. Why hadn't he noticed it before? Leaning across, he picked it up and looked at it. It felt very cold, as though it had just been brought in from the garden. David. David must have brought it for her. He frowned angrily then, throwing it down on the bedside table, and he walked purposefully out of the room.

CHAPTER 15

"How can he have gone back to London?" Joss sat up in bed, her elbow on the pillow, and stared at Lyn. "Why?"

Lyn shrugged. "I think he and Luke had words about something." She was stacking coffee cups onto her tray.

"What do you mean, they had words?" Joss frowned, shocked. "What about?"

"Can't you guess?" Lyn stood looking down at her. "He thinks David fancies you."

Joss opened her mouth to protest. Then she shut it again. "That's silly."

"Is it?"

"You know it is. David and I were colleagues. Yes, he's fond of me and I of him, but that's all it is. Luke can't think anything else. It's crazy. Damn it all, I'm pregnant!"

"He thinks David has been giving you flowers."

"Flowers!" Joss was astonished. "Of course he hasn't given me flowers. And even if he did, what's wrong with that? Guests often bring their hostesses flowers."

Lyn shrugged. "Ask Luke."

Joss lay back on the pillows with a deep sigh. "Lyn." She ran her fingers gently over the bed cover. "What kind of flowers does he think David gave me?"

Lyn gave a small laugh. "Does it matter?"

"Yes, I think it does."

"Well, you'll have to ask Luke. I don't know."

"I will. He can't order our friends out like that!"

"I don't think he ordered him out. He just went. It's a shame. I like David. We need visitors here to cheer us up."

Her voice was light, casual, but Joss frowned, distracted for a moment from her own worries. "Is it too lonely for you, Lyn? Are you missing London?"

"No. 'Course not. I've told you before." Lyn picked up the tray.

"I feel so guilty that you've got to do so much while I'm stuck here in bed." Joss reached out and put her hand on Lyn's arm. "We'd be lost without you, you know."

"I know." Lyn softened the abruptness of her answer with a grin. "Don't worry. I'm tough. Looking after this house is easy and you know how much I love Tom." She paused. "Dad just rang, Joss. The last set of results were good."

"Thank God!" Joss smiled. "You must go up and see her again, Lyn. Whenever."

"I shall."

"I would go if I could, you know that."

Lyn gave a tight smile. "Of course you would," she said. She hitched the door open with her elbow, the heavy tray balanced in her hands.

"Simon is coming later. He said not to tell you or you'll get your blood pressure up!" She grinned again. "Yoga breathing and meditation for you, madam, and then if you are sufficiently calm and laid back, maybe he'll let you come downstairs."

He did in the end. Gentle walking. No housework, and don't try to carry Tom. Those were the instructions.

The first moment she had on her own in the study she picked up the phone and rang David. "Why did you go like that — not even saying goodbye?" Luke had driven over to Cambridge for the rest of the day in pursuit of spares. She couldn't ask him.

She heard the hesitation in his voice. "Joss, I think maybe I've come down once too often to see you."

"What do you mean?" Joss frowned. "Lyn thinks you had a row with Luke. You can't have. No one rows with Luke."

"No?" He paused. "Let's just say that Luke and I had a small disagreement over something. Nothing serious. I just thought maybe it was time to come home and do some preparation for the new term. No sweat."

"What did you have words about?" She glanced at the door. The house was silent. Lyn and Tom had gone for a walk.

"He feels maybe I am encouraging you too much in your obsession with the house." He did not mention Luke's sudden strange hostility. The accusation, sudden and frenzied, about the rose.

Joss was silent.

"Joss, are you still there?"

"Yes, I'm here. I didn't think he minded."

"He doesn't mind your interest. He's interested himself. He just doesn't want you to get things out of proportion."

When Luke got back she pounced on him. "What on earth do you mean, quarreling with David and sending him away like that? If you have a problem with him doing research on the house, tell me, not him. I asked him to do it!"

"Joss, you're becoming obsessed —"

"If I am, it has nothing to do with David!"

"I think it has." Luke tightened his lips.

"No. Besides, it's more than that, isn't it. You've got some crazy idea that he's in love with me."

"I don't think that's crazy, Joss. It's obvious to everyone, including you." He sounded very bleak. "You can't deny it."

She was silent for a moment. "He's fond of me, I know. And I of him." She met Luke's eye defiantly. "That doesn't mean we're planning a raging affair, Luke. You're the man I love. You're the man I married, the father of my children." She rested her hand on her stomach for a moment. "Luke." She hesitated. "Did this start off as a row over some flowers?"

Luke shrugged. "A rose is usually a love token, I believe."

"A rose." She went cold all over.

"He left a rose on your pillow." Luke's face was set with anger. "Come on, Joss, even you can see the significance of that."

She swallowed. The rose, when she had found it on her bedside table, had been cold and dead.

She knew it had not come from David.

For a long time she said nothing else about the house or the family, reading her mother's diaries in private and, between stints of writing, climbing to the attic only when Luke was out or safely ensconced beneath the car. David did not come again that term, nor did he send her any more cuttings or notes gleaned from his research.

Taking advantage of Lyn's baby-sitting and making trips to Mothercare and others to research the book her excuse, Joss made one or two visits to Ipswich and Colchester. She went to libraries, looking at books on local history, borrowing tomes on medieval costume and food and fifteenth-century politics. Given the all clear by Simon, on the condition she rested whenever she felt tired, she drove around the countryside, astonished to find that, away from the house and the strained atmosphere with Lyn, she felt happier and more positive than she had for months.

Coming home exhilarated and inspired, she wrote and wrote, hearing the story inside her head almost as if it were being dictated to her by Richard himself. She began to think that the story was like a charm. As long as she thought about it and stopped thinking about the family into which she had been born, the house remained gentle and benign, content to sleep with its memories, content perhaps that she was weaving its story into her novel and exorcising its legends by putting so much of it down on paper.

Sometimes, when it was her turn to do the

lighter chores she was still allowed, she would straighten up from sorting clothes or dusting or washing up and listen intently, but the voices in her head were only those of her own imagination. Perhaps the ghosts had gone. Perhaps they had never been there at all.

A few weeks later, Gerald Andrews came. On the backseat of his car was a pile of books. "I thought I would leave them for you. Just for when you have time. No rush to give them back." He shrugged. "I have to go into hospital for a hip operation next month. When that's all over may I come again and bring my friends? I so want to be there when they see the vaulting." He smiled conspiratorially and she said she would look forward to seeing him then. She put the books in the study, in a pile behind the chair. Luke would never notice a few more among so many.

For several days she ignored them, then she realized they could be fruitful sources for her novel. One by one she brought them out when she wasn't writing and scoured the pages for information.

It was all there — especially in the Victorian guidebooks to East Anglia. The legends, the rumors, the ghost stories. Belheddon Hall had had a reputation as long as it had stood.

Outside, a short gray February leached into March. Her stomach had at last rounded a little in this her fifth month as though acknowledging that spring was on the way. There were golden whips on the willow trees, hazel catkins in the hedge. Snowdrops and primroses gave way to daffodils. Hidden under her steadily growing manuscript was her family tree. She had filled in details covering more than a hundred years now — births, marriages, and deaths. So many deaths. It was compulsive. She pushed the pile of paper aside and read about the house again. Her excursions became fewer, and as she moved around the house with dustpan and brush or piles of clean clothes and towels for the various cupboards and drawers or took her turn — less often because she hated cooking as much as Lyn loved it — at the hot stove in the kitchen, she found she was again listening for voices.

Climbing to the attic, almost against her will, when Lyn and Luke and Tom were out in the stable yard, she moved slowly through the empty rooms, listening intently. But all she could hear was the wind, soughing gently in the gables, and she would go back down to the bedroom or to the study with a sigh.

She was mad, she knew that. To want to hear the voices again was idiotic. But they were the voices of her little brothers, her only contact with a family that had gone forever. She began to ignore her writing, deliberately challenging her theory that the intensity of her concentration on the book had driven Georgie and Sammy away, but without her writing there was an empty space inside her — that thought made her smile wryly as she patted her steadily swelling stomach — an empty space which left her feeling frustrated and unfulfilled.

Luke noticed her restlessness and tried to help. "Lyn wondered if it would be fun to take Tom to the zoo. He's had so few excursions since we moved here. Shall we make a day-trip of it? All of us go? It'll get you out of the house." He had noticed that her own private excursions had stopped.

She felt her spirits rise. "I'd like that. It would be fun. Tom will love it!"

They settled on the following Wednesday, and Joss began to look forward to the trip. Her aimless visits to the attic stopped and she helped Lyn prepare Tom for the animals, looking at pictures of elephants and lions and tigers and telling him stories about the other animals they thought they would see there.

On Tuesday night Tom was sleepless with excitement. "It's our own fault." Wearily Joss stood up. They were sitting at the kitchen table finishing supper when the baby alarm crackled into life for the second time that evening. "It's my turn. I'll go and see to him."

She let herself into the great hall, hearing Tom's cries for real now, not through the plastic alarm on the kitchen dresser. Hurrying to the foot of the stairs, she peered up into the dark and reached for the light switch.

The shadow on the wall at the angle of the stairs was clearly that of a man. Hunched toward her menacingly, it hovered above her as she clutched at the banister. Paralyzed with fear, she stood for a moment staring up toward it, Tom's screams echoing in her ears.

"Tom!" Her whisper was anguished as she put her foot on the bottom step, forcing herself to move toward it. "Tom!"

One of its arms was moving slightly, beckoning

her onward. She froze, willing herself upward, craning her neck upward toward the landing. Luke's waterproof jacket was hanging jauntily from the carved acorn knob at the top of the stairs. What she had seen was its shadow.

That night she had a nightmare which woke her shivering and sweating. In her dream a huge metal drum on legs had walked slowly toward her across the room. On top of it a jaunty tricorn hat belied the evil expression in its two rivet-stud eyes. Its arms, like giant linked paper clips, were stretched out toward her, its method of propulsion hidden by the gleaming aluminium of its body. She awoke with a start and lay there, too afraid to move, her heart thundering in her chest. Beside her, Luke stirred and groaned. She listened intently. Beyond his gentle snores there was silence. No sounds from Tom. No sounds from the house. There did not seem to be a breath of wind outside in the garden.

When she awoke at last it was with a splitting headache. She sat up and groped for the alarm clock and then fell back on the pillow with a groan. She could hear Lyn talking cheerfully to Tom as she got him up. The little boy was giggling happily. Of Luke there was no sign.

By the time the others had had breakfast she knew she couldn't go with them to the zoo. Her head was spinning and she was so tired she could barely move.

"We'll put it off, go another day." Luke bent over her, concerned.

"No." She shook her head. "No, you can't disappoint Tom. You go. I'll go back to bed and sleep the rest of the morning. Then I'll do some work on the book. Honestly. I'll be fine."

She waved them off, torn by Tom's tears when he found his mummy wasn't coming after all, and then, her head throbbing, she turned back toward the house.

It was after two when she awoke. The morning sun had gone and the sky was overcast and sullen. As she made her way downstairs, she could hear the wind in the huge chimney.

Making herself a cup of tea and a marmite sandwich, she sat for a long time at the kitchen table before at last reaching for her jacket.

At the edge of the lake she stopped, her hands in her pockets, watching the gusty wind blow sheets of black ripples across the water. Staring down into its depths, she hunched her shoulders against the cold, deliberately fending off the thought of a little boy with his jam jar of tadpoles bending toward the water on the slippery bank.

She tensed at a sound behind her. Turning, she surveyed the lawn. There was no one there. She listened, straining her ears to separate sounds from the roar of the wind in her ears, but there was nothing.

Turning, she began to walk slowly back toward the house. Another cup of tea and she would go back to the book. She had wasted too much time daydreaming; she had a novel to write.

Sammy!

One hand on the mouse the other on the key-board, she looked up, listening. Someone was running down the stairs.

Sammy! Play with me!

Holding her breath, she stood up slowly and tiptoed toward the door.

"Hello? Who's there?" Reaching out to the doorknob, she turned it slowly. "Hello?" Peering out into the hall, she squinted up the staircase into the shadows. "Is there someone there? Sammy? Georgie?"

The silence was electric, as if someone else too were holding their breath and waiting.

"Sammy? Georgie?" She was clutching the doorknob as though her life depended on it, a thin film of perspiration icing her shoulder blades.

She forced herself to take a step out into the hall, and then, slowly, she began to climb the stairs.

"You know better than to ask me for sleeping pills." Simon sat on the chair next to her in the study. He was watching her closely. "Come on now. What is it. You're not afraid of the birth?"

"Of course I'm afraid. What woman isn't." Joss hauled herself up from her chair and went to stand at the window with her back to him, wanting to hide her face. Outside, Lyn and Tom were playing football on the grass, his latest game, zoos, finally exhausted. "Not too near the water," she wanted to shout. "Don't go too near." But of course Lyn wouldn't let him go too near. Even if she did, there was a solid wall of vegetation around the lake now — dead nettles, brambles, a tangle of old man's beard.

Sammy

The voice calling was loud in the room. It was the third time she had heard it that morning. She swung around and stared at the doctor. "Did you hear that?"

Simon frowned. "What? Sorry."

"Someone calling. Didn't you hear?"

He shook his head. "Come and sit down, Joss."

She hesitated, then she went and perched on the low chair opposite him. "I must be hearing things." She forced herself to smile.

"Maybe." He paused. "How often do you hear 'things,' Joss?"

"Not often." She gave an embarrassed smile. "When we first moved here I began to hear the boys — shouting — playing — and Katherine — the voice calling out for Katherine." She shrugged, finding it difficult to go on. "I don't want you to think I'm ready for the men in white coats. I'm not mad. I'm not imagining it —" She paused again. "At least I don't think so."

"Are we talking about ghosts?" He raised an eyebrow. Leaning forward, his elbows on his knees, he looked at her intently, studying her face.

She looked away, unable to meet his gaze. "I suppose we are."

There was a long silence. He was waiting for her to say something else. She gave a nervous laugh. "Women grow fanciful in pregnancy, don't they? And, thinking about it, I've been pregnant

206

since we moved in."

"Do you think that is what it is?" He leaned back in the chair, crossing one leg over the other, almost too deliberately casual.

"You tell me. You're the doctor."

He took a deep breath. "I don't believe in ghosts, Joss."

"So I'm going mad."

"I didn't say that. I think you have been physically and mentally exhausted since you moved into the house. I think you have allowed the romance and history and emptiness of the place to play upon your mind." He sighed. "I suppose if I told you to take a holiday you would say it was out of the question."

"You know Luke can't go away. He's got three cars to work on now." They were even discussing his taking on some help.

"And it's out of the question that you go away without him?" He was still studying her face. She was too thin. Too pale.

"Out of the question." She smiled.

Why did he get the distinct impression that her answer had, in fact, nothing at all to do with Luke. He shook his head. "Then you must be firm with yourself, Joss. More rest. Real rest. More company. I know that sounds a contradiction, but you have a real treasure here in Lyn. I know she would welcome visitors and take the strain off you. You need distraction and laughter and, not to put too fine a point on it, noise."

She laughed properly this time. "Simon, if you knew how awful that sounds! I'm not lonely. I'm not suffering from the quiet, and I'm sure I'm

207

not having delusions."

"So you believe in ghosts."

"Yes." One word, half defiant, half apologetic.

"When I hear or see something myself, then I'll believe you." He stretched, groaned, then stood up. "Well, I'm afraid I can't help with the sleeplessness. Gentle walks in the fresh air, cocoa or malted milk before bed and an easy conscience, that's the best prescription a doctor can give." He turned to the door and reached for the handle, then he stopped. "You are sure you're not afraid, Joss?"

"No." She smiled reassuringly. "I'm not afraid."

The attic was full of bright sunshine. It showed up the marks of rain and dust on the window, and made the air dance with sunbeams. It would make the perfect setting for one of the scenes in her book — just like this — the hot sun, the smell of centuries, old oak, the dust, the absolute silence. Puffing slightly after the steep stairs, Joss went straight to the trunk by the wall and threw back the heavy lid. She had only managed to open the padlock a few days before. Not wanting to ask Luke to cut it off for her, she had sat there for an hour with a hairpin and suddenly, easily, the lock had clicked back and the hasp swung open. Elated, she had lifted the heavy lid and stared inside. Books, letters, papers — and an old bunch of dried flowers. She had picked them up and stared at them. Roses. Old dried roses, colorless with time, tied with silk ribbons. Laying them gently on the floor beside her, she began to look through the paper. From the depths of the chest drifted a musty smell of cedar and old brittle paper.

In the bottom of the box she had found John Bennet's diary — the John Bennet who had married her great grandmother in 1893 and nine years later, in 1903, had disappeared without a trace.

The last entry in the diary, which seemed to cover, on and off, about five years, was dated April 29, 1903. The writing was shaky, scrawled across the page. "So, he claims yet another victim. The boy is dead. Next it will be me. Why can't she see what is happening? I have asked that the sacrament be celebrated here in the house and she refuses. Dear sweet Jesus save us."

That was all.

Joss sat on the closed trunk, the book open in her lap staring out of the dusty window. The sky beyond was a dazzling ice blue. Dear sweet Jesus save us. The words echoed through her head. What had happened to him? Had he run away, or had he, as he feared, died? She looked down at the book again, leafing through the pages. Until the last few entries the handwriting had been strong, decisive, the subject matter on the whole impersonal — to do with the farm and the village. She had found the entry for little Henry John's birth. "Mary had an easy delivery and the child was born at eight o'clock this morning. He has red hair and looks much like Mary's father." Joss smiled, wondering if that was a touch of humor. If it was, the reason for it had long gone.

Farther back she found the entry where his

marriage to Mary Sarah in the spring of 1898 was similarly laconically described. "Today Mary and I were married in the church at Belheddon. It rained, but the party was I think a merry one. We have waited so long for this marriage I pray that it may be joyous and fruitful and that happiness will come now to Belheddon Hall."

Joss chewed her lip. So, even then, he knew. Where had John Bennet come from? How had he and Mary met? It was all there. His father was a clergyman in Ipswich; his mother had died some time before. He himself had trained for the law, and for several years he seemed to have been a partner in a firm of solicitors. When he married he gave up the partnership — presumably to manage Belheddon, which had been at that time a large and prosperous estate, with farms and cottages and hundreds of acres.

The diary fell in her lap and she leaned back against the wall, staring at the shadows on the far side of the attic. The hot sunshine, the heavy carved mullions, the arched roof beams: the combination sent a network of dark shadow over the wallpaper, shadow that looked — almost — like the figure of a man. She frowned, trying to focus, conscious suddenly that her heart was beating faster than normal. Her palms had grown moist. She pressed them hard on the lid of the trunk on which she was sitting, taking comfort from its solidity, and glanced at the doorway. It seemed a hundred miles away. The attic was unnaturally quiet. The usual creaks and groans of the timbers, the soft soughing of the April wind, all had faded to silence.

"Who are you?" Her whisper seemed crude and violent in the emptiness. "Who *are* you?"

There was no answer. The shadows had re-arranged themselves, back into a crisscross of architectural shapes.

Swallowing nervously, she pushed herself up until she was standing upright. The diary fell unnoticed to the floor and lay facedown, the pages splayed at her feet.

"In the name of Jesus Christ, go!" Her voice tremulous, she found her hand tracing the age-old pattern from head to heart, from shoulder to shoulder, the protecting, blessing cross. Slowly, step by step, she sidled toward the doorway, her eyes fixed on the wall where she had seen — thought she had seen — the shape of a man. Her back to the wall, she edged out of the room, then she ran. She ran through the attics, down the steep stairs, down the main staircase, through the great hall and into the kitchen. There, panting, she threw herself into a chair and buried her head in her arms on the table.

Slowly her panic subsided and her breathing calmed. She pressed the heels of her hands into her eyes. Then reflexively she cradled her arms around her stomach. She was still sitting there when Lyn came in with Tom in his buggy.

"Joss?" Lyn abandoned the baby buggy and ran to the table. "Joss, what is it? What's happened? Are you all right?" She put her arms around Joss's shoulders. "Is it the baby? Are you in pain?"

Joss smiled weakly and shook her head. "No, no. I'm fine. I just had a bit of a headache, that's all. I thought I'd make a cup of tea, and I felt a bit dizzy."

"I'll call Simon."

"No." Joss shouted the word in a panic. Then more gently she repeated it, "No. Don't fuss, Lyn. I'm OK. Honestly. I was sitting down and I stood up too suddenly, that's all." She dragged herself to her feet and went over to Tom, releasing his harness and humping him to his feet. "There, Tom Tom. Did you have a nice walk?"

The things she had heard, children's voices, the voices of her own brothers, they had nothing to do with whatever had scared generation after generation of grown men and women in the house. Georgie and Sammy had been born long after their grandparents and great-grandparents had died. John Bennet, Lydia Manners — they could not have heard the laughter of Georgie and Sammy in the attic. Controlling herself with an effort, she picked up the kettle and carried it to the tap. No one else had heard anything. No one else seemed worried. Perhaps Simon was right. She had got herself into a silly neurotic state as a direct result of her pregnancy. Perhaps all the pregnant women in her family had the same wild fancies. The idea struck her suddenly as ludicrous, and she found as she turned with the filled kettle to put it on the hot plate that she was smiling.

Lyn noticed and smiled back. "Before I went out, David rang," she said abruptly. "I said we wanted him to come down. I said I thought it would cheer you up. He was a bit iffy about it but he said he would. Next weekend. Is that all right?"

"Of course it is."

"I told Luke."

"Good." Joss glanced at Lyn. "How did he take it?"

"OK. I told him it wasn't just you who liked David. And not all of us are married." Lyn's face had colored slightly, and Joss found herself studying her sister with sudden perception. The normally colorless complexion, the slightly surly demeanor, had been replaced by a sparkle that Joss had never seen there before. She sighed. Poor Lyn. Sophisticated, intellectual, and well-read, David would never fancy her in a million years.

At first the weekend went well. David arrived loaded with wine for Luke ("Now that so much of yours has been taken away, I reckoned a donation to help top up the cellars would be appreciated — when is the auction, by the way?"), books for Joss, a pretty porcelain vase for Lyn, and a massive black teddy bear dressed in a crocheted lace jumper for Tom. He insisted on helping Lyn cook lunch, admired the latest car in the coach house, met Luke's new part-time assistant, Jimbo, a twenty-year-old apprentice mechanic from the village, and, Joss felt, avoided her as much as possible.

Determined not to show how hurt she felt, she declined the offer of a walk with the others after lunch and climbed instead to the bedroom, where she flung herself down on the bed. Exhausted, she was asleep in seconds.

In her dream she seemed to be looking down upon herself as she slept. The figure standing near the bed was clearer now. It was tall, broad-shouldered, clearly a man, or all that was left of the spirit of what had once been a man. It moved closer, looking down at her, stooping slightly to rest a hand as transparent and light as gossamer on her shoulder under the cover. Gently, imperceptibly, the hand moved down to rest on the hump of her stomach, almost caressing the baby which nestled there in the safe darkness of her womb. The room was unnaturally cold, the atmosphere electric. Joss groaned slightly, and moved in her sleep to ease the discomfort in her back. The figure did not move. It bent closer. The icy fingers brushed lightly across her hair, her face, tracing the line of her cheekbone. With a cry of fear Joss awoke and lay staring up at the tester of the bed. She was perspiring slightly and yet she felt desperately cold. Shivering, she pulled the covers around her more closely. The shadow had gone.

It was early evening before she had a chance to speak to David alone. Luke had gone over to see the Goodyears and it was Lyn's turn to put Tom to bed. Sitting opposite Joss in the study, his legs stretched out to the fire, a glass of whiskey in his hand, David scrutinized her appreciatively for a moment, then he grinned. "So, how is authorship?"

"Fine. Good fun. Hard work."

He took a sip from his glass. "I had lunch with Gerald Andrews last week. I don't know if he told you, but he's about to go into hospital, poor man. He's very frustrated. He won't be able to help us with our research after all. We talked about you quite a bit."

"And?"

"And —" He paused in mid breath as though changing his mind about what he was going to say. "Joss, have you ever thought about selling Belheddon?"

"No." She said it uncompromisingly, without even a second taken for thought. For a moment neither of them said anything, then she looked him in the eye. "Why?"

Uncomfortably, he put down his whiskey glass. Rising, he went over to the French doors and stared out across the moonlit lawn. It was very bright out there, but cold. There were still traces of the previous night's frost lying in the shade of the hedge.

"We felt that maybe the stories about the house might be depressing you a bit," he said after a moment.

"Did you mention this to Luke?"

"No."

"Well, please don't. I'm not the slightest bit depressed. Why should I be? It is in the nature of history that most of the players are dead."

His face cracked into a smile almost against his wishes. "I couldn't have put that better myself."

"David. What about you and Luke? Is it all right?" She looked away from him, a little embarrassed.

"It's fine. I wouldn't be here otherwise." He did not turn around. There was a long silence and at last she stood up. Coming over to stand next to him at the window, she decided to change the subject.

"Something Gerald said stuck in my mind. He noticed that Belheddon nearly always passed down through the female line. That is why everyone has different surnames even though they are related. Matrilineal descent, he called it. I checked up on it afterward on the family tree I've been drawing up. It's true. No son has ever lived to inherit Belheddon Hall. Not once. Ever."

She did not look at him as she spoke. Her eyes seemed to be focused on a distant point on the water of the lake, where the moon glittered on the gray surface, turning it into a diamanté cloak.

"We hoped you wouldn't notice."

"No exhortations to ignore it, to believe it is just coincidence?"

"What else could it be?" His voice was bleak.

"What else indeed." Her voice was flat. She went back to her chair and threw herself into it.

"Have you told Luke about this, Joss?" David followed her to the fire. He stood with his back to it, looking down on her.

She shook her head. "I tried telling him about the diaries, the letters. He didn't want to know. It was you who told me not to ram my inheritance down his throat. How can I tell him that this house is cursed?"

"It isn't. I'm sure it isn't." In spite of himself he shivered.

"Isn't it? Do you know how many accidents have happened here over the years? Over the centuries? And never to a woman. Never. Only to men. My brothers, my father, my grandfather

— only my great grandfather escaped, and you know why? Because he saw it coming. He wrote in his diary that it — it — was going to get him next." Her voice had risen. She slumped back in the chair suddenly. "Perhaps it did get him. All we know is that he disappeared. We will never know whether he ran away or something awful happened to him. Perhaps he was cornered in the woods or the lanes, or in the garden, and his body was never found."

"Joss, stop it." David sat down on the arm of her chair and reached for her hand. "This is ridiculous. It is coincidence. It has to be coincidence."

"Then why did you want me to sell it?"

He smiled ruefully. "Because in each of us, however down to earth and boring, there is a tiny, treacherous bit of superstition."

"And that bit believes the devil lives at Belheddon." Her voice was very small.

David laughed. "Oh no, I didn't say that. No, not the devil. I don't believe in the devil."

"That, if you don't mind my saying so, hardly proves that he doesn't exist."

"True. But I'm happy with the theory. No, whatever happened here, it is a mixture of things. Tragic accident, like your brothers and your father — all things that could happen in any family, Joss, and probably have. In the past, maybe there was some other factor at work. Maybe the water was contaminated and the germs affected boys more than girls; maybe there was a sex-linked gene in the family which made the male children weaker, susceptible to — something."

"A sex-linked gene making the male children more susceptible to falling into the pond?" Joss forced a smile. "Not very convincing, David."

"No, but as likely as any other theory."

Behind them the door opened, and Luke looked in. His eyes immediately went to the arm of the chair where David's hand rested on Joss's. "I see I'm interrupting." His voice was cold.

"No, Luke. No." Joss levered herself from the chair as David moved away. "Listen. There is something I must tell you. Please — listen."

Coming in, he closed the door behind him. His face was white. "I'm not sure I want to hear this."

"Well, I want you to listen. There is something you must know. I've tried to tell you, but —" She shook her head and looked helplessly at David. "It's to do with the house. We — I — think there is a curse on it."

"Oh, please." Luke pushed her away. "Not that again. I have never heard such crap. A curse! That's all we need. In case you've forgotten, we have to live here. You can't sell. That was a condition of your mother's will. If you want to leave, we lose the house. We have no money, no job. Here I can work. You can write your stories. Lyn and your parents can come if they want. There is room even for your friends." He glared at David. "I must say, David, I'm surprised you're still encouraging her in all this. I thought you had more sense."

"I do think there is something in what she says, Luke, old boy." David looked distinctly uncomfortable. "You should listen to her. I don't

218

think the house is cursed — maybe it is just an accumulation of old stories and circumstances, I agree, but it does seem strange — too strange to be entirely coincidence — that so many things have happened here over the centuries."

"And you think the devil lives here? Satan himself, complete with pitchfork and furnace in the cellar?"

"No. Not that. Of course, not that."

"I should bloody well think not. Have more sense, David. Joss is pregnant. The last thing she needs is someone winding her up and encouraging her in all this stupidity. Simon Fraser had a word with me. He says she's got herself in a state. She's supposed to keep calm. And I find you holding her hand, discussing with her the possibility that our son will die."

There was a sudden total silence. Joss went white. "I never said that," she whispered. "I never mentioned Tom."

"Well, that's what this is all about, isn't it? The sons of the house dying. The voices in the dark. Little boys in the cellar." Luke rammed his hands deep into the pockets of his old cords. "I'm sorry, Joss. I just want you to realize how preposterous this sounds. Your family are dead. They are all dead. Like all families, some of them died young and some in old age. Obviously, the farther back you go the more likely they are to have died unexplained and unsatisfactory deaths — that is the nature of those days. They had no medicine, no surgery. Children died all the time, that is why Victorians had so many children — to try and up the ante a bit. Luckily, we

219

are living in a more enlightened and scientific age. End of problem. Now, if you will excuse me, I'll go and finish up in the coach house. Then I suggest we all have supper and forget this whole sorry rigmarole."

The door shook as he closed it. Joss and David looked at one another. "Not an easy man to convince," David said quietly, after a minute. "Besides, Joss, I do think that he is in many ways right. Relax. Try and put it all out of your mind, but maybe be a little on your guard as well."

"On my guard against what?" With a shiver, she stood closer to the fire. "In the diaries he is described as 'he' or 'it.' Something or someone who terrified sane, rational, educated women."

And killed little boys. She did not speak the words out loud.

"And you, who are also sane, rational, and educated, have seen nothing. And you have heard nothing — nothing but some voices, trapped like echoes within the fabric of the house." He smiled. "Come on, Joss. You know the sign against the evil eye, don't you." He raised his two forefingers and crossed them in front of her face. "Be ready if he or it ever manifests. Otherwise, forget it. Tom loves it here. It's a great place. All houses have dangers. Cellar stairs and ponds are obvious dangers, and an unsupervised youngster could fall foul of them anytime in history or today. You take precautions, you watch him, Lyn clucks around him like a mother hen. No one could do more."

"I suppose not."

So, he claims yet another victim. The boy

220

is dead. Next it will be me. Why can't she see what is happening . . .

Could so many people have imagined the same thing? Had they all read each other's diaries, perhaps sitting in this very room, taking comfort from the fire as their hair stood on end and their toes curled with terror in the darkness of long gone winter nights? Somehow that didn't seem likely.

The kitchen was deliciously warm and bright and sane. Lyn glanced at them as they walked in. She had just put a cake in the oven and her face was shiny with the heat of the stove. On the floor in the corner, Tom was playing with his Duplos, building a castle with some very questionable symmetry. Self-consciously she rubbed her face on her sleeve. "Luke just went out muttering," she said. "I gather he thinks you two are around the bend."

"Something like that." Joss forced a smile. "Anyway, we have been well and truly reprimanded, and, full of repentance, we are going to help you set the tea things." She was gazing at Tom, needing suddenly to hold him in her arms.

"Great." Lyn did not seem that enthusiastic. "He says you think the house is cursed." She frowned. "You don't really think that, do you Joss?"

"No, of course she doesn't." David hauled himself up to the table beside her. "Now, what can I do to help? I feel a cookery lesson coming on."

Lyn glanced at him archly. "I suppose I could

make some biscuits." She blushed.

The magic word had an immediate electrifying effect on Tom. Scattering brightly colored plastic bricks all over the floor, he scrambled to his feet, dodged effectively past Joss's outstretched hand, and ran toward them. "Me cook bickies," he announced firmly, and standing on tiptoe he grabbed a wooden spoon from the table.

Joss watched them for several minutes. Her back ached and she was feeling peculiarly tired. Lyn was flirting openly with David, and after an initial show of reluctance he had obviously decided to humor her. When Joss finally wandered out of the kitchen and back to the study, no one noticed her go. David and Lyn, covered in biscuit mixture as much as Tom, were laughing too much to hear the sound of the softly latching door.

In the great hall she stopped and looked around. Lyn had put a huge vase of daffodil buds on the table, and in the comparative warmth of the house they had opened. The glorious scent filled the room. It was a happy smell, one that reminded her of spring and optimism and rebirth. She stood for a while looking down at the flowers, then she went through into the study. On the chair where she had been sitting lay a rosebud. She stared at it. David would not have put it there. He would not have done anything so stupid! Putting out her hand, she touched it. It was ice cold, frosted, already growing limp in the heat of the room, the white petals falling open, it was collapsing as she watched. Distastefully, she picked it up and looked at it closely. There was something sad and decadent about it — something unpleasant that she couldn't quite put her finger on. She looked at it for a moment longer, then with a shiver she threw it on the fire.

CHAPTER 16

As she lay back, Joss craned sideways to look at the image of her baby on the screen. She could see it clearly this time — the fetal shape, the little arms, the legs, the pulsing swirling life.

"Can you tell if it's a boy or a girl?" she asked. The question had been seething inside her all morning.

"If I can, I'm not allowed to tell." The radiographer calmly went on with the scan.

"I need to know." Joss's voice was tense. "Please. I do need to know."

"Oh come on, Joss." Luke was with her, sitting on a chair nearby, peering in some confusion at the strange blobs and swirls which showed his child. "It's more fun not to know. It's not as though we mind, either way, as long as he or she is healthy."

"I need to know, Luke." Her voice was fierce. "Please. Can't you tell me? I shan't breathe a word."

The woman stepped back from the bed. "It's the hospital's policy not to tell mothers." She pulled a wad of tissues from a box and began to rub away the gel from Joss's skin. "But in fact, my dear, I don't know. Not the way your baby is lying. So you must wait and see. Not long now. Twenty-eight weeks and as far as I can tell the little one is absolutely fine. No trouble there at all." She smiled as she covered Joss up. "Now, you get up in your own time while I fill in the form, and you can have a picture to take home." Sitting down, she scooted her chair across the floor to her desk.

"Luke. Make her tell me." Joss's eyes filled with tears.

Luke stared at her. "Joss! What on earth is the matter? We agreed we don't mind what it is."

"Well I do mind. I want to know."

The radiographer had put on a pair of wire-rimmed spectacles. She turned and peered over them at Joss. "Mrs. Grant. I told you I couldn't tell you, even if I wanted to." She frowned as she stood up and threw the glasses onto her desk. "Now, you mustn't get yourself in a state. That's not good for you. Not good at all."

In the car going home Luke said nothing until they had reached the outskirts of the town. "Come on, Joss. What is it? She said the baby was fine."

"I need to know, Luke. They'd tell me in London, I'm sure they would. Don't you see? If it's a boy, it's in danger —"

"No!" Luke slammed on the brakes. "Joss, that is enough. I will not listen to any more of this. It's crazy. Tom is not in danger. That baby, boy or girl, is not in danger. You are not in danger. I am not in danger." Behind them a car hooted and edged past them. The driver lifted the middle finger of his hand as he passed. "You are not to worry. Listen, I am going to ask the rector to come in and talk to you. Would you feel better if he blessed the house, or exorcised it or something? Would that put your mind at rest?"

Exorcizo te, in nomine Dei + Patris omnipotentis, et in nomine Jesu + Christi Filii ejus, Domine nostri, et in virtute Spiritus + Sancti . . .

With a sigh, Joss leaned back in her seat and slowly shook her head. What was the point? It had already been tried.

Luke called him anyway three weeks later. James Wood sat on the edge of his chair and listened politely to Joss and then again to Luke as the May sunshine poured in through the windows. Then he smiled. "I am always prepared to bless a house. I usually do it when people first move in. I pray for their happiness in the house and that it should be a sanctuary and a home." He shook his head slowly. "But I normally pass ghosts over to a colleague who specializes in such things."

Joss forced herself to smile. She liked the rector and had enjoyed going occasionally to his services in the church, but his reaction to their request did not inspire her with any confidence "Your blessing would be wonderful, rector. Thank you." She glanced at Luke. He was looking away from her, seemingly studying the fire, and she could not see his face.

They both sat, heads bowed, there in the study

226

while he prayed over them, then they stood in the great hall while he said another short prayer, presumably designed to cover the rest of the house. It was as he was leaving that he turned to Joss. "My dear. You told me, I think, that you had visited Edgar Gower? Have you spoken to him about your troubles?"

She shook her head. "He's still away." She had tried to ring him almost every day over the last month or two, hoping he might be back from South Africa.

"I see." He sighed. "He would be the man to help you, I feel sure. He knows Belheddon. He knew your mother and father. And he is more sympathetic than I to the ideas you are putting forward." He looked shamefaced for a moment. "I have never seen a ghost or experienced anything remotely supernatural outside my own religious experience. I find it hard to understand."

Joss put her hand on his arm. "It doesn't matter. You have done your best."

The trouble was, his best might not be good enough.

For several weeks she thought it had worked.

The weather had grown steadily warmer; Luke's vegetable garden was beginning to take shape. In the middle of the month, Luke went up to London for the wine auction.

"I wish you had come with me, Joss." He was full of excitement. "It was amazing! We're rich!" He seized her hands and whirled her around. "Even after they've taken their cut, we will have about twenty-seven thousand pounds! No more

227

worries for a bit. Oh Joss!"

Joss, buoyed up with energy and optimism, threw herself into her writing again. Working with Lyn in the house, cooking, helping Luke with his accounts, she tried very hard to put her worries out of her head. The house was at peace. The atmosphere had lost its tension. The spring sun had swept away the shadows.

Then about an hour after he had been put to bed on Friday night, Tom had another nightmare. The adults had just sat down around the kitchen table when his screams rang out from the baby alarm. All three jumped to their feet. Joss, in spite of her increasing bulk, was there first.

The crib had once more moved across the nursery floor to the corner near the window. Tom was standing in the corner, his face red, tears streaming down his cheeks, his eyes tight shut. "Tin man," he bellowed. "Me see the tin man. Me don't like him!"

"Don't pick him up, love, he's too heavy for you now." Luke's admonition came too late as Joss swung him up out of the crib and hugged the little boy to her, feeling his legs straddling her rib cage, his small arms tightly clinging around her neck. "What is it? What tin man?" She buried her face in his hot little neck. "Sweetheart, don't cry. You've had a bad dream, that's all. There is no one here. Look, Daddy is going to put your bed back where it belongs."

Luke was looking at the floor. "I had wedged those castors so they couldn't move. I can't think how he's managing to rock himself across the room like that. He must be remarkably strong."

228

He straightened the bed, still miraculously dry, and reached out his arms for his son. "Come on, sausage. Let Daddy carry you."

"Who is this tin man he sees?" Joss was looking at Lyn. "I thought I asked you not to ever read him *The Wizard of Oz* again! It's upsetting him."

Lyn shook her head impatiently. "I haven't, Joss. As far as I know we haven't even got a copy. We are reading Babar books, aren't we Tom —" She broke off as Luke tried to lower Tom into the bed. The child's scream was piercing. "He'll have to come down. Let him fall asleep with us. I'll bring him up later." Fussing, she followed Luke as he carried the little boy downstairs, bringing with her his comfort blanket and his black teddy bear. In the doorway she paused. "Joss? Are you coming?"

"In a second." Joss was staring around the room. "Let me just look. Maybe it's a shadow or something that he sees."

She heard their footsteps cross her and Luke's bedroom, then clump across the landing. In a moment they had walked downstairs and she was alone. She looked around the room. Behind the thick curtains it was still daylight outside, but the room was brightly lit now from the center light, the floor a litter of Tom's larger toys, the small ones neatly put away in his play box. In the corner his chest of drawers stood between the door and the wall, on it the shaded night lamp. There was nothing there that could possibly frighten him. Aware that her own heartbeat was thudding uncomfortably fast in her ears, Joss went to the door and switched off the main light, then she walked back and stood by the crib, looking around. The shaded bulb hardly penetrated the murky corners of the room. Standing beside the crib, she could see the huge multicolored plastic ball the Goodyears had given him, the bright rag rug, and the toy box itself, cardboard, but covered by Lyn with thick sticky-backed scarlet and blue paper, almost in the corner of the room, the heaped toys spilling out of the top. The curtains were pulled tightly across the window. She frowned. The curtains were moving, sucked in and blown out as though by a strong draft. Nervously, she stepped toward them.

"Who's there?"

Of course there was no one there. How could there be? But the window was shut. It was very cold. Outside one of the late frosts that so often blight an English May was turning the garden silver, and she had shut it herself when she kissed Tom good night earlier. So why were the curtains moving? Her heart in her mouth, she was there in two steps, flinging back the multicolored curtains to expose the windows behind. The reflection of the lamp shone back at her, somewhere behind her shoulder. There was no stirring from the fabric now except that which she had caused by her own impetuous movement. She shivered.

Katherine. Katherine, sweet child, won't you talk to your king?

His eyes followed the girl as she flitted through the rooms of the house. From behind the heavy curtain of rippling, ebony hair, she flirted with eyes the color of speedwells, her laughter echoing through the rooms.

It was intensely cold over here by the window. Far colder than the rest of the room. Quickly Joss dragged the curtains closed again and turned.

It was standing right behind her, a shadow between her and the lamp. Between one second and the next it was there, blocking out the light, towering over her, and then it was gone.

"Oh." Her involuntary gasp seemed a pathetically small sound in the dimly lit room. She stared around frantically, but there was nothing there, nothing at all. She had imagined it.

Lyn glanced up at her as she entered the kitchen. Luke was cuddling Tom, sitting on the rocking chair by the range and already the little boy's eyes were closed. "Come and sit down, Joss. I'm just rewarming supper. He'll be asleep in a minute and we'll snuggle him up in a blanket on the chair."

"I don't think we should let him sleep in that room alone anymore." Joss flung herself down at the table and put her head in her hands. "I'd rather he slept in with us. We can move his crib into our bedroom."

"No, Joss." Luke frowned over Tom's head. "You know as well as I do that that is the thin end of the wedge. He'll never go back on his own if we let him sleep with us now. Besides, with the baby coming so soon you need your rest. Let him stay where he is."

"He'll be all right, Joss. Honestly. All kids have nightmares from time to time." Lyn was watching as Luke stood up carefully and lowered the little boy onto the chair where he had been sitting. Tucking him up with his blanket, he slipped the teddy bear in next to him and stood for a moment looking down at his son's slightly flushed cheeks, listening to his regular breathing.

"I suppose so." Joss stared at the little boy, her heart aching with love.

"I know what you're thinking, sweetheart." Luke came over to her and dropped a kiss on the top of her head. "All those children who have gone before. Don't. It's stupid and it's morbid. That was then. Now is now. Children nowadays have far better prospects."

In her sleep Joss stirred. A smile touched the corners of her mouth and she gave a small moan. Gently, not waking her, the bed covers were slowly eased back and her night shirt fell open, exposing her breasts to the starlight.

She woke heavy-eyed while it was still dark. She stared up at the ceiling for a moment, disoriented, and then reached across with a groan to find the alarm clock. It was half past four. What had woken her? She listened. Tom had not woken the night before when at last Luke had carried him upstairs, snuggling down at once with his teddy and turning over with his back to them, his arms around the furry creature's body, but even though there was no sound from Tom's room, she knew already that she would have to get up and see that he was all right.

Heaving herself carefully out of bed, she stopped for a moment, looking back toward

Luke's humped form. She could barely see him — just the outline in the light from the landing which streamed through the half-closed door. He did not stir. Reaching for her bathrobe, she padded on bare feet through to Tom's room and pushed open the door. The room was cold. Far colder than the rest of the house. Frowning, she went to the radiator and checked the switch and thermostat, which had been left on in case the weather should suddenly revert to winter. It was hot beneath her hand. Shivering, she went over to the window. It was open only a crack. Her own reflection as she peered out into the darkness of the garden was dim — a silhouette, backlit by the night-light. As she peered, she could see the dull gleam of water far away at the end of the lawn, reflected in the starlight.

If you look you will find the house was nearly always inherited by daughters.

Gerald Andrews's words ran suddenly through her head as the baby kicked beneath her ribs. It would be a boy. She knew it with absolute certainty. A brother for Tom, and they were both in terrible danger. Closing her eyes, she took a deep breath, trying to stifle the cry of anguish which seemed to be rising inside her from the very depths of her soul. No! No! No! Surely to God it was not possible. It could not be possible. Her hands cradled over her stomach, she turned slowly, her whole body clammy with fear, expecting it to be there again — the tall, broad figure between her and the crib. There was nothing.

For a long time she sat, her arms wrapped

around her knees, uncomfortably plumped on Tom's beanbag, her eyes fixed on the sleeping form, hunched under his quilt. From time to time the little boy snuffled and smacked his lips, but otherwise he slept undisturbed. Slowly, her lids dropped.

As her head fell forward, she jerked awake. In the semidarkness she felt a moment of confusion. She couldn't see Tom anymore. The crib, black with shadow, stood empty. Scrambling desperately to her feet, she staggered toward him, realizing only after she half fell that her legs had gone to sleep.

He was there, almost invisible in the pool of shadow, but still safe, still asleep. With a small sob she turned away. Hesitating in the doorway, she glanced back. The room was warm again now. It seemed snug and safe and almost happy. She was overwhelmed suddenly by a longing for Luke.

Rubbing her eyes, she made her way back to her own bed. The wedge of light was still shining through the door from the landing, and for several minutes she stood staring down at him. He was curled up in the same position as his son, his face slightly flushed, relaxed and happy in sleep. Instead of a teddy bear, he was cuddling a pillow. Smiling, she reached for the knot securing her bathrobe. As she slipped it off and threw it across the foot of the bed she glanced back at the landing. It was empty. Quiet. Nodding to herself, reassured, she pulled back the covers, ready to climb into bed. On her pillow lay another rose.

Backing away she stared at it in horror. "Luke!" It came out as a strangled whisper. "Luke, did you —" Put it there, she was going to ask, but already she knew he had not. None of the roses had come from Luke.

Staring down at it in horrible fascination, she crossed her arms over her breasts. She felt sick and degraded. It was on her bed, her pillow, where earlier her head had lain, defenseless, asleep. For all she knew, he — it — had been standing there, watching her.

Shuddering, she backed away from the bed. "Luke!" She reached for the light switch. "Luke!"

"What is it?" With a groan, he turned over and peered at her, his eyes gummed with sleep, his hair tousled. Like this he looked more like Tom than ever.

"Look." With a shaking hand she pointed at the pillow.

"What?" Groaning, he sat up. "What is the matter with you? Is it a spider?" He peered around myopically. She had never been afraid of spiders.

"Look at the pillow!" she whispered.

Luke stared at the pillow. He shook his head. "Can't see it. It must have gone. For God's sake, Joss, it's the middle of the night!"

"There. There!" She pointed.

"What?" Wearily he climbed out of bed and pulled the covers right back, exposing the pale green sheets. "What is it? What are we looking for?"

"There, on the pillow." She couldn't bring herself to come any closer. From where she stood she couldn't see it, but it was there.

Without touching it she knew how it would feel. Ice cold, waxy.

Dead.

"There is nothing here, Joss. Look." His voice had lost its grumpiness as sleep left him and suddenly he was gentle. "You must have dreamed it, darling. Look. Nothing. What did you think was here?"

She took a step closer peering at the pillow. "It was there. In the middle. A flower. A white flower." Her voice was shaking.

Luke looked at her hard. "A flower? All this panic for a flower?" Suddenly, he was cross again.

"Flowers don't just appear in the middle of the night. They don't drop onto your pillow from nowhere." She flared up defensively. "For God's sake. Do you think I would be afraid of a real flower?"

"What sort of flower was it then?"

"Dead."

He sighed. For a moment he seemed at a loss what to say, then slowly, almost resignedly, he started pulling the covers back across the bed. "Well, whatever it was, it's not there now. You dreamed it, Joss. You must have. There is nothing there. Look. Smooth sheet. Smooth duvet. Smooth, clean, fresh pillows. And I for one am getting into bed and going to sleep. I am tired."

She gave a small humorless smile. "I'm not going mad, Luke. It was there. I know it was there."

"Of course it was there." Irritated, he thumped the mattress beside him. "Are you coming to bed, or do you want to go and sleep in the spare room?"

"No. I'm coming." Tears of anger and humiliation and exhaustion welled up in her eyes. Quickly, not giving herself time to think, she made for the bed and climbed in. Luke's energetic stripping of the linen had left the bed cold and pristine. It no longer felt cosy. Reluctantly, she lay back and stared up at the tester as he leaned across and switched off the light. "Now, please let us get some sleep." He hunched the pillow around his shoulders. As he fell asleep, he remembered only briefly the rose he had found on her pillow once before. The rose he had accused David Tregarron of leaving there.

Miserably, she turned away from him.

Beneath her cheek the hard stem of the flower was cold and very sharp, the petals like soft wax.

CHAPTER 17

"Is there somewhere she could go and stay for a few days — away from here?"

Simon Fraser's quiet voice penetrated Joss's brain at last. It was two weeks later.

"No, I can't go. I mustn't. I have to stay here."

"Why, exactly, Joss?" The doctor was sitting on her bed holding her hand. The clock on the bedside table said it was ten minutes to four. Outside it was slowly growing light.

She shook her head. "I just want to be here. I have to be here. This is my home." Her desperate need to stay in the house was irrational, she knew, but she could not fight it.

"Your home seems to be giving you nightmares at the moment. This is the second time in two weeks that Luke has called me out. You are tired and overstressed." Simon smiled at her patiently. "Come on, Joss. Be sensible. Just for a few days so that you can have a good rest, be pampered, stop worrying about Tom and the baby."

"I'm not worrying —" She could feel the house listening, pleading with her to stay.

"You are. And it's understandable. You are per-

238

fectly normal, you know. You have probably been sleeping badly, and when you do sleep, you dream violently. The weather has suddenly grown hot and the baby is lying heavy on your stomach, as my old grandmother used to say. After all, there's not long to go now. What are you? — thirty-six weeks? There is nothing wrong with you — or the house — but just at the moment I think it would be a good thing if you were separated. Luke will look after things here, and Lyn will take care of Tom. There is nothing for you to worry about. Lyn has told me it might be nice if you were to go up to London to see your parents. I know things there are not exactly ideal, with your mother ill, but I understand from Lyn that all the tests have been reassuring and she is on the mend and they would be happy to have you, so I think that is a good idea. An ideal solution."

"Luke?" Joss stared at him. "Tell him I can't go."

"You can go, Joss. I think you should. Just to give you a bit of a change."

"No!" It came out as an undignified shriek. She struggled to get out of bed, pushing past Simon, who stood up and began to pack his bag. "I will not go. I won't. I'm sorry, but this is my home and I am staying here." Barefoot, she rushed past Luke and into the bathroom, where she slammed the door. She was hot and shaking, a pain somewhere up under her ribs. Stooping over the basin, she splashed cold water onto her face and then stared up into the mirror. Her cheeks were flushed, her eyes bright, tears still clinging to the spikes of her eyelashes. "They can't make me leave." She spoke out loud to her reflection. "They can't force me to go."

She could still hear her own screams ringing in her ears and feel the waxy imprint of the rose against her cheek — the rose which was never there when she awoke.

"Joss?" There was a soft knock at the door. "Come out. Simon is leaving."

She took a deep breath. Pushing her hair out of her eyes, she turned and unlocked the door. "I'm sorry, Simon." She gave him a determined smile. "I'm a bit tired and overwrought, I admit it. All I need is some more sleep. I am so sorry Luke called you out again."

"That's OK." Simon lifted his bag from the bed. "As long as you are all right." He gave her one more intense look from beneath his bushy eyebrows. "Keep calm, Joss, please. For the sake of the baby. Stay here, if that is what you want, but don't let the place get to you, and" — he gave her a stern look — "I think we should consider the idea that you might have the baby in hospital after all. Just a thought!" He gave a sudden beaming smile. "Now, I'm for my own bed, and if you are sensible that's what you two will do as well. No more alarums and excursions please. No, Luke, don't show me out. I know my way by now." He lifted his hand and disappeared toward the stairs, leaving Luke staring at his wife.

"Joss." Suddenly he seemed incapable of saying anything else. He shrugged. "Do you want a cold drink or something?"

She shook her head. She sat down on the edge of the bed, sheepishly. "I'm sorry, Luke. I really am. I don't know what came over me. I suppose I was dreaming. But you shouldn't have called Simon, you really shouldn't. The poor man has enough to do with people who are really ill." She hauled herself up onto the high mattress and lay back against the pillows. "It felt so real, I thought I really did feel something, you know. Another of those dead roses." She shuddered.

He sighed. "I know, Joss. I know."

She found it impossible to sleep again. The lights out, the sheet, which was all she could bear over her in the hot room, rearranged, she tried to get herself comfortable beside Luke. But sleep eluded her. The house was completely silent, the room still shadowy, but outside as the sun rose out of the sea behind the field she could hear the chorus of birds. She stared at the windows, watching the morning star fading between the mullions behind the half-drawn curtains. Beside her Luke grunted and sighed and almost at once began to breathe deeply and evenly. His body, heavy and hot, seemed to mold itself into the mattress, secure, safe, reassuring, while she lay, rigid and afraid, every part of her body aching and uncomfortable. She shut her eyes, screwing them up tightly, trying to focus on sleep.

In the corner of the room the shadow that was never very far away stirred and seemed to shiver, an insubstantial wraith. Near it a spider tensed and fled beneath the coffer which stood in front of the window.

When Luke awoke, to the not-very-tuneful singing of his small son from the nursery, Joss was fast asleep. The room was full of bright sunshine, and he could hear a pigeon cooing soothingly in the tree outside the window. The first days of June had brought a heat wave, and it was already very hot. He looked down at Joss for a moment. Her face was still flushed, pressed against the pillow. There was a frown between her eyes and she looked as though she had been crying in her sleep. With a sigh he slid out of bed, careful not to wake her, and padded across toward the little boy's bedroom.

She was still asleep an hour later when he brought her a cup of tea and the mail. Putting the cup down gently on the bedside table, he went to stand looking down on the garden. Behind him the shadow in the corner stirred. It moved away from the corner and hovered in the center of the room. There was no question now that it was anything other than a man. A tall man.

Joss stirred and turned over to face it, but she did not open her eyes. In her sleep, her hand went protectively to her stomach and rested there. Luke did not move. With a sigh he rested his forehead against the glass, savoring the coolness of it. His head ached. His eyes were gritty with lack of sleep. When he turned back toward the door, he did not see the shadow which had drawn near his wife. Rubbing his face with the palms of his hands, he reached for the handle and let himself out onto the landing, closing the door behind him. In the bedroom the shadow bent over the bed. The slight indentation on the sheet was the only sign of where it touched her.

Joss had tried the number four times that week. Once again this morning it rang with no reply. Putting down the phone, she put her head in her hands and stared down at the desktop without seeing it. Her sleep after the doctor had gone had been shallow and troubled; she had woken herself twice with her own whimpering, staring up at the bed hangings above her head. When she got up she felt stiff and uncomfortable, unable to eat any breakfast. All she could think about was the need to speak to Edgar Gower. With a shaking hand, she dialed his number and at last there was a reply.

"It's Joss Grant. You remember? Laura Duncan's daughter."

Was it her imagination or was the pause at the other end longer and more uncomfortable than it ought to have been.

"Of course. Jocelyn. How are you?"

In her anxiety she ignored his question. "I need to see you. Can I come up to Aldeburgh today?"

Again the pause. Then a sigh. "May I ask what you want to see me about?"

"Belheddon."

"I see. So. It has started again." He sounded resigned and a little cross.

"You have to help me." She was pleading.

"Of course. I'll do everything I can. Come now." He paused. "Are you calling from Belheddon, my dear?"

"Yes."

There was a moment's silence. "Then be very careful. I will see you as soon as you can get here."

The coach house was empty and locked. Luke was nowhere to be seen, and there was no sign of Jimbo. The Citroën had gone. Joss stared at the place it was usually parked in dismay. There had been a heavy thundershower an hour before and she could see the dry patch on the gravel where it had stood. Going back into the kitchen, she shouted for Lyn. There was no reply. There was no sign of her or Tom. Running to the back door, she looked at the hooks where the coats usually hung. Lyn's mac was gone. So was Tom's and so were his little red gum boots. They had gone out with Luke without telling her, without saying good-bye or coming upstairs to see if she were all right.

For a moment she was panic-stricken.

She had to go now. She needed to see Edgar Gower without delay. Lyn's car. Puffing, she ran out to the coach house. Lyn's car stood in one of the open coach bays. It was locked. "Oh, please. Let the keys be here." Turning, she sped back into the house. The keys were not on the shelf by the back door where Lyn sometimes threw them. They were not on the dresser or the kitchen table. Setting her teeth grimly, Joss walked through the house to the stairs. Her hand on the rail, she looked up toward the landing, suddenly reluctant to go up there. There was no one there. Nothing could hurt her. Her mouth dry, she put her foot on the bottom step and began slowly and quietly to climb.

In her bedroom the shadow stirred. It drifted slowly toward the door.

Katherine, I love you!

Halfway up the stairs Joss stopped, dizzy. Gritting her teeth, hanging onto the banister, she pulled herself up step by step, increasingly weary, and turned toward Lyn's door. Pulling it open, she stepped into the room.

Lyn's room was as always spotlessly tidy. The bed was made, the cupboard closed. No clothes lay strewn about, no books or papers. Her belongings, on the dressing table and the high Victorian chest of drawers, were meticulously arranged in small piles. The car keys were there, next to the hairbrush and comb.

Grabbing them, Joss turned to the door. It was closed. She stared at it, her stomach churning suddenly. She had not closed it and there had been no draft. Although Lyn's window was open, the curtains were not moving at all. Taking a step toward it, she was conscious suddenly of how quiet the house was. There were no sounds anywhere.

The door was not locked. Pulling it open, she stared across the landing toward her own bedroom. The skin on the back of her neck was prickling. There was someone there, she could sense it; someone watching; someone pleading with her to stay. Closing her eyes for a moment she took a deep breath, trying to steady herself.

"Who is it?" Her voice sounded very odd in the silence. Defiant and frightened. "Luke? Lyn,

245

are you home?" There was no sound.

She had to look. Slowly, plucking up her courage, she forced herself to move toward the doorway. She was torn. She needed to escape; she wanted to stay; she wanted to surrender to that languid ecstasy which had overwhelmed her once as she lay on her bed. She could feel it pulling her, soothing, gentle. Hesitantly, she took two more steps toward the room and looked in. There was no one there. It was completely empty.

CHAPTER 18

Her hand shook so much she could not get the key into the lock of the mini. Desperately, she tried again, glancing over her shoulder across the courtyard toward the house. The back door was closed. She had slammed it behind her but not paused to double lock it. Too bad. She was not going back now. Closing her eyes, she took a deep breath and tried to steady herself before bringing the key toward the lock again. It clicked against the car's paint work, slid toward the slot, and at last engaged. She turned it and wrenched the door open. Diving headfirst into the seat, she wedged herself behind the wheel, pulled the door closed behind her, and pushed down the locks, then she sat for a moment, her head resting against the steering wheel. When she looked up the courtyard was still empty; the back door still shut. Huge swaths of blue sky were spreading now between the thundery clouds.

A note. She should have left a note. Oh God! They would wonder where she was. She looked beside her to the passenger seat where her shoulder bag should be lying, chucked there as she got in. It wasn't there. It was still lying on the kitchen table together with her house keys. Almost as soon as she thought of it she knew she was going to do nothing about it. They would guess when they saw Lyn's car was gone that she had driven somewhere and she could phone them once she got to the Gowers'.

In the drive, she pulled up and for a moment sat staring over her shoulder at the front of the house as she tried to steady her breathing. The windows were all blank. There were no faces looking down at her from her bedroom window.

The roads were almost empty. She made good time as far as Woodbridge and was setting off northward when she happened to glance at the petrol gauge. It was hovering over empty. She had been driving fast, concentrating on putting as much space between her and Belheddon as possible, thinking about Edgar Gower and what she was going to say to him when she got there.

If she got there.

Without a handbag she had no money.

"Shit!" She didn't often swear, and certainly not alone, out loud. "Shit shit shit!" She banged the steering wheel. "Oh, please, let there be enough to get me there."

Leaning across, she pulled open the glove compartment and rummaged through the tapes and sweets Lyn had left there. She found a couple of fifty pees, her fingers sorting through the contents while her eyes were still fixed on the road ahead of her. All she needed was another pound and she could perhaps get a gallon — enough to get her there. A garage loomed ahead, its ugly

248

neon sign bright in the rain-swept landscape, and she pulled in, avoiding the pumps, drawing up near the air and water. With both hands now and the help of her eyes she began to ransack the glove compartment. Sweet papers, tapes, shopping lists tumbled to the floor. How strange that Lyn, so meticulous at home, should be so messy in her car. She smiled as she realized that most of the sweet papers related to Tom and then she frowned, wondering just how many sweets Lyn gave him. Her fingers closed over another coin. Five pence. Please, please, let there be some more money there.

In the end she found three pounds in scattered coins around the car — one coin under the floor mat, one down the side of the seat, another on the shelf under Lyn's sunglasses. Relieved, she backed the car up to a pump, put in the petrol, and at last was on her way again.

She drew into Aldeburgh as a heavy thundery shower of rain began to fall. It was very hot. Pulling into the square, she climbed stiffly out and ran, awkwardly because of her bulk, toward the Gowers' house. The door had opened before she got there. "I saw you from the window, my dear." Dot pulled her in. "Are you soaked? You should have brought an umbrella, you foolish child!"

In no time at all, it seemed to her, she had been dried, reassured, settled into a comfortable chair in Edgar's study, and given a glass of iced lemonade. Edgar had waited behind his desk while his wife fussed around Joss and only when she too had at last settled onto the sofa by the window did he come forward and sit down.

His face was very serious as he reached for his own drink. Then he glanced at Dot. "She is expecting a baby," he said with a slow shake of the head. "I should have guessed."

"We can all see that." Dot sounded impatient.

He gave a deep sigh. "So, Joss. What can I do for you?"

"What do you mean? Why is it significant that I'm expecting a baby?"

Edgar Gower shrugged. "Perhaps you should tell me first why you wanted my help."

"You know about Belheddon. You know what it was that haunted my mother and grandmother. You know what happened to my brothers. You know about the roses."

He frowned. "I know a certain amount, my dear. Not perhaps as much as you might be hoping. Tell me what has happened. From the beginning."

"I went to see John Cornish after you gave me his name last year. I tried again and again to ring you and thank you. It turned out that I had been left the house in my mother's will. She said if I turned up within seven years of her death I was to inherit it. As you know, I did. It came at the right moment for us. My husband had lost his business and we were penniless. We moved in, even though it was fairly run-down and we are living there now. Myself and my husband and my sister — my adoptive sister, that is — and my son, Tom." She scarcely noticed as Dot leaned forward and took the empty glass out of her hands. "I found diaries and letters in the house. My mother and my grandmother seem to have been haunted by something. They were very afraid. And now —"

She couldn't go on. Afraid that she was going to cry, she reached for a handkerchief and found a wad of crumpled tissues in the pocket of her skirt.

"And now it is your turn to be afraid." Edgar's voice was matter-of-fact, unemotional. "My dear, I received your letter. I'm sorry. I hadn't got around to replying as yet. Perhaps I wasn't sure what to say. You have made me feel very guilty. Can you tell me what has happened since you arrived in the house?"

"Roses." She found the laugh she was going to give came out as a sob. "It sounds so silly. To be haunted by roses."

"In what way are you being haunted by roses?" Unseen by Joss, Edgar gave his wife a quick worried glance. She was sitting, lips pursed, Joss's glass still in her hand.

"Just that. They keep appearing. Dried roses — no, not always dried, sometimes fresh and cold — almost slimy —" She shuddered. "On my desk. On the table, on my pillow —"

Edgar sighed once again. "At least roses are unthreatening. You have never seen anything else?"

She shook her head and then shrugged. "I don't know. I don't think so. But I sometimes wonder if Tom has."

"Tom is your son?"

She nodded. "He's only two. He doesn't understand. But something frightens him. He has

251

bad dreams. I'm sorry. I really am. I can't sleep anymore. I'm so afraid. They want me to leave the house. To go away until the baby is born, but I don't want to do that. It's my home. My family home. And I've been part of the family for such a short time."

He nodded. "I can understand that, my dear. But nevertheless I'm not sure that they're not right."

"There must be something else I can do. Something you can do. Is it the devil? Does he really live at Belheddon?"

She expected him to laugh, to shrug, to deny it absolutely, but instead he frowned. "There have been exorcisms at Belheddon. Several, I think. I know your mother had one carried out before I came to the parish, and I myself blessed the house and celebrated Holy Communion there on one occasion. Your grandmother too may have done the same. There was a history going back many centuries of reports of ghosts and even of devils, though I don't myself believe it is the devil or even one of his minions." At last he permitted himself a little smile. "No, I think there is an unhappy spirit in the house. And I think it finds itself attracted to women. I don't think you yourself are in any danger, Joss. None at all."

"But what about the others?"

He looked up and met her eye. For several seconds he said nothing. "I think you should be aware that it is possible that it is in some way more hostile toward men. And boys."

"So hostile that no boy has ever lived to grow

up in the house."

He shrugged unhappily. "Your brothers' deaths were recorded as accidental, Joss. Both seemed terribly, terribly sad accidents, the kind of thing that can happen anywhere in any period. I really don't know if there was anything sinister about them. I was with your mother after the deaths of both boys, and she never for a moment seemed to suspect anything else. She would have told me if she had, I'm sure of it. And yet —" He stood up, shaking his head uncomfortably and went to stand at the window, looking down at the sea, which looked black and oily beneath the thunderclouds. Running his finger around the inside of his collar, he turned at last. Perspiration was standing out on his forehead. "Joss. I do not want to alarm you, but I am not happy about you and your family staying at that house. Why not go away for a few weeks. When is the baby due? Surely you could stay with friends or family until then."

"You could even come here, my dear," Dot put in. "We'd be happy to have you. All of you."

Joss shook her head slowly. "I don't know. I don't want to go away. Belheddon is my home now. I love it so much." She shrugged. "And the others don't feel anything. Luke loves it there too. It's perfect for him. He can run his business from the courtyard, and he's doing really well. He would think it a tragedy to leave now, just when it's all coming together. And I . . . I'm happy there."

"What about your son?" Dot's voice was sharp.

"Dot!" Her husband rounded on her. "Young Tom will be fine. Joss is a different woman from her mother. She can cope. She can keep them all safe, I'm sure she can."

Joss stared at him. "What exactly does that mean?" Her own voice had suddenly become hard with suspicion.

"It means that your mother became nervous and lonely after your father and brothers died. And who can blame her. She was not a strong woman at the best of times, and she became a little neurotic. I think she imagined a great deal of what she thought went on in the house."

"What sort of things did she imagine?" Joss was watching him intently.

He did not meet her eye. "She imagined she heard things, saw people. She thought things were being moved about. Toward the end she was hallucinating — of that there is no doubt. When her French friend suggested she move away from Belheddon, for a long time she was too afraid to go. She seemed to feel that someone was keeping her there. We — that is, the village quack and I — thought it was the memory of the boys — and of course your father. Nothing could have been more understandable. Harder to understand was her resolve to give you away. No one understood that. No one." He shook his head.

"She did it to save me." Joss was twisting her fingers into the cotton of her voluminous shirt. "She wrote me two letters, which John Cornish gave me. One said she hoped one day I would understand why she had given me away; the other said that it was my father's idea that I should

254

be allowed to inherit Belheddon and that she could not leave until she had arranged that I should, even though it was not what she wanted. My father died before I was born, so presumably he left some kind of will which included his unborn child." She shrugged. "He must have loved me."

Neither of the Gowers reacted to the illogicality of this remark. Edgar merely slowly shook his head. "They both loved you, my dear. Your father was so pleased your mother was going to have another baby after all the unhappiness in the house. His accident was the most dreadful tragedy. My hope is that the happiness of having a young family in the house again will wipe out all the sadness once and for all."

"And the unhappy spirit you were talking about?"

He glanced at his wife. "I think what I will do is have a talk with one or two colleagues who know more about these things than I do. I have an idea what we should do, but I need to consult. Will you trust me?" He smiled. "And above all be brave. Remember, prayer will act as a shield and a strength. I will come and see you as soon as I have worked out what to do. And now" — he took a deep breath — "I think what we are going to do is give you a decent lunch to fortify you before you go home."

Home! She hadn't rung. They would be wondering what on earth had become of her.

When she finally got through, Lyn was furious. "Who said you could take my car? I was going home this afternoon and Luke needs the Citroën. What were you thinking about? For God's sake,

255

Joss, you could have guessed we were only down in the village. What the hell is the matter with you?" The angry voice echoed around the Gowers' living room. Joss's hosts had withdrawn tactfully to rummage in the kitchen and begin to make lunch.

Joss looked out of the window toward the sea. "I'm sorry, Lyn. I really am. It was urgent."

"And what am I supposed to do? Isn't it bad enough having to look after your bloody family every second of the day, without you taking my only means of escape!"

There was a long silence. Joss's attention had come back sharply to the phone. "Lyn —"

"Yes, Lyn. What would you do without Lyn?" The voice had grown more shrill. "I'm sorry, Joss. But it is too bad. I am fed up with it all. I know you can't do much at the moment, but why should it all fall on me?"

"Lyn, I am so sorry. I thought we'd talked it through. I had no idea you still felt like that."

"No. You have no idea about a lot of things." The resentment in the voice was unabated. "You live in your own happy little world, Joss, and see nothing of what is going on around you. That's always been your trouble and now it's ten times worse. I don't know what this bloody house has done to you, but it is not good."

"Look, I'll come back straight away —"

"Don't bother. Luke is going to drive me to the station. And now I've got to go and get Tom's lunch. You'd better see you're back in time for his tea because Luke is going to be in charge all afternoon!"

Joss sat staring at the receiver in her hand for several minutes after Lyn had banged down the phone. Lyn was right. She had been so involved with the house and the book she had not noticed that Lyn was unhappy and restless again. She did take Lyn for granted. Lyn would look after things. She always had.

Wearily, she stood up and made her way toward the kitchen. It was a small room, warm and cheerful, full of flowers and scarlet French cooking pans, decorated with Provençal pottery. It made the kitchen at Belheddon look very dark and Edwardian in contrast. She took the chair that Edgar Gower proffered and sat down heavily, her elbows on the small littered kitchen table.

"My sister is furious. I pinched her car without asking." She tried to make it sound like a joke, but her exhaustion and worry were beginning to wear her down. "It sounds as though she's had enough of us."

Dot sat down opposite her. "Come here to stay, Joss. Bring your little boy. I would love to look after him. It would be no trouble. It would give your sister a rest and I am sure your husband wouldn't mind being on his own if he has a business to run. Ask Edgar. I am a sucker for children and our grandchildren live so far away. I can only indulge myself once a year. You would be doing me a kindness." She reached across the table and took Joss's hand. "Stop trying to take it all on your own shoulders, Joss. Let other people help."

Joss rubbed her hands up and down her cheeks wearily. "I feel tempted. It would be nice to get away — just for a few days."

She meant it, she realized suddenly. No more listening for children's voices. No more glances over her shoulder into the dark shadows of her bedroom. No more stomach-turning fear each time Tom awoke screaming from a nightmare.

"Good. Then that's settled." Pushing back her chair, Dot stood up. "Go home and pack up some things, put Tom in your own car this time, and bring him to us. This afternoon I shall get the rooms ready. We have a couple of lovely spare rooms in the attic. A bit of a climb, I'm afraid —" She paused, eyeing Joss's figure. "If it's too much, then Edgar and I will move up there and you can have our room. The trouble with this house is it's tall and thin. Everything on top of each other." She beamed happily. "Now, let me make up a salad and we can all get on."

The salad was delicious with homemade dressing, whitebait fresh from the beach, and homemade bread, followed by strawberries and cream. At the end of the meal Joss felt calmer, and it was with something like optimism that she walked back to the car, with borrowed money in her pocket for petrol, amid promises to return with Tom the next morning.

Tom and Luke were in the kitchen when she arrived home. Tom was filthy — still covered, obviously, with his lunch, together with a great deal of black motor oil. Luke's mood was as black as his son's hands and face.

"Were you out of your mind, taking Lyn's car like that? Couldn't you have left a note? Anything?

258

That woman has given me complete hell, thanks to you, and it wouldn't surprise me at all if she didn't come back. Then where will we be?"

"Don't be silly, Luke." Extricating herself from Tom's ecstatic welcome at seeing his mummy again, Joss was reluctant to abandon her good mood. She went to the sink and squeezed out a sponge. Kneeling, she began to sponge the little boy energetically. "Of course she'll come back. I'm sorry I upset her, I really am. She was only miffed with me because she had an arrangement this afternoon. But there was no need for her to behave like that. I know Lyn. She'll be terribly sorry once she's cooled down. You'll see." She sat Tom down and gave him one of his books. "Lyn has a self-esteem problem. If she doesn't think people are acknowledging her full worth, she gets really cross. But it doesn't last. I shall grovel all over the place when she comes back. And," she hesitated, "Luke, I've arranged to go away for a few days with Tom. That will give her a break. And you."

"You've arranged to go away for a few days!" Luke echoed. He was standing hands on hips watching her. "You have arranged to go away for a few days! And were you going to tell me about this or is this a spontaneous decision too?"

"Don't be silly." She didn't look up. "I am telling you now. I went to see the Gowers in Aldeburgh and they have suggested that I go and stay with them for a few days to give everyone here a rest. Dot says she will look after Tom. She loves children."

"I see. And who exactly are these people?"

"The Gowers. You remember. It was Edgar Gower who gave me John Cornish's address right at the beginning. He was my parents' rector here."

"And why, may I ask, did you find it so urgent to go and see them this morning that you had to drop everything, leaving the radio on, half the lights, no message, doors unlocked! Can you imagine what we thought when we got home and found the house abandoned?"

Joss bit her lip. "Oh, Luke. I am sorry. I was going to leave a note, but then —" She stopped abruptly. She couldn't explain to Luke her wildly swinging emotions, her longing, and then the fear and terror she had felt; she couldn't tell him about the panic as she sat in the little car groping for the ignition. How could she? "I forgot. I'm sorry," she finished lamely. "I really am sorry. I didn't mean to frighten everyone. Blame it on my sleepless night. I don't think my brain was functioning very well this morning."

Throwing the sticky sponge on the table, she went to him and put her arms around his neck. "Please, don't be cross. I was hoping you might drive Tom and me up there tomorrow. Then you can meet the Gowers and bring the car back for when you need it. I'll make it up to Lyn, don't worry. She needs this job as much as we need her, so I don't think she's going to quit just like that."

"Don't you be so sure." Disengaging himself from her arms, Luke turned away. "And don't forget if, God forbid, your mother does get worse, Joe won't be able to look after her on his own.

260

He's going to need help."

"Oh, Luke." Joss slumped miserably on a chair, confused and guilty that for a moment she had been going to correct him. Adoptive mother. Not mother. Never real mother.

He stood looking down at her for a moment, then his face softened. "Well, let's hope that doesn't happen for ages yet. I'm sure it won't. Not before the baby comes, anyway. And you're right. Lyn will come around. So, we'd better get ourselves organized. Maybe I can take a couple of hours off tomorrow to take you up there, if it's what you want. Simon certainly said you should get away for a bit, so perhaps this is a good idea after all."

Katherine! Sweet Jesus, Katherine, don't leave me.

Neither of them heard the voice from the echoes. In the silence of the kitchen, only Tom looked up. "Tin man sad," he said conversationally. He picked up his coloring book and then threw it down on the floor.

Luke had taken the chair opposite Joss. "You look very tired, old thing," he said gently. "I'm sorry I snapped. Only Lyn can talk like a cheese grater at times."

Joss smiled. "I know. She's my sister."

Adoptive sister.

Wearily, she got to her feet and went to put the kettle onto the hot plate. When she turned around Luke had scooped the little boy off the floor. "Come on, Tom Tom, let's get Mummy settled in the study, and then we'll go and work in the garden for a bit so she can sit and have her cup of tea in peace."

Joss smiled. Slowly she followed them through into the great hall. Halfway across it she stopped. The room was very cold after the sultry heat everywhere else. The stormy bronzed sunlight barely seemed to filter across the gray flagstones. She must put some new flowers on the table, bring in a few more lamps to brighten the room up.

Katherine. Sweet Katherine. I need you.

Uncomfortably, she looked around. Something was wrong in the room. There was a resonance in the air, a movement, as though someone or something had spoken. She shook her head, aware that the small hairs on the back of her neck were beginning to move.

"Luke!"

Her voice sounded raw and out of place in the room. In the distance, from behind the study door, she could hear Tom's giggle and then his father's deep laugh. They were tidying the room, playing, making a game of it, waiting for her. So why could she not move?

"Luke!" It was more urgent this time. Louder. But still they did not hear her.

Katherine, I can't live without you. Don't leave me . . .

There were words in her head, hurtling around her brain, but she could not hear them properly.

262

Confused, she turned around, her hands to her face.
"Luke!"

Katherine.

"Luke, help me."
She groped for the chair by the empty fireplace and sat down, her head spinning, her breath painful, concentrating on a patch of brilliant sunlight which had appeared on the floor near her. A prism of green and blue and indigo floated over the cool flags and then was gone. She looked up at the window. The sky was leaden again, heavy with purple cloud, and the garden appeared to be growing dark.

She took a deep breath. It was easier this time. And another. He — it — had gone.

"Joss? Are you OK? What are you doing there?" Luke appeared in the doorway.

She smiled at him. "Just a bit tired suddenly. I was watching the sunlight on the floor." She levered herself out of the chair. "I'm coming."

"It's all ready for you. Come and sit down." He was studying her exhausted face. The strain was more than just physical. He could see the fear in her eyes.

"Joss —"

"A cup of tea, Luke. It solves everything. Then tomorrow I'll go away for a bit, just to rest. That's all. I'll come back. Soon."

She was not talking to him, and they both knew it. Luke glanced around the room. As he put his arm around his wife's shoulders and led her into the study, he swore under his breath.

CHAPTER 19

A wave of pain took her and carried her in the warm seawater, brushing against the soft green weed. She flailed with her arms and splashed desperately, trying to reach the land, but the swell, inexorable, powerful, had her in its grip and pulled her onward toward the horizon. Someone was standing there on the shore, waving at her. She could see his distress as he reached out toward her. It wasn't Luke. It was a tall man, fair, broadshouldered, and she could feel his pain mingling with her own. Again she tried to call out to him, but the warm seawater washed into her mouth and she felt her cry smothered before it had left her lips. He was growing smaller now, more distant, standing up to his thighs in the waves, gesticulating desperately in her direction, but a new momentum of pain had taken her and she turned her back on him, curling up in the water to become one with her agony.

Surfacing, blinking the salt drops from her eyes, she looked back at last. She could hardly see the beach now; his figure was all but invisible against the glare of sunlight, but she could feel his love, like a tangible web which enfolded her and drew her slowly back. The pain was there again, hovering on the edge of consciousness, deep inside her, part of her, drawing her bones and muscles apart, with pitiless, torturing fingers. As she curled her body into another crest of anguish, the figure disappeared and the line of the beach vanished below the horizon.

Thunder rumbled in the distance and a flash of lightning illuminated the sky. She opened her eyes and saw that darkness had come to the sky save where the storm flickered and rumbled on the horizon. A zigzag of light tore the sky apart suddenly and the thunder reverberated closer, vibrating through the water. She trod the waves, trying to get her bearings, and it was then she saw the flowers. Roses, their white petals floating and slowly disintegrating on the waves all around her. She reached toward them, feeling their flesh as cold and slimy and dead, and at last she opened her mouth to scream.

"Joss! Joss, wake up!"

Luke sat up and bent over her, shaking her shoulder gently. "Joss, you're having another bad dream."

With a groan, Joss turned toward him, wrenching her eyes open. Lightning flickered at the bedroom window and she could hear the rumble of thunder in the room. So it had not been a dream at all. She stared into the darkness, confused, her head aching with exhaustion, clinging to the last remnants of sleep as once again the pain began to build.

"Luke." With a groan she curled around her

stomach. "Oh, God, I think it's the baby. Contractions! And it's not due for another two weeks! Can you phone Simon?" She was fully awake now, clenching every muscle against the building pain. Relax. Go with it. Breathe. "Oh, God! They're coming quickly. I think you'd better call an ambulance." She gritted her teeth as Luke shot out of the bed and, turning on the light, made for the door. Relax. Let it come. Ride with it. Breathe.

Oh, Christ, she had to get out of the house!

Waiting for the peak of the pain to pass, she sat up. A flash of lightning lit the window for a blinding moment and in the brightness which filled the room she saw the figure clearly, standing in the corner. It was the man from the beach — tall, fair-haired, broad-shouldered.

"No!" Joss pushed herself up off the bed and backed away, blinded in the sudden total darkness, putting the bed between her and the corner as another flash of lightning followed the first. He had gone. There was no one there. She clutched the bedpost as another wave of pain began to build. Oh, God, this is what bedposts were for! In the old days. The days she was writing about in the book. She braced herself against it desperately. Luke! Where was Luke? She had to get out of the house. Away from him — from it — away to a nice bright, noisy, safe hospital where she would be surrounded by people and technology and there would be no shadows at all.

"Luke!" She raised her voice at last. "Luke, where are you?" She had to pack, to try and

266

get dressed. There was no time for an ambulance. Luke would have to drive her to the hospital — ring them to say she was coming. Oh, God, it was coming again, the pain, inexorable, building like a great monster inside her, pulling her body this way and that as she clutched the bedpost, pressing her face against the old black wood.

Another flash of lightning tore through the room and she opened her eyes, fixing her gaze on the corner. It was empty. There was no one there. Only the shadow of the cupboard across the floor. Outside, through the open window, she could hear the sudden downpour of rain, a hiss on the canopy of leaves, a drumming on the grass of the lawn. The sweet smell of wet earth flooded up into the room and at last Tom began to cry.

"Tom Tom! I'm coming!" She staggered toward the door. "Luke! Luke, where are you?"

The corridor was dark, and the door to Tom's bedroom was almost shut. She pushed it open and stared into the room. Tom was sitting huddled in the corner of his crib, his hands to his eyes. As she pushed the door farther open he began to scream, long, high-pitched, mindless screams of pure terror.

"Sweetheart, don't be afraid. It's only a silly old storm." As she hurried across the floor toward him the pain began again. Gritting her teeth, she grabbed the little boy from his crib and held him against her, conscious of the wet diaper and damp pajamas pressed against her breast.

His little arms were around her neck and he was sobbing convulsively as she stood breathing deeply, trying to control the pain, feeling his weight dragging her down.

"Tom Tom, I'm going to have to put you down for a minute, darling —" She could hardly speak. Desperately, she tried to disengage herself, but the more she tried to loosen his grip, the more tightly he clung, terrified by her frantic efforts to dislodge him.

"Joss? Where are you?" Luke appeared in the doorway suddenly. "Oh, Joss, darling. Here, let me take him."

She was kneeling by the cot, her arms round the child, panting as the wave of pain receded once again. "Oh, Christ, how can this happen? Why does it have to be now, when Lyn's away?"

He tried to loosen Tom's grip, but the little boy was screaming hysterically, beyond all reason, as another sizzling flash seemed to cut through the room.

"That's struck something awfully close." Luke disengaged the child's arms by force and dragged him from Joss's neck. "Come on, sweetheart. Can you walk? I think we should go downstairs. You can lie on the sofa in the study."

As he swung Tom up into his arms the night-light on the table in the corner went out.

"No! Oh please, no!" Joss climbed to her feet, hauling herself up on the bars of the crib. "Have they all gone out? Luke? Are you there? I can't see you!"

Panic was rising in her voice.

"It's all right, Joss. Don't move. Stay where you are and I'll get a flashlight. There's one by our bed. Don't worry, I've got Tom Tom. He's all right."

The child's screams receded slightly as Luke groped his way out of the room and along the corridor, leaving Joss alone.

"Luke!" Her own cry echoed in the silence. "Luke, don't leave me! Is the ambulance coming? Luke, please." Darkness pressed against her eyeballs like a physical blindfold. She could feel the heavy velvet blackness of it all around her. Holding her hands out in front of her, she groped toward the crib, sobbing. She could hear nothing but the blanketing silence around her, see nothing. Then she heard Tom crying. His little footsteps in the hall. "Mummy. Find Mummy." He was sobbing so hard his breath was coming in little hiccups.

"Tom Tom." She called out to him, facing the door in the darkness. A brilliant flash of lightning showed the door opening and the small face peering around it. "Mummy!" He ran to her and threw his arms around her legs.

"Where's Daddy, Tom Tom?" The dull ache in her back was growing stronger again.

"Daddy find matches." The small face was buried in her nightshirt.

"Oh, God." The pain was swelling around her. She took a staggered step around Tom toward the cot, and gripped the rail, gritting her teeth.

From the doorway a pale flickering light appeared, throwing immense shadows as Luke appeared down the passage, a candle in his hand.

"Luke, thank God. Is the ambulance coming?" Her knuckles whitened on the crib rail as another contraction began to build. Feeling her pain with her, Tom began to scream again. In an instant Luke was beside her, an arm around her shoulders, holding her as the waves of pain built.

"How long?" She spoke through clenched teeth. "How long till it gets here?"

"I can't get through, Joss." He caught both her hands in his. "The phone is dead. It must be the storm. I'm going to drive over to Simon's —"

"No!" Her cry of alarm ended as a sob. "Don't leave me."

"Then I'd better drive you to hospital myself. Let's grab your dressing gown and we'll go straight there. We can do it in forty minutes. It's all right, love. We'll make it." He squeezed her hand harder. "Come on. There'll be someone there who can take care of Tom Tom as well."

Even as he said it he knew that it was too long.

"No!" This time it was a cry of real anguish. "Luke, I don't think there's time. They're coming too quickly." Perspiration beaded her upper lip and ran down her neck. It streamed between her breasts as the pain spread across her back like a tightening vice. "Luke, I don't know what to do."

"Of course you do. You've done it before."

She shook her head. "Luke, you're going to have to deliver him. Oh, God!" With a groan she fell to her knees, her arms clutched across her stomach in an attempt to ward off the new pain.

"Tom? Tom Tom, come to Daddy." Desperately, Luke tried to disengage the little boy from his mother as he clung more and more tightly to her. "Come on, old chap. Let's get Mummy back to her bed. She's not feeling well. She's got a tummy ache and we're going to have to look after her for a bit. Are you going to help me?" He was resorting to force now, unclasping the child's fingers from Joss's nightshirt, pulling him away. "Can you walk, Joss? Can you get back to our room?" He was shouting to make himself heard above the screams of the child. "Tom. Please. Let go."

"Let him be, Luke." Joss was panting. "You're frightening him more. Tom Tom," she said as she put her arm around the little boy as the contraction passed and hugged him against her. "You've got to be very brave and very grown up. Mummy's all right. She's going to be fine." Was he too little to tell him what was happening? They had hardly mentioned to him yet the possibility of a new brother or sister. The baby wasn't due for two or three weeks. Dear God, and there was no one to help. She bit back tears of panic and frustration, gritting her teeth against a new wave of pain as she felt the little boy's grip relaxing a little. "Stay with him here, Luke, while I get back to bed. See if you can calm him down and get him to sleep." She pulled herself upright on the bars of the crib and turned toward the door.

"Mummy!" Tom's little hands reached out after her.

"Take him, Luke." She couldn't hide the pain much longer.

Luke grabbed the child and lifted him into his crib. Tom's screams doubled in intensity.

"Oh, sweetheart, don't!" Joss held out her hand toward him, then as the pain seized her she stepped back and doubled over with a groan. Relax. Go with the pain. She gasped as she felt her bones beginning to wrench themselves apart.

"Go, Joss. Go to bed!" Luke was trying to force Tom to lie down. "Go on. He'll calm down once you've gone."

The pain was receding, her body resting momentarily, gathering itself for the next battle. She turned and, closing her ears to the screams, she headed back toward the bedroom.

The bed. She must put something on the bed to protect that deep old mattress — a mattress which must have been the place of dozens of births in its time. Desperately, she tried to keep her mind on the practicalities. What was it they say in films about home births? Hot water and towels. Lots of hot water and towels. Hot water, she was sure someone had said, was just to keep the husband occupied. Towels were in the linen cupboard, a huge old oak press on the landing outside the bathroom. A million miles away.

"Oh, God!" She couldn't bite back her cry of pain. Surely it was going to happen any moment.

She could see the bed, its posts and draperies illumined suddenly in a lightning flash; it seemed an insubstantial thing, a wavering oasis with its crewelwork embroidery hangings, flowers of fantastic mossy green and dull reds and ochres entwined with tortured stems and tendrils climbing the bedposts in sinuous undulating spirals. The curtains were moving, fading, swelling, one moment diaphanous, as transparent as mist, the next

272

growing heavy and thick, the ribs of woollen stitching as thick and corded as a man's wrist. Joss let out a sob. It was too far away. She couldn't move. In the intense darkness which followed every flash the great black bulk of the bed had moved away. It was out of reach, beyond some invisible barrier she couldn't penetrate. Luke. Where was Luke? Dear God, help me, please.

Then he was there — a hand on her arm, a pressure at her shoulder, comforting, guiding, pushing her gently across the room. Another flash of lightning; she could see nothing now but the imprint of the window mullions, thick scarlet brands on her retina.

Groping, she reached for the bed, dragging off the heavy counterpane with its thick stitching, and throwing it to the floor.

"Luke — find something to put under me."

She could see a flickering light appearing in the passage now. Luke was there, the candlestick in his hand. "It's all right, love. I've thought of that. I've got something." His voice came from the doorway. The spare waterproof sheet from Tom's chest of drawers, then some towels, then he was helping her up into the cool soft bed. "Hang on, sweetheart." His hand on her forehead was hot, nervous, unlike the other hand, the cool hand which had guided her to the bed. Her eyes flew open. Luke had put the candle down beside the bed. He had only just come into the room . . .

She turned on her side with a groan as a new wave of pain hit her, curling herself around it, conscious with some distant part of her mind that she could smell roses in the air.

"Luke!"

"I'm here, darling. Pant. Remember, they told you to pant." He was pulling a sheet over her.

"You're going to have to deliver it."

"I'd already worked that out for myself." She could hear the wry tone in his voice.

"Tom!"

"Tom's asleep. He was completely worn out. Once you'd gone he was settled in seconds, the poor little mite." He reached for her hand and clasped it tightly. "So, tell me what to do."

"Boil some water to sterilize some thread and scissors. Then find the baby clothes. They're stored in the bottom of Tom's chest. The blankets are there too. Don't wake him." She groaned, clutching his hand. "You were there when Tom was born. You saw what went on. I was up the other end, remember?" She managed a laugh, which ended as a sob.

"I remember." Luke scowled. "There was a doctor and two midwives and I closed my eyes at the crucial moment."

"Go. Luke. Get the water going." She was drifting away from him again, into a sea of pain.

She had no idea how long he was gone. It seemed like a month of pain, a few seconds' respite — then he was there again with the saucepan and more towels, a pile of shawls and tiny white garments. She turned her head toward the window. It was growing faintly less dark. There hadn't been a rumble of thunder for awhile now and the flashes of lightning were growing less intense, just flickering faintly on the horizon out to sea.

The smell of the roses was stronger now as Luke moved around the bed to rub her back. She lay still, staring up into the darkness of the shadowy tester, her body relaxed, painfree for a few blessed seconds.

And then it began to build again. She didn't remember screaming in the hospital, but then they had given her something for the pain. The pain, the fear, the awful voice in her head.

Katherine!

He was there in the shadows, in his usual place near the window, the tall man with the sad eyes. She hadn't seen him before. Not so clearly. Not for sure. She reached out her hand to him and smiled. "I'll be all right." She mouthed the words, but no sound came out. Not until she screamed again.

"Joss!" Luke's voice was suddenly excited, full of awe. "I can see its head."

It was a boy. Holding him, dried and warmly wrapped, in her arms, Joss looked down at the small head and nestled him against her chin. She looked up at Luke and smiled. "Congratulations, doc."

He grinned. "He looks OK, doesn't he?"

"He's fine." The baby was making small contented snuffling noises, his face very red against the white of the blankets. Outside it was full daylight now, the garden cool and cleansed by the rain, lying silent beneath a pall of white mist. Exhausted, Joss lay back and closed her eyes.

The silence was total. Luke had checked that Tom was all right and found the little boy sleeping peacefully, his thumb in his mouth. With the lights and phone still disconnected, he had tiptoed off through the shadows of the early morning house to put the kettle on again — this time for tea.

The slight pressure on the blanket was so gentle that she hardly noticed it. Smiling as she drifted off to sleep, she eased her aching body into a more comfortable angle around the crooked elbow which held her new son and pushed her head deeper into the pillow.

She was jerked awake by the baby's sudden squeal.

"What is it? Little one?" Sitting up she peered down at the tiny face, screwed up now into screams of unhappiness. "Oh, sweetheart, quiet." She stared around the room. The cold had come back. The terrible, all-encompassing cold which was the cold of the tomb. "Luke?" Her voice was lost in the ceiling beams, panic-stricken. "Luke?"

He was there. Somewhere.

Desperately she held the baby to her. "Luke!"

A boy. Oh sweet Jesus, why couldn't it have been a girl? She realized suddenly that she was crying. Deep, body-shaking sobs of exhaustion and fear.

She was still crying when Luke came back with the tray of tea things. "Joss, what is it, love? Is something wrong?"

"He's a boy." She was holding the baby tightly against her.

"Of course he's a boy." Luke sat on the bed. "Come on, sweetheart. There's nothing wrong. Jimbo will be here in an hour. I'll send him straight off for Simon and he can come and give you both a checkup. Come on, love, there's nothing to cry about." He leaned forward and touched the baby's tiny hand. "So, what are we going to call him?"

Joss looked up at him. Her cheeks were still damp with tears, her eyes reddened, her face pale with exhaustion. "I'd like to call him Philip."

Luke frowned. "After your father? Won't that upset Joe?"

She nodded miserably.

"Then let's think of another name to go first. A name that has no complications — then he can have Philip and Joe as his second and third names." He smiled.

"Ever the diplomat." She regarded him wanly. "So. Think of a name."

"We don't have to decide at once." He looked down at the sleeping infant. "Why don't you rest. Later, when you're feeling stronger, we'll do some brainstorming, OK?"

He had found the little crib basket, and lined it with sheets. Taking the baby gently from her, he laid him in the basket and tucked the blankets around him. "There. Rest now, Joss. Everything's all right. When the phones are back on I will ring Lyn, and Alice and Joe. They'll all be so excited." He stooped and kissed her forehead. Then he tiptoed out of the room.

In the shadows the anger and fear had begun to build again once more.

CHAPTER 20

"Well, you both seem extremely well, considering." Simon put away his stethoscope and tucked the baby's little shirt back down under the blankets. He had examined Joss and the baby and inspected the afterbirth. "I suppose I should have expected some kind of rebellious move like this!" He grinned. "Didn't like the idea of a high-tech birth, you said, if I remember?"

Joss laughed. She was sitting on the edge of the bed, fully dressed, drinking a cup of tea.

Simon reached for his own cup.

"I don't think we need send you to hospital. As far as I can see everything is fine. As I said before if I remember, take it easy, don't do too much, and I will ask the midwife to call later this morning." He glanced at the lamp by the bed. "Have you got your electricity back yet up here?"

Joss shook her head. "No electricity and no phone. I'm pursuing the primitive birth thing to its ultimate conclusion."

"I see." Simon stood up. "You modern women never cease to amaze me. Well, I must go on my rounds. Don't hesitate to send for me if there are any problems, no matter how small."

After he had gone, Joss lay back, exhausted, on the pillows. Outside, the mist had lifted to leave a beautiful hot day. A sky the color of cornflowers arched above the garden, reflecting in the lake at the end of the lawn. The house was very quiet. Luke had driven over to Janet Goodyear with Tom, hoping she would look after him for a few hours and hoping even more that the Goodyears' phone was working. If ever they had needed Lyn it was now. Stretching, Joss stared up at the tester, then slowly she moved her head on the pillow to look toward the front window. The room was full of sunshine. There was nothing there to frighten her. Luke had thrown open the window and she could hear the birds and smell the wet freshness of the earth and the grass, mixed with honeysuckle.

Edgar! She sat bolt upright. Edgar was expecting her. Damn the phone. Sliding off the high bed with a surge of sudden energy, she went to the baby's basket, which was standing on the chaise longue near the back window, and peered in. He was asleep, the small lids, blue-veined, a fringe of dark lashes on the soft cheeks. He had thick dark hair, like her and Luke, and it stood up on the top of his head with every appearance of having the same wild individuality as his father's. She smiled. Tom had taken one quick look at his new brother and seemingly lost interest. As far as she could see, he was none the worse for the traumas of the night. In fact, he seemed remarkably cheerful — more so at the thought of visiting Janet and the basket of kittens at present occupying the prime spot in front of her stove.

Slowly and a little painfully, Joss made her way downstairs and through the great hall toward the kitchen. Luke had left the mail unopened on the kitchen table. Pulling the kettle onto the hot plate, Joss opened her first letter while she was waiting for it to boil. It was from David. "A few more pieces of the jigsaw," he had written in his neat small script. "I've found a wonderful old book which mentions Belheddon several times." Folded into the envelope was a thick wad of photocopied pages. Joss looked up as the kettle began to steam. Putting the letter down, she made herself a cup of tea and then, feeling shaky, she sat down, picking it up again. David went on: "It was published in 1921 and tells some half dozen stories of mystery and mayhem all set in East Anglia. I remember your telling me about John Bennet who disappeared sometime at the beginning of the century. Well, the author of this book has the story. It's weird. Are you sitting comfortably? Then read on . . . David."

Joss put down the letter and extricated the folded pages which were with it. David had photocopied about six, and spreading them out in front of her, Joss began to read.

One of the many legends attached to beautiful Belheddon Hall, an ancient manor house set in lovely rolling parkland on the edge of the sea, concerns the family who lived there within very recent times. Mary Percival inherited the house on the death of her mother in 1884 when she was just twenty years old. A determined and resourceful young woman by all accounts, she resolved to run the huge estate single-handed, rejecting all offers for her hand, offers of which, as may be imagined, there were many.

As far as we can gather, Mary was an attractive and popular member of the community and when at last she gave her heart it was to the handsome son of a Suffolk clergyman who was practicing as a lawyer in Manningtree, a town some miles from Belheddon. John Bennett was a year her senior, and on their marriage abandoned the law in order to help Mary look after the estate. This heavy responsibility he took over completely within a few months as Mary waited for the birth of her first child. Henry John Bennett was born in October 1900 and two years later his sister Lydia Sarah followed.

As far as is known all was contentment within the Bennett household, and the first sign of a problem in the house was noted by the local rector, a Doctor Robert Simms. In his memoirs there are several references to Belheddon Hall, and he was called to perform a Service of Exorcism in the house on at least two occasions. Dr. Simms was called to the Hall in the winter of 1902 after servants reported sightings of an apparition, variously described as a knight in armour, a Martian, and astonishingly a "tripod" (this was four years after the appearance of The War of the Worlds by Mr. H. G. Wells) and a monster foretelling the end of the world. In the course of the next year the Bennetts found *it impossible to keep servants at the Hall. One after another they left and their replacements departed in similar short order. Only a few months later, in the spring of 1903, tragedy struck the family. Little Henry John died as the result of a terrible accident.*

This is where the mystery begins. There is no record of how or why he died. It was presumably no ordinary childhood malady which carried him off. The shock and horror throughout the county precludes that.

Joss laid down the sheets of paper and reached for her teacup thoughtfully. She gazed into the depths of the tea, remembering. She was sitting in the attic, the brilliant blue sky outside the windows, with John Bennet's diary lying in her lap. The words sprang out at her as they had then.

So, he claims yet another victim. The boy is dead. Next it will be me.

She was not at all sure she wanted to go on reading this. Folding the pages, she stood up and pushed them into the pocket of her trousers, then, picking up the cup, she made her way slowly and a little painfully through to the great hall. The room was bright, sunshine flooding in through the rain-smudged windows and casting moted beams across the floor. The flowers she had put on the refectory table only yesterday had shed petals all over the black polished oak and there was a dusting of sticky pollen around the silver bowl. With a shiver, she glanced around the room and then she headed for the staircase.

She realized as she looked down into the crib that her heart was thudding with fear. What had she expected? To find something awful had happened to her baby? She gave a smile. He was awake, his little fists waving aimlessly free of his shawl.

"Hello, stranger," she whispered. Stooping, she scooped him up into her arms. Carrying him over to the chair by the window, she settled herself comfortably so she could look out over the garden, and slowly she began to unbutton her blouse.

Ned. The name came to her out of nowhere. Edward. There were no Edwards in her family as far as she could remember. Frowning, she tried to picture the family Bible downstairs in the study. And there were certainly none in the Davies family. "Edward Philip Joseph Grant." She repeated the names to herself out loud. "Not a bad handle for a very small chap." She dropped a kiss on the fuzz of dark hair.

When he was once more asleep, she went over to sit on the window seat and only then did she pull the photocopied pages from her pocket once more.

Stories continued to circulate throughout the next few months and must have distressed the bereaved family enormously. Mr. and Mrs. Bennet became increasingly unsettled and Dr. Simms was repeatedly sent for to the Hall. Then at the end of July in that year John Bennet disappeared and, despite countrywide attempts to find him, was nowhere to be found.

No trace of him was ever discovered at the

time, but some fifteen years later rumors began to circulate around the Essex-Suffolk border as to what had really happened.

An elderly man was reported to have been seen in several different hostelries, claiming to be the missing John Bennet. He looked like a man in his eighties (John Bennet would by now have been about fifty-five, a year older than his wife) with white hair, vacant eyes, and a severe nervous twitch. Word of his presence on the Suffolk border of course reached Mary Sarah, living still at Belheddon Hall with her only surviving child, Lydia, now a young lady of sixteen. The demons of Belheddon had, it seemed, been laid to rest after the disappearance of the master of the house. Mary Sarah, it is reported, denounced the man as an impostor and refused to see him. He on his part refused to go to Belheddon Hall and when asked about his life in the intervening years became vague and troubled.

Nothing more would have been heard of him, perhaps, had he not been discovered unconscious on the steps of the church in the village of Lawford. The rector had him carried into the rectory and there he was nursed back to a semblance of life. The story he told the rector was never divulged officially but a housemaid in the rectory said that on several occasions her duties took her into the rector's study to stoke the fire while the two men were talking. The story the visitor was unraveling filled her with horror.

John Bennet, so the story went, and so he claimed to be, was walking in the garden at

Belheddon one evening as dusk was falling when he was confronted by something which had the appearance of a man encased in the armor of yesteryear. The figure, at least seven feet tall, strode toward him, its hands outstretched toward him.

As Bennet turned to flee, his foot slipped in the mud at the edge of the lake and he fell awkwardly upon his back. To his terror, the apparition stooped over him and proceeded to lift him in the air. Before he knew it he found himself hurled into the water.

When he surfaced and looked around, trying to see his assailant, there was no sign of him. The banks of the lake were empty and there was nothing to be seen in the darkness but the outlines of the nearby trees. Swimming to the far bank, Bennet, if indeed it was he, climbed out, but his sanity, already unhinged by the death of his only son, had completely deserted him. Instead of making his way to the house and safety, he remembered fumbling for the latch on the gate into a back lane, and running, still dripping with ice cold water, into the coming darkness. It was the last thing, or so he claimed, that he remembered, before waking up in the rectory fifteen years later.

What happened to the man who told this story no one knows. He remained in the rectory for several days, then one night he let himself out into the darkness from which he had emerged and was never seen again.

Joss let the pages fall into her lap. From where

she was sitting she could see the lake across the grass, concentric circles forming on its glassy surface among the lilies as fish came up for flies.

A man in medieval armor? The tin man? She closed her eyes against the glare of the sunlight on the water.

She was awakened by Luke's hand on her shoulder.

"Hi. How are you?" He had brought her a cup of tea, which he set down on the small table beside her.

She stared at him blankly for a moment, then she sat up, leaning toward the crib. "Is Ned OK?"

"Ned?" For a moment Luke paused, head to one side. "Yes, I think I like that. Edward Grant. He's fine." Luke stood looking down at the baby fondly.

"And Tom?"

"Tom is happy as a clam. I've left him with Janet for the day. And their phone was working, so I've rung your Edgar Gower and he and his wife are going to drive over tomorrow to see you. I've rung Lyn and she is coming back immediately, and some good news: she said Alice's tests are encouraging. The biopsy showed no malignancy. So, sweetheart, you don't have a single thing to worry about in the entire world! And another piece of good news. My parents are back. I rang them in Oxford just in case and they got home last night! They send all their love and congratulations and they're longing to see their new grandson!"

Joss smiled. On the floor, the photocopied pages

which had slipped from her knee were scattered around her feet. "So, all that and a perfect husband and a cup of tea as well."

"All that!" He sat down on the window seat. "Oh, and Jimbo has brought you a box of chocolates!"

Janet brought Tom back while Luke was collecting Lyn from the station that evening. Stooping over the baby, she examined the sleeping child with the same dispassionate eye she had turned on their cooking range. "Bit small, I suppose, but very pretty," she announced. "Well done, you!" She straightened and turned her back on the baby, the inspection complete. "A bit dramatic, even for Belheddon, wasn't it? Giving birth in a thunderstorm like that!"

"I suppose so." Joss lifted the baby out of his basket. "The midwife has been twice and so has Simon, so I'm being kept a strict eye on!" She glanced up at Janet. "You and Roy were here when Edgar Gower was rector, weren't you?"

Janet nodded. "He'd been here years when we bought the farm."

"What did you make of him?"

Sitting down, she unbuttoned her shirt and put the baby to the breast. Janet looked the other way, but Tom, fascinated, leaned against her knees and poked at the small ear with his finger.

"A man of fire and steel — so different from dear gentle James Wood. Come here, Tom." She hauled the little boy onto her knee. "Luke rang him, you know, from our place. He wanted to come over now, today, straight away. He sounded terribly worried." She eyed Joss for a moment.

287

Joss's face was hidden by her curtain of hair as she looked down at the baby in her arms. "Joss —" She paused. "Listen, I know we've all made a bit of a drama out of the stories about this house. One does. It's" — she hesitated — "it's fun, I suppose. Dramatic, spooky. Everyone loves a good ghost story. But you mustn't take it too seriously. Edgar was a bit —" She stopped, searching for the right word. "Superstitious, I suppose. A mystic. Some people might have said a bit of a nutter. Some members of the PCC used to have terrible doubts, you know. Not quite the thing at all in a conservative parish. The thing was, he and Laura used to wind each other up. Nothing really out of the ordinary happened here, you know. Just a series of terrible tragedies. Laura just couldn't accept that they were accidents. She needed to believe there was more to it than that. But these things do happen. Families have the most rotten runs of luck and then it changes suddenly." On her knee, Tom, his fingers wound into her pearls, had closed his eyes. She hugged him gently. "He's exhausted, poor lamb. A new brother and the promise of his very own kitten when it's old enough to leave its mother. You don't mind, do you?"

Joss looked up at last. "Of course not. We need a cat. That would be lovely."

"And you won't worry anymore?"

"Not if the cat is black." Joss managed a smile.

Janet shook her head. "They're all splodgy. Calico cats. But just as lucky."

She stood up carefully, holding the sleeping child. "What shall I do with him?"

"Can you put him in his crib? Through there, on the left." She sighed as Janet disappeared with Tom. Was that what it was? Imagination. A superstitious man and a hysterical woman in a hot-house environment: isolated, bored, lonely.

She cocked her head suddenly at a noise above her head. Mice playing in the attic, or children?

Dead children.

Generations of little boys, their shouts and laughter still echoing in the roof timbers of the house.

"Lyn!" Joss threw her arms around her sister and hugged her. "I'm so sorry about the car."

Lyn smiled. "All forgotten. You were obviously under stress." She looked around as she dropped her bags on the floor. "So, where is the latest little Grant?"

"Upstairs. They're both asleep. Oh Lyn, I don't know how we would ever manage without you!"

"You can't. It's as simple as that." Lyn looked at her for a moment before turning away and heading toward the door. "So, are you going to show me?"

They stood for several minutes by the crib, staring down at the sleeping baby. Gently Lyn reached in and touched the little hands. Her face softened. "He's gorgeous. You haven't asked me about Mum." She was still concentrating on the baby.

"Luke told me. It's not malignant."

"You might have rung her!" Lyn looked up at last. "You might have told her about the baby!"

"Lyn, I couldn't!" Stung, Joss spoke more

loudly than she intended and the baby stirred. "The phones have been out of order since the storm. Luke must have told you. That was why we were stuck here on our own, for God's sake!"

She stooped as Ned let out a wail of anguish and she scooped him out of the crib.

"OK. I'm sorry. Of course you couldn't. Here, let me hold him." Lyn reached out her arms. "But ring as soon as you can, Joss. It would mean so much to her. He is her grandson, remember." She said it with a note of defiance in her voice.

Joss frowned. Laura's grandson. A son of Belheddon.

"Of course."

Joss woke at the first sound of a whimper from Ned. She lay for a moment in the darkness staring toward the window where the garden was as bright as day in the moonlight. In the silence she heard the sharp yip yip of a little owl and again Ned gave a little cry. Sitting up, trying not to disturb Luke, she pushed her feet over the side of the bed and reached for her cotton bathrobe. The room was cold. Too cold. She glanced around with a shiver. Was he there, lurking in the shadows, Tom's tin man? The man without a heart. The alien intruder. The devil of Belheddon.

The moonlight was flooding the small basket bed as she crept over to it and stared in. Ned's face, turned away from the brightness, was alert. He appeared to see her at once, and she saw a small fist appear from beneath the swaddling, waving in the air. She stood for a moment looking down at him, overwhelmed by such a flood of love and emotion that she was incapable for a moment of doing anything. Then at last she picked him up. Kissing him, she carried him to the seat by the window. Before she sat down, she stood for a moment staring down into the garden. The central casement between the mullions was open a crack. She pushed it slightly, surprised to find that the sweet night air which flooded in was considerably warmer than the air in the bedroom. For a moment the balmy beauty of the night overwhelmed her. She stood staring down and only the distracted crying of the baby in her arms brought her back to the present. Pushing her nightshirt off her shoulders, she put the baby to her breast, still staring down toward the lake. A cloud shadow drifted across the grass. She frowned. The night was very silent. She stood there for several minutes, lulled by the gentle rhythmic sucking of the baby, conscious of the gentle snores of her husband in the bed behind her, then, tired, she lowered herself at last into the chair. It was as she was preparing to move the baby to the other breast that she heard the nightingale. Entranced, she stared up at the window. The pure notes poured on and on, coming, she supposed, from the woods behind the church. The sound filled the room. Standing up again, she walked back to the window and looked out. Two children were playing in the moonlight near the lake. She stiffened. "Georgie. Sammy?"

Sensing the change in her mood at once, Ned stopped sucking and turned his head away, screwing up his little face to cry. Her mouth had gone dry. "Sammy?" She breathed the name again. "Sammy?"

"Joss?" Luke stirred and turned toward her. "Everything all right?"

"Everything is fine." Shushing the child, she rocked him against her gently, realizing suddenly that the nightingale had stopped singing. And the figures in the moonlight had disappeared.

"Come back to bed."

"I'm coming. As soon as he's asleep again."

Tucking Ned back into his little bed at last, Joss straightened wearily and stretched her arms. She could hear the nightingale again now, more distant, echoing in the silence of the garden. "Can you hear it?" she whispered to Luke. "Isn't it beautiful?"

There was no answer.

Turning, she stared at the bed. Luke's face lay in shadow, the heavy drapes of the bed curtains half pulled across by his head as though warding off the moonlight. With a smile, she turned back to the window. On the sill, silver in the moonlight, lay a white rose.

She stared at it for several seconds, feeling the scream mounting in her throat. No. She must be imagining it. It wasn't there. It could not be real! Taking a deep breath, she shut her eyes, her fists clenched, and counted slowly to ten, hearing the clear liquid notes of birdsong louder and louder in her brain. Then at last she opened them again and stared down at the stone sill.

The rose had gone.

CHAPTER 21

Leading the way into the sun-filled study next morning, Joss set her tray of coffee and biscuits down on the desk. The midwife had gone just as the Gowers arrived. They stood just inside the doorway now staring around the room.

"Why, it hasn't changed at all since your mother was here," Dot said in evident delight. "Oh, Joss, dear, this is such a lovely room. And is this the little one? May I see?" Ned was sleeping in his crib beside the open window. She stood looking down at him for several seconds, then she turned and smiled. "Edgar? Come and look. I think this house is blessed. I think all the unhappiness has gone."

Her husband stood looking down into the crib as she had, then his face too relaxed into a smile. He glanced up at Joss. "My dear, the last time I came into this house I performed a service of blessing and exorcism for your mother. I think it worked. Dot is right. The atmosphere has changed completely. I will never forget the anguish and fear and hatred which seemed to pervade the very walls on that occasion. I felt as though I were wrestling with the devil himself. But now . . ." He shook his head wonderingly. "This place is full of joy and light." Turning to the fireplace he stood for a moment with his back to it, then he lowered himself into an armchair. "May I suggest something?"

Joss gestured Dot toward the other chair and then turned to pour out the coffee. "Of course."

"I think it would be nice to baptize the little one as soon as possible. Would you allow me to do it? Unless of course you have already made plans in that direction."

"Well, no, we hadn't." Joss passed him a cup. "I must discuss it with Luke, but I think that would be wonderful. Tom Tom was christened in London."

"Soon." Edgar's brilliant blue eyes were fixed on her face.

Joss frowned. "You are still worried."

"No. But I believe in taking no chances. I know that to many people the baptism is merely a social occasion — a marker to place the child in the community — but it has a far more important purpose than that: to save and protect the child in Christ's name. You do not need to send out invitations."

Joss sat down, suddenly very weary. "You mean you want to do it now."

"It would be best."

"Here. In the house."

"In the church."

"Would James Wood mind?"

"I shall ring him first, of course." Edgar sat back in his chair slightly and sipped his coffee.

"My dear, I'm sorry. I don't mean to railroad you into this. You need time to think and discuss it with your husband, of course you do. I can always come back. Or Wood can do it." He smiled, pushing the shock of white hair back out of his eyes. "There is no need for an indecent hurry. I was filled with such unease about this house, but it was not necessary. I can sense that. I think the problems have gone. Perhaps your poor mother, God rest her soul, brought them on the house with her unhappiness." Putting down his cup, he stood up restlessly and wandered back to the window, glancing down at the sleeping baby as he did so. Then he swung around. "May I wander around the house a little? Forgive me. Call it professional interest."

Joss forced a smile. "Of course."

He nodded. "Stay and talk to Dot. She'll tell you what an insufferable boor I am, and you can moan about my ideas as much as you like!"

In the hall he stood still, gazing up the staircase. For a moment he did not move, then slowly he reached into his pocket for his crucifix.

The staircase was dark. Groping on the wall, he found the light switch and flicked it down. The lights were dim — a bulb had gone halfway up at the corner of the stairs and the flight wound up into the shadows. Taking a deep breath, he put a foot on the bottom step.

Ignoring Lyn's room, he made his way at once into the master bedroom and looked around. The four-poster was the same, the heavy cupboard by the window, the rugs, the chairs. The only differences came from the clothes scattered around, the books piled on the window sills, the flowers in vases on the chest of drawers and the shelf by the chimney breast and the small crib by the back window with its trail of white shawls, the attendant piles of small garments, the garish plastic changing mat, and huge bag of disposable diapers.

Standing in the middle of the room, he listened intently.

Katherine.

Was that a voice in the echoes? He remembered from last time the anguish, the pain that permeated the very plaster of the walls of this room, the conviction that if he tried harder he would be able to hear the voice that seemed to scream its agony beneath this roof.

A pox on you priests. Why could your prayers not save her?

With a sigh he turned around, then, taking a deep breath and squaring his shoulders, he knelt on the rug at the end of the bed and began to pray.

When he returned to the study Dot and Joss had been joined by Lyn and Tom. "I was telling Lyn that we thought we might have the christening early," Joss said slowly as Edgar appeared. She was tight-lipped. "She doesn't feel it would be right."

"Of course it's not right." Lyn was clearly angry. "You can't do it without Mum and Dad. They would be desperately hurt." She turned on Joss. "I don't know what's the matter with you! Doesn't the past mean anything to you at all? All the years they have treated you as their daughter, loved you, cared for you! Now this bloody house comes into the picture and dear old Joe and Alice are so much rubbish you'd rather forget about!"

"Lyn!" Joss stared at her. "That's not true. That's absolute nonsense and you know it! We're not talking about a christening to thwart Mum and Dad's chances of a nice party, we're talking about saving a baby who might have a terrible accident at any moment!"

There was a shocked silence.

"Joss, dear." Dot cleared her throat. "I am sure there is absolutely no danger of little Ned having any kind of an accident. Edgar had no business frightening you like that. And I don't think we should discuss it anymore at the moment. Edgar, a christening is a family occasion and it's important that Joss's parents have a chance to be here. A few days or even weeks are going to make no difference whatsoever." She sounded really cross.

Edgar shrugged. "I'm sure you're right, dear." His eyes contradicted the meekness of his tone. They were plainly angry. "Very well, may I suggest we leave the discussion now. Should you wish me to baptize little Ned I shall do so, of course. Otherwise, fix it up with James Wood, but I beg you to do it as soon as possible." He cleared his throat. "Dot, I think we should be going. Jocelyn has only just had a baby and she must be very tired." He smiled suddenly. "He is a beautiful child, my dear. Congratulations. Don't let my wittering on frighten you. Enjoy the baby and enjoy the house. It needs happiness — the best exorcism of all."

As soon as the Gowers' car had disappeared up the drive, Joss turned on Lyn. "What on earth is the matter with you? How dare you think I am trying to cut out Alice and Joe. That's an outrageous thought. What kind of person do you think I am?"

Lyn was unrepentant. "I am beginning to wonder. I think all your newfound grandeur has gone to your head."

"Lyn!"

"Take a look at yourself, Joss." Lyn scooped Tom up into her arms. "Now, I'm going to get lunch. May I suggest you rest or something as the lady of the house should!"

Joss stared after her as the door closed. Then, miserably, she turned toward the pram. Picking Ned up, she cuddled him for awhile before carrying him to the chair and sitting down. Closing her eyes, she tried to relax. It was natural for Lyn to be jealous. She had every reason. Joss had a husband, children, a beautiful house — it must seem like untold riches to Lyn, who had failed to find a job at all for the last year, and had been unemployed until Joss and Luke had offered her this one. Joss dropped a kiss on Ned's little head.

In her arms the baby slept. Closing her own eyes, Joss, worn out, let her head rest against the chair back and drifted into sleep.

She was awoken by screams as Ned suddenly slipped from her arms.

"Ned! Oh, God!" She grabbed at him in time to stop him falling to the floor and clutched him against her. She was shaking. "Oh my little love, are you all right?" Ned was crying hard, small high-pitched screams of distress which tore at her heart.

"Ned! Ned, little one, hush." She cradled him to her, cursing herself for falling asleep.

"Joss?" It was later. Luke put his head around the door and then came in.

Joss was sitting by the window, the baby at her breast, listening to the tape of Chopin nocturnes which had been her favorite listening for the last week. "How is he?"

"OK." She bit her lip.

"Lunch is nearly ready. I hear the Gowers were here."

She nodded. "I suppose Lyn has told you."

"She's very upset. You know, Joss, you're not handling her very tactfully." He sat down opposite her, watching fondly the cameo before him of mother and child. "I've warned you. We have to be careful. We don't want to lose her. Don't forget, you have a job to do. That publisher was serious about his contract. You're not just playing at the hobby of writing now. It's for real. With real money. You can't risk losing Lyn."

Joss nodded. "I know. And I didn't mean to

upset her. Or you. It was Edgar who thought it so important that Ned be baptized."

"And he will be. Just as soon as we've got a date organized when Alice and Joe can get here. And my parents too, Joss. Don't forget them. They haven't even seen the house yet."

"She's going to neglect Tom, you know." Lyn turned from the cooker where she was stirring a saucepan of soup as Luke came in.

"Nonsense." Luke sat down at the table with a four-pack of Fosters he had taken from the fridge. "Here, like one?"

"No thanks. She is." She turned back to her soup. "Poor little Tom Tom really was the Davies' grandson. Ned — you're not really going to call him that, are you? — is the Belheddon child." Her voice stressed the last two words with heavy sarcasm. "Believe me, Luke, I know her."

"No, Lyn, you're wrong." Luke shook his head adamantly. "Terribly wrong."

"Am I?" She flung down her spoon and turned to face him. "I hope so. But I want you to know I love little Tom as if he were my own. While I'm here he will never be second best."

"He will never be second best with Joss or me either, Lyn." Luke kept his voice steady with difficulty. "Where is Joss now?"

"With the baby, I don't doubt."

"That goes without saying, Lyn." Luke took a deep swig from his can. "The baby is two days old, for God's sake!" Unable to contain his irritation with her any longer, he turned and walked out of the kitchen. In the courtyard he stood still for a minute staring up at the sky, taking deep breaths to calm himself. Silly bitch. Stirring it. The rivalry and antagonism that had always been so close to the surface between the sisters was beginning to get to him. He took several more gulps of lager as a thin brown face, creased with anxiety, appeared around the coach house door. "Luke, that you? Can you come a minute?"

"Sure, Jimbo. On my way." Putting his thoughts about Lyn firmly out of his head, Luke tucked the empty can into the garbage as he passed and disappeared into the oil-smelling interior of his domain.

Lying awake, staring toward the window, Joss could feel every muscle in her body tense. There was no sound from either of the children; the house was silent. Her eyes were gritty with sleep. She moved uncomfortably, trying not to disturb Luke, totally alert suddenly. Something was wrong. Swinging her legs over the side of the bed, she padded across to the crib to look down at little Ned. She had been feeding him every couple of hours during the day, but now he was fast asleep at last, his little eyes tight shut in the shaded light of the lamp.

On bare feet she passed through to Tom's room and gently pushed open the door. Holding her breath, she tiptoed in and stood for a moment looking down at him. He was sleeping peacefully, his cheeks pink, his hair tousled, his covers for once pulled up around him. Smiling, she gently touched his cheek with her finger. Her love was so intense it was like a pain squeezing around her heart. She could not bear it if anything happened to either of them.

She glanced toward the window. There was no wind tonight. No draft touched the curtains. There were no shadows in the dark.

Silently she pulled the door half closed behind her and went back to her bedroom. Luke had moved in his sleep, sprawled across the bed, his arm outflung on the pillow. Beside his hand she could see something lying in the dip where her head had been. Her stomach lurched with fear. For a moment she was too scared to move. Her throat clamped shut and she felt the cold trickle of sweat between her shoulder blades. Then Luke moved. With a mutter he turned over, humping the duvet over him and she saw the mark on the pillowcase flatten and stretch and vanish. It had been no more than a crease in the cool pink cotton.

The christening was fixed for ten days later — a Saturday — which gave the Davieses and the Grants, the godparents and other guests, time to assemble at Belheddon. It was a thundery day, reminiscent of the night of Ned's birth, and the humid air was heavy with the scents of the wet garden. The night before, Janet had helped Joss with the flowers in the church.

"You look tired, love." Deftly Janet slit the stem of a rosebud and inserted it into her vase. "Look, aren't these lovely? I thought we'd put them around the base of the font." She had produced a basket of white roses from her garden, their tightly furled buds still glistening with raindrops, the tips of their petals blushing slightly to a gentle pink.

"Roses. Bring her roses. Cover her with roses."
He could not stop his tears. Slowly, gently, he brought his lips to the cold forehead. He knelt beside her while they brought the flowers. White roses in heaps, their fragrant petals covering her like soft snow.

Joss stared down at the basket. "Oh, Janet." She felt a sudden churning of fear in her stomach.

"Whatever is it?" Janet dropped the basket at her feet and reached out a concerned hand. "Joss. Aren't you feeling well?" Joss had gone as white as the flowers.

Shaking her head, Joss moved away and sat down at the end of the back pew. "No. No, I'm fine." She shook her head. "Just a bit tired. I've been trying to make some headway with my writing and I'm feeding Ned about every two hours." She forced herself to smile, but her eyes were drawn back again and again to the roses. "Janet, do you mind? Can we put them somewhere else? Perhaps over there, by the choir stalls. I know they're lovely. It's just —"

"Just what?" Janet frowned. She came and sat beside Joss, putting her hand firmly over Joss's as they clutched the back of the pew in front. "Come on. Tell. What is it? They're only roses, for goodness sake. The best I could find in the rose garden for my new little godson." With Lyn already Tom's godmother, it had been an easy and unanimous choice for Joss and Luke to pick

Janet as one of Ned's three godparents.

"I know. I'm being silly."

"So. Explain."

Joss shook her head. "Just a silly phobia. Thorns. You know. 'Round the font. Everyone will catch their dresses. And Edgar will rip his surplice." She laughed unsteadily. "Please, Janet. Don't be hurt. They're beautiful. Exquisite. Just put it down to postpartum neurosis or something like that."

Janet stared at her for a moment, then she shrugged. She stood up. "OK. Roses on the windowsill up there. And what around the font? How about these?" She gestured at a bucket full of lupins and delphiniums and marguerites.

Joss took a deep breath. "Lovely. Perfect. Just what the doctor ordered. Here, let me help."

It was late by the time they had finished, locked the church, hidden the key, and gone back inside the house for a quick drink before Janet made her way home. Lyn had long since put Tom to bed and pushed supper onto the back of the stove. "Luke and I have eaten," she said from the sink as Joss walked in. "If you want yours it's there, keeping warm."

Joss sighed. "Thanks. Any sign of David?" Against strenuous disapproval from Luke, she had asked David to be one of Ned's godfathers. The other was to be Luke's brother, Matthew.

Lyn shook her head. "He rang to say he'd be late leaving London and not to wait supper. He probably won't be here till ten or eleven."

"And Mum and Dad?"

"They should be here any minute. They rang

too. They stopped for tea with the Sharps and they were coming on after that. Their rooms are all ready." Lyn had been dusting and sweeping and polishing in the attic, making beds and arranging flowers for the last two days. "No one else is coming tonight. Luke's family are going to be here for lunch tomorrow, which is for family and godparents only, then everyone else will arrive for the christening itself and stay on to tea afterward." She was obviously still ticking items off mentally as she stared around the kitchen.

"You've been a brick, Lyn. You've done everything." Joss opened the cupboard and rummaged for the bottle of Scotch. She found two glasses and poured herself and Janet small drinks.

Lyn stared at her. "You're not going to drink that?"

"Why not?" Sitting down at the table, Joss picked up the glass.

"Because of your milk of course."

There was a moment's silence, then Joss took a sip of the whiskey. "I'm sure Ned wouldn't begrudge me this," she said firmly. "And he may as well start as I'm sure he will go on. If he gets hiccups in church it's too bad."

"Right. Well, I can see it's none of my business." Lyn, tight-lipped, made for the door. "I'll see you later."

"Oh dear." Janet raised her glass at Joss and smiled. "Are you behaving badly, my dear?"

Joss nodded. She took another sip from the glass. "It's not as though she's had any kids of her own!" she burst out suddenly. "She acts as though she knows the lot."

"She is their nanny, isn't she?" Janet leaned back in her chair, her eyes on Joss's face. "She probably feels it's part of her brief. Besides, she's had training for it, hasn't she?"

"She's had training for absolutely nothing except cooking." Joss stood up restlessly and walked around the table to the stove. She pulled the saucepan forward and peered into it. "She's done a bit of temping, and she's the kind of person who can clean and organize a house naturally."

"That doesn't make her less intelligent or less sensitive, Joss," Janet put in gently.

"Oh, I know." Joss came back to the table and sat down. "Oh Janet, that sounded so awful of me. It's not as though I'm not grateful. We couldn't survive without Lyn. It's just that she makes me feel" — she spread her hands helplessly — "so inadequate. In my own house. I take ages to sort something out and polish it. She comes in and does it in thirty seconds. But she does it in such a cold, efficient way. She doesn't feel anything —" She shrugged. "It's hard to explain."

Janet smiled. "No it's not. You are just too very different personalities. And that has nothing to do with being adoptive sisters. My sisters and I can't get on either and one of them is my twin. Accept that you're different, Joss. Martha and Mary, if you like. You should complement each other. But you are both, I think, feeling threatened by the other at the moment and that's silly. Forgive a comparative outsider commenting, but perhaps I can see it. You're too close. Lyn is feeling very insecure. After all, you hold all the trump cards. It's your house, your children, your family, and you are the one who has a burgeoning career as a writer. All that." She reached for the bottle and poured herself another Scotch. "I won't give you one, in deference to Ned's hiccups. As his godmother, I'm probably the one he'll be sick over in church." She laughed loudly, one of her great guffaws. "Come on, love. Too much stress and not enough fun makes everyone miserable. Probably you and Lyn should leave Luke in charge one day and take yourselves out on a day off. That would sort it."

Joss smiled wearily. "Would it? I wonder." She sighed. "Yes, you're probably right."

When Alice and Joe arrived, Joss flung herself into her mother's arms. "I was so worried! All those tests! Half the time Lyn didn't tell me until it was too late, what was happening."

Alice held her at arm's length and studied her face. "I don't need to see you every day to know you care, you silly child." She pulled Joss back into her arms and gave her a hug. "You're a clever, clever girl. Another beautiful grandson is the best medicine I could possibly have! And a christening party is the best celebration. I'm going to enjoy myself here, Joss. And I want to see you doing the same."

Lunch was a great success. Lyn had laid the table in the dining room, loading the sideboard with cold meats and salads, whole grain bread, cheeses and fruit and white wine from the bottles remaining in the Belheddon cellar. Tea was already prepared and ready in the great hall, the refectory table with its huge bowl of gladioli groaning under plates and cups and a vast array of plastic-wrap-covered sandwiches and cakes and biscuits. The pièce de résistance, the christening cake, made and iced by Lyn, was standing by itself on a table near the window and beside it stood a dozen bottles of champagne, a contribution from Geoffrey and Elizabeth Grant, who had driven over from Oxford.

It was Joss who had taken them on a quick tour of the house before lunch. "My dear, it's more beautiful than I ever dreamed!" Geoffrey put his arm around her shoulders and gave her a hug. "You and my son have the luck of the devil."

He did not notice the look she gave him as she led the way through into the great hall. "Nothing here is to be touched until later or Lyn will kill us," she said, staring around at the feast already spread before them.

"That girl must have worked so hard." Elizabeth went over and examined the cake. "What a treasure. Why on earth hasn't some man snapped her up?"

Joss shrugged. "I just hope they don't. At least not for awhile. I can't live without her at the moment." She glanced around the room, frowning. It felt fine. Happy. There was no atmosphere; there were no shadows, no echoes in her head. She was beginning to wonder if she had imagined the whole thing.

Smiling, she turned to Geoffrey. "You can stay a few days, can't you? I'm afraid our facilities are a bit primitive, whatever it may look like

308

on the surface, but we'd like it so much if you can. And Matthew. Luke misses him so much, you know, now he's got the job in Scotland."

Geoffrey nodded. "They were always close, those two. Never mind. Life goes on. It makes occasions like this even more special, my dear. And this is the most special we've had for a long time."

CHAPTER 22

In spite of the distant rumbles of thunder and the darkness outside the stained-glass windows of the church, the christening service was full of charm. Cuddling Ned to her, Joss looked around at the twenty or so guests clustered around the font and felt a tremendous elation, which increased as she passed the baby to Edgar Gower.

She glanced from Edgar to James Wood, who stood beside him. Lucky baby to have two vicars at his christening. A double blessing. A double safety net. She glanced at David and found him watching her with a slightly absent frown on his face. Was he thinking the same thing, she wondered? Was this belt-and-braces christening enough to ward off the horror which had sent John Bennet fleeing forever from his home? She looked up in spite of herself at the window where Janet had placed the huge foaming bowl of white roses and she shuddered.

There was a touch on her shoulder. Luke. He was looking down at her with an expression of such tenderness that she felt a lump in her throat. She reached for his hand and together they heard their son named Edward Philip Joseph before the world.

David managed to maneuver Joss into a corner halfway through tea. Around them guests were devouring cake and drinking champagne or tea with equal enthusiasm. Tom, covered in cake and icing and melted chocolate, worn out with the excitement, had curled up on one of the sofas and was fast asleep, while the star of the show, sleeping equally peacefully, was in his pram in the study where it was quieter.

The great hall rang with shouts and laughter. Wine flowed and the boards groaned beneath their load of food.

Katherine and Richard, hand in hand, led the dancing and their faces glowed in the candlelight.

The king's gift, of heavy silver, filled with white roses, stood in the place of honor on the high table.

With it came his love.

"So. It's going well." David raised his glass. "Well done. A wonderful spread."

"Thanks to Lyn." Joss, clutching a teacup, was longing to sit down; she was wobbly with exhaustion.

"You read the photocopies I sent you?" David reached over to the table and helped himself to a couple of egg sandwiches.

She nodded. "Let's not talk about it now, David." Even the thought of the contents of those few sheets of flimsy paper sent a shiver down her spine. "Edgar thinks this — all this" — she waved her hand behind her as the crescendo of conversation steadily increased — "will help to make the house a happy place again. No more shadows."

David shrugged. "Good. There's more to discover, though, you know. Going right back into the past, there is something or someone at the root of all this and I want to find out what or who it is."

Joss looked up at him, half amused, half irritated. "What if I don't want you to? What if I tell you I want to stop all this."

He looked shocked. "Joss, you can't mean that. You can't not want to know!"

She shook her head and shrugged. "I don't know what to think. I'm confused. If it were somebody else's house, David. Someone else's problem. But I live here." She gazed around the room as though looking for some clue which would tell her what to do. "Supposing the truth is too awful, David? Supposing it is insupportable?" She held his gaze for several seconds, then slowly turned away.

It was very late before everyone went to bed that night, Luke's parents and Matthew in the two attic rooms which had been made hospitable, David in the spare room where he usually stayed. It was an airless muggy night, the occasional flicker on the horizon and the almost inaudible grumbles of thunder betraying the fact that storms were still prowling around.

Exhausted, Joss threw herself on the bed, still

fully dressed. "I don't think I have the strength to have a bath."

Luke sat down beside her. He gave a great contented sigh, stretching his arms above his head. "I really enjoyed today, Joss. It's so nice having Ma and Pa and Mat here. They love the house, did they tell you?" He smiled, reaching over to kiss her. "Come on, sleepyhead. Climb out of your dress. It'll get spoiled if you sleep in it. I'll go and check on Tom and Ned."

Ned had been allocated his own small bedroom, opposite Tom's. A crib, a pine chest of drawers, and now lots of shiny christening presents adorned the room, which Lyn had papered in a pattern of teddy bears and balloons. Luke peered in. The baby was fast asleep, his little hands lying half clenched above his head on the pillow, his face pink. Above him hung a mobile of small red fire engines, a present from his godfather, Mat. "He needs something he can use now," Mat had said cheerfully. "The mug is boring. He won't need it till he's about twenty. I wasn't sure what babies like when they're this big, or" — he had peered into the pram doubtfully — "to put it another way, small." The mobile was perfect. Already Ned had spent a happy half hour seemingly gazing at it before he drifted off to sleep.

Tom was fast asleep too, lying on his tummy, his bedclothes tumbled at the end of the bed. Luke left them.

Even with the windows thrown open it was too hot to breathe. He stood for awhile in the bathroom sluicing cold water over his face and head, then at last he climbed into bed and lay staring into the darkness.

He was woken much later by a piercing scream from Tom.

"Christ! Joss, what's that?" He was out of bed before he was properly awake and before he realized that Joss wasn't there. Scrabbling for the light switch, Luke ran into Tom's room. The little boy was lying on the floor beside his crib amid a tangle of sheets, sobbing his heart out.

"Tom? Tom, my God, what happened old chap?" Scooping him up into his arms, Luke was trying to comfort the little boy as Joss appeared in the doorway. In her white cotton nightdress she looked almost ethereal for a moment as she peered in. "What's wrong?" She looked odd to Luke. Vague. Spaced out.

"Where on earth have you been?" he shouted. "Didn't you hear Tom crying? He fell out of bed!"

Joss frowned. "Tom?" She stared around. "He can't have. The crib side is up." She took a step into the room. "I was feeding Ned." She reached to touch Tom's head with her fingertips, then she stooped and picked up the tangled sheets. "He must have climbed out. I'll remake his bed and you can settle him down again."

Shaking out the small white cotton sheets, she smoothed them over the mattress, tucking them in. "OK? Do you want to put him down now?"

"He won't go, Joss. He's too upset." The little boy was clinging to his father's neck, his face red with screaming, tears pouring down his cheeks and nose.

Suddenly Joss too was near to tears. "Luke — I can't cope. I'm too tired. You'll have to deal with him." She was white and strained. "Do you mind?"

Luke stared at her, then his face softened. "Of course not, sweetheart. Off you go. Go to bed."

It was a long time before he climbed back in beside her.

It was Joss who moved first. "What's the time?"

"About three, I think. Sorry. Did I wake you?"

She grimaced. "I couldn't sleep. Too tired. Is Tom OK? I can't think why he didn't wake everyone."

"He's settled now. Poor little chap. Joss —" He turned to her and propped his head on his arm. "Joss, when I changed him — he was covered in bruises."

"But he was all right."

"Yes, he was all right."

"He must have got them falling out of bed." Her voice was blurred with exhaustion. "Don't worry. He'll be OK."

The next morning the storms had cleared away out to sea and the air was fresh and bright.

Matthew was entranced by everything he saw. Standing next to his brother on the terrace at the back of the house, he took a deep breath and beamed. The same height and coloring as Luke, with dark hair and dark, hazel eyes, he had inherited a crop of freckles from his mother which gave him a carefree, unruly appearance that made him irresistible to women. "I'm going to say it again, brother. You're a lucky, lucky sod!" Mat clouted Luke affectionately across the shoulders. He raised his hands above his head and took a deep breath of the sweet air. "It's a heavenly place for kids to grow up. I heard young Tom playing in the attic behind my bedroom this morning. God, I wish you and I had had somewhere like this when we were kids!"

"You heard Tom in the attic?" Luke stared at his brother, surprised. "Well, that's somewhere he shouldn't have been. He's too young to go off up there on his own. I expect he was looking for you or Ma."

"Georgie. He was calling someone called Georgie." Mat stepped onto the lawn. "Come on. I want to see your fish. Are there carp in that lake?" He set off over the grass, leaving Luke staring at him thoughtfully.

"You know Tom's covered in bruises." Lyn had come up behind him, her bare feet silent on the warm York stone terrace.

"I know. He fell out of his crib."

"When?" Lyn stared at him in horror.

"Last night."

"And where was Joss? Why didn't you call me?"

Luke shook his head. "Joss was feeding the baby. I didn't call you because there wasn't any need. I coped." He smiled. "Come on. Let's go and find a carp for Mat."

David was watching them from the study window. He stepped back as Joss came in behind him and he felt his heart turn over. Her exhaustion had forged her dark beauty into something ethereal. He closed his eyes, willing himself to put

316

all his lustful thoughts out of his head, and with a supreme effort kept his voice steady. "Kids OK?"

She nodded wearily. "Two grannies baby-sitting. I thought I'd have a sit-down for a minute." She glanced out of the window where Luke and Mat and Lyn were strolling down across the grass toward the water.

"Poor old Joss. But sorry, old thing. No time for resting. I want you to come with me back to the church. There's something I want to check."

"No, David." She threw herself into a chair. "I told you, I don't want to think about all that now. I really don't."

"You do, Joss, if it puts your mind at rest." He squatted down in front of her and reached for her hand. "I had a long talk with your rector yesterday — the old one with the white wild hair — and I put one or two thoughts I'd been having to him for his views." He stared up into her face. "I think he and I may have similar theories on this one, Joss, and I think that whereas he is coming at it from an intuitive angle, I as a historian have the edge. I know where to look for the proof."

"Proof?" She rested her head against the back of the chair, her eyes on his face. "What sort of proof?"

"Evidence. Gossip. Chronicles. Records. Letters. Not proof perhaps that would stand up in a court of law, but nevertheless something to substantiate and explain what has happened here in the past."

"And stop it happening again?" She looked at him wearily.

"Until we know what it really is, we won't know how to fight it, Joss."

"And the answer is in the church?"

"Maybe." He stood up and held out his hand again. "Come on. Take the opportunity, while the grandmas are here and on call and still delighted with their new grandson. Take advantage of the chance. It probably won't last."

"All right." She grasped his fingers and let him pull her to her feet. "Let's go and look."

The path to the church, cut back neatly for the christening, was lined with pink roses, cascading in heavy curtains from the wild rosebushes, nestling between hedgerow trees and curtains of ivy. Underfoot, the soft moss, greened by the thundery rain, allowed them to walk silently as far as the door. Reaching for the handle, Joss swung it open and they stepped down into the dim cool interior.

"Don't the flowers look nice." David pulled the heavy door closed behind them.

"We didn't come to see the flowers." She averted her eyes from the window with the white roses. One of them had blown and she could see the petals on the floor, drifting over a grating.

"Up here." He headed toward the chancel steps. "Gower said to look under the carpet."

They stood looking down at the faded Persian runner which lay between the choir stalls. Even in the dim light they could see the richness that had once been there. David crouched and flicked back one corner of the rug. "Good Lord. Look.

He's right. There's a beautiful brass under here."
He dragged the carpet back, revealing the ex-
quisitely elaborate detail of an inlaid brass about
six feet long.

"It's a woman," Joss said after a moment. She
grimaced. What else would it be at Belheddon.

"A beautiful rich woman." David stood with
his back to the altar so he could see her the
right way up. "Gower said this was only un-
covered in 1965 when they took the floorboards
up because of dry rot. The original stone floor
had been covered to raise it at some point."

"Who is she, do we know?" Joss joined him
with her back to the altar. "Margaret de Vere.
See." He pointed to the ornate lettering. HIC
JACET . . . MARGARET . . . UXOR . . . ROBERT
DE VERE . . . MORETE IN ANNO DOMINE 1485.
He glanced at Joss. "This is Katherine's mother!"

Katherine!
She had seen the king's gaze following the
girl around the hall and she had long ago sensed
his lust.

"Husbands can be disposed of, my lord." Her
eyes narrowed as she smiled.

He frowned and shook his head.

The presence of the woman made his flesh
crawl. But still his whole body ached to have
the girl.

Squatting by the elegant pointed feet of the
woman on the floor before them, David leaned
forward and touched the cold brass with a tentative finger. "Margaret de Vere was accused of

sorcery and fortune-telling, which was their way of saying witchcraft," he whispered. "It was even rumored that she had brought about the king of England's death. The king being Edward IV — the king who came to Belheddon."

There was a long silence. Joss's first reaction, incredulous disbelief, wavered. At Belheddon anything was possible.

"What happened to her? Was she burned or did they hang her?" Joss stared down at the aquiline features beneath the ornate headdress.

"Neither. Nothing was ever proved. She died at home in her bed."

"At Belheddon?"

"At Belheddon."

They both stared down at the floor.

"Do you think she was a witch?" Joss asked at last.

David shook his head thoughtfully. "I don't know. I wondered if we would find a clue. Some kind of symbol on the brass perhaps. You know, the way you can tell whether a crusader reached Jerusalem or not by whether or not his feet are crossed. I've always wondered if that is true or not!"

Joss managed a smile. "You mean we're looking for a heraldic broomstick?"

He shook his head. "Witchcraft wasn't so much a cottage industry then. It was a far more aristocratic pastime at this period, don't forget. The court was riddled with accusations. There were rumors about Elizabeth Woodville, Edward IV's queen, and the Duchess of Bedford, her mother, and at least one of his mistresses, Jane Shore —"

"Surely a lot of those accusations were part of Richard III's propaganda against the princes who were Elizabeth's sons." Joss sat down in the front choir stall, still staring down at the brass.

"But not all. Accusations had been made against Elizabeth Woodville from the start, because no one at court could understand why King Edward married her. There was this young, tall, handsome, romantic king, and he meets this widow, who is a Lancastrian, has two children already, is not even particularly beautiful, in the middle of a forest, and within days and against everybody's advice he's married her! Perhaps she did bewitch him." He smiled. "And there lies our problem. No historian worth his solid, scientific salt would believe it. It must have been something else. Something dynastic."

"Or just her beautiful blue eyes?" Joss smiled.

He scowled. "Or was there no smoke without fire? Did these women and others like her — the Duchess of Bedford or Margaret de Vere here — actually find a means of summoning the devil to help them achieve their ends?"

The atmosphere in the church appeared to have dropped several degrees.

Joss shivered. Did he really believe that? "You're talking about Satanism, David, not witchcraft," she said at last.

"Devil worship." He glanced at her. "Don't tell me you're one of those women who believe that witchcraft was some kind of goody-goody, never-hurt-a-fly paganism which does no harm to anyone and is the feminist answer to the patriarchal, misogynist church!"

Joss smiled. "Something like that, perhaps." She found herself staring into the shadowy nave. "But not in this case. Here, I think you may be right."

Almost unwillingly she looked down at the brass at her feet, picking out one by one the details from the ornate curlicues of the surround. Were there hidden symbols there, clues she could not see or recognize?

"You believe that she" — she gestured at the floor — "conjured the devil here, at Belheddon?"

"I think maybe she did something rather strange. Enough to make people suspicious. I've a few more sources to look up before I try and formulate a theory."

"I think it will be very hard to find proof, David." Joss gave him a tolerant grin. "We're dealing with a field here which is not amenable to the kind of reductionist study you are used to."

He stooped again and began dragging the carpet over the brass. "That won't stop me trying, old girl," he said cheerfully. "Not now I've got my teeth into it."

She stared down for one last time as he pulled the rug across the cold, haughty face of the woman on the floor and she shuddered. "It would be wonderful if you could find a way to end all the unhappiness."

"We'll find a way, Joss. You'll see." He reached out for her hand. "Come on, let's go back to the house." Did she realize, he wondered, just how beautiful she was looking — more so every time he came to visit the house — every time he set eyes on her?

CHAPTER 23

Alice was alone in the study reading one of the pile of copies of *Good Housekeeping* she had brought for Joss and Lyn. She looked up as Joss walked in and put it down with a smile. "Hello, love. How are you? I've seen hardly anything of you, you've been so busy."

Joss sat down near her and, reaching forward, took Alice's hand. "I'm sorry. What with the christening and everything. How are you, Mum?"

"I'm fine. Just fine. Still a bit tired, but better every day for knowing there's nothing terribly wrong with my insides." Alice scanned Joss's face carefully. "Don't do too much, Joss. Let Lyn help you as much as she can, won't you?"

Joss gave a wry smile. "I think Lyn feels she's doing enough already."

"Rubbish." Alice sounded suddenly brisk. "That young lady has more energy than she knows what to do with. And she's worried about you, Joss. You've not long ago had a frightening birth and on top of that there's this big house to look after." She stared around the room with pursed lips. "I can see it's a joy for you, but it's a big

323

responsibility as well. You let Lyn help. And your dad and I will too, if you'll let us. You've only got to ask. Joe . . ." She took a deep breath. "Joe feels you might be a bit reluctant to have us here, dear, seeing as it's your real mum's house, but I told him you would never, never feel such a thing. I'm right, aren't I?"

Joss slipped to her knees beside the sofa and put her arms around Alice. "How could he even think such a thing? You've been more to me than real parents ever could, you know that. You always used to tell me I was special because I was the chosen baby. I really believed it." And Lyn, who had once heard her father say it to Joss when no one knew she was there, had never forgotten or forgiven the fact that she was not chosen. She just arrived. Joss hoped Alice and Joe would never find out that little source of some of Lyn's bitterness.

"Right, dear." Alice pushed her away gently and edged herself forward so she could climb off the sofa. "Now that's settled, let's go and find the others. I let Elizabeth and Geoffrey take that baby out in its pram, and I reckon it's time this set of grandparents had a go, don't you?" She chuckled. "So, where's little Tom got to?"

Joss shrugged. "There are so many people looking after him I've lost track. He's having the time of his life with so much attention."

"Yes, well. Don't let him get spoiled." Alice pursed her lips as she opened the door. "And Joss, remember what I said. Rest. You're looking peaky."

Mat was standing in the great hall looking up

at the picture over the fireplace. He grinned at Alice and then caught Joss's hand. "A word before you rush off, sister-in-law."

She looked up at him in surprise. "I am popular today."

"Popular and, as your mother said, peaky. Luke's worried about you, you know, Joss."

Joss shook her head. "Why on earth is everyone so concerned suddenly?"

Mat looked down at her, his dark eyes, so like his brother's, deeply troubled. "David Tregarron has no business worrying you about the house. Luke says he's winding you up, frightening you deliberately."

"That's not true!" Joss was indignant.

"Luke thinks it is. Being Luke, he's not about to say anything, Joss. At least not to you. He knows you value David's friendship, and he knows you'd resent him interfering." He paused. "David's in love with you, isn't he?"

"That's none of your business, Mat."

"Oh, I think it is. Be careful. Don't hurt Luke."

"Mat —"

"No, Joss. Let big brother speak." Mat gave his slow, intimate smile. "He's worried sick and not just about David. He says you're hearing voices, seeing things, scaring yourself witless, and all that is not good, especially when you have a new baby in the house. Thinking there is some kind of a threat to the baby is crazy, Joss. You must get that idea right out of your head. You do see that, don't you?"

Joss was silent for a moment. "I appreciate your talking to me, Mat," she said at last, firmly. "But

325

there is nothing wrong with me. You must tell Luke I'm OK. I'm not imagining things, and I'm not letting David wind me up. I promise." She glanced at Mat and smiled. "And Luke knows that whatever David feels for me, I'm not in love with him. I promise."

"You've no business complaining to Mat about me!" Joss cornered Luke alone at last in the coach house. "All you are doing is worrying him and your parents absolutely unnecessarily. What on earth were you telling him, anyway?"

"Only that I was worried about you. And I did not complain to him. He had no business speaking to you." Luke looked at her wearily. "Joss, I don't think you realize how much strain you are under."

"I realize perfectly well, thank you. And there is nothing wrong about it. I gave birth only a couple of weeks ago! Ned cries a lot. I am feeding him myself, I am missing a lot of sleep. What is so odd about my feeling strained?"

"Nothing." Luke put down the spanner he had in his hands and came toward her, wiping his fingers on the seat of his overalls. "Come here, you gorgeous, clever lady and let me give you a kiss."

He put his wrists on her shoulders, drawing her toward him, dangling his oily hands behind her head so as not to touch her with his fingers. "Don't take it wrong that I worry, Joss. It's because I love you so much." He looked into her eyes. "Now, I've got some good news for you. This old bus is just about finished. She'll be off home next week, if all goes well, and I've had two new inquiries, one of which is a definite for full restoration jobs. At this rate, I might even be able to pay one or two of the bills by the end of the year."

Joss laughed. "That's brilliant!"

"And what about you? How is the book going? Are you getting any work done at all with both our families encamped in the place?"

"No. Of course not." She gave him a playful cuff on the side of the head. "But I think I'm allowed a few days off while my favorite parents and in-laws are in residence. Plenty of time to write again once they've gone."

He grinned. "The trouble is we might not get them to go away. They love it here so much."

"I'm glad." Walking back to the door, she stared out into the yard where Jimbo was industriously polishing two great disembodied headlamps. "He's a godsend, isn't he."

"Certainly is. Who knows. Next year I might just look for another one like him."

Joss frowned. "With all this talk about me, no one has said anything about you looking tired, Luke." She reached up and touched his face. He was pale and thin, his eyes reddened from lack of sleep. "No one sympathizes with the father, do they. It's tough."

"Very." He nodded vigorously. "Don't you worry. I'm playing for all the sympathy I can get from my mummy and daddy right now." He laughed. "It's nice having them here."

In the yard, as though sensing their eyes upon him, Jimbo had turned and looked at them. He raised a hand, and Joss waved back. "I'd better go and find Tom. No one seems to know who's looking after him."

"He's loving all the attention." Luke shook his head fondly. "We'll have trouble when they all go." He hesitated. "Have you heard when David is leaving?"

Why — can't you wait to get rid of him? Joss was about to reply, but she swallowed the comment. David was going anyway. "He's driving up to town this evening. It's still term time, don't forget."

"Well, as long as he doesn't decide to come down here for the whole summer." He softened the words with a smile.

"He won't." She reached out and touched his hand. "It's you I love. Never forget that, Luke."

There was no sign of anyone indoors. She hurried through the rooms, calling, but the house was deserted. From the study window she could see Elizabeth and Alice strolling across the lawn. Elizabeth was pushing the pram, an expression of intense concentration on her face, while Alice was talking nineteen to the dozen, gesticulating as she walked. Joss smiled fondly and turned away from the window. Tom could be with Mat or with Lyn or Geoffrey or Joe or even David. Someone would be keeping an eye on him. So why was she so uneasy? She knew why. Because they could all so easily be thinking the same thing.

"Tom!" She whispered his name. Then "Tom!" louder. Heading for the staircase, she ran up into his bedroom. It was deserted and tidy, as was

Ned's. There was no one in her room or Lyn's or David's. She stood at the bottom of the attic stairs and stared up. The Grants' bedrooms were there, and little Tom had plodded up at least twice to find them.

Slowly she climbed the flight and stood on the landing, listening. The attic was very hot. It smelled strongly of rich, dry wood and dust, and it was quite silent.

"Tom?"

Her voice sounded indecently loud.

"Tom? Are you up here?"

She went into Elizabeth and Geoffrey's room. It was strewn with clothes; the small chest of drawers was littered with items of makeup and Elizabeth's strings of beads and Geoffrey's tie, torn off as soon as possible after the christening guests had left the day before and not replaced. The bed was a low divan — nowhere under it to hide. There was no sign of Tom. He wasn't in Mat's room, either. She stood in the middle of the floor looking around, listening to the scuffling from behind the far door, the door which led into the empty attic, which stretched the rest of the length of the house.

There were footsteps, the sound of a piece of furniture being moved, a suppressed giggle.

"Tom?" Why was she whispering?

"Tom?" She tried a little louder.

Silence.

"Georgie? Sam?" Her voice was shaking.

The silence was so intense she could feel someone listening to her, holding their breath. The attic was hot beneath the roof, sweet-smelling, dry. Slowly, almost as though she were sleep-walking, she moved toward the far door. She put out her hand to the key and turned it. The silence deepened. As she pushed open the door it became something tangible, opaque, heavy with threat.

"Tom!" This time her shout was loud, high-pitched, bordering on panic. "Tom, are you there?"

Pushing the door back against the wall, she stepped into the empty room and looked around. The light was shadowy, full of dust motes. A bee, trapped against the glass of the window, buzzed frantically, yearning for the sunlight and flowers of the garden. Another door on the far side of the room stood half open. Beyond it the shadows were thick and warm. "Tom?" Her voice was shaking now, the panic heavy in her throat. "Tom, where are you darling? Don't hide."

The giggle was quite near this time, a child's giggle, half stifled, very close. She swung around. "Tom?"

There was no one there. Almost running, she dived back into Mat's bedroom and looked around. "Tom!" This time it was a sob. Retracing her steps at a run, she plunged through the first two empty attic rooms to the third and last, the one with an end window overlooking the court-yard. "Tom!" But there was no one there and no answer save the single panicked sound of the bee against the window. Passing slowly back through the empty shadowy rooms, she walked over to the small window and forced it open, watching the bee soar with sudden palpable joy up into the sunshine. There were tears on her cheeks, she realized, tears pouring down her face. Her throat was tight and her heart thudding unevenly under her ribs. "Georgie, is that you? Where are you? Sammy? Is it you?"

Unsteadily, she made her way back through the Grants' bedroom to the top of the staircase, peering down, trying to see through her tears. "Tom? Where are you?" Sobbing, she sat down on the top step as her strength drained from her. She was shaking, exhausted and terribly afraid.

"Joss?" It was Mat, peering up from the landing. "Is that you?" He took the stairs two at a time. "Joss, what is it? What's the matter?"

"Tom." She was shaking so much she could hardly speak.

"Tom?" He frowned. "What about Tom? He's down in the kitchen with Lyn."

Joss was clasping her knees; raising her head, she stared at him. "He's all right?"

"He's all right, Joss." He stared at her, searching her face for a clue to her behavior. Sitting down on the step next to her, he put his arm around her shoulders. "What is it, Joss?"

She shook her head, sniffing. "I couldn't find him —"

"He's OK. Honestly." He hugged her, then he stood up and reached down for her hand. "Come on, we'll go and see him."

She looked up at him, pushing her hair out of her eyes, aware suddenly of how she must look. "I'm sorry, Mat. I'm so tired —"

"I know." His grin was so like Luke's it tugged at her heartstrings. "That's babies for you, I guess. Not enough sleep."

331

She nodded, climbing wearily to her feet. "Don't say anything. Please."

"Scout's honor." He raised two parallel fingers to his forehead. "On one condition. You have a sleep this afternoon. A proper one, letting us take care of the kids so there is nothing to wake you, nothing to worry you. Agreed?"

"Agreed." She let him take her hand and guide her down the stairs, feeling a little foolish as, following him into the kitchen, she found a room full of people, noise, and laughter, and at the center of all the activity an unconcerned Tom, kneeling up on a kitchen chair and drawing with large plastic crayons on a huge sheet of paper.

"There you are, Joss." Lyn looked up from the worktop where she was chopping onions. Her eyes were streaming. Pushing her hair out of her eyes with the back of her wrist, she grinned. "We couldn't think where you'd got to."

She looked too cheerful, almost frenetic.

"Where's Luke?" Joss asked. He was the only one missing from the cheerful gathering.

"He went out to have a word with Jimbo," Lyn said, turning back to her onions. "Then he's coming in for lunch. Are you going to feed Ned first?"

Joss nodded. She could see the baby asleep in the pram by the dresser. He seemed able to sleep through any amount of noise at the moment, and for that fact she gave a quiet prayer of thanks. "Sit down, Joss." Mat guided her by the shoulders to a chair. "I was just telling Joss that she needs to rest," he said firmly as she collapsed into it. "I think this afternoon the doting grandparents and uncles and godfathers should remove the junior Grants from the premises and allow their mum to have a really good sleep."

"First rate idea." Geoffrey smiled. "You do look washed out, Joss my dear."

Washed out, she thought much later as she climbed the stairs to the bedroom. I suppose that's one word for it. She felt almost sorry for the others. In spite of the heat, they felt duty-bound, she suspected, to go for that one last walk before setting off in their various directions. The Grants to Oxford — Mat was spending another couple of days with his parents before setting off back north — David and her parents to London. In some ways she was glad they were going. Having so many people in the house was exhausting, but in other ways she was sorry. While they were there, there were people to keep an eye on the children, people to create noise — critical mass — within a large house, drowning out the other sounds, the sounds that came from the silence.

Sitting on the edge of the bed, she kicked off her sandals and lay back on the pillow. She had drawn the curtains against the sun and the room was shadowy, the heat stifling. She could feel her eyes closing. Relaxing on top of the duvet, she could feel some of the aching tension easing out of her bones, the heat and the darkness behind her eyelids like a warm bath of peace. Sleep. That was all she needed to soothe away her fears. Sleep, undisturbed by a crying baby or the restless, hot body of her husband next to her in the bed. Poor Luke. He was out in the coach house with Jimbo working among the smells of oil and gasoline and the heat of sun-warmed metal.

The weight on the side of the bed was so slight she barely noticed it. For a moment she lay there, eyes still firmly shut, resisting the lurking flutters of fear, then slowly, reluctantly, she opened them and looked around. Nothing. The room was still. There was nothing near the bed which could have caused the slight frisson of movement in the air, the almost unnoticeable depression of the bed-clothes near her feet — nothing beyond the stir-ring of the bed curtain in a stray breeze from the window. Feeling her mouth dry and uncom-fortable, she swallowed and closed her eyes again. Nothing to worry about. Nothing to be afraid of. But the moment of relaxation had gone. She could feel the uncomfortable trickle of adrenaline into her system — nothing dramatic, nothing star-tling, just a premonitory priming of the nerves. "No." Her whisper was long drawn out, an-guished. "Please, leave me alone."

There was nothing there. No shadow in the corner, no strange half-heard echoes in her head which seemed to come from some unrecognized aural receptor which had nothing to do with her ears, nothing but a shred of instinct telling her that all was not well.

Pushing herself up on her elbow, she could feel a trickle of perspiration running down her face. Her hair was sticky; it needed washing. More than anything, she realized suddenly she would love a long, cold bath, somewhere she could wal-low sleepily with the door locked, and the humid heat of the afternoon kept at bay.

Swinging her feet to the floor, she dragged herself off the bed, realizing at once that she was still dizzy and aching with exhaustion. Padding on bare feet across the cool boards, she headed for the bathroom and, putting the plug in the bath, turned on the taps — mostly cold — and tipped in a little scented oil. Her face, as she examined it in the mirror, was white, damp, and — even to herself — exhausted. There were dark rings over as well as under her eyes, where the lids were sunken and drawn, and her body, as she peeled off her thin cotton skirt and blouse and underwear, was ugly — still swollen, her breasts huge and blue-veined, damp with sweat. She scowled at herself, tempted for a moment to veil the mirror with a towel. The idea made her smile as she stooped to turn off the tap and step gingerly into the cool water.

The bath was definitely an improvement on the bed. She smiled to herself, every time she climbed into the huge old-fashioned bath with ornate iron legs, at the thought that such things were now the height of expensive fashion. Cool, supporting to her back — it felt solid and somehow secure. She lay back until the water lapped around her breasts, her head against the rim, and closed her eyes.

She wasn't sure how long she had slept but she woke to find herself shivering. Chilled, she sat up with a groan and hauled herself out of the water. She had left her watch on the shelf above the washbasin. Grabbing it, she looked at it. Nearly four. The others would be back from their walk soon, and Ned would be wanting a feed. Snatching her cotton robe from behind the door, she went back into the bedroom. It was just as before — hot and airless. Pulling back the curtains, she stared down into the garden. It was empty.

Reaching for her hairbrush from the dressing table, Joss began to brush her hair vigorously, feeling the residual tension from her forehead and the back of her neck receding with every stroke. Throwing it down, she was reaching into the drawer for fresh crisp clothes when she glanced up at the mirror and felt her stomach drop. For a split second she didn't recognize the face before her. Her brain refused to interpret the image. She could see eyes, nose, mouth, like gaping holes in a waxen mask — then, as shock-driven adrenaline flooded through her system, the images regrouped, cleared, and she found herself looking at a frightened facsimile of herself — eyes, huge; skin, damp; hair, disheveled, her bathrobe hanging open to display the heavy breasts — breasts which for a fraction of a second had felt the touch of a cold hand on the hot fevered skin.

"No!" She shook her head violently. "No!"

Clothes. Quickly. Quickly. Bra. Shirt. Panties. Jeans. A protection. Armor. Outside. She must get outside.

The kitchen was empty. Throwing open the back door, she looked out into the courtyard. "Luke?"

The Bentley had been pulled out of the coach house. It stood gleaming gently in the sunlight, strangely blind without the two huge headlights, which still stood on a trestle table just inside the open double doors.

"Luke!" She ran across the cobbles and stared in. "Where are you?"

"He's gone out for a walk with the others, Mrs. Grant." Jimbo appeared suddenly from the shadows. "With his ma and pa being here and that, he thought he'd take the chance."

"Of course." Joss forced a smile. "I should have thought of that." She was conscious suddenly of how hard Jimbo was staring at her. The young man's face had fascinated her when she first saw it. It was thin, brown, with strangely sleepy slanted eyes, the planes of the cheeks and brow bones flattening into Slavic features of startling dramatic cast. She could never see him without picturing him on a pony, a rag tied around his head, a gun brandished in one hand as he galloped over the plain. It had been something of a disappointment when, unable to resist it, she had asked him if he could ride and he had looked at her askance with the unequivocal answer, "No way."

"You all right, Mrs. Grant?" The soft local vowels did not fit the hard features. Nor, she had to admit, did the eyes: the strange all-seeing eyes.

"Yes. Thank you." She forced an uncomfortable smile.

"You look tired, Mrs. Grant."

"I am." She began to turn away.

"The boys been keeping you awake, have they? I seen them when I stayed at yours with my mum when I was a lad. She says they always come back when there are folk in the house."

Joss stared at him. "Boys?" she repeated in a whisper. He wasn't talking about Tom and Ned.

"All the lost boys." He shook his head slowly. "Like Pe'er Pan. I didn't like the house. My dad said I might get taken too, but Mam had to caretake here sometimes for Mrs. Duncan before she packed up and went to live in Paris. And I had to come too then."

Joss's mouth was dry. She wanted to turn and run, but, pinned by his sly gaze, she was suddenly rooted to the spot.

"Did you ever see them?" she managed to whisper at last.

He shook his head. "Our Nat saw them though."

"Nat?" Joss could feel the tightness in her throat increasing.

"My sister. She liked it up here. Mam used to clean for Mrs. D and she often brought us to play in the garden while she was working. Nat would play with the boys." His face darkened. "She thought I was a wimp because I didn't want to. I thought she was loopy. I wouldn't stay. I'd go and hide in the kitchen and get under Mam's feet or if she got cross I'd nip through the hedge and go home. No matter how often she tanned my backside I wouldn't stay."

He looked remarkably cheerful about it now.

"But your sister liked it here?"

He nodded. "Well, she would, wouldn't she," he said cryptically. He reached for a soft cloth and began buffing the huge headlamps.

"You don't mind working here now, though?" Joss said thoughtfully.

He grinned. "Na. I don't believe in that stuff anymore."

"But you think I do?"

He winked. "I heard them talking about you. I didn't think it was fair. After all, it's not just you, is it. Loads of people have seen the boys."

And the tin man without a heart?

Joss wiped the palms of her hands across the front of her shirt. "Does your sister still live in the village, Jim?"

He shook his head. "She got a job in Cambridge."

She felt a sharp pang of disappointment. "But she comes back? On visits?"

He didn't look too sure. With a shrug, he rubbed at an almost invisible speck of rust. "Not often."

"And your mother?"

He shook his head. "When Mam and Dad split up, Mam went to live in Kesgrave."

"Does your dad remember this house in my mother's time?"

Jim shrugged. "I doubt it. He wouldn't set foot in the place." He looked up at her and again she saw the narrow, calculating look. "He didn't want me to take this job."

"I see." She supposed she didn't need to ask why. Too many local tradesmen had explained with a shudder why they would not want to live here themselves.

She sighed. "Well, Jimbo, if you see Luke tell him I was looking for him, OK?"

"OK, Mrs. Grant." He was smiling. As she turned away she felt rather than saw him straighten up from the lamp and stand watching her as she retraced her steps across the courtyard.

The French doors in the study were open onto the terrace. Standing just outside on the cool stone, she surveyed the rather motley collection of garden furniture they had assembled from the outhouses around the courtyard. There were two Edwardian recliners — a little rotten, but remarkably solid considering their age. Two wicker chairs, chewed by mice, but again just about serviceable, and a couple of decidedly dodgy deck chairs both within days of the ultimate split which would deposit their occupants unceremoniously onto the floor. She smiled involuntarily as she always did when she looked at them. Enough to make the owner of an upmarket garden center go prematurely gray. To sit at this moment in one of those long, Edwardian recliners, which smelled of damp and age and lichen, even though they had cooked for weeks now on the terrace, would be heaven. With a cup of tea. Just for a few minutes. Till the others came back.

She turned back into the study. She ought to take the opportunity to write, now while the house was quiet. She looked guiltily at the pile of neatly printed pages on the desk. It was nearly three weeks since she had touched it. Picking up the last few pages, she glanced at them. Richard — the hero of her story, the son of the house, whose tale came so easily to her pen that she wondered sometimes if it were being dictated to her — had he been one of the lost boys? Were there generations of boys like George and Sam haunting the attic of the house? She shuddered. Had Richard in real life not survived his adventures to live happily ever after, as he was going to in her story, but fallen prey like her brothers to another of the accidents and illnesses which plagued the sons of Belheddon? "Please, God, keep Tom and Ned safe." Throwing down the pages, she went back to the doors. Geoffrey and Elizabeth had appeared on the far side of the lawn. Behind them she could see Joe and Alice with the pram just coming through the gate. They must have all walked across the fields and down to the low red cliffs above the estuary. Mat had appeared now, with Tom Tom sitting on his shoulders, and Lyn beside him and, last of all, Luke. They were all laughing and talking and for a moment she felt a wave of utter loneliness, strangely excluded from the group even though they were of all the people in the world those closest to her.

She watched as they approached her across the grass.

"Did you sleep well?" Luke greeted her with a kiss.

She nodded. She stooped and lifted Ned from the pram. He was fast asleep, oblivious to the world. Hugging him against her, she felt the ache in her breasts, the need to feed him. She glanced at Lyn. "Shall we have tea soon?"

"Sure." Lyn was relaxed and smiling. Her tee shirt had slipped off one tanned shoulder; her legs, long and slim, were dusted with sand beneath the frayed, cut-off jeans.

"You all went on the beach?" she asked.

Lyn nodded. "Mat and I took Tom down to

make sand castles. It's glorious there today." She stretched her arms languidly above her head. Joss saw Mat's eyes go involuntarily to Lyn's breasts, outlined so clearly under the thin blue tee shirt. He was looking remarkably cheerful.

"I'll take Ned up and change him." Joss headed for the stairs as the others trooped, talking loudly, toward the kitchen.

She glanced warily around her bedroom. The sun had moved around slightly and the room was cooler. In her arms, the baby had opened his eyes. He was gazing up into her face with unwavering concentration. She dropped a kiss on the end of his nose, overwhelmed with love for him. No one. No one was ever even to think of harming him or she would not be answerable for her actions. Sitting down in the low chair by the window, she gazed down at his face, overcome with love as he dozed off again, seemingly not ready yet to be fed. Breathing in the heavy scent of mown grass and roses from the climber outside the window, she felt herself grow drowsy, and as her eyelids became increasingly heavy her arms began to loosen the hold on the baby, almost as if someone was gently taking him from her —

"Joss? Joss, what the hell are you doing?" Lyn's shriek brought her back to the present with a jerk of terror. Snatching Ned from her, Lyn had turned on her with the ferocity of a spitting cat. "You stupid idiot! You could have killed him! What were you doing?"

"What — ?" Joss stared at her blankly.

"His shawl! You had his shawl over his face."

"I didn't." Joss looked around, confused. "He

342

didn't have a shawl. It was too hot."

But it was there, still wrapped around him, covering his head and face and trailing from Lyn's arms as the baby began to scream.

"Give him to me." Joss snatched Ned from her. "He's hungry. I was just going to feed him, that's all. He's all right. He's just hungry."

She cuddled the baby to her, unbuttoning her shirt. "Go and make tea! I'll be down soon."

She watched as Lyn backed away toward the door. Her sister's face was preoccupied and uneasy as she let herself out onto the landing.

"Silly Aunty Lyn." Joss guided Ned's mouth toward her nipple with her little finger. "As if I would hurt you, sweetheart." Lowering herself back onto the chair near the window, she gazed out at the garden as Ned suckled, relaxing back against the embroidered tapestry cushion which Elizabeth had brought as a house-warming present.

On the bed, the rose which lay on her pillow wilted in the last rays of the sun as it moved across the window into the western sky and one by one the petals fell, small white patches on the rich colors of the crewelwork bedcover.

CHAPTER 24

The house was very quiet after the departure of the family. As each stifling airless day followed the one before, Luke and Joss and Lyn found themselves growing increasingly listless. Even Tom was subdued, missing the posse of adoring grandparents. Each morning after feeding Ned and putting him down to sleep, Joss disappeared into the study where, with the French windows wide, she would sit in front of the computer wrestling with Richard and the climax of her story.

Twice David phoned, the last time before he set off to spend the summer in Greece. "Just to see how you are. Is the book going well?" He did not mention his research into the house anymore and she did not ask.

Out in the courtyard, the Bentley went, to be replaced by a 1936 SS and then a Lagonda. In the shadowy coach house, the coolest place in Belheddon save for the cellar, Jimbo and Luke worked early in the morning and late in the afternoon, saving the hot midday for a swim in the sea, sandwich lunch, and then a siesta under the trees. During the long evenings Luke and sometimes Jimbo too would work in the garden until dark.

Lyn, ignoring all warnings about the sun, stretched out on one of the old chairs, firmly plugged into her Walkman, while the children slept in their bedrooms. Twice she had written to Mat. He had not replied.

At her desk, Joss stared out at her sister and frowned. In spite of the liberal application of sun oil, Lyn's legs were peeling, pink flaky patches appearing through the brown. Lyn was constantly watching her. Ever since that afternoon when Lyn had snatched Ned from her arms, Joss had the feeling she was being checked on. She shook her head wearily and stretched her arms above her head, easing the cramp from her muscles. Tom and Ned were both growing fast, seemingly thriving in spite of the heat. Were it not for Tom's nightmares, all would have been peaceful. Simon, called in at last at Lyn's insistence, gave Tom a complete checkup and blamed the heat. "He'll settle down once it's cooler, you'll see." The arrival of two kittens from the Goodyears' farm, christened with due ceremony by Tom Kit and Kat, cheered him up enormously but did not stop the dreams. If they were dreams. Getting up, night after night, to feed Ned and see to Tom, Joss was growing more and more tired and her tiredness was beginning to show. The book was going badly. The story wouldn't progress, and Lyn was getting on her nerves. Often now, when she picked him up, Ned would start to scream. She would hug him and comfort him but, as though sensing her exhaustion and her distress, he would cry all the harder. And every time he cried, Lyn would be there, reaching out for him, trying to take him, looking at her accusingly.

"You see! When I hold him he stops." She would croon over the baby and then look up in triumph.

"It's normal, Joss," Simon said gently. "Babies often cry when their mums pick them up because they want her milk. It's frustration and hunger because they can smell it so close. Lyn has nothing Ned wants, so he doesn't bother."

Lyn was not convinced.

The hot weather broke at last at the beginning of September. Torrential rain hurtled across the gardens, and the roof began to leak. Wearily, Joss and Lyn trudged up and down to the attic with buckets and washing-up bowls, and Tom caught a violent cold. Wiping his nose for the hundredth time as they all huddled in the kitchen, Joss had sent him off to play before going out to the door to collect the mail. Glancing through it, she paused, looking at one particular envelope, then she threw the whole pile on the table. "Bills," she said casually. "Bills and more bills."

"In that case I'm going out to the cars." Luke stood up, stuffing the last piece of his toast into his mouth. "Like to bring us out some coffee at about eleven? That would be nice." He glanced at Lyn and then at Joss. "Please?" he wheedled.

They both laughed. "We'll toss for it," Lyn said. She stood up and began to stack the dishes.

It was Joss who carried out the two steaming mugs and a pile of homemade cookies later, leaving Lyn with the washing. Her raincoat collar pulled up against the cold wind and streaming rain, she ducked into the coach house and put the mugs down on the bench amid a pile of brake drums and shoes and old spanners.

"Where is he, Jimbo?"

"Under the car." Jimbo jerked with his thumb toward the chassis blocked up in the middle of the coach house.

Joss crouched down. "Grub's up!" She peered down to see Luke lying on his back, groping above his head in the car's intestines. "Great." His voice was muffled. "Thanks." He began to push himself out. As his face appeared, black and grinning from beneath the wing, the car with no warning lurched suddenly sideways. "Luke!" Joss's scream brought Jimbo leaping to her side.

"Watch out. The axle stands are slipping." Jimbo's warning shout as Luke rolled clear was drowned by the crash as the car body slid down onto the ground.

Luke stood up shakily. "Close one!" He wiped his forehead on the back of his hand.

"Luke. You were nearly killed." Joss had gone white.

" 'Fraid so. Never mind. I wasn't." He turned to Jimbo, who was bent over the jack. "What happened?"

Jimbo was ashen. He shook his head. "Must have been knocked, I reckon."

"Knocked?" Joss looked from one to the other. "By me? It must have been me?" She was distraught. "Oh God, I'm so tired these days I can't see what I'm doing."

Luke shook his head. He came and put his

347

arm around her. "You weren't anywhere near the car, Joss. Anyway, it doesn't matter, love. No harm done. These things happen."

"Oh, Luke." Her knees had begun to shake. "It was me! Luke, I could have killed you."

"Take more than that to kill your husband, my dear." Luke grinned. He reached for one of Lyn's biscuits. "Go on. Forget it. I'm OK."

The rain clouds had blown themselves out by lunchtime and the afternoon was crisp and glorious. Leaves scattered across the lake, and the lily pads flapped playfully on the water. Standing side by side, Luke and Joss were silent as they watched a heron take off on the far side of the lake and flap laboriously over the hedge with indignant raucous squawks of complaint. One of the kittens, half hidden in the undergrowth, had been stalking it with exaggerated care. As the huge bird lifted above its head the small cat turned and fled toward the house. "Are you OK?" Luke glanced at her sideways. "You're not still worrying about that silly accident with the car, are you?" Joss's face was pale and strained. There were dark circles under her eyes.

She gave a wan smile. "Not really." In her shock at what had happened she still couldn't believe the fact that she had been nowhere near the jack handle when the car began to move. In theory she knew perfectly well that the accident had not been her fault, but deep down inside she wasn't certain.

"Are you sure?" He was studying her face. Something was wrong. More than just the tiredness. He turned back to look at the water, screwing up his eyes against the glare from the sun on the dancing ripples. "Have you heard from David recently?" he asked. He kept his voice casual.

For a moment she didn't answer. Then she shook her head. "Not for ages. Why?"

"I just wondered."

He rammed his hands into his pockets with a shiver. The autumn wind was growing cold. He had seen the envelope lying in the pile on the kitchen table and he had recognized the writing, just as she must have. It had been bulky and sealed with tape. The stab of rage he had felt when he saw it was irrational and violent. Why hadn't he thrown the thing on the stove? Why hadn't he opened it and read it? After all, he could guess what was in it: more about the bloody house. At first she had ignored it — left it on the table to be lost in a swirl of newspapers and shopping lists — then at lunchtime he saw that it had disappeared. Tear it up, he thought. Please, Joss, tear it up.

He took a step or two nearer the steep bank, staring down into the water to where goldfish and tench flitted among the roots of the lilies, faint shadows in the water — water which was deceptively deep.

"Luke." Joss's voice came from farther away now.

Luke swung around. He frowned. He couldn't see her. A raft of ripples crossed the water, rocking the floating leaves. Near the far bank a moorhen ran lightly across the lily pads, scarcely rocking them, giving sharp croaks of alarm.

"Joss? Where are you?"

There was no warning, no sound of steps, just the sudden, firm, violent push from two hands squarely planted in the small of his back as, with a shout of surprise and fear, he felt himself hurtling down the steep bank and into the water. No longer glittering gold, it was brown, sandy, cold, and very very deep. His eyes open, he found himself staring around the murky depths of the pond, then, arms flailing, he fought his way to the surface, choking, feeling the weed and lily stems clutching at his legs, pulling him back. His head broke the surface and he took great gulps of air, clawing at the leaves around him. "Christ almighty, Joss, what did you do that for?" He was apoplectic with anger and fright. "You could have drowned me!"

"Luke? Luke, what happened?" Joss was standing a few yards away. Her face was white. "Here, catch my hand." She stepped gingerly down the bank and stooped toward him.

He grabbed her fingers and hauled himself dripping onto the bank. "I suppose you think that was funny?" He glared at her, shaking himself like a dog. "For pity's sake, Joss!"

"I don't think it was funny at all," she retaliated. Then her mouth twitched very slightly at the corners. "Oh, Luke, but you did look funny, suddenly hurling yourself into the water. What on earth made you do it? Did you slip?"

"Slip? You know bloody well I didn't slip. You pushed me."

"I didn't." Her face was a picture of injured

350

innocence. "How could you think such a thing?"

He was taking deep breaths, trying to catch his breath. In the cold wind, he was suddenly shivering violently. "Well, I'm not going to argue the toss now. If I stand here much longer I'll get pneumonia." He turned toward the house and strode away up the lawn. Joss stood still, looking after him. Her sudden hilarity had gone as swiftly as it had come. She hadn't pushed him. She had been standing several yards away from him when he had suddenly given the surprised shout and hurtled forward into the water. He hadn't slipped; he hadn't jumped. He looked as if he had been pushed. But if she hadn't done it, who had?

She shuddered, looking around. The moorhen had disappeared. The bright autumnal sun had vanished behind a cloud, and the garden was suddenly very bleak and cold. She watched as Luke disappeared around the side of the house toward the kitchen, then she turned and looked back at the dull black surface of the lake, the lake where Sammy had died, and she shuddered violently. Dear sweet God, it was starting.

Lyn was in the kitchen making pastry when Joss made her way in through the back door and hung up her jacket in the hall. She glanced up at Joss over the rolling pin and raised an eyebrow. "Luke is pretty pissed off with you," she said. Beside her, Tom, his sleeves rolled up, was kneeling on a kitchen chair rolling out his own small piece of dough. He was covered in flour. "What on earth made you do it?"

"I didn't do it, Lyn." Joss went to the stove and lifted the kettle. She reached for a mug. "I wasn't anywhere near him."

"So he jumped in by himself?"

"He must have slipped. Do you want some coffee?"

Lyn shook her head.

"Daddy all wet," Tom observed. He stuck his thumb into his dough and made two eyes. Then he gouged out a smiling mouth.

"I'll take him up a hot drink." Joss spooned coffee into two mugs and stirred the hot water. She added milk. "I didn't do it, Lyn," she repeated firmly. "Really I didn't."

Luke was running a bath. He was tearing off his sodden clothes as Joss came into the bathroom. "Here," she said. "Coffee, to thaw you out. Are you all right?" There was a long bleeding scratch on his leg.

"Yes, I'm fine." He lowered himself into the hot water and reached for the mug. "Sorry to be so cross, but it wasn't my idea of a joke, Joss."

"Nor mine." She sat down on the lid of the lavatory. "I didn't do it, Luke. Honest. You must have slipped. I was miles away from you. I saw you just take off suddenly."

He leaned back and closed his eyes, sipping at the hot drink. "If you say so."

"Luke, I think we should leave Belheddon."

"Joss." He opened his eyes and looked at her. "We've discussed this before. I'm sorry, but it's impossible. Even with the money from the wine. You must see that. The terms of your mother's will say we can't sell it; we still need to earn a living, and our only chance is to persevere with my restoration and with your writing. Well, I suppose you can do your writing anywhere, but the cars, no. I need space for that. Space and covered accommodation, and now I need Jimbo. That lad is worth his weight in gold. He has a real feel for old cars. And here I can put the fiasco of Barry and H&G behind me. They're never going to catch the bastard. It's no use my thinking they will. I needed a new life, Joss. And here we have room for Lyn too. It's perfect in every way." Putting down his coffee, he reached for the soap and began lazily to lather his arms. "I know you're nervous about the stories about this house, but they are so much crap, you must know that at heart. You mustn't let people wind you up. People like David." He glanced at her again, searching for any reaction, and his face relaxed into a smile. "I'm glad in a way you thought it funny, watching your husband hurtle into fifteen feet of ice-cold water. I haven't seen you laugh for a long time."

"I didn't laugh."

"Well, smile, then. Joss, I know it hasn't been easy, love. Coming here, with all the memories and stories about your family. I do understand."

"Do you?" She stared at him thoughtfully.

"Yes, I do." He sat up, the water coursing off his shoulders and arms, and reached toward the towels. She took one and passed it to him. "I also understand it's not easy seeing Lyn spending so much time with the little boys, when you have to lock yourself away in the study writing."

"I'm terrified the story won't be any good when it's finished."

"It will. After all, they've seen a chunk of it, and they know what's going to happen. It will be fine."

"Do you think so?" She hugged her arms around herself.

"I know so." He stood up and, wrapping himself in the towel, put his arm around her, and she found herself enveloped in a warm steamy hug that smelled of soap and radox. "Forget the ghosts, love. They don't exist. Not in real life. Wonderful for novelists and historians and old biddies in the village, and even retired vicars looking for jobs as exorcists, but not for real. No way. OK?"

She gave a tight smile. "OK."

"So, let me get dressed and we'll go down and drink to Belheddon Enterprises, and confusion to the ghosts of yesteryear. Agreed?"

"Agreed."

Tom's first scream brought Joss to her knees on the bed as she was dragged violently out of her dreams. "Luke, what is it?"

"It's OK. It's another nightmare. I'm going." Luke was out of bed in a flash. Behind him, Lyn appeared in the doorway, dragging on her dressing gown.

Tom was standing in the middle of the floor. Joss reached him first and picked him up.

The child clung to her, sobbing. "Tom Tom fall. Tom Tom fall on the floor." He buried his head in her neck, nestling into her curtain of hair.

Lyn let down the side of the crib. "For goodness

sake, Joss. Look. You didn't fasten the side properly. The poor child could have been badly hurt." Crossly, she began to remake the tangled bed.

"Of course I fastened the side properly. I always check." Joss glared at her over Tom's head.

Lyn sniffed. "If you say so." She smoothed the sheets efficiently and turned back the blankets. "Come on, Tom Tom, let's see if you need changing before I put you down." She reached for him and Joss felt the child relinquish his tight grip on her neck and transfer it to Lyn's. She clutched at him. "Tom Tom, stay with Mummy," she said firmly. "I'll do it. You go to bed, Lyn."

Lyn stared at her. "Why? I'm offering."

"I know you're offering and I'm grateful, but I want to do it myself."

Lyn relaxed her hold on Tom and stood back. "OK, please yourself. Shall I check on Ned?"

Joss shook her head. "No. I'll go to him when I've done this. He'll be ready for his night feed soon. Go to bed, Lyn."

She sat the little boy down on his changing mat and began to unbutton his pajamas. He was still sniffling miserably as she laid him back and eased off his trousers, conscious that Lyn was hovering in the doorway. Half hidden by the plastic toddler's diaper, a huge black bruise was developing on Tom's leg. Undoing the plastic tabs, she took off the nappy and gasped. The bruise covered his whole hip.

Lyn had seen it too. "Dear God, how did he do that?" She came and peered at the little boy.

Joss stared at it, horrified. "Tom Tom, sweetheart! Oh you poor little lamb!" She ran her fingers gently over the bruise. "How did you do it? Let Mummy see. I'll put some arnica cream on it. He must have done it falling out of the crib." She rolled up the wet diaper and, putting it into the bucket under the table, she reached for the talcum powder and a dry diaper from the packet.

"He didn't fall." Lyn suddenly bent closer. "Look. Those bruises on his leg. The marks of fingers." She stood back suddenly and stared at Joss. "You must have done it. You!"

Joss, having smoothed on some soothing cream, was easing the little boy's hips onto the fresh pad, folding it over, sealing the sticky strips. She looked up at Lyn furiously. "How could you say such a thing!"

"Luke. Look." Lyn swung around to Luke, who was standing by the wall watching. "For Christ's sake, Luke, say something. She's hurt him. Her own child."

"Lyn!" Joss repeated angrily. "Luke, listen to her!"

"You know that's not possible, Lyn," Luke said quietly. "You're being silly. Joss would never hurt Tom. Never."

"No, I wouldn't! How dare you!" Joss took a deep breath. "Go to bed, Lyn," she repeated. "You're obviously tired. Let me get on with settling Tom down." She was keeping her temper with difficulty. "I would never hurt him in a million years, and you know it. The poor little boy has had a horrid fall out of his crib, and he's bruised, but that's all. He's fine now, aren't you, Tom Tom?" She pulled on his pajama bottoms and buttoned them back to the top. Then she sat him up. "OK, soldier, let's pop you back to bed."

"Tin man gone?" Tom refused to lie down. He stood in the bed, holding on to the bars, staring past her into the corner of the nursery. Joss bit her lip. She could feel a small worm of panic beginning in her stomach. "No tin man, Tom. That's your bad dream. He's gone. Silly tin man. He didn't want to frighten you. He's gone away now." She saw Luke and Lyn exchange glances over her head. "Come on. Let's tuck you up."

The night feed was the only one she was still giving Ned from the breast. It had seemed to make sense to wean him slowly onto the bottle so Lyn could take over more of the feeds herself, but this last one, in the quiet depths of the night, she had been reluctant to relinquish, even though it added to her exhaustion. As she sat with the baby cradled in her arms, she knew she would hang on to this precious moment each night as long as she could, when Ned was hers and hers alone.

It had been a long time before she could persuade Luke and Lyn to go to bed and leave her to settle Tom. When at last they had gone, she had sat down beside his crib and read him a story and soon, very soon, his eyes had closed. Kissing him, she had, self-consciously, made the sign of the cross over him before tucking in his blankets and tiptoeing out of the room.

As she sat with the baby cradled in her arms,

she found her thoughts going back to Lyn. It was as though her sister didn't trust her. Or was it just that she was jealous, without babies of her own? She frowned, picturing the bruises on Tom. It was not the first time the little boy had fallen and been bruised, and she was sure that Lyn must have seen those bruises too. Bruises from falls. They must be. After all, he was growing more adventurous now, banging his head on the corner of the kitchen table, nearly tipping over his high chair. Bruises were normal in a toddler. But what about nightmares? His nightmares about the tin man.

She sighed. They were not nightmares. She had seen him, sensed him, too, in the corner of the room, Tom's room, her own bedroom and the great hall, watching from the shadows, no more than a shadow himself, yet always there, waiting. Waiting for what? Even the kittens had sensed him, she was sure of it. Neither of them liked the great hall, avoiding it where possible, or, if intent on finding her in the study, scampering through with huge eyes and flattened ears. She shivered, her arms tightening around the baby, and Ned stopped sucking. He gave a resentful whimper and opened his eyes to look up into her face. She smiled at him and dropped a kiss on the dark hair. "Sorry, little one."

Her thoughts went back to David's letter. After she had picked the envelope up off the breakfast table, she had put it on her desk in the study unopened. David's letters were no longer seized and torn open with eager anticipation. Now she dreaded them, although she didn't have the willpower to ask him to stop writing. She had sat down at the desk and drawn her mug of coffee to her, cupping her hands around it, staring sightlessly out of the window. In front of her the pile of manuscript pages was very little higher than it had been a month before. Her long sessions in the study were more and more unproductive. Sitting at the desk, her ears straining for sounds from the depths of the house — a whimper from Ned, a cry from Tom — she could not concentrate on the story unfolding before her. And always there was the fear that she would hear the others — the lost boys.

Reaching for the computer switch, she had watched the screen as her program came up, sipping at the steaming coffee. Then her eye had fallen again on the envelope. With a sigh, she reached for it and slipped her finger under the flap.

No photocopies this time, just several pages of David's closely typed script. She pictured his old battered portable — sometimes to be seen on the staff room table, more often lying tossed and abandoned in the back of his car, the case covered in torn travel labels. He typed with two fingers — often crossed, as he explained to anyone who came face to face with his efforts — but there was no sign here of the rows of X's which so often littered his work. Where he had hit wrong keys he had left the results uncorrected.

Dear Joss — Hope my godson flourishes. Give him a kiss from me.
Re: the tin man. I think I know who/what

he is!!!! Maybe!!! I've been following up on Katherine de Vere and her witchy mother. There are some wonderful records of court proceedings extant. They didn't entirely get away with it, you know. Margaret was actually arrested in 1482. She was taken from Belheddon to London but before she could be brought before the court she demanded to see the king — Edward IV. He interviewed her in the Tower. It is not recorded what she said but the charges were immediately dropped and she left London laden with gifts. It's my guess that she had something on him, as they say, and that that something was to do with her daughter Katherine. King Edward had visited Belheddon four times the previous year and on each occasion he stayed several days — once for ten days, which was comparatively unheard of. What was the attraction? The place was hardly a political center in any sense and, taking time off from the war/ruling the country, was not a particularly expedient action at that time. One contemporary source says Margaret bewitched him to fall in love with her daughter. The idea was that Elizabeth Woodville would die and he would then marry Katherine de Vere.

The Belheddon De Veres were close kin of the earls of Oxford, and the political implications were enormous if they could net the king and ally themselves by marriage to the white rose . . .

Joss put the letter down and rubbed her eyes wearily. The white rose. It seemed almost corny, but did King Edward present white roses to his girlfriends? Is that where they came from? Or did Margaret de Vere use them in her magic spells to conjure the love of a king for the daughter of a minor noble who lived at the easternmost edges of his kingdom? She shuddered. Leaning forward, she pulled open a small drawer. She had put one of the roses in there, at the beginning, before they had begun to fill her with such dread.

She poked around among the pencils and stamps and sticks of sealing wax, but there was no sign of it now. Not even the crumbs of brittle petal in the bottom. The drawer, when she pulled it right out and held it up to her nose, smelled of camphor and dust, nothing more. She took a deep breath, sliding the drawer back into place, and picked up the letter again.

Of course, we will never know how much of all this was malicious gossip and rumor, and how much if any was based on fact.

Fact: Elizabeth Woodville outlived her husband.

Fact: Katherine de Vere married a man who died in mysterious circumstances only six months later.

Fact: Katherine herself died a month after that, probably in childbirth.

The king died seven months after that in 1483 at the age of 40. He died suddenly and unexpectedly at Westminster. The death was considered suspicious by many and at that point all the accusations of witchcraft resurfaced and various people were accused of procuring his death. Among them was Margaret de Vere, who was rearrested. Apparently she counterclaimed against the king, blaming him for Katherine's death. Why? My suspicion is that King Edward was the father of the child that killed her. I'm leaping to conclusions here, Joss, as you will immediately point out, and being shockingly unscientific and even romantic in my deductions, but perhaps some of this makes sense? What do you think? Could our ghost be King Edward — a tin man in armor?

Must go. Have got to teach lower fifth about Disraeli and Gladstone, God help me. If I could talk about Dizzie's racy novels and Glad's girls they'd pay attention. To the Irish question — not a hope! See you all soon. Regards to Luke and Lyn. D.

Slowly Joss refolded the sheets of paper and reinserted them into the envelope, which she stuck into one of the pigeonholes of the desk. Then she sat for a long time staring out of the window, lost in thought.

CHAPTER 25

The barometer in the dining room was falling steadily. As the winds increased the following day, rattling the windows and howling around the chimneys, the family congregated in the kitchen. By four o'clock Luke had sent Jimbo home and he too was sitting at the kitchen table, a dismantled carburetor spread out before him on a newspaper. He glanced up at Joss, unable to contain his curiosity any longer. "Was that a letter from David yesterday morning?"

Joss was cutting up pieces of fruit for Tom's tea. She glanced up at him, knife raised. "It was. He sends you both his regards."

"And has he found out any more history about the house?" He held the housing from one of the twin carbs of the SS up to his mouth and, breathing on it heavily, he rubbed the gleaming aluminium with a duster.

"A bit. Apparently King Edward IV visited here on several occasions. David thinks he fancied one of the daughters of the house." She scooped pieces of chopped apple and banana onto a saucer and put it in front of Tom. There was no way they could see that she was holding her breath, straining her ears toward the hall, wondering if someone was there, listening, someone who might resent her light, almost flippant tone.

Lyn was studying a recipe book with a frown, pencil in hand, as she noted down ingredients on her shopping list. "Of course, it would be a king," she observed quietly. "No lesser mortal would dare to chat up a Belheddonist."

Luke raised an eyebrow. He caught Joss's eye and grinned. "Not bad. A Belheddonist. I like that."

Joss laughed uncomfortably. "Is that what we are too?"

"Lotus eaters, one and all." He began stacking the pieces of metal back into an old cardboard box. Standing up, he walked over to the sink to wash his hands under the tap. "So, shall I put on the kettle?"

Joss nodded. "Then I'd better get back to work. I don't seem to be making much progress at the moment." Her deadline was not very far off, and twice now she had had letters from Robert Cassie asking her if she thought she would complete the book on time. They had only added to her guilt.

It wasn't until Joss had retreated to her study, cup of tea in hand, and Lyn had set Tom drawing pictures at the table with a box full of crayons, that Lyn sat down opposite Luke. "What really happened yesterday?"

"Yesterday?"

"You know what I mean, Luke. The lake."

"I fell in."

"Fell?"

"Yes, fell." He looked up and met her gaze. "Leave it, Lyn. I've told you before. This is between Joss and me."

"Is it? And is it between you and her when she hurts the children? You don't think those bruises on Tom came from the fall, do you? There were fingermarks, for God's sake. And Ned. How many accidents has he had now? Little ones, admittedly. A fall here and there, a blanket over the face. What about the things we don't know about? What is it going to take for you to pay attention, Luke?" She stood up and paced up and down the floor a couple of times. "Can't you see what's under your nose? Joss can't cope. She's depressed. It's all getting too much for her. I think she's hurting them. She's doing it. It's a plea for help, Luke, but who knows how far it will go? You have to do something."

"Lyn, you don't know what you're saying!" Angrily, Luke thumped the table with his fist. "You're her sister, for God's sake —"

"No. No, Luke, I'm not her sister. Not anymore. That's been made perfectly clear. But I still love her like a sister." She pushed her hair out of her eyes angrily, "and I can see what's happening. This house, the family, even these bloody ghosts she thinks are here — everything is combining to make her depressed. She's not writing, you know. I've looked at that manuscript on her mother's precious desk. She got to page one hundred forty-seven three or four weeks ago, and she's written nothing since. She just sits there, brooding."

"Lyn, it may have escaped your notice but she's

365

trying to do a lot of the housework as well as feed Ned and write a book. And why is she doing housework? Because you feel you're being asked to do too much! She's tired, Lyn."

"Yes, she's tired. I'm tired. We're all tired. But we don't go around hurting the children."

She became aware suddenly that Tom had put down his crayons and was staring at her and Luke solemnly, eyes huge, thumb in mouth. "Oh, Tom, darling." She ran to him and picked him up, swinging him onto her hip. "Aunty Lyn is going to look after you, sweetheart, I promise."

"Lyn." Luke controlled his temper with difficulty. "Please, don't ever say things like that again. It's not true. Joss would never, never hurt the children."

"No?" She glared at him. "Why don't we ask Tom?"

"No!" He stood up, sending the chair shooting backward across the floor. "No, Lyn that's enough. Have some common sense, please!"

Angrier than he had been for a long time, he slammed out of the kitchen and into the hall, aware of Tom's gaze, thoughtful somehow beyond his years, fixed unwaveringly on his back.

In the great hall he stopped in the middle of the floor and took a deep breath. He was letting Lyn get to him and it was crazy. He could see what she was up to — undermining Joss, trying to win him and the children away from her, planting seeds of doubt. Damn it, she almost had him believing it was Joss who had pushed him into the lake.

Around him the room seemed suddenly very

silent. Ramming his hands down into the pockets of his cords, he shivered, staring down at the empty hearth. A mound of cold ash lay between the firedogs, a scattering of small twigs around it. The room was very cold. He could feel the chill striking up from the flagstones into his bones. He was conscious suddenly of the sound of the wind in the great chimney. It was moaning gently and every now and then, as a stronger gust shook the house, the sound changed and took on a strange resemblance to laughter — children's laughter.

"Joss!" He turned abruptly and strode toward the study.

She was standing staring out of the French windows at the dark garden. The computer, he noticed, was not even switched on.

"Joss, what are you doing?" He saw her guilty jump and the way she reached for the curtains, pulling them quickly across to shut out the darkness almost as though she didn't want him to see what it was she had been watching. He also saw the surreptitious gesture she made to wipe away the tears on her cheeks.

"Joss, what is it? Why are you crying?"

She shrugged, still not looking at him.

"Joss, come here." He drew her into his arms and held her against him. "Tell me."

Wordlessly, she shrugged again. How could she tell him her fears? They sounded crazy. They were crazy! The images which haunted her dreams and her waking hours were no more than that — images which derived from some archetypal nightmare world where Luke was being threatened on every side and Ned and Tom were in danger of their lives and other people, people she didn't know, were running, fearful, through the house.

The young man writhed in pain, spittle froth-ing at the corners of his mouth, his hands clutch-ing at hers.

"Katherine! Sweet wife! Hold me."

"Richard!" She pressed her lips against his hot sweating forehead and soothed him gently.

"I'm done for, sweetheart." He retched again, his body contorted. "Remember me."

"How could I forget," she whispered. "But you will get well. I know you will get well." She was crying so hard she could hardly see his face.

He shook his head. He had read his doom in his mother-in-law's eyes. "No, my love, no. I have to leave you."

He too was crying as he died.

"Is it the book? Are you having trouble with the book?" He was talking softly, his mouth pressed against her hair. "Joss, you mustn't let things get out of proportion, love. It doesn't mat-ter. Nothing matters so much that you let it make you ill."

His arms around her were strong. Within their embrace she felt completely safe, and yet John Bennet had been strong; her own real father had presumably been strong, and what had happened to them? With a violent shudder, she pushed Luke away. "Take no notice of me. I'm being silly.

It's lack of sleep, that's all."

"Joss, you know Lyn has offered —"

"Oh, I know she has offered." The emotion in Joss's response astonished her as much as Luke. "I don't want her taking over Ned's life. I don't want her doing every single thing for him. I don't want him to think she is his mother. I want him myself, Luke. I want to look after him! She's stealing him from me."

"Of course she isn't, Joss —"

"No? Take a look at things." She tore herself out of his grip and went to stand in front of the computer. The screen was a reproachful blank.

"You take a look at things, Joss." Luke kept his voice deliberately even. "You and I are employing Lyn to be the children's nanny. We are giving her board and lodging and a small wage to do a job. That was supposed to help both of you. She needed a job and I suspect a home away from Alice and Joe for a bit to give her some independence, and you wanted space to write a book and get on with doing up Belheddon and researching its history. After Tom was born, you felt the restrictions of looking after a small child very badly, if you remember. Having Lyn here wasn't a plot to deprive you of the boys, Joss. It was to help you. If it's not working, we'll tell her to go."

Sitting down at her desk, Joss put her head in her hands. Wearily she rubbed her temples. "Oh, Luke. I'm sorry. I've been feeling as though my life has been running away with me. As if it is living me instead of me living it!"

He laughed. "Silly old Joss. If ever there was a lady in charge of her own destiny, it's you."

Joss put both children to bed while Lyn was making the supper and they were sitting around the table in the kitchen when Janet arrived. Shedding her raincoat in the back porch, she came in, her cheeks whipped pink by the wind, her hair wet and tangled. "I've got something for my godson in the car." She accepted the offer of a cup of coffee with alacrity. "It's so gorgeous I had to bring it straight over. Until he's old enough I thought his brother will adore it too."

"Janet, you spoil them. First Kit and Kat, and now — what is it?"

Janet beamed. "All right. I can't wait. I'm no good at building suspense. Come and help me, Luke. It's in the back of the car."

They disappeared outside the door, letting in a waft of wet night air.

Joss glanced at Lyn. "Have we got enough to offer her supper? Roy is still away at some conference or other so she's on her own."

"Of course we have." Lyn nodded vehemently. "You know I always make enough for two or three meals."

"Great." Joss nodded. "Lyn, I'm sorry I've been a bit of a bear."

Lyn turned to the stove so that Joss couldn't see her face. "That's OK." She was going to add something else when the door reopened and Luke staggered in carrying a wooden rocking horse.

"Janet!" Joss's squeal was one of genuine pleasure. "It's the most beautiful thing I've ever seen!"

Hand-carved in painted dapple gray, the horse had a rippling black mane and tail and a red leather bridle and saddle studded with brass-headed nails.

"Tom is going to adore it." She stroked the shining mane as Luke set it down on the floor by the dresser.

"I always thought there should be a rocking horse at Belheddon." Janet picked up her mug and warmed her hands on it. "I was so sure there must be one hidden away somewhere that I sent your brother, Luke, on a secret mission to the attic when he was here for the christening."

"You sent him up to the attic?" Joss stared at her, amused.

Janet nodded. "No sign of a rocking horse, he said. It was originally going to be a christening present, but then I realized how long it was going to take to make. There's a waiting list with this chap near Sudbury who makes them."

She chuckled as Kit and Kat, climbing languidly from their basket by the stove, crept up to the horse and, feigning indifference, inspected it from a safe distance before pouncing at the long tail.

"Another of your wonderful craftsmen." Luke put his arm around Janet's shoulders and gave her a hug. "Clever girl. I had no idea old Mat was poking around in the attic. He did that very discreetly." He glanced at Joss, but her attention appeared to be fully on the horse. "Shall we see if Tom is still awake? If he is, he can come down

371

to see it while Janet's here. As it's a very special occasion."

Janet nodded. "Oh please. Would you? Just this once? I know it was a silly time to bring it, but I only collected it this afternoon, and I couldn't wait."

"I'll get him." Luke strode toward the door. "It's the sort of surprise he'll probably remember all his life."

The kitchen was warm, full of succulent smells from the cooker. Kit and Kat, having examined the new acquisition in great detail, were curled up once more, safe in their basket, when there was a click and then a crackle from the baby alarm standing on the dresser. "Joss!" Luke's voice was tinny, distant, but sharp with anxiety. "Where is he, Joss?"

Joss stared at the dresser. "What do you mean, where is he?" But he couldn't hear her. Her frantic question shouted into the speaker of a one-way system was lost in the silence of the kitchen.

"Christ!" Lyn pushed away the bottle she had been opening so violently it fell over and rolled to the edge of the table, splashing wine onto the flags. "What's happened now?" She looked at Joss for a fraction of a second before she made for the door.

The three women ran for the staircase and found Luke standing in Tom's bedroom. The bed was neat and appeared unslept in. "The baby alarm was switched off. Where is he, Joss? Where did you put Tom?" His voice was shaking as he caught her arm.

"What do you mean, where did I put him?"

372

Joss stared down at the little bed in disbelief. "He was here. I tucked him in. He had his rabbit." A cold lump of something like stone seemed to have settled in her stomach as she stared around wildly. "He was here. He was fine. I read him a chapter of Dr. Seuss — look, here's the book." It was lying facedown on his chest of drawers near the night-light. She stared down at the new candle in the holder. She no longer entirely trusted the electricity. "I lit it. I remember lighting it . . ."

"Where is he, Joss?" Luke's grip tightened on her arm.

She shook her head. "He was here."

"For God's sake, she's obviously not going to tell us. We've got to look." Lyn's voice was shaking. She turned back out of the room and crossed the narrow corridor into Ned's. The baby was fast asleep. There was no sign of Tom in there.

"He's in the attic," Joss whispered suddenly. "I think he's in the attic with the boys." She didn't know how she knew.

The others stared at her for a moment and she was the one to run first toward the attic stairs. "Tom —" Her scream echoed around the house. "Tom, where are you?"

He was sitting contentedly in the middle of the double bed in the attic room that had been occupied by Elizabeth and Geoffrey Grant. Before him, in the middle of the eiderdown, was a box of wooden animals. At the sight of the faces in the doorway he beamed at them contentedly. "Georgie's toys," he said happily. "Tom play with Georgie's toys."

"How many times do I have to tell you, I put him to bed." Joss sat down at the table and put her head in her hands. "He was all right. I read him a story. I tucked him in. I put the side of the crib up and checked it. I lit the night-light and I turned on the baby alarm."

Tom had gone back to his bed with only a token protest, after twenty minutes' ecstatic rocking on the horse, asleep almost as soon as his head touched the pillow. Making sure the alarm was on this time, they left him and came back down to the kitchen.

Luke was watching her soberly. "Perhaps you ought to see Simon, Joss," he said tentatively. "Honestly, it might be the best. I'm sure it's no more than lapse of concentration or something because of your tiredness."

"There is nothing wrong with me." Joss rubbed the palms of her hands up and down her face several times, hard. "For God's sake, why will no one believe me?"

She was conscious of Lyn and Luke exchanging glances. It was Janet who came up to her and gave her a hug. "I believe you, Joss. I think there's something funny in this house. And I think you should all leave. Come and stay with me. We've plenty of room. I'd love to have you." She glanced at them all again. "Please."

"That's kind of you, Janet." Luke spoke firmly before Joss had a chance to reply. "But there is no need. There is nothing odd about the house which isn't in my wife's imagination. She has been scared by a lot of silly stories, and the sooner

374

we admit that, the better. I'm sure she's fine. All she needs is to rest. I'll get Simon to come over tomorrow and prescribe something."

"Luke!" Joss stared at him. "How dare you! It's me you're talking about. You sound like a Victorian patriarch! I am not imagining things, and I did not take Tom upstairs and leave him in the ice-cold attic to gratify my lurid imagination. And where did those toys come from, is anyone going to tell me that? I've never seen them before. If they were Georgie's, how did Tom Tom know? Oh, Luke, how could you think that I would terrify my own child like that!"

"He wasn't terrified, Joss," Janet said quietly. "Whatever happened and however he got up there, he wasn't terrified. He was having a good time with those toys, and that's the main thing, surely. There is no harm done."

"There's a great deal of harm done." Lyn's hands were shaking. Sitting down abruptly, she chewed her lip, trying to stop herself sobbing out loud. "When will someone realize that the children are in danger?"

"I agree." Joss met her eye steadily. "The children are in danger. But not, for God's sake, from me!"

"There is no danger." Luke gave a deep dramatic sigh. "My God, this is what happens when you have a house full of hysterical women. For heaven's sake, pull yourselves together. This is the twentieth century. The nineteen-nineties. Lyn, let's have supper. Please! We'll forget all this for now. Tom Tom is asleep and safe and the alarm is on, so there is nothing for us to worry about for now."

There was a moment's silence as all three of them looked toward the dresser where the small white plastic baby alarm sat between a bowl of fruit and the coffee jug. From it came the sound of gentle snuffling snores.

CHAPTER 26

"Tom Tom, are you awake?" Joss lowered the side of the crib gently and touched the little boy's cheek with a cautious finger. "Tom Tom, can you hear Mummy?"

He mumbled and stirred slightly in his sleep.

"Tom Tom, who was it that took you upstairs to play with Georgie's toys?" she whispered.

There was no reply. The little boy began to breathe deeply and evenly again, his eyes tight shut, his thumb in his mouth. Joss watched him for a few minutes in silence. Across the passageway, Ned, fed and changed, had snuggled back into his own small crib and both rooms, lit by the gentle glow of night-lights, were warm and safe. The sound of the wind playing among the gables of the house emphasized the silence and the gentle breathing of the sleeping child.

With a sigh, she turned away from the crib. Lying on the chest of drawers, just within the pool of light thrown by the night-light, lay a white rose.

She stared at it, feeling suddenly sick. It had

not been there when she walked into the room.

Don't scream.

Don't wake them.

Taking a deep breath, she clenched her fists, then slowly she turned around to face the window. There was always a pool of deep shadow there, where the faint candlelight never reached. The room felt the same as usual. It wasn't especially cold; there was no strange half echo in her head. A stronger than usual gust of wind blew, and she saw the curtains move slightly. Her palms were sweating. Stepping closer to the crib, she gripped the rail on the side. "Go away," she mouthed silently. "Go away. Leave us alone." She was aware suddenly that Tom's eyes had opened. He was watching her, his thumb still in his mouth. He caught her eye and gave her a big smile. Withdrawing the thumb, he held out his arms. "Kiss Mummy goodnight."

She smiled at him and bent over the crib, stroking his hair. "Goodnight, little chap."

"Tin man take Tom to play with Georgie's toys," he murmured sleepily. Already his eyes were closing.

Joss felt her heart do a somersault with fear. Stepping away from the crib, she studied the room again. There was no one there. Even the shadows were empty.

The rose was fresh, velvet to the touch and sweetly scented. It did not fall to pieces. She carried it into the bathroom, and for a moment she was tempted to try and flush it down the lavatory. Instead, she threw open the window and leaned out into the wind. As she dropped it, it vanished

out of sight into the darkness like a puff of this-
tledown. When she closed the window again, she
found her finger was bleeding where she had
caught it on one of the thorns.

"Joss? What time did you get up?" Luke came
into the study, rubbing his eyes, at about six-
thirty. "Ned's crying. You said you wanted to
do his morning feed." He groaned, running his
fingers through his hair. "God, it's cold in here.
Why on earth haven't you lit the fire?"

She stared at the hearth blankly. It had been
about half past two when she gave up all attempts
to fall asleep and, careful not to wake Luke,
had crept out of bed and come downstairs.
She had lit the fire then and, wrapped in a
rug, had curled up in the armchair, cradling
Kit on her knee and gazing into the flames.
Obviously, she had fallen asleep in the end.
The room was freezing.

With a groan she tried to straighten her legs.
"I couldn't sleep and I didn't want to disturb
you. Can you make us a cup of tea while I warm
his bottle?"

He nodded. "Of course. Five minutes."

Joss tucked Ned warmly inside her dressing
gown and, sitting down, abandoned herself to the
silence of the early morning and the gentle rhythm
of the baby's sucking as she gave him his bottle.
When the door opened and Lyn appeared, she
was almost asleep.

"Joss! What are you doing?" She too was carrying a newly warmed feeding bottle.

Joss opened her eyes. "I'm giving my son his breakfast."

"But that's my job!" Lyn was fully dressed, her hair neatly brushed.

"Didn't you see Luke in the kitchen? He's making tea. He should have told you I was doing it. I'm sorry, Lyn. Could you get Tom up?"

Lyn swallowed a retort and, banging down the bottle on the table, turned on her heel. "Perhaps next time you want to do it, you'll let me know so I don't have to get up at dawn."

"Oh, Lyn, I'm sorry —"

"No. That's OK. I'm just reminding you."

Already she had gone. With a sigh, Joss dropped a kiss on Ned's head, listening as Lyn's voice changed from nagging sarcasm to bright and cheerful. "Good morning, Tom Tom. Time to get up, sweetheart. Tom Tom?" The tone abruptly turned sharp with fear. "Oh God, Tom!"

"Lyn? What is it?" Joss stood up. Dropping Ned into his crib, she ran toward Tom's room, pulling her dressing gown around her. "Lyn, what's happened?" Behind her the baby was screaming with indignation.

Lyn had lifted Tom from his crib. "Quick, he's choking on something. He's turning blue."

"Push his tummy — quickly —" Joss grabbed the little boy, folding him across her arm. With two desperate gasps Tom coughed up a tiny wooden bird, vomited a trail of bloody spit, and began to cry in short rasping sobs.

"Tom!" Joss hugged him. "Tom, darling —"

"Sweet Jesus, why did you give him these? You must have known he'd put them in his mouth!"

Lyn had picked up a handful of the tiny birds which were scattered all over his bed.

"I didn't give them to him." Joss was trying to soothe the sobbing child.

"Hush, darling, please. Tom — please stop crying. It's all right now. Everything's all right now."

"Blood! Joss, there's blood all over the bed!" Lyn pulled back the covers. "Oh, God, Tom. Where's he bleeding?"

"He's not bleeding." Joss was managing to soothe him at last. "He's OK. Just very frightened, that's all."

"I'm going to call Simon. Look at the blood around his mouth —"

"It's only a tiny bit, Lyn. He's all right —" Joss was calming down far more quickly than Lyn now that the initial panic was over.

"He's not all right. Where did the blood on his sheets come from?"

"I expect from me. I pricked my finger last night. It wouldn't stop bleeding."

"So you were in here last night. It was you who gave him the toys." Lyn's voice was a mixture of accusation and triumph at catching her out.

"I am allowed in my own child's bedroom, Lyn." Joss's temper suddenly snapped. "And I never gave him those animals. I told you. I wouldn't be so stupid!"

"Well then, who did? Tell me that. Luke?"

"No, of course not Luke."

"Then who? Go on Joss, as you know so much. Who?"

"I don't know who." Joss cradled Tom's head against her shoulder. "Look, Lyn, go and ring Simon. Perhaps he could look in on the way to the surgery. Go on," she repeated as Lyn hesitated.

Reluctantly, Lyn went through to the bedroom. Behind her, Joss carried Tom through to Ned's room. "Will you stand close to Mummy while I see if your little brother needs a burp before I change his diaper?" She set Tom down on the floor, disengaging herself from his arms with difficulty. He had stopped crying at last. While he hung onto her dressing gown with one hand, the thumb of the other had found its way back into his mouth. Stooping over the screaming Ned, she picked him up and held him against her shoulder.

"Who gave you those little birds, Tom Tom?" Joss kept her voice as casual as she could as she gently rubbed Ned's back. He was quiet at last.

"Georgie." The thumb came out long enough for the one word.

Joss took a deep breath, trying to steady the sudden jolting of her heart. "I know they're Georgie's toys, but who put them in your crib?"

"Georgie." He reached for her sash and began to swing the ends of it backward and forward.

"Tom." She moved Ned to the other shoulder and crouched down to put her free hand around Tom's shoulders. "Darling, what does Georgie look like?"

"Boy."

She swallowed hard. Her mouth had gone dry. "What sort of boy?"

"Nice boy."

Ned was already asleep when she tucked him back into his crib. Then she squatted down in front of Tom once more and took his hands in hers. "Tell me about him. Is he bigger than you?"

Tom nodded.

"And what color is his hair? Is it like yours?" She fingered Tom's curls. He nodded. "Like Mummy's hair."

"I see." There was a lump in her throat which would not go away. "And the tin man, Tom. Was he there too?"

Tom nodded.

"Did he play with the toys?" Her breath felt as though it were being squeezed between ribs of steel. She couldn't breathe properly.

Tom nodded again.

"And you're not frightened of him anymore?"

Tom nodded a third time.

"You mean you are frightened?"

Tom's eyes filled with tears. "Don't like tin man."

"Tom —" She hesitated. "Tom, has he ever given you a rose to play with?"

He looked at her uncomprehendingly. "A flower — a white flower with prickles —" The other roses hadn't had thorns — none of them had had thorns.

Shaking his head, Tom poked at her skirts with his finger.

"Why are you frightened of him, Tom?"

He stared at her with huge eyes. "Tom go see horse."

Joss smiled. "You like the horse, Tom?"

He nodded vehemently.

"Right then, let's go and see him. You can have a ride while Aunty Lyn and I get breakfast."

The doctor was in the kitchen with Luke when Joss and Tom arrived downstairs. The two men were seated at the table over cups of coffee, talking in subdued tones, which ceased the moment she appeared. Joss felt a moment's unease as she caught Simon's speculative gaze on her, but she smiled and greeted him amicably. "So, Luke, what happened to my cup of tea? I was waiting for it with my tongue hanging out." Tom had released her hand and run straight to the rocking horse.

"Sorry, I got delayed." Luke stood up and went to lift him onto it. "Jimbo wanted the keys to the coach house. He got here early."

Simon, relaxed, in an open-necked shirt and heavy sweater, took another sip of his coffee. "So, it doesn't look to me as though there were much wrong with that young man of yours."

"There isn't." Joss picked up the coffeepot and shook it experimentally. "You managed to get here very quickly, Simon."

"Lyn caught me on the car phone. I was on my way back from the Fords'. Their fifth was born in the early hours." He grinned wryly. "Someone needs to tell Bill Ford to tie a knot in it or they'll end up with fifteen in as many years." He chuckled. "Forget I said that. Most unprofessional. So, young master Grant, I gather you've got a bit of a sore throat this morning. Didn't your mummy ever tell you not to put things into your mouth?" He opened his bag and produced a flashlight and spatula.

"What were you thinking about, Joss, to leave such small toys in his crib?" Luke stopped pushing the horse and stood back out of Simon's way.

Joss took a deep breath. "I did not give them to him. I am not a complete fool!"

"Then who did? It wasn't Lyn or me."

"I asked Tom who gave them to him." Joss had poured her own coffee. Turning away from them, she stood for a moment looking through the window out into the courtyard. The doors of the coach house were open and the light poured out into the still dusky yard.

"And what did Tom say, eh?" Simon's voice was carefully neutral as he peered at Tom's throat.

Tom pushed the spatula away. "Georgie gave Tom toys," he said helpfully.

"Georgie?" Simon switched off the flashlight. "And who is Georgie?"

There was a silence. "Georgie does not exist." Luke's voice was suddenly repressive.

"I see." Simon went back to the table and picked up his cup. "An imaginary friend."

"No." Joss spoke sharply from the window. She did not turn around. "Not imaginary. If he was, how could he give Tom the toys?"

"Right." Simon glanced at Luke, who shrugged. "Luke, would you mind?" He gestured toward the door with his head. He waited until Luke had let himself out into the courtyard before standing up again. "Why don't I give you a bit of a push, old chap." He went back to the horse. "There's no problem here, Joss. Just a fright. A bit of bruising locally, nothing more. So" —

he glanced at her, noting the tense shoulders — "tell me how you are."

"I'm fine." Her voice was still tight.

"Really fine?" He was still gently pushing the horse's glossy dappled rump.

Joss turned. "What has Luke been saying to you?"

"He's worried. He thinks you're doing too much."

"He thinks I'm going around the bend."

"Do you?"

He expected her to flair up at the question. Instead, she left the window and sat down at the table, her coffee cup in front of her. "I think I'm beginning to wonder."

"So. Who is Georgie?"

"My brother."

"Your brother?" He looked astonished. "I didn't realize you had one."

"I don't." She looked up. "He died in 1962, two years before I was born."

"Ah." There was only the slightest hesitation in the rhythm of his pushing as he noticed Tom's sudden tension. Releasing his viselike grip on the red leather reins with one of his hands, the child raised his thumb to his mouth. Simon frowned. "Where's Lyn?"

Joss shrugged. "Listening at the door?"

"Oh, Joss, hey, come on." Simon walked over to it and opened it. The hall was empty. "I'd like Lyn to come and give Tom here his breakfast before he starves so much he turns into a little tiny frog, and I want you and me to have a little talk. Lyn?" His shout was surprisingly loud.

386

They both heard the slap of her exercise sandals on the stone flags as she answered the call. She had not been far away.

"So, tell me what's going on." In the study, Simon took up a stance in front of the fire. Lyn had already made it up, Joss noted. It was burning merrily, filling the room with the sweet smell of fruitwood.

"What did Luke tell you?"

"That he thought you might be suffering from postnatal depression."

"And do you think I am?"

"I think it unlikely. Maybe you're tired and maybe you're a bit depressed — show me a new mother who isn't — that doesn't mean it's anything serious. How are you sleeping these days?"

"All right." It was a lie and they both knew it.

"And you're still breast-feeding?"

She nodded. "Just one feed a day."

"I'd better take a look at that young man while I'm here, too."

"Simon." She walked restlessly over to the desk. "I did not make Georgie up. You heard yourself that Tom has seen him."

"I heard. So tell me about it."

"If it were just me, Simon, I'd wonder if I needed putting in a straitjacket, but it's not." She shook her head. "Other people have seen them too."

"Them?"

She sat down. "Are you taught that irritating, unflappable tone of voice at medical school?"

He smiled. "On day one. If you can't do it,

387

they kick you out straight away."

"So you can sound as if nothing in the whole wide world can surprise or shock you."

"Nothing can, Joss, believe me."

"So, if I say the house is haunted, you won't turn a hair?"

"Not even one of my gray ones."

"I've heard Georgie and Sammy, my other brother, and there's something else." She couldn't hide the slight quaver in her voice.

"Something else?"

"Tom calls him the tin man. I think maybe he's wearing armor."

There wasn't a trace of a smile on her face. Simon noted the dark shadows, the pale skin, the trapped dull look behind her eyes.

"What particularly interests me is how Tom came by these toys. You and he think Georgie gave them to him. Does that mean that a ghost is capable of carrying things? The toys were clearly themselves real."

"I don't think they have any trouble carrying things at all." She was thinking of the roses.

"And that includes people? I gather Tom was taken up to the attic and has also fallen or been thrown from his crib."

She bit her lip, nodding.

"Have you asked him who took him up to the attic?"

"He says it was the tin man."

"Who you think is a man wearing armor. Do you believe him?"

"Who else could have done it? Luke and Lyn were in the kitchen."

"Joss, you haven't been suffering from any headaches lately? Dizzy spells? Lapses of memory?"

"Oh I see. You mean I did it. Of course, we had to come to that, didn't we."

"I have to check every possibility. You must see that."

"Right. Well, you've checked. Have you asked Lyn and Luke the same question? After all, either of them could have slipped out of the kitchen. Either of them could be lying too."

For the first time he looked uncomfortable.

"I thought not. I assure you, Simon, I am perfectly sane."

"And the bruises, Joss. On Tom. Did Georgie do that? Or the tin man?"

Her eyes flashed dangerously. "He fell from his crib!"

"And you're sure of that?"

She hesitated. "What else *can* I think? Simon, it wasn't *me*."

He looked at her for several seconds, then he shook his head. "No, I don't think it was. Joss, if you are unhappy here, would it be possible for you to go away for a bit — with the children? To stay with friends, or family. Just to give you all a change of scene."

She shook her head. "Luke won't go."

"I'm not suggesting Luke go too. Just you and the children."

"Not Lyn?"

He put his head on one side slightly. "Do you want Lyn to go with you?"

She shrugged. The idea of going away without

Lyn suddenly seemed very inviting. She looked up at him. "I sometimes think it would be lovely to have the boys to myself."

"That is not something you need be ashamed of, Joss. It's perfectly natural to want your babies to yourself. Lyn is an extremely efficient lady, I can see that. Someone you would be very thankful for under normal circumstances, but maybe she has taken just a bit too much on herself and you are feeling a bit left out?"

Joss sniffed. "Now you're playing the psychiatrist."

He laughed. "That's day two of being a medical student." He gave a deep sigh. "Listen, I have to go home and have a bath and grab some breakfast before going off to surgery. Think about a holiday, Joss. Give yourself a bit of a break. I think this house and its memories have got on top of you a bit." He moved away from the fire reluctantly and Joss followed him back toward the kitchen. Lyn was tidying up when they walked in and Joss caught the look of inquiry she threw toward Simon. "I'm afraid they're not going to section me, yet, Lyn," she said.

Lyn shook her head. "Of course they're not. I hope you've ticked her off, Simon, and told her to rest more."

"Indeed I have." Simon grabbed his jacket. "Farewell, ladies. I'll let myself out."

Straight across the yard to the coach house and Luke, Joss noted, as she watched him from the window. She turned to face Lyn. "I'm sane, sober, and exonerated," she said softly. "Please don't suggest anything else in future, Lyn."

Lyn raised an eyebrow. "If there was no need, I wouldn't dream of it."

"Good. We could manage without you, you know."

Lyn flushed a deep red. "That's up to you."

"Yes." Joss looked at her thoughtfully. "Yes, it is."

CHAPTER 27

Luke's office was an old suitcase in which he kept all his paperwork, to be produced once in a while and spread across the kitchen table, held in place by a cup of coffee, an apple, and a plate of bread and cheese. An office day was not to be interrupted by anyone, but on this occasion Lyn ignored the warning frown he gave her as she walked in. "Luke, I have to talk to you. Now, while Joss has taken the children out."

"Oh, Lyn, not again." With a groan, Luke pushed back a pile of bills and reached for his glass.

"Yes, again. How many times do I have to warn you? Something awful is going to happen and it will be your fault. You can't see what's happening in front of your nose."

"I can see, Lyn. There is nothing happening. Joss is coping very well. The children are happy — partly thanks to you, partly thanks to their mother, who adores them. They are in no danger from her or from anyone else. If you would just let this stupid idea go and let us all relax and get on with life I would be a lot happier."

Lyn closed her eyes and took a deep breath. "There were bruises on Tom's arm again this morning."

Luke frowned. "I helped bathe him last night, Lyn. The bruises are what's left from his fall."

"New ones. Luke, for pity's sake, please, you have to believe me. It's a plea for help. That's what they always say when a mother starts knocking her kids around."

"Joss is not knocking the kids around, Lyn." Luke stood up abruptly. "I don't want to hear any of this, do you understand? I can't believe you would say all this about your sister."

"She's not my sister, Luke. That's the point." Lyn's voice was suddenly bleak. "She has made it very clear. She is the la-di-da lady of the manor, I'm just an uneducated girl who is no better than a nursery maid in her eyes."

Luke stared at her, shocked. "Lyn! You know that's rubbish! Joss doesn't think that at all. How could you even imagine it?"

With a little half laugh, Lyn shrugged. "Quite easily, under the circumstances. You may as well know, Luke, I'm only staying because I love little Ned and Tom so much and I think they need me. Otherwise I would tell her to stick her job!"

He stared at the door open-mouthed as she went out, slamming it behind her.

"Lyn —" His cry of protest hung unheard in the air.

"My goodness you've walked a long way!" Janet pulled Joss into the hall of the farmhouse and helped her negotiate the double buggy around

393

the corner into her own kitchen. "You idiot. In this weather too." The afternoon had degenerated into a cold, blustery gray, laced with spinning leaves and icy needles of rain. "I'll run you back when you've had a cup of tea." She smiled as Tom, cheeks scarlet from the wind, ran to throw his arms around the neck of the old Labrador, who had risen from beside the stove to meet him with wildly wagging tail. "Joss?" Sharp-eyed, she caught sight of the tears on Joss's cheeks before her guest bent to release the baby from the cocoon of blankets which kept him warm. "What is it? What's happened?"

"Nothing." Holding Ned close, Joss shrugged. "Lyn thinks I'm hurting them, Janet."

"She what?"

"She thinks I'm battering the children." She sniffed hard. "Look at Tom's arm."

Janet stared at her for a moment, then she went across to Tom and the dog. "Here Tom Tom, let me take your coat off, then we'll find the bicky tin." Pulling off the little boy's jacket and gloves, she pushed up his sleeves. On his left arm was a series of bruises which looked exactly like fingerprints. She swallowed hard. Pulling down the sleeve, she straightened and went to find him a biscuit. "Most for you and only a tiny tiny bit for Sim, Tom. He's getting so fat." She handed the boy a piece of shortbread, then she glanced at Joss. "That wasn't an accident."

"No." Joss spoke in a whisper.

"If it wasn't you, who could it have been?"

"Not Luke."

"Of course not Luke."

"Not Lyn. Oh, Janet, she adores him."

"Then who? And don't tell me that a ghost did that, because I won't believe it. That was done by a real person, Joss. Come on, think. He must have been playing with someone. What about that Jimbo boy who helps Luke? His mother and sister were both a bit strange. Have you ever left Tom with him?"

Joss shook her head. "That happened last night, Janet. Luke helped me bathe him. Those marks weren't there then. And when Lyn dressed him this morning, there they were."

"And she thought you'd done it?"

"I'm the only one who goes to the children at night."

"Joss —" Janet plonked the biscuits down in front of her on the table and caught her two hands in a warm firm grip. "Is there any possibility you could be sleepwalking?"

Joss stared at her. For a moment she hesitated. "No. No, of course not."

"You don't sound entirely certain."

"Well, how can I be? But surely, Luke would have heard me. He'd know."

"Yes, I suppose he would." Climbing to her feet again, Janet went to lift the heavy kettle off the stove. "OK. Let's think of something else." She poured boiling water into the teapot. "What does Tom say?"

Joss shrugged.

Janet looked at her sharply. "You have asked him?"

"Not this time."

"Oh come on, darling, you can't not ask." Janet went down on her knees in front of the little boy, who was gamely trying to save some of his biscuit, now a soggy remnant of crumbs, from the Labrador's enthusiastic lick. "Go on, give it to Sim. You'll have to have another one. You can't eat it after he's woofed it!"

Tom giggled. "Sim's woofed it!" He was delighted with the word.

"And you can woof the next one. So, Tom Grant, you look as if you've been fighting a war. Who did this to you then?" She pulled the little boy's sleeve back again gently.

Tom half glanced at it, his attention still on the dog. "The tin man."

Behind them, Janet heard Joss make a strangled sound that was half gasp and half sob.

"And when did this nasty old tin man do this?" She asked cheerfully.

"At bedtime."

"Why didn't you call your mummy and daddy when he came?"

"Did."

Tom pulled another biscuit from the tin she was holding and broke it in half.

"But they didn't come?"

"No." He shook his head.

"Why not?"

"Don't know."

"What did the tin man do?"

"Hurt Tom."

Janet bit her lip. "Did he try to pick you up?"

Tom nodded.

"But you didn't want to go?"

Tom shook his head.

"Why not?"

"Don't like him."

"Tom, what does he look like? Is he big and tall like daddy?"

Tom thought for a moment, and the dog, taking its chance, neatly removed the biscuit from Tom's grasp. Tom smiled impishly at Janet. "Sim wants 'nother one."

"Sim's a greedy pig. Tell me about the tin man, Tom."

"Like Daddy."

"And what does the tin man look like?"

"Cat food."

"A cat food tin?" Janet stared at him, then she looked up at Joss, suppressing a giggle with difficulty. "Are we talking a bedtime story here?"

Joss shrugged. She was smiling, but her face was very white. "Tom, tell Aunty Janet about the tin man's face. What does he look like? Has he got a beard like the milkman?" Their milkman's beard fascinated Tom, who took every opportunity — of which there were mercifully few — to tug it.

Tom shook his head.

"Does he wear a hat? A big tin hat?"

Tom shook his head again.

"Once he gave you some of Georgie's toys. Has he ever given you anything else?"

Tom nodded. "Flowers. Prickly flowers. Tom pricked myself."

"Joss, what is it?" Pushing the tin of biscuits into Tom's arms, Janet climbed to her feet and went to Joss, who had sat down abruptly at the kitchen table and put her head into her arms.

"Roses. White roses."

"Right." Janet was suddenly brisk. "I don't believe what you're telling me, but whatever it is, I don't like it one bit. You are not going back to that house. I want you to stay here. All of you. There's loads of room. We'll go and collect some stuff when you've got this cup of tea inside you, and then we're all coming back here. Understand?"

Joss nodded weakly.

"Would you like that, Tom?" Janet gave him a hug. "Come and stay with Sim?"

Tom nodded. He glanced at Joss. "Tom have Sim's puppy?" he said hopefully.

Janet laughed. "Not a chance, old son. Poor old Sim is not the puppybearing type." She glanced back at Joss. "Drink."

CHAPTER 28

There was no sign of Luke as the two women entered the kitchen at Belheddon. In the courtyard, where they had left Janet's Audi, the coach house was locked and in darkness.

Joss frowned. Normally by now Lyn would be cooking supper, but there was no sign of any preparation. "I'll go and see where they are." She pushed Ned into Janet's arms. "Tom, you stay here. Show Aunty Janet how well you can ride your horse."

The great hall was in darkness.

"Luke? Lyn?" Joss's call seemed indecently loud to her own ears. "Where are you?"

The house felt empty. One of the bulbs in the wall light by the door had gone out and the other one gave a weak light which scarcely reached the far wall as she switched it on. The wind was moaning gently in the chimney as she reached the bottom of the stairs and peered up into the darkness.

"Katherine!" He drew her toward him gently. "My little love. Come, I won't hurt you." He

cupped his hands around her breasts and kissed the nape of her neck, then expertly he began to undo the lacings of her gown.

Naked, she turned to him, her body young and firm, her skin as white as milk. She did not shrink as he pulled her nakedness against him; her eyes were strangely blank.

As he kissed and groaned and sweated she gazed slit-eyed into the distance.

She was listening to the echoes.

Joss could feel the small hairs on her forearms pricking. "Lyn? Are you up there?"

Her voice sharpened. "Lyn?" She groped for the light switch and turned it on.

He was there. She could feel him, and this time he was not alone.

Immobile, with one hand on the banister, she waited a few more seconds, trying to force herself to put her foot on the bottom step — then she turned and ran.

In the courtyard she stood taking deep breaths of the frosty air, trying to steady the panic churning inside her.

"Joss?" Janet's voice from the doorway was sharp with alarm. "Joss, what is it?"

She shook her head, not trusting herself to speak, hearing Janet run toward her, feeling Janet's arms around her shoulders, shivering so much she could not think as she turned and buried her face in Janet's coat.

The headlights of Lyn's car cut a swath across the darkness before it turned through the archway and came to rest, focused full on them.

400

"Joss, where the hell have you been?" Lyn threw herself out of the car. "Luke and I have been frantic. Where are the boys?"

Joss stood transfixed by the beam of the headlight, unable for a moment to speak, and it was Janet who answered. "The boys are here. They're fine." The calmness of her voice cut through the icy wind. "Nothing is wrong. We wondered where you were."

"I told you I was taking them for a walk, Lyn." Joss moved at last, stepping out of the lights. From the darkness she stared around, no longer blinded. "Where's Luke?"

"He went across the fields after you."

"But why? You knew where I was going."

"I knew you were going for a walk. Hours ago. In broad daylight. Joss, for God's sake, you had two tiny children with you!"

"I told you I was going to Janet's," Joss interrupted firmly.

"No. No, Joss, you didn't. You said you were going for a walk along the cliff. A walk in the sun. Couldn't you have rung from Janet's when you found yourself there? It was too much trouble, wasn't it! And now I see Janet had to bring you home." Leaning into the mini to turn off the engine and the lights, she could see for the first time Janet's car parked in the darkness.

There was an awkward silence. Janet frowned uncomfortably, then she cleared her throat. "I offered to bring them back if Joss stayed to have a cup of tea with me, Lyn. If you want to blame anyone, then blame me. Where is Luke now, by the way?" Behind her, Tom appeared in the door-

401

way. He stood for a moment on the step and then jumped off it, running to Janet and sliding his hand into hers.

"He went after her." Lyn slammed the car door.

"When?" Joss swung around, and stared out through the courtyard arch into the dark gardens.

"Hours ago."

"So, where is he now?"

"I don't know." Lyn shook her head wearily. "He never came back. Why do you think I got in the car and started driving around? I've been up the cliff lane and down to the village. There's no sign of him."

"Was it daylight when he left?" Joss grabbed her sister by the shoulders. "It's dark now, Lyn. I went over to Janet's hours ago. So where is he now?" She could feel a sour churning in her stomach.

The only light now came from the lamp in the back hall, spilling out in a pale wedge into the thick darkness. Silhouetted in the light were Janet and Tom, hand in hand, their shadows, one short, one long, stretching over the cobbles almost to Joss's feet.

"Come in, Joss." Janet's voice was clear in the silence. "And you, Lyn. There's no point in standing out here and freezing. I'm sure Luke's OK. He's probably arrived at the farm by now and is trying to work out where we all are. Come on."

After a moment's hesitation, Lyn turned away from Joss. Stooping, she swept Tom up into her arms, detaching him from Janet and disappearing into the house.

Janet waited. "Joss?"

"He's out there, Janet. In the dark." Joss couldn't keep the terror out of her voice. Quotes from David's letter kept nudging into her head. "John Bennet . . . walking in the garden at Belheddon . . . was confronted by something . . . his sanity, already unhinged by the death of his son, completely deserted him . . . he remembered running into the darkness . . . Something . . . a figure, at least seven feet tall . . . ."

Janet reached out and put her arm around her again. "Joss —"

"He's out there, Janet. Can't you feel it? In the darkness. Watching us?"

"Luke, you mean?" Janet followed her gaze, but could see nothing.

"No, not Luke. Him. The devil. The monster that haunts Belheddon."

With a sigh, Janet shook her head. "No, I can't feel him. I can't feel anything. I'm too cold. Come in and have a hot drink —"

"He's looking for Katherine."

"Who's Katherine?" Janet's voice sharpened. "Joss, for goodness sake!"

"He kills everyone who stands in his way." Her stomach churning, her legs unsteady, Joss clutched at Janet's hand. "We have to find Luke. Janet, you have to help me."

The latch on the gate was jammed. Frantically, she scrabbled at the ice-cold metal, trying to lift it. "Janet!"

"Joss, I don't think this is a good idea." Janet was beginning to feel the fear. It was contagious. She looked around as a sudden icy wind ruffled her hair, listening to it swirling through the branches of the chestnut trees, and wishing, just for a moment, that it would stop so she could listen in the silence. "Joss, let's go inside. It's silly to go out there. We don't know where he is and we'd never find him in the dark."

The latch had lifted at last with a metallic click and the gate swung open. Above them the half-moon swam high behind a veil of streaming cloud. It gave enough light to see the leaf-strewn lawn as a paler gray in a monochrome world. Running onto the grass, Joss stared around — beyond the moon dusk, the shadows were black and unyielding, hiding everything and nothing.

Janet stepped beside her and caught her arm again. "Come inside, Joss." She spoke more urgently than she intended. "Please."

"He's out there, Janet."

"No he isn't." Janet wasn't sure whether they were talking about Luke or — or who? She felt another cold wash of fear drench her shoulder blades. "Joss, the children need you. You must be there for them. You have to pack and come back with me. Now. I have a feeling that we'll find Luke waiting at the farm when we get there."

"I suppose so." Joss was still hesitating. As she stared out into the shadows there was a movement near them and she tensed, feeling her heart flip somewhere under her ribs. For a moment she could see nothing, aware that Janet was staring at the same spot, then suddenly Janet's cheerful laugh broke the silence. "It's Kit and Kat, look!"

The two small cats hurtled out of the darkness, tails at right angles to their bodies, intent on a fast and furious game of chase culminating in a huge leap which took both animals high in the air before they disappeared into the wintry rose beds on the far side of the lawn.

The tension was broken. Without a word, Joss followed Janet back into the courtyard and watched as she fastened the gate behind them. Seconds later they were in the house.

Janet flung herself down at the table and put her head in her hands. "If you offered me a black coffee I'd probably say yes."

Without a word, Joss went to put the kettle on.

Janet rubbed her face with her hands. "What was that all about, Joss?"

"I told you."

Janet looked at her searchingly for a moment, then she stood up and went to the phone. "I'll call the farm. Maybe Luke is there. He knows where I hide the key."

She let it ring for a couple of minutes before hanging up. "Of course, he may not have gone in when he found we weren't there."

"He isn't there, Janet." Joss stared down at her hands, aware that they were shaking. "He's out there, somewhere."

Like John Bennet. Like her father.

"Get the children's things, Joss." Janet stood behind her, giving her shoulders a quick massage, a firm reassuring pressure.

Nodding, Joss stood up, ignoring the strange reluctance to leave the house which clung to her like a sticky, entrapping net. "Lyn must have taken the boys upstairs. I'll pack a case. Do you want to wait here?"

Janet shook her head. "Perhaps I'll come too. Give you a hand."

The kitchen, always so warm and welcoming, seemed very safe as they opened the door into the hall. The draft, sweeping under the front door, was icy.

The two women hurried across the great hall toward the staircase and, not giving herself time to think, Joss led the way up. Lyn was in Ned's room, changing his diaper. Tom, in his own room across the narrow passage, had tipped his playbox on the floor and was happily stirring the resulting mess.

"Lyn, I'm taking the children over to Janet's for a couple of days." Joss bent to pick up a small jumper from the floor. It was there again — the reluctance to leave, the certainty that it would be easier to stay.

"You're welcome to come too, Lyn." Janet smiled at her as Lyn looked up from the baby, a tin of talcum in her hand.

"It would be nice if you would come," Joss went on without enthusiasm. "Or if you want to take a couple of days' break so you can go and see Mum and Dad, I know they'd love that."

Lyn went back to her task, deftly folding and taping before replacing Ned's jumpsuit and sitting him up. "Is Luke back then?" She swung the baby onto her shoulder.

Joss shook her head. "There's no sign of him." She bit her lip. "Lyn, exactly what time did he go out?"

"About an hour after you."

406

"And you haven't heard anything from him since at all?"

Lyn shook her head. "He probably got thoroughly pissed off looking and went down to the Swan."

Joss gave a faint smile. "I wish I believed that." She glanced at Janet. "I can't go till I know he's safe. I'm going after him. Watch the children, Lyn. Don't let them out of your sight." She reached over and planted a kiss on Ned's head, then she turned and ran out of the door.

"Joss!" Janet called after her. "Wait. I'll come with you!"

"No. Stay and watch with Lyn. Don't leave the boys." The words floated over her shoulder as she took the stairs two at a time and disappeared.

Lyn looked at Janet and pursed her lips. "She needs a rest badly."

Janet nodded. "It will be good for her to have a bit of a break. This house is getting to her." She glanced around with a shudder. "Do you think there really is something here?" Her voice had dropped to a whisper.

Lyn smiled. "Of course not. Simon says it's a touch of postpartum depression. He seems to think she's doing too much. He obviously doesn't realize who does all the work around here. If anyone needs a rest, it's me." Her voice was tart. She laid Ned in his crib and tucked the blanket over him.

"You're going to leave him up here on his own?" Janet stood back out of the way as Lyn whisked around the room, tidying powder and diapers into neat piles.

"I'll put on the baby alarm. He'll be all right. If he cries, we'll hear him, and Tom Tom can come downstairs for his tea now. She'll probably be hours, then she'll be even more worn out when she gets back." Lyn gave a deep sigh. "It's not easy to work for your own sister, Janet —" She paused. "Adoptive sister, I should say. We are not allowed to forget our station." She banged a drawer shut.

Janet frowned. "You know, I think you do her an injustice, if I may say so. She loves you like a sister." She gave a sudden snort. "I should know. I've got three and we all fight like cats and dogs half the time. But that doesn't mean we don't love each other dearly. All for one and one for all if anyone comes between us. Don't underestimate the strain all this has been on her, Lyn. Finding her family and this house has been an enormous emotional shock. You and your parents are probably doubly precious to her. You are there for her, and always have been. Her real mother is something out of a dream which has, I suspect, some pretty nightmarish qualities."

Besides, there is something frightening about this house. She stopped herself saying it out loud in time. "Come on. Let's feed this young man, then when Joss comes back we can pop them all in the car and I'll take them back to the farm for a few days."

She glanced back through the door into Ned's bedroom. He was lying in his crib gurgling happily. She could see his arms waving in the air. Air that had grown suddenly strangely cold.

The beam of the flashlight was very thin as Joss ran across the lawn toward the gate. To her right, the black water of the lake reflected the frosty starlight, glittering between the darker patches where the water lilies, soggy and submerged with the heavy autumn rains, barely broke the still surface. As she walked silently through the frosted grass, a squawk and sudden rush of wings and water showed where she had disturbed a roosting duck.

The gate was swollen and hard to open. Pushing it with all her strength, she let herself out into the lane and stopped, shining the flashlight in front of her. The hedges, newly slashed by a hedge trimmer, showed raw torn spikes of white wood. In the distance an owl gave a series of sharp quick cries as it floated on silent wings over the field.

She swallowed, gripping the flashlight more tightly. Luke would have assumed that she would go down the lane as far as the footpath toward the cliffs and then follow it across the short rabbit-cropped turf to where the land dropped sharply toward the beach. It was one of her favorite walks, easy to manage, even with the buggy, and led around in a wide circle either back to the house or, if one took another path, across the newly planted winter wheat to the back of the farm. The whole walk was, she supposed, about three miles. She shivered. It was bitterly cold and the night seemed very quiet. Gritting her teeth, she began to walk briskly forward, shining the flashlight to right and to left into the hedges and down into the deep ditches which lined the lane.

"Luke!" Her voice was thin and lacked strength in the immensity of the silence. "Luke, are you there?" He could have fallen, twisted his ankle — or worse. He could be anywhere along the route. She stopped, shining the flashlight down into the ditch where it widened between the angle of two fields. Drainage pipes deep beneath the black newly plowed soil were pouring water beneath the mat of nettles and bramble, making the ditch sound like a fiercely running river. As she walked slowly on, the flashlight picking out the coral pink berries of a spindle bush at the angle of the lane, she heard the indignant metallic shout of a disturbed moorhen on its roost.

"Luke!"

Her boots were uncomfortable on the frosted ridges of the lane. "Luke, where are you?"

She swung around suddenly, flashing the flashlight behind her. Her heart had started thumping wildly. But there was nothing there.

How far from the house would he — it — travel? She swallowed, standing still for a moment, listening carefully.

"Luke?" It came out as a whisper now.

Suddenly she was running, the beam of the flashlight flailing in front of her as she slid and stumbled, turning onto the footpath across the grass.

She was panting violently when she reached the edge of the cliff. Standing still, she stood staring down at the sea. The tide was high. In the patchy moonlight she could see the water, a slate-

colored heaving mass, silently shifting immediately below her. There was no beach to be seen.
The tide was as high as she had ever seen it.
Raising her eyes, she looked out toward the
horizon. She could see the lights, a long way off,
of a huge North Sea ferry moving purposefully
and at surprising speed toward Harwich. For a
moment she was comforted by the thought of
the huge vessel, with its crowds of passengers
and steadily beating engine; then she became
aware once more of the immense expanse of the
sea around it and she found herself shivering violently again.

The path was so easy to see on the clifftop
that she switched off the flashlight, walking
quickly on the short grass. She could see a long
way and there was no sign of another human
being. Or anything else. She was conscious of a
sudden soreness on her lips and she realized she
had been biting them in the cold wind. She could
taste the sharp salt of blood on her tongue.
"Luke!" The call was fruitless. Stupid. A waste
of her voice, but the sound of it comforted her
as she trudged on.

She switched the flashlight on again when she
came to the midfield path, following the frozen
mud track over the newly sprouted winter wheat,
on up the hedgerow and toward the old orchard
at the back of the farm. She was miles from
Belheddon Hall here. Surely there could be no
danger. No danger other than the normal hazards
of the track. The flashlight wasn't so bright now.
She flashed it ahead into the gray tangle of old
apple boughs.

"Luke!" Hoarse with exhaustion, she felt hot tears well up suddenly in her eyes and splash down onto her cheeks. "Luke? Are you here?"

There was no reply. Behind her, on the field a flock of peewits called to each other, gossiping in the starlight which was suddenly as bright as day as the clouds rolled back.

CHAPTER 29

With Tom settled in his chair with a plate of cheese sandwiches, Lyn sat down at the kitchen table opposite Janet.

"Lyn, don't underestimate Joss's worries about the children." Janet hesitated. "Not all her concerns are imaginary, you know."

"The ghosts, you mean."

Janet nodded. "This house has a reputation for strange happenings — a reputation which goes back hundreds of years. I don't think they should be completely written off." She smiled, half apologetically. "There are more things in heaven and earth and all that."

Lyn raised an eyebrow. "I think it's all rubbish. I don't believe in ghosts and I never have. What you see is what you get in this world. And this world is it. Nothing else afterward." She got up and, going to the tap, drew herself a glass of cold water.

"And you can see no possibility that you might be wrong?" Janet spoke mildly, hoping her rising antagonism didn't show.

Lyn shrugged. "I may not be as well educated

as Joss, but I know enough to realize that religion is no more than glorified crowd control. It's brainwashing on a vast scale. Wishful thinking. Man is so arrogant he can't believe he can just stop being." She sat down and put her glass down in front of her. "You will have gathered that I'm a bit of a cynic."

Janet gave a wry smile. "Just a bit."

"Joss, besides being overeducated in my view, is also a bit hysterical." Lyn sighed. "Something which is obviously hereditary, judging by all this stuff her family have put in their letters and diaries. And of course the village believed them. Everyone loves a good ghost story. So do I, as long as one remembers that that is all it is. A story."

"So, you're not worried about Luke."

Lyn shrugged. "I'm a little worried, I suppose, in that he has been gone a hell of a long time. But I don't think he's been attacked by ghosts and demons. And I don't think Joss will be either. I would hardly have let her go off on her own if I thought there would be any danger out there."

"No, I don't suppose you would." Janet's voice was a little bleak. "Obviously, a few days' change of scene will benefit Joss and the boys, though, don't you agree?"

Lyn shrugged. "I suppose so. Anyway, I'd be glad of a break, to be honest. It all gets a bit incestuous around here — the atmosphere is dreadful sometimes."

"The atmosphere between Luke and Joss?"

Lyn shook her head. "Not exactly. Just Joss and her theories, I suppose. She believes it all so passionately I sometimes think she could make it happen by sheer willpower." She glanced up suddenly, her head to one side. "Is that someone at the door?"

Janet felt a small shiver of apprehension. She glanced over her shoulder. An icy draft swept through the kitchen and then stopped as suddenly as it had come as the outer door was banged shut.

"Lyn, has she appeared yet?" Luke stood in the doorway, still in his jacket. His gaze took in Janet and then Tom, earnestly stuffing bread and cheese into his mouth and his expression softened. "I see she has. Was she with you, Janet?"

Janet nodded. "I'm sorry. It all seems to have been a misunderstanding."

"And where is she now?" He stripped off his jacket.

"She's gone to look for you." Lyn stood up, automatically reaching for the kettle. "She thinks the ghost has got you."

"Oh my God, not that again." Sitting down, he gave a deep sigh.

"Luke." Janet leaned forward on her elbows. "Listen, please don't dismiss everything Joss is saying out of hand —"

"The trouble is, you encourage her!" Luke shook his head. "The last thing she needs, if you don't mind my saying so, is local gossip egging her on in these wild fantasies of hers. There is nothing wrong in this house. There is no danger to the children and there never has been. It's all in her head. A story. Make-believe. A romantic fiction she's concocted, with herself as the lead heroine. Don't you see, Janet? It's all part of her background. Adopted. A dreamer, bless her. Suddenly, fact seems to be even better than any fiction she ever dared invent for herself, and it's all got out of hand. Just leave her alone and she'll get over it."

"She was thinking of taking the children over to Janet's for a few days, Luke," Lyn put in quietly. "To get away from the atmosphere here."

"No!" Luke banged his fist on the table. "No, Janet, it's kind of you, but absolutely not. I'd be grateful if you'd just leave her alone."

"It's for her to decide, Luke, surely." Janet spoke as calmly as she could.

"No. It isn't. Not in this case. This is a matter between her and me."

"But —"

"Janet." He stood up abruptly. "Please, don't think me rude, but I'd be grateful if you could leave us now. It's time for Tom to go to bed. Please allow Joss and me to work this out for ourselves."

Janet stared at him open-mouthed. Slowly she pushed back her chair. She took a deep breath. "Very well. If that's the way you want it. Poor Joss." She glanced at Lyn, who had gone very pink. "Take care of them all. Tell Joss I'm there if she needs me."

No one spoke until she had gone. "That was very rude, Luke," Lyn said mildly. "She's a nice woman."

"She is sometimes an interfering busybody." He stood up. "I'm going out to check the garages are all locked up for the night."

416

Lyn sat for several minutes after he had gone, then with a sigh she stood up and turned to Tom. "Ready for your drink, young man?"

Pulling the carriage house door open, Luke stood staring at the bonnet of the Lagonda. In the light of the fluorescent strip which ran down the ceiling of the garage, the pale blue paintwork gleamed softly. Folding his arms across his chest, he sank into deep thought, listening as the sound of Janet's Audi died away in the distance.

"Luke?" Joss's voice was hesitant. "Luke, is that you?" She had appeared at the gate of the courtyard.

He sighed. "It's me."

"And you're all right?" Her chilled hands fumbling with the latch, she pushed the gate open and came toward him. "Oh, thank God! Luke, I thought something awful had happened to you!"

"Which is exactly what I thought about you earlier." He put his arms around her and held her close. She was shivering violently. "Why on earth didn't you say you were going out for the entire afternoon?"

"I did. I'm sure I did."

He smiled ruefully. "Well, never mind. You're all back and safe now." He pushed her away gently. "Come on, let's go back indoors. Lyn will be getting supper on."

"Where's Janet's car?" Wearily Joss looked around.

"She's gone."

"Gone? But I was going over there. I was taking the boys —"

417

"I told her it was a bad time, Joss. I need you here." He took her hand.

"Luke!" She pulled away from him. "You don't understand. I have to get them away from here. I have to." The net was closing; she could feel the lethargy, the reluctance, the pull of the house like a huge magnet, holding her close.

"No, darling. You don't. I think it's time we got this quite straight, don't you. An awful lot of what has been going on has been totally in your imagination. You have to admit it. Lyn and I are here to help you. There is no threat — none at all — to the boys. This ghost business is just so much hysterical rubbish on the part of people like David and, let's face it, Janet herself. Come on. Let's go indoors. We'll talk about it after supper."

"Luke —"

"Later, Joss. Come on. It's bloody cold out here. Let's go in."

He pulled the carriage house door shut and clicked the padlock into place, then he held out his hand. Reluctantly, she took it.

The kitchen was very warm after the frost outside. Tom, surrounded by toys, was playing on a rug in front of the television, halfheartedly watching cartoons while Lyn was peeling potatoes. She glanced up as they appeared. "At last. The whole family together. If you're going upstairs, Joss, you might look in on Ned. He sounds a bit restless." She dug her peeler energetically into a deep eye.

Joss stared at her. Then she turned and ran from the room.

There was a single lamp on in their bedroom. Tearing off her jacket she threw it down on the bed before hurrying toward Ned's little nursery. There was no sound from him now, just the soughing of the wind in the bare branches of the creeper outside the windows. She pushed open the door.

"Ned?" she whispered. She crept toward the crib. "Ned?"

He was lying on his stomach, his small fists clenched on either side of his head.

"Ned?" She bent over him. He was very still. In sudden panic she pulled back the covers. "Ned!"

Her sharp cry woke him with a start and he jumped. As she gathered him up into her arms he was screaming indignantly.

Lyn was in the room in seconds, with Luke just behind her. "Joss, what is it? Is he all right? We heard you on the baby alarm."

"He's fine." Joss cradled him gently in her arms, soothing him. "I didn't realize he was asleep, that's all, and I woke him up, poor little darling." She was shaking like a leaf.

Lyn noticed. She glanced at Luke, then she held out her arms for the baby. "Come on, Joss. You're cold and tired. Why not have a hot bath while I get supper? I'll take Ned and put him back to bed." She took Ned and gave a grimace. "I'll change him quickly first. Go on. No arguments. Have a nice bath. Get Luke to bring you up a drink."

Laying the baby down on his changing mat, she began to strip off his pajamas. Joss was just leaving the room when she heard Lyn's sharp intake of breath, hastily swallowed. She stopped and turned, in time to see Lyn pointing to Ned's arm. "What is it? What's wrong?"

"Nothing, love. Ned's had a bit of a bash, that's all. I expect he's knocked his arm against the crib." Lyn was frowning.

"Let me see —" She was frantic.

"No need. Nothing to worry about. Hardly a mark." She pushed her gently out of the room and Joss found herself staring at the closed door.

Exhausted, defeated and cold, she was suddenly too tired to argue. Walking slowly back into their bedroom, she kicked off her wet shoes and began to unfasten her jeans. Running hot water into the huge old-fashioned bath, she tipped in some bath oil and stood in front of the swiftly steaming mirror, slowly brushing her hair. How had Ned got bruised? Had she done it when she pulled him out of the crib? It was quite possible. She had been in such a panic. Or had something else been near him? Something, or someone. Her knuckles whitened on the hairbrush. Putting it down, she unbuttoned her shirt and pulled it off. Then her bra. Her breasts were still heavy and blue-veined; she surveyed them miserably through the condensation before turning to bend over the bath, stirring the water with a hand which still tingled with cold.

Katherine.

The sound had mingled with the rush of water in her head. For a moment she didn't react. Then

420

slowly, she turned off the taps. The skin of her back was crawling. Not looking around, she groped behind her for the towel on the rail, her fingers flailing in the air till at last they connected with it. Grabbing it, she pulled it off the rail and whisked it around her.

Katherine.

It was louder this time, easy to hear above the drips from the taps. She backed away from the bath. Wraiths of steam hung in the air, condensing on the walls. The water was growing cooler already as she stood with her back to the wall.

Katherine.

It was stronger again. No possibility of its being her imagination. She stared around wildly, clutching the towel around her breasts.

"You give her to me, but she does not love me!" The king stared in anger at the woman who stood so arrogantly before him. "I did not want a whore, madam. You promised me love in exchange for my adoration! I take her to my bed and she lies like a wax doll in my arms!"

Turning to pick up the goblet of hot wine, he did not see the woman tense at his words, nor the expression of feral cunning which flitted across the strangely golden eyes.

"Joss? Can I come in?" It was Luke's voice

that brought her out of her panic-stricken daze. She flung herself at the door and slid back the bolt.

"Why on earth did you lock it?" He had a couple of glasses with him. "Come on. I thought I'd talk to you while you have a soak. Lyn's getting supper and Ned is fast asleep." He grinned at her, then, as he noticed her white face, his smile died. "What's wrong?"

"Nothing." She shook her head. She was trying desperately to get a grip on herself. "Nothing's the matter. I'm just much tireder and colder than I thought." She took the glass, sipping at the white wine gratefully. "Sit yourself down and talk to me."

With him there she would be safe. Glancing around in spite of herself, she dropped the towel and hopped into the bath, lowering herself with a groan into the steaming water.

"Better?" Luke was watching her carefully. He could see clearly the signs of strain and agitation. Closing the lid of the toilet, he sat down on it and leaned forward, elbows on knees, studying his wife. She was still very beautiful, her body already more or less recovered from the birth, the only sign of which was a wonderful voluptuousness of breasts and belly which he found a great turn-on. Leaning forward, he put a hand gently on her breast. "Nice."

She smiled sleepily, submerging beneath the bubbles, feeling the water and Luke's presence comforting, reassuring. Closing her eyes, she reached up to touch his hand. "You're sure Ned was OK?"

"He was OK." His voice was calm, but he frowned suddenly. The bruises on Ned's arm had definitely been the marks of fingers. "Here." He lifted her glass and passed it to her. "Drink." Slipping onto his knees beside the bath, he pulled up his sleeve and, putting his hand into the water, he ran his fingers down and over and around her breasts, feeling the slipperiness of the bath oil on her skin, gently massaging and rubbing, sliding his hands on down over her belly.

She took a sip of wine, giving a quiet groan of pleasure. "Does it matter if we're late for supper?"

He smiled. "Not in the least. Lyn is putting Tom to bed. I said you'd look in later and say good night, but we both know he'll be asleep by then." His hand was still moving rhythmically over her breasts, making little choppy waves in the bathwater.

"Luke —"

"Sssh." He bent over and kissed her on the lips. "Am I going to get in there with you?"

She giggled. "We'd never fit."

"Then you'd better get out."

"I don't want to. It's cold out there."

He laughed. Standing up, he pulled the heap of towels from the towel rail and spread them on the floor. "Come on. You won't feel cold with your husband to keep you warm." He was pulling at his belt, sliding it through the loops, unzipping his jeans, then suddenly he swooped and she felt his arms slide under her. "Luke, you'll strain something!" She smothered another giggle as he heaved her out of the bath and laid her dripping on the heaped towels. Kneeling astride her, he

423

leaned forward and pressed his lips on hers.

Katherine gazed up at him and smiled. Her arms went around his neck and her lips, soft and sweet as cherries, seized greedily on his. "My love," she murmured. "My king."

With a groan he caught her to him, his hands running over every inch of her body, his tongue greedily questing over her face, her neck, her breasts, glorying in her heat and in her passion.

His cry of triumph and possession hung in the rafters above the bed and rang around the shadowy spaces of the house.

Contentedly, Joss put her wet arms around Luke's neck, pulling him closer. "Love you," she whispered. She opened her eyes sleepily, reveling in his warmth, running her tongue over the roughness of his cheek, gazing unfocused into his eyes. "Luke, I want to take the children away tomorrow," she whispered. "Just for a few days. Please."

He frowned. She felt his body tense. "Joss —"

"Luke. Please. Humor me." He was on the same side as the house, wanting to keep her there — not wanting her to go. She reached up to nibble his ear. It had, she realized, become suddenly very cold in the bathroom. She had begun to shiver in spite of the warmth of his body above hers. He had lifted his head to look down at her and she saw the anger in his eyes. "Joss —"

"Please, Luke."

She reached across him to pull at one of the towels, trying to cover her legs. "I'm getting cold,

Luke —" She was shivering so violently her teeth had begun to chatter. Suddenly she found it difficult to breathe. His weight on her was intolerable, pressing on her chest. Panicking, she pushed at him violently. There was something over her face, pushing over her nose and mouth, an invisible weight, pushing her into the floor. With a violent wrench she threw Luke off and staggered to her feet. Running over to the window, she threw it open, leaning out into the icy wind and taking deep gasping breaths of air.

"Joss?" Luke's voice behind her was sharp with concern. "Joss, what on earth is it? What's wrong?"

She couldn't speak. The stone of the mullions was freezing against the skin of her breasts, her fingers were locked onto the ivy-covered sill. She gave a great wheezing gasp, followed by another. "I'm sorry . . . couldn't breathe . . . I need a drink, Luke . . . water —" It was pressing in behind her now — the sense of someone close to her, breathing down her neck, closer, pressing against her. Luke had grabbed her glass of wine from the rim of the bath. Chucking the contents into the foamy water, he ran to put it under the tap and brought it to her. Wrapping her dressing gown around her naked shoulders, he pushed the glass into her hand. "Here. Drink this." She turned and took it in shaking hands.

The figure standing behind Luke was absolutely distinct. A man taller than Luke, and older, a man with anguished blue eyes and graying fair hair, a man with fury and pain etched into every angle of his face. As she met his eye he raised his hand toward her, then as she watched he dissolved into the steam of the bathroom and in a few seconds he had gone.

The wineglass slipped from her fingers and crashed to the floor. Slivers of glass scattered around her bare feet but she didn't notice them. She stared over Luke's shoulder for several seconds in shocked disbelief.

"Joss? Joss, what is it?" Luke swung around to look where she was staring. "What is it? What's wrong? Are you ill?"

She couldn't speak. He had been so real. So clear. The figure that had been only shadow and a sense of oppression to her before had shown himself clearly in all his pain and anguish, and she had made eye contact with him. He had been real. For those few brief seconds he had been as real to her as Luke was now. Blinking hard, she stared around, aware for the first time of the icy wind blowing in through the opened casement.

Somewhere outside the shriek of a fox rang out of the darkness. Luke leaned past her and pulled the window closed. "Come on, Joss. Into the bedroom. Let's get you warm. Mind your feet, there's glass everywhere."

He pulled the towel around her again, and put his arm around her shoulders.

"We have to go, Luke. Now. I have to take the children away." She grabbed his shirt and made him face her. "Luke, you have to understand. The children are in danger." She pushed past him and ran through into the bedroom, treading on a piece of glass which sliced diagonally into her toe. Grabbing at her dressing gown, she pulled it on properly. "Call Lyn. Tell her to help us. We'll take them over to Janet now. Luke. Don't look at me like that, for God's sake! Do it!" She slid her bleeding foot into a slipper and pushed her hair back off her face. "Quickly. Don't you understand? He has become strong enough for me to see him! The boys are in danger."

She ran through into the hall and stood outside Tom's room, staring in. The little boy was asleep, the night-light burning steadily on the table by the window. "Let him sleep, Joss." Luke came up behind her and peered through the door. He put his hands on her shoulders. "Come on, love, you're overwrought. Let it be. Come to bed and I'll get you some supper."

The shadow was there again — by the window in its usual place. Her mouth went dry; she stared, not daring to take her eyes off it. It was moving. Moving toward the child's crib. She could see the shape distinctly now — a man's shape, a tall, broad-shouldered man, his figure bulked grotesquely by some kind of breastplate beneath the flowing cloak.

"The tin man!" She didn't realize she had spoken out loud. She turned and caught at Luke's arm. "Look! You don't believe me? Look, for God's sake! Get him. Get Tom before it's too late!"

Luke put his hands on her arms. "Joss —"

The shadow was closer now, nearly at the crib. It was bending, reaching out —

With a scream, Joss flung herself into the room. She could feel it — a solid presence between her and Tom. Frantically, she reached into the crib and grabbed the small boy by the arm. Hauling him out bodily, she flailed out at the figure behind her. "Go away! Leave us alone! *Luke!*"

Above Tom's screams, she could hear Luke's voice, but she couldn't reach him. The figure was between her and the door. In her arms, Tom's cries were piercing. Across the landing she could hear Ned crying too —

Clutching Tom against her chest, she tried to run toward the door. Something was holding her back. Something was trying to snatch Tom from her.

"Joss!" Lyn's voice reached her through the screams. "Joss, give him to me!"

Lyn was there somewhere. Lyn was trying to help.

She stared around frantically, fighting her way through the blue folds of the swirling cloak, feeling a mailed hand on her arm, the fingers biting into her flesh as she clung to the screaming child.

She was losing him; she could feel her hold slipping. The strength of the man was too much for her. "Luke!" Her frantic sob was drowned by Tom's screams as he was wrenched from her arms, and then suddenly it was all over. The figure had gone.

Joss collapsed on the floor sobbing. "Tom . . ."

"I've got him, Joss." Lyn's voice was tight with fear.

"Take Tom downstairs, Lyn, and get in the car. Now." Luke was standing over Joss. He pulled her to her feet. "What the hell were you playing at? You nearly killed that child! I saw

428

you do it! I *saw* you! What the hell is the matter with you, Joss? You should be in hospital. You're not fit to look after the children." His voice was shaking. "Lyn's right. I should have listened to her weeks ago. I'm sorry, darling. But I'm not taking any more risks. I'm taking the children. Now. Do you understand? Are you listening to me, Joss?" He caught her arms and dragged her around to face him. "I'm sorry, darling. I know you're not yourself. But I can't risk this happening again."

"Luke?" She was staring at him. "Luke, what are you talking about —"

He stared at her, then with a sigh he let her go. "I suggest you have a good night's sleep. Then if you've any sense you'll ring Simon in the morning and get him to sort you out. Once I've got the children away safely I'll come back and we'll decide what to do."

He strode out of the nursery and across into Ned's little bedroom. Scooping a pile of clothes and diapers into a bag, he lifted the screaming baby out of his bed. "Go to sleep, Joss. Have some rest. We'll sort this out tomorrow."

"Luke!" She was standing staring at him in bewilderment. "Luke, what are you doing?"

"I'm taking the children away, Joss. Now. Before you hurt one of them really badly. I didn't believe Lyn. I wouldn't let her ring Simon. But she was right. It was you all along."

"Luke —" Her knees had gone weak. She couldn't run after him. All the strength had drained out of her. "Luke, wait —"

For a moment his face softened. "I'll come back,

Joss. Later. When we've taken the boys to Janet's. I promise, darling."

Then he had gone. She heard his footsteps, running down the stairs, and then there was silence.

"Luke." It was a whisper. She stared around the empty nursery, the silence somehow more shocking after the noise of the children's screams. The flame of the night-light flickered a little and steadied. Her own shadow, humped and grotesque in the candlelight, crouched against the wall near the crib, huge and menacing. She stared at it in confusion, hugging her dressing gown around her. In her left slipper the blood from her cut foot oozed steadily through the soft sheepskin, staining it red.

"Luke?" The small, querulous cry of protest had no strength. "Luke, don't leave me."

She heard the sound of the car clearly. Outside in the drive the headlights arced across the frosted trees for a moment, then disappeared in the direction of the village.

Tom's favorite teddy bear was still lying discarded in the crib. He would never get to sleep without it. Picking it up, Joss stared down at the silky brown fur and small beady eyes. It was wearing a yellow knitted jumper. Hugging it to her, she sank to her knees and began to cry.

It was some time later that the pain of the stiffness in her legs made her move. Staring around the room, she realized the night-light was flickering, the wick only a fragment in the last liquid drops of translucent wax. Still clutching the teddy bear, she dragged herself to her feet

430

and made her way back into the bedroom. The house was bitterly cold. She could hear the wind now, knocking the creeper against the windows. There was a hollow moaning from the chimney. Outside, the clouds were building and it was beginning to sleet. Her slipper was stiff with dried blood and her foot hurt. Making her way toward the door, she went out onto the landing.

At the top of the stairs she stopped and looked down. They had turned the lights off; the great hall was in darkness. She swallowed, her right hand clinging to the newel post at the top of the banisters, listening to the wind howling in the huge chimney. It was very cold downstairs. They hadn't lit a fire in the vast fireplace for days, and the chill of the autumn nights had penetrated deep into the room. She took a deep breath and put one tentative foot on the stairs, hearing the protesting creak of the oak. Her heart was thudding so loudly she could feel it in her ears. It made her feel dizzy, disoriented. She took another step down, the landing light throwing her shadow down before her. There was something lying on the stairs a few steps down in the shadows. She frowned. The others must have dropped something in their hurry. She took another step, staring at the soft glow of the polished wood on the step. It was white. A rosebud. She stood still, clinging to the banisters, staring at it, bile rising in her throat.

"Leave me alone," she whimpered into the darkness. "Do you hear me? Leave me alone. What have I done to *you*?"

There was no reply.

She took another step down, still holding onto the wooden handrail as though her life depended on it, and stepped carefully around the rose. Its scent was sweet and delicate, reminding her of early summer. She took another step, sliding away from it warily, and then another and another. A gust of wind hit the house and she felt the chimney shudder with the strength of it. Another two steps and she would be able to reach the light switch, illuminating the great hall, throwing gaunt reflections back from the glass, cold behind undrawn curtains.

Katherine. I'm here, Katherine.

One more step. Her hand reached out, the fingers grasping for the switch.

Katherine. Sweet lady, don't die. Wait for me, Katherine. Why did your mother not send for me, Katherine? A pox on her for her hatred and her scheming.

The light came on with a sharp click and she stood, her back pressed against the wall, staring out into the room. A dusting of ash had blown out of the hearth, scattering across the stone flags. On the polished table the chrysanthemums which Lyn had picked a week earlier in the garden had wilted, their petals showering in a ring of sticky pollen.

I curse the child that killed you, Katherine. Would that it had died instead of you. Come back to me, Katherine, love of my life and my destiny . . .

"Stop it!" Joss shook her head, pressing her hands to her ears. "Stop it!" The words were there, hammering inside her skull, echoing strangely without form. "Stop it! Leave me alone!"

She took a step out into the room, shivering violently, her hands crossed tightly across her chest. Opposite her, the door into the main hall seemed a lifetime away. She took another step, afraid to run as though it might provoke some kind of pursuit. Another gust of wind; a movement in the hearth caught her eye, and she stopped again, staring at it as a shower of white rose petals floated gently into the room from the chimney and settled on the flags. In the kitchen the two cats, cuddled together in their basket, awoke suddenly, their fur on end, and fled as one across the kitchen floor and out of the cat flap into the wind and icy rain.

"No." She bit her lip. "No, please." Only another few steps and she would be through the door down the hall and into the kitchen, then out of the house. She took another step, her eyes straining into the corners of the room, then at a sound behind her she whirled around.

The door of the study had slipped off its latch and swung open as with a violent crash the French windows, not properly fastened last time they had been opened, flew open onto the garden. Wind and rain lashed through the room as the doors were hurled back against the wall. Running back, she stared around in despair. Sleet was pouring into the room, soaking the carpet. She flew to the window and wrestled the doors shut, then, switching on the desk light, she locked them and pulled the curtains closed, out of breath with the effort. The papers on her desk were scattered across the room. She surveyed them miserably. The manuscript of the book — notes, letters, some of her mother's things, all strewn across the carpet, some of them, near the window, soaking wet. She left them. Running back to the door, she stopped dead.

The figure was standing in the doorway to the great hall, huge and clear as he had been in the bathroom. There was no armor now. He was dressed in black and purple, his dark blue cloak swinging from his shoulders as he raised a hand toward her.

Her reaction was reflexive. She turned and, wrenching open the nearest door, that of the cellar, she dived through it, taking the steps three at a time into the darkness. Sobbing, she fled across the first cellar out of the diagonal light thrown down the steps from the hall and into the total darkness of the second. Crawling behind the empty wine bins, she pressed herself against the cold damp bricks and held her breath.

The cellar steps creaked. Moaning, she crouched smaller, hiding her head in her knees, her arms clutched around her. She could feel him near her, his presence like an electric charge in the darkness.

Katherine. Come to me.

"No." She had stopped breathing. She could smell the roses — their scent filled the air around her.

He was close to her now, having no difficulty finding her in the darkness, seeing not a strange woman hiding among the wine bins of a twentieth-century cellar but the love of his life, lifeless on a bier — lifeless until he could breath life into her with his love and tear the child from her, the child that had stolen her life.

Katherine.

He put out his hand to touch her hair, scattering around her the rose petals they had used to pack her coffin. She was moving. She was alive, the wraith he had seen flitting through the house, the woman who was so like his dead Katherine that he had grown confused. One more time. Make love to her one more time and waken her with the sheer force of his love.

With a groan he gathered her against his chest, pressing his cold lips against hers.

Katherine!

She could feel the strength of his arms, the enveloping, stifling softness of the velvet wrapped around her, pinioning her arms, sapping the last of her resistance.

Katherine!

His breath on her cheek was icy, his fingers, as they began to open her dressing gown, felt like those of a frost-rimed statue in the center of a winter fountain.

"No." Joss's pitiful whisper was no more now than an exhalation of breath. Katherine was there; Katherine was inside her head. Her stomach knotted with fear and lust, she was looking out of Katherine's eyes.

"Edward! My lord!"

His hands were on her breast now, his kisses raining on her throat, her breasts, her belly. *Sweet child, you are alive.* She couldn't move. Paralyzed at first with fear, she could feel tremors of excitement coursing up her legs and into the muscles of her belly. Her breath was coming in short, shallow gasps. Her dressing gown had fallen completely open and now there was nothing between them: the soft velvet and the brocade and the silk had all gone. All she could feel was the hard urgency of his flesh.

Looking down into Katherine's eyes, Edward of England smiled. Gentleness was forgotten. This was his sweetheart, his woman, the mother of his child, the love promised and paid for in a pact with darkness.

Holding her wrists tightly in his massive fists, he kissed her again, enjoying her feeble struggles, knowing the fear in those brilliant blue eyes would turn soon to a lust and passion to match his own.

Katherine!

With a shout of triumph he entered her warm flesh and sank his face, sobbing, into the dark silken halo of her hair.

CHAPTER 30

"Joss?" Luke walked into the kitchen and stared around. The room was silent. Kit and Kat were curled up on the rocking chair near the range, a mass of black and white and orange fur. He sighed. She must have gone to bed. He had left Lyn and the children at Janet's, and from there he had phoned Simon; then he had climbed once more into the car and driven back through the lashing sleet.

With a sigh, he reached for the whiskey bottle out of the cupboard and poured himself a small measure, which he drank straight. Putting down the glass, he walked through into the great hall. Behind him Kit and Kat, scampering down the hall after him, stopped in the doorway. Their game forgotten in an instant, they turned and fled, their fur on end, their tails bushed. The light was on and Luke stared around. There was ash all over the floor where the wind had blown back down the chimney.

"Joss?" He strode across toward the door and looked out into the hall at the foot of the stairs where the lights were on as well.

The door into the study was closed. Pushing it open, he stared in. The room was a mess with paper all over the floor and the desk, the carpet soaked. He walked across to the window and, pulling back the curtain, stared out through the glass. The door had obviously been opened. Was Joss out there? But the key was in the lock on the inside. Turning, he surveyed the mess again for a minute, then he ran out of the room and raced upstairs, two at a time. "Joss? Where are you?"

On the rug in Tom's bedroom he could see slight traces of blood. Was she hurt? His stomach turning over with fear, he stared around, but there was no other sign of Joss; not in their bedroom, or in Ned's. He did a quick search through Lyn's and then on up to the attic. She was nowhere to be seen.

Cursing himself for having left her alone, he walked back downstairs and into the study once more. It was only then that he spotted the teddy bear, lying on the floor behind the door. She must have dropped it. He knew they hadn't taken it with them — it had been a matter of extreme distress to Tom when he found Ted had been left at home.

"Joss?" He felt the stirrings of unease again. "Joss, where are you?"

He walked out again to the foot of the stairs. It was very cold there. He shivered, glancing around again. In the great hall, in the shadow of the minstrel's gallery, it was very dark. He could hear the wind in the chimney. For some reason the house felt strangely sinister. No wonder Joss was afraid. He sighed. Turning, he looked back upstairs.

If she wasn't in the house, that left the gardens and — his mind shied away from the idea — the lake. It was as he was turning to walk away that his eye caught the cellar door. Surely earlier that day it had been closed and locked? They were so careful about locking it.

The door was slightly open, the cold draft playing around his ankles in the hall undoubtedly coming up from the cellar stairs. "Joss?" There was a tight knot of fear in his stomach as he pushed the door wide. "Joss, are you down there?" He leaned in and clicked on the electric light, peering down the staircase. It was very cold; he could see the dull gleam of condensation on the bottles nearest to him. Reluctantly, he put his foot on the first step. "Joss?" It was too silent.

He stopped, about to turn back, then on second thought he went on down. She was not in the first cellar. He ducked through the arch into the second one, remembering the fear he had felt the first time he had set foot down here. He could hear something now. It sounded like someone laughing. He swung around. "Joss?"

The laughter stopped suddenly, as though cut off by a knife.

"Joss? Where are you?" It hadn't been her voice, he was sure of that. It sounded more like children. "Joss?"

The silence was tangible. He could feel the small hairs on the back of his neck stirring. "Who's there? Come out. I know you're here somewhere!"

He stepped farther into the cellar, firmly trying to push the thought of Joss's little dead brother out of his mind. "Joss! Is that you?"

It was shadowy in here. The single bulb, suspended from the vaulted ceiling, did little to illuminate the end of the wine racks and the bins on the far wall.

Slowly he moved toward them and his gaze was suddenly caught by a dark shadow on the floor in the corner. "Joss? Joss, oh my God!"

She was lying in the far corner, wedged between two of the bins, still wearing her dressing gown. It had pulled open and he could see her white breasts, her bare legs, her slipper half off, encrusted with dried blood.

"Joss!"

She did not move.

"Joss? Dear God, are you all right?" He was beside her on his knees, feeling for a pulse. Her skin was ice cold and she appeared to be deeply unconscious; the pulse, when he found it, was faint and irregular, fluttering beneath his finger like some tiny thing which could die at any moment. "Joss! Hang on, my love." He didn't dare move her. Pulling off his jacket, he laid it over her, then he ran for the cellar steps.

He nearly collided with Simon in the hall.

"Sorry. I did ring the back door bell, but no one heard so I came in."

"Simon. Down here. In the cellar. She's unconscious. Oh, God, I shouldn't have left her! I was so stupid! I just wanted to get the boys away from her —"

Simon frowned as he followed Luke down the

440

stairs. "Did she fall down the stairs, do you think?"

"I don't know. If she did, she managed to crawl a long way before she collapsed. Look, she's through here."

Simon pushed past him. Like Luke, he felt for her pulse, then gently he ran his fingers down her neck and arms, feeling her bones. "I don't think anything's broken. There is just this massive bruise on her forehead. It looks as though she caught it on the corner of the wine rack here, do you see?" He continued his examination. "I don't think she's had a fall, Luke. It looks more as though she was trying to hide here — see how her hand is clasped around the side of this bin?" He loosened her fingers with some difficulty. "Just to be on the safe side I won't try and move her. I'll call an ambulance." He glanced up. "Run up and get some blankets so we can keep her warm until they get here." He reached into his pocket for his mobile phone. "Go on, man. Hurry."

"Luke?" Joss opened her eyes slowly. "Luke, where am I?"

He was sitting by her bed in the small, darkened room off the main ward. The only light came from a lamp on the table in the corner.

"You're in the hospital, love." He stood up and came to her. "How are you feeling?"

She frowned, screwing up her eyes. "I've got a headache."

"I'm not surprised. You've got an awful bump on the head. Do you remember how it happened?"

She lay for a minute, staring at the opposite

441

wall, her concentration fixed on a small print which showed a bluebell wood in spring, then at last she shook her head. Her mind was a total blank.

"I think you fell down the stairs." He took her hand and pressed it, drawing up a chair near her with his foot. "We found you unconscious. Oh, Joss, I'm so sorry. We shouldn't have left you alone. I feel dreadful about it."

"The boys?" She gave a deep sigh, her eyes still closed. "Are they OK?"

"They're fine. Lyn is with them at Janet's."

She smiled. "Good."

"Joss?" He paused, looking down at her exhausted face. "Do you remember anything about what happened this evening?"

For a moment there was no response, then she gave a small groan.

"Does that mean no?" He squeezed her hand.

"That means no." It was a whisper.

"Do you want to go to sleep, Joss?"

There was no reply. When Simon looked in some twenty minutes later, Luke was still sitting by the bed, holding her hand. He looked up.

"She came to for a few minutes, then she fell asleep."

"Did you call the nurse?"

Luke shook his head. "There wasn't time."

"Was she lucid?"

"Sleepy. She didn't seem to remember what had happened."

Simon nodded. He reached for her hand and took her pulse again. "There is bound to be some concussion after a bang like that on the temple. Luke, can I suggest you go home and get some sleep yourself. I doubt she'll wake again before morning now, and if she does the hospital will take care of her. Come again in the morning. Not too early, OK? Provided there's no real structural damage to that poor old head of hers — and we're pretty sure there isn't — the duty psychiatrist will pop in to see her tomorrow morning. We need to find out what she was doing in the cellar — why she fell — if she did. And we have to get to the root of the other problem with the children. It's far more common than you may realize in women who have given birth reasonably recently — there is a tremendous strain, you know, and if the hormonal system is not quite running as it should it can just tip someone over into doing things they would never in a million years do under normal circumstances. As the boys have you and Lyn to look after them, I'm quite sure that at this stage we can sort this out in the family. So, don't worry." He walked over to the window and looked out across the darkened car park toward the sleeping roofs of the town. "I might suggest, Luke, that you find somewhere Lyn could take Tom for a while so Joss can have a complete rest. Joss has more or less stopped breast-feeding now; she's told me that Ned has begun to sleep through the night, so she might consider letting him go too. I don't want to separate her from him, of course, unless she agrees, but we'll have to take the advice of the psychiatrist." He turned. "Is there somewhere Lyn could go? Grandparents perhaps?"

Luke nodded. "Both sets would have them like

a shot. But Joss —"

"Joss may need a complete rest, Luke. I'd quite like her to get away from that house for a bit. From what you've told me, it seems to be at the root of her problems. She's had a tremendous emotional shock, you know, inheriting that house and all the history that goes with it — and with the birth so soon after you moved, she hasn't really had time to adjust. I think a couple of weeks in the sun might do the trick. Any chance you could arrange that?"

Luke looked gloomy. "Money's a bit tight. I could probably manage something."

"Well." Simon folded his stethoscope. "Just give it some thought. We can all discuss it tomorrow when we see how she is."

The psychiatrist, bearded, gray-haired, and gentle, sat on her bed, sharing her grapes as he talked. He pulled no punches. "A touch of what we call puerperal psychosis, I think." His calm voice was strangely comforting in spite of the intimidating words. "From what your husband and your GP say and from your own story, I'd say that's the problem. It can make you imagine all kinds of very frightening things." He glanced at her from under bushy eyebrows. "Very frightening." He paused. "You are sure you can't remember what happened to make you go down into the cellar?"

Joss shook her head. There was a wall in her mind — a wall of impenetrable blackness — a wall behind which she did not want to look.

He waited, watching her thoughtfully, the si-

444

lence drawing out between them.

"No." She shook her head again, compelled to speak at last by his silence. "No, I can't remember."

He nodded. "Well, as I said, I've spoken to your GP and your husband and they both feel very strongly that what you need is a bit of time away from everything." He was silent for a minute, thinking. "I'm going to give you some tablets and I'm going to allow you to go away for a few days with your husband." He paused and then went on carefully. "I think your doctor mentioned to you the possibility of leaving the children behind. How do you feel about that?"

Joss shook her head. "Not happy. Of course, not happy, but Lyn would look after them, I suppose. I . . ." She hesitated. "I do want to rest. To sleep." To feel safe. She didn't say it out loud, but the fear was there, lurking; the fear in the house. She closed her eyes, letting her head fall back onto the pillow.

He was watching her closely. He couldn't decide whether she was suppressing the memory of what had happened to her consciously or not. Or was it just that she didn't want to tell him. On the whole he thought it was a genuine amnesia, induced by shock. The interesting thing would be to find out exactly what had caused it.

He stood up, tweaking the bedcover straight behind him. "So, enjoy your break. And I shall need to see you as soon as you get back. Just to see how you are."

"Paris?" Luke stared at her in astonishment.

445

He had expected protests at the thought of leaving Tom and Ned, refusal to leave the house, not this sudden, almost feverish desire to cross the Channel.

"We needn't go for very long. The doctors are right. It's just what I need." She had been reluctant to leave Ned and Tom with Lyn, but the suggestion that Lyn take the boys to Oxford to stay with the Grants had mollified her. She knew how much Tom adored his Granny Liz, and their big house could easily absorb three visitors and two small cats, whereas the small terraced house in London where the Davies lived would have bulged uncomfortably however much Alice and Joe would have loved to have them.

"I suppose we could afford it with the wine money." Luke smiled. "The only real problem is time. We've promised the Lagonda by the end of next month and there's a little Austin Seven coming in next month too, but if I can persuade Jimbo to keep things ticking over while we are away I reckon we could do it. Yes. Why not? It would be fun."

CHAPTER 31

Putting down the telephone, David sighed. He had been trying to phone Belheddon for three days. Where were they all? He paced up and down his small study once more, glancing at the piles of books and notes on his desk. There was so much information here. So much to tell Joss. Frustrated, he stared down at the notes he had been making that morning. He had planned to go down to Belheddon over half term and now he couldn't find them. Time was so precious when you were tied to a job like his.

He made up his mind in the time it took to pace toward the door and back to the window — four large steps, that was all. He would go down there anyway. Joss had to know what he had discovered. She had to know it as soon as possible.

The coach house door was standing open when he turned under the arch and brought the car to a rest near the kitchen door. He could see the lights on and hear from somewhere deep inside the raucous beat of heavy metal being played on something, the tone of which left a lot to be desired. Rather apt, he thought with a wry grin as he climbed out of his car and made his way toward the noise. "Hello? Luke? Anyone at home?"

The radio was switched off abruptly and Jimbo appeared from the back of the garage, wiping oil off his meaty forearms. "Hello, Mr. Tregarron." He gave a grin.

"Jimbo. Where are Luke and Joss?"

"They've gone to France."

"France?" David stared at him in shock. It had not crossed his mind that they might not be there at all.

"Went two days ago. Joss had a bit of a fall. She hadn't been well so they thought they'd get her away for a break."

David was shocked. "What happened? Is she all right? My God, I didn't know!"

"No, she's OK. They'll be back at the end of the week."

"I see." David felt deflated. His shoulders slumped. He hadn't realized just how much he had been looking forward to seeing Joss again. "And Lyn and the children? Are they still here?"

Jimbo shook his head. "They've taken the cats with them and gone off to stay with Mr. and Mrs. Grant. Somewhere near Oxford, I heard."

"That's a bit of a blow. I was hoping to stay a couple of days."

"I've got the keys, if you want. Don't s'pose they'd mind if you use the house." Jimbo turned to the workbench which ran down the side of the coach house and rummaged among his tools.

He produced a bunch of keys. "Wouldn't do no harm for the place to have some heat on. They asked me to keep an eye on things, but I haven't been in." He folded his arms with a gesture of finality.

"I see." David hesitated. "You don't have a phone number for them, I suppose?"

Jimbo shrugged. "I was told if there was a problem to get in touch with Mr. Goodyear at the farm."

"Right." David glanced over his shoulder toward the back door. He felt strangely reluctant to go in on his own. "Supposing I have a brew up. Would you like to come in and get some coffee?"

Jimbo shook his head. "I'd as soon stay out here."

"Right," David said again. "Fair enough. I'll go in and have a look around then."

He put his hand out for the keys. As he turned toward the back door, he felt Jimbo's eyes following him. The young man's expression was far from reassuring.

The kitchen was ice cold. The range was out and the room was unusually tidy. He flicked on all the lights, wondering if they had an electric kettle. If they didn't, he would have to fire up the stove and wait while the heavy iron kettle boiled. He scowled. The weekend was not turning out quite as he had hoped.

By the time he had made the coffee and carried a mug out to the coach house, Jimbo had gone. He stared at the padlocked doors in disbelief, then reluctantly he turned back toward the house.

He established a base camp in Joss's study, clearing her notes and manuscript into meticulously arranged piles on the floor under the table, well out of the way, and spreading out his own material in its place. He had had only a brief struggle with his conscience about whether he ought to stay in the house, uninvited as he was. But he had been given the keys by Jimbo, who was, it seemed, in charge, however unlikely that appeared to be, and he was after all Ned's godfather, which made him almost a relation, and he was certain, had Joss been there, that he would have been made welcome. Whether Luke would have been quite so welcoming he did not consider quite so closely.

He sat down at Joss's desk and began to read through his notes. First thing in the morning he was planning to visit the church. There were several things he wanted to check against the brasses and plaques, but until then he wanted to get a feel of the house.

He glanced up at the fire, which had been left ready laid. It was crackling merrily, already throwing warmth into the room. His research seemed to prove that the original house had been built on the site of a Roman villa; the building as it stood was certainly a substantial manor house in its own right by the early fifteenth century, probably a hundred years before that. It was the fifteenth century he was interested in, however. And in particular the reign of King Edward IV.

He ran through the dates again in his head. Three times, Edward had come to East Anglia in 1482. On two of those occasions Belheddon was mentioned by name and on the third by implication. David had made a chart of the king's movements. It was exactly nine months after his last visit that Katherine de Vere had died. For two weeks in the month of her death he had visited Castle Hedingham. In the previous year he had spent several weeks at Belheddon and in the year before that two visits of a week each. Katherine's marriage, he was prepared to bet, had been arranged by the king's command to give the king's bastard a father. The poor young man had not lived to enjoy his rather dubious honor; within months he had died. Of natural causes, or at the hand of a jealous man who could not bear to see his mistress as another man's wife? Probably they would never know.

David sat for a moment, staring out of the window. All those facts were, near enough, just that: fact. He had guessed perhaps at motive, and he had certainly guessed that the child that had killed Katherine was the king's, but the rest was the stuff of record. The remainder of his research had moved well beyond the realms of what was acceptable to a serious historian. He found himself smiling, alone as he was, in something like embarrassment. This was the matter of Margaret de Vere and her witchcraft. That she was accused was fact. That she had been arrested twice was fact. That she and the women accused with her were guilty as charged was something dismissed as rubbish by historians. The women had been framed by the supporters of Edward's brother, Richard. But. He ran over the facts again. The first time Margaret was arrested, it was by Edward's orders, shortly after a visit by him to Belheddon Hall. There was no question then of her being framed by anyone — unless it was by Edward himself, and why would he want to frame (and, by implication, get rid of) his hostess, the mother of the young woman he loved? Unless she opposed him. But surely it made no sense at all to oppose a match, even one on the wrong side of the blanket, with the king himself? No ambitious woman of the period would do that if she were in her right mind.

Unless she really was a witch.

He had trouble with this. Big trouble. Witchcraft could not be real. Or could it? Feminists always thought accusations of witchcraft were macho-male-misogynist politically inspired, didn't they? Witchcraft either did not exist at all, and was drummed up as a charge by these fearsome women haters, or was a harmless, indeed benevolent, remnant of some pre-Christian paganism dating from a Golden Age which had never existed. But which antagonized a male-macho-etc. Christian hierarchy.

Supposing neither was true? Supposing the witchcraft as practiced by Margaret de Vere was real, effective, and as malevolent as popular myth described it?

He gazed into the warm, cheerful depths of the fire and wished Joss were here. He would like to argue this out with her. Without her acerbic comments to keep him in line, he was floundering deeper and deeper into a mire. Could Margaret have killed and/or cursed King Edward IV? And could that curse, effective five hundred

452

years later, still be blighting the house where she had uttered it? The thought which haunted him, one that had arrived unbidden as he lay sleepless one night in his London flat mulling over the problem, was a simple one. Did Margaret de Vere kill her daughter's baby by the king? And had the curse, raging out of control, threatened every boy baby born in the house ever since?

He shuddered. Not the best thing to think about if he was going to spend the night alone in the place. Not the best thing at all.

He stood up and went to stand near the fire, stooping absentmindedly to throw on a log. It was very quiet without the others there. He stared down into the flames, watching them lick greedily over the wood. Quiet and somehow brooding. He gave himself a mental shake. He did not believe in ghosts, nor the power of the occult. It was an intriguing theory, but one based solely on the superstition and gullibility of its audience. It might — would — have worked in the fifteenth century. It could still work presumably in the twentieth but only by association; it relied on rumor and fear and ignorance to give it energy. He turned his back on the fire, massaging his backside in the warmth. Yet Joss believed it. She was neither ignorant nor gullible, nor, as far as he could remember, superstitious. He frowned. She was, though, a woman with two small children and through them desperately vulnerable.

The sound of scuffling in the hall was very small. He hardly heard it above the crackle and hiss of the fire. Stiffening, he listened, every ounce of his attention fixed, not conscious before just how twitchy he had been. He felt the sweat start out on the palms of his hands. It couldn't be the cats. It was his imagination — or, at worst, mice.

Cautiously, he tiptoed away from the fire toward the door, listening as hard as he could, cursing the fact that the dry log he had thrown on was crackling and spitting merrily and noisily behind him. He put his hand on the doorknob and waited, his ear to the paneling. Nothing. There was no sound. He stood there for a couple of minutes before gently beginning to turn the knob.

The hallway outside was in darkness. He frowned. Had he forgotten to turn on the light? Of course, it had not been dark when he came into the study. The early dusk of November had fallen swiftly and like a blanket across the garden. Pushing the door wide so the light from the study fell across the floor, he took a step forward, his hand raised toward the light switch.

The scuffling came from above him this time, on the broad staircase, where it swept around out of sight into the darkness. It took all his resolution not to dive back into the study and slam the door. Instead, he took another step forward and turned on the light, then he looked up. Silence. His back to the wall, he listened, frowning. He had the very strong impression that there was someone up there, sitting on the stairs, just out of sight.

"Who's there?" His voice sounded shockingly loud. "Come on. I can see you."

There was a suppressed gurgle of laughter — a child's laughter — and then he heard the thud of footsteps as someone ran on up the stairs. He swallowed hard. Children from the village? Or Joss's ghosts. He licked his dry lips, not moving. "Sam? Georgie?" This was ridiculous. All he was proving was that he was as superstitious and gullible as the next man when it came to spending a night alone in a haunted house. "Come on, Tregarron. Pull yourself together." He spoke under his breath. "You've got to go up there. You've got to search the place. Supposing they're thieves. Or vandals!" He did not move. His limbs seemed anchored to the spot. Behind him the study was warm and welcoming. His coffee was getting cold. Cautiously, a step at a time, he retreated into the study, leaving the lights on, and pulled the door closed. Mug in hand, he went sheepishly to the telephone and picked it up. The Goodyears were in the phone book.

"I didn't realize that Joss and Luke were away. I feel a bit of a fool — here on my own — I wondered if I could ask you both over for a drink. I'm sure they won't mind." He glanced at the windows, seeing his own reflection, upright, tense, on the edge of the chair, staring back at himself in the glass. He should have drawn the curtains at once, before he phoned.

"Oh, I see." He tried to keep the disappointment and fear out of his voice as Roy explained that they were going out. Laughing, he brushed off Roy's apology. "Not to worry. Next time, perhaps. No, no. I'm going back to town early tomorrow. Goodnight." He replaced the receiver with a shaking hand. Getting up, he went to the curtains and pulled them across, then he wandered over to the desk and stood looking down at his meticulously written notes.

Georgie!

He looked up at the door, shocked. The voice had been so close. So clear.

Georgie!

He clenched his fists. They're only children. They can't hurt me.

What am I saying. They don't exist.

His mind was whirling into activity now. Superstitious nonsense. Idiot. Ignoramus. I don't believe this.

Slamming his notes into a pile, he strode toward the door and threw it open. There was no one there. Moving swiftly toward the stairs, he ran up them two at a time, not giving himself time to think as he reached for the landing light. "Where are you?" His voice was stronger now. "Come on. I want you out of here." He strode into Joss and Luke's bedroom. It was tidy, strangely impersonal without them there, and empty. Swiftly he headed for the door, searching Ned's little room, then Tom's. Both were empty. He went into Lyn's next, then, not giving himself time to think, he ran on up toward the attic, searching the two spare rooms, pausing at last before the door that led through into the empty rooms. Surely there was no need to search those? But of course there is, he lectured himself furiously. Don't be a fool. Pulling open the door, he hesitated, staring into the darkness. There appeared to be no light switch here. Perhaps there were no lights. He could smell the slightly damp, cold smell of emptiness and disuse, and at last he conceded defeat. He closed the door again and turned back to the stairs.

A small painted wooden car lay discarded on its side on the top step of the staircase. He stared down at it, his arms and back crawling with fear. It had not been there a few moments before. If it had been, he could hardly have avoided seeing it. He would have fallen over it. He stared down at it in horror, then, overcome by curiosity, he bent and picked it up. It was about four inches long and two inches high, crudely made and painted a bright blue, though the paint was worn and chipped. He turned it over in his hands, then, slipping it into the pocket of his jeans, he ran on down the stairs, leaving all the lights on behind him.

In the kitchen the stove had heated up enough to put something in the oven. He rummaged through the freezer and found a foil-wrapped package labeled steak and kidney pie. Heaven knows how one was supposed to cook it, but he supposed if he stuck it in the oven until it was done it would be all right. He put the whole thing, foil and all, into a baking tin, put it in the oven, and reached for Luke's whiskey on the dresser. Then he pulled out the car. Standing alone on the kitchen table, it looked shabby and forlorn — and distinctly old. Toys these days were made of plastic or metal; they were brightly colored and nontoxic. This looked as though it would be eminently toxic. The paint was flaking off even as he touched it. He frowned. Ghosts didn't have toys. Or did they, if they were little boys, trapped in a house where they would never grow up? He frowned, taking a deep swig of Scotch, hoping that Margaret de Vere, if she was guilty of witchcraft as charged, was having a really bad time in hell.

One of the books he had brought with him to show Joss was a history of magic in the Middle Ages. He had left it on her desk in the study. Putting down his glass, he went to fetch it, gathering up an armful of books while he was there to bring back to the comparative warmth of the kitchen. It felt more comfortable there. He would read while he was waiting for his foil-wrapped package to cook or self-destruct, depending on which happened first. Pouring another drink and slopping in some water, he spread the books out and opened the book on magic.

Twice he looked up, listening. It was strange how the silence at this end of the house was companionable, not threatening. He felt safe here, even content, as slowly the smell of cooking steak and rich gravy began to permeate the room.

Procuring people's deaths by magic was a common enough charge in the Middle Ages; any sudden death was immediately suspect. With minimal medical knowledge and even less forensic, what else was there to fall back on? He sighed, flicking through the book. He was right, wasn't he, in dismissing magic as nonsense? His gaze strayed to the little car on the table near him. Supposing Margaret de Vere had real power? Had she caused the king to fall in love with her daughter? Had she gone on, when her scheme had gone tragically wrong, to bring about the downfall of both king and bastard child? Was it possible? If so, where had she got the knowledge from? Picking up the car, he turned it over and over in his hands as though seeking inspiration from the small wooden toy. The legends of the devil at Belheddon went back into the mists of time. They seemed to pre-date Christianity. She must have known about them too. Was that where she had got her power?

He gave an involuntary shudder. Putting down the car, he got up and went to the oven, pulling the baking tray out with hands padded with dish cloths. He examined his supper. Inside the foil there was a solidly frozen amorphous lump inside a gloriously rich mess of gravy and meat. The pastry appeared to have disintegrated into a soggy mess. He shrugged, pushing the whole lot back in the oven again. No doubt it would taste nice, whatever it looked like.

Did she conjure the devil? Did she swap her eternal soul for power? He wished he had paid more attention to the stories and legends which he had always dismissed as philosophical hogwash. He was beginning to feel grave doubts about all this.

On a sudden impulse he went to the dresser and pulled the phone book out from its position under the telephone. Edgar Gower's Aldeburgh number was listed.

The clergyman listened carefully as David spoke. He was sitting at his desk overlooking the blackness of the sea, twiddling a pencil in his hand. From time to time he made notes, frowning. "Dr. Tregarron, I think you and I should meet." He shifted in his seat slightly so the reflections moved in the window. He was watching the lights of a fishing boat far out at sea, moving slowly up the coast. "When will you next be coming up to East Anglia?"

"I'm here. Now." David carried the phone to the table and sat down. The smell of steak and kidney was getting stronger and more mouth-watering.

"Here?" The voice at the other end of the line had sharpened.

"I came up this morning. I'm at Belheddon." He reached out and put his finger on the roof of the little car, running it up and down the table.

"I see." There was a long pause. "You're there alone, I gather?"

"Luke and Joss have gone to Paris."

"And the children?"

"I understand they're with their grandmother."

"But not at Belheddon."

"No. Not at Belheddon." There was a moment's silence as both men had the same thought: Thank God.

"Dr. Tregarron." Edgar could no longer see the ship. "A thought has struck me. If you would like to drive to Aldeburgh, we are only about an hour away. It would be good to talk this over, and" — he added casually — "you might like to stay the night here."

David closed his eyes, overwhelmed by a rush

of relief. "That's good of you. Very good."

The urge to abandon everything and leap into his car was very strong. It was his pride which stopped him. He would eat his supper, collect his books and papers, and then check the house and turn off the lights before he left. He glared at the whiskey bottle. He had probably had too much of the damn stuff to drive without some food inside him anyway.

The pie, though messy and in some part disintegrated, was good. He ate it swiftly with relish straight out of the foil. Washing up his fork and glass, he banked up the stove and then turned toward the door.

He forced himself to go upstairs first, turning off the lights, closing doors. The house was quiet, even benign. Checking Joss and Luke's room, though, was different. He stood for a moment in the center of the floor, listening intently. The silence was heavy, almost tangible. There had been some sort of shift in the atmosphere. It was as if someone or something was watching him. He swallowed hard. Heading for the door and clicking off the light, he went out onto the landing. He could feel it there too: a brooding resentment, a chill that had nothing to do with the physical cold in the house.

Ignore it. Collect the books and go. He put his hand on the top of the banisters and looked down. In the bright cold light of the hall he could see the toys lying all over the floor. Cars, like the one he had left on the kitchen table; pieces of meccano, a pencil box . . .

"OK." He spoke out loud, his lips dry. "Point

taken. I'm on my way." It took an enormous amount of willpower to walk down the stairs, to step over the scattered toys, and go into the study. He looked around, expecting to see something in there as well, but the room seemed much as he had left it. The fire had died down and it was cold, but otherwise the room felt friendly, almost safe. He prodded the fire flat and put the guard in front of it to be doubly safe, then heaped his papers and books together into his arms. One quick glance around and he was ready. Switching off the light, he closed the door behind him.

In the hall he hesitated for a moment, then, stooping, he scooped some pieces of meccano and a car into his pocket. "I'll bring them back, lads," he said out loud. "Just want to check something."

The giggle behind him came from the staircase out of sight beyond the curve. He glanced up. He was not going to go up or run away. They were only kids. Kids teasing. They couldn't hurt him.

Could they?

Hesitating, he glanced up again. "So long, boys," he said softly. "God bless."

Pulling the back door shut behind him, he heard the lock click. He threw his books into the car and climbed in. It was only as he slammed the locks down that he realized he was shaking all over. It was several seconds before he could get his key into the ignition. As the car shot through the courtyard arch and out into the drive, he glanced once into the rearview mirror. The windows of the house were all once more blazing with light. Putting his foot on the accelerator, he skidded down the drive and out into the road.

CHAPTER 32

They had picked up a taxi at Les Invalides after an easy flight from Stansted to Orly and gone straight to their hotel near the Etoile. Joss was very quiet. Each time Luke looked at her she seemed more withdrawn and pale. By the time they had paid off the driver and found their room, she looked as though she were about to collapse.

"Do you want to ring mother and see how the boys are?" He sat down next to her on the bed. Outside, the traffic was roaring down the street, tires rattling over the *pavé*. They could smell coffee and garlic and wine from the café across the road opposite their window as their net curtains blew inward on a strong draft. He stood up and went to close the window, then he sat down next to her again.

"So, what are we going to do?" He took her hand after she had made the call. "They're well. They're happy, and they're absolutely safe, so you have nothing to worry about except how we are going to amuse ourselves!"

Joss took a deep breath and as she let it out she could feel her tension dropping away. She was safe. The children were safe. Luke was safe. Outside, the roar of traffic down the road, only slightly muffled by the closed window and its swath of white net curtain, was a comforting balm. Unexpectedly, she threw herself back on the bed and stretched her arms luxuriously above her head. Later she would think about her mother's Frenchman, but now, just for a while, she needed to relax. For the moment Belheddon was very far away. She had escaped.

Luke looked down at her and smiled. "Paris seems to be doing you good already."

"It is." She reached up to him. "I think you and I should have a little rest and then, this afternoon, do you know what I would like? To go on a *bateau mouche*. I haven't been on one since I was a child."

Luke laughed. He leaned over her, kissing her forehead and her cheeks and then her lips. "I think that sounds like an excellent plan."

As his fingers moved expertly down the row of buttons on her blouse, she tensed for a moment, but the black wall in her mind held firm and, relaxing again, she put her arms around his neck and abandoned herself to his attentions.

Mary Sutton stopped as she walked across the village green in the dark, returning home late after the bus had dropped her at Belheddon Cross, and she watched the car screech out of the gates of the Hall, scattering mud and stones behind it as it turned west through the village. She gazed at its retreating taillights until it was out of sight, then she turned and thoughtfully studied the

464

driveway. The Grants had gone away, Fred Cotting, young Jimbo's dad, had told her that. The house was supposed to be empty.

It was a clear cold night, and as she stood in the entrance gateway she could see the house in the starlight. The windows were dark now and uncurtained, the glass black, unreflective.

She hesitated, gripping the top of her capacious handbag very tightly with both hands. Little Lolly would have wanted her to keep an eye on the place. That was what Laura's brother Robert had called his little sister. Robert, who had died, aged fourteen, falling out of that great chestnut tree which guarded the front of the house. She hadn't told Laura's daughter about those two boys, Laura's brothers. She could see that Jocelyn could barely cope with the idea of her own brothers' deaths.

Mary pursed her lips. Slowly she began to walk up the drive. She did not think the car which had left in such a hurry could have been a burglar's. No one in its entire history had burgled Belheddon Hall. No one dared. So, who had it been?

She stood on the front gravel staring up at the house, feeling the waves of emotion coming off it: the fear, the hate, the love, the happiness; feeling the blessing woven by little boys' laughter, and behind it all the ice-cold venomous evil which poisoned the very air itself.

Gripping her bag even more tightly, she began to walk around the house. Every door and every window was locked, and at each she muttered a few words and traced the sign of the sealing, pointed star. Her powers were long unused, weak compared to those of Margaret de Vere, but her loyalty to little Lolly and her daughter was absolute. They would have whatever strength was left to her.

"It's strange how much better things feel in daylight." David had produced the back door key and inserted it in the lock.

Behind them the coach houses were still locked fast. There was no sign of Jimbo, though it was nearly eleven in the morning.

"Darkness doth make cowards of us all," Edgar commented tersely. In his hand was a black briefcase. "I can't tell you how glad I am you came to us last night. It's strange, but the subject of black magic and witchcraft has never really surfaced here before. Poor Laura and I never looked beyond the actual presence of malign influences. I know she was very conscious of the tragedy of Katherine, but as far as I know she never suspected her or her mother of any influence on the house."

He followed David into the kitchen, which was warm and welcoming, the stove still banked from the night before.

Turning on all the lights, David reached for the kettle. "So, what happens now?"

Edgar frowned. He put his briefcase down on the table. "While you make us a cup of coffee each, I think I will have a walk through the house. Just get the feel of things a little." He gave a grim smile. "What Margaret de Vere did was probably not done openly and in public. It would

466

have been done surreptitiously, in secret, without witnesses other than her accomplices, if she had any. I may be able to tell where it happened."

"She must have known she would be sentenced to death if she were caught." David reached into the fridge for a jar of instant coffee.

"Indeed. But I suspect she was confident in her allies. The devil is a powerful friend."

David shivered. "Let's hope the church is stronger," he muttered. His fervent plea went unheard as Edgar disappeared into the passage.

Their meeting the night before had lasted long into the night. David's books and papers were spread all over Edgar's desk in the window of his study, and as the night cleared and the stars appeared they glanced from time to time up at the uncurtained window to see the luminous blackness of the sea with the trails of silver and white as small uneven waves crisscrossed the incoming tide. It was half past four before Dot at last managed to chase them to bed, David in the attic bedroom which looked out to sea, and only five hours later when she woke them with cups of tea and toast. In twenty minutes they were on the road back to Belheddon. In Edgar's case was holy water, wine and bread, a crucifix, and a Bible.

The great hall was very cold when he walked into it. He stared around, shivering. Outside was brilliant sunshine, and the low November sun was slanting in at the windows, throwing patches of warm light on the flagstones. He saw the dead flowers and frowned. Bad vibes. He grinned to himself. There were things that even his New Age dotty daughter could teach him, and vibes was one of them. Vibes mattered. He walked through to the study, stepping over the scattering of toys on the floor at the foot of the stairs, and pushed open the door. Sunlight filled the room. It was warm and welcoming. He felt a quick surge of anger. This was such a beautiful house. A home. A family home for hundreds of years, and yet it was blighted — blighted by the spite and greed of one woman, if David's theory was to be believed. A woman who had used her daughter to lure a king, who had conspired to have the king sleep with that daughter, and who, when she found he was not prepared to abandon his wife to marry the girl, had used her evil arts to cause her death and probably his as well.

He stood thoughtfully in front of the fire. She had been very powerful, Margaret de Vere, if they were right. She had enlisted the help of the devil, and somehow her viciousness had survived the centuries to threaten the occupants of the house to this very day. He went over in his mind the things he would do. The rite of exorcism was powerful. He had done it here before when he had been licensed by the bishop to perform the service. And he had come here with holy water to cleanse the house on more than one occasion, both before and since. Why had that not worked? Why had nothing worked? Was it that he was not powerful enough?

He swallowed his doubts quickly, gazing around the room again. On each occasion before, he had addressed his exorcism to some unspecified evil

468

— probably male — not identifying his quarry. This time it would be different. He intended to address Margaret de Vere by name and banish her forever from the house.

Edgar found David opening a biscuit tin. "All right?" David sounded anxious. He had been gone longer than he realized.

"All right." Edgar wished he felt stronger. He sat down at the table and helped himself to one of the blue earthenware mugs. "We'll do it in the great hall, I think. It's the center of the house, and wherever she cast her spells and wove her charms, it is the whole house that needs to be freed from her."

"And can you release the boys?"

Edgar shrugged. "I hope so."

David grimaced. "I feel as though I'm taking part in some fairy story written by the brothers Grimm. Magic. Witches. Trapped enchanted children. It's grotesque."

"It is." Edgar put down his mug. Suddenly he could not face coffee or biscuit. "Come on. Let's get on with it, shall we? The sooner the better."

Picking up his briefcase, he led the way through into the great hall once more. The sunlight had gone. In the short space of time while he had been in the kitchen, the skies had grayed and the room had filled with gloom. "Can you get rid of those flowers, old chap. I'll spread my stuff out here on the table." He unpacked the cross and stood it before him.

Georgie.

The voice from the stairs was loud and quite clear.

The vase of flowers slipped from David's hand and crashed to the floor, spilling slimy green water and dead flowers over his feet and onto the flags. "Christ! Sorry." The stench from the water was overpowering.

"That's all right. I'll help you clear it up. Careful, don't cut yourself." Edgar stooped down next to David, picking up slivers of broken glass. "I should have warned you. There may well be manifestations."

"What sort of manifestations?"

Edgar shrugged, his hands full of glass and flower stems. "Noises. Lights. Banging and crashing. Evil doesn't like being dispossessed."

David took a deep breath. "I'm trying to think of this as historical research."

"Don't." Edgar spoke sharply. "Bring this all through to the kitchen and we'll find something to mop up the water. This is not an experiment for your amusement. This is serious beyond words." He threw the mess in his hands into the bin and reached for a floor cloth, wringing it out in the sink. "I want that room spotless. Foul water is not something we want in there."

Obediently, David helped him clean the floor, and finished it off with a spray of disinfectant from the bottle under the sink. Only when order was completely restored would Edgar, his hands washed and dried, go back to his unpacking. David stood close to him, wishing the sun would come out again. He was finding the darkness of the room oppressive in spite of the lights. "Shall

I find some candles?" He had expected to find them part of Edgar's kit.

The other man nodded. "It would be helpful."

They were, David remembered, in the cupboard under the gallery. He walked over to it and pulled open the door. A toy car fell out at his feet. He stared down at it, feeling suddenly rather sick.

Sammy.

The call was from the opposite doorway. He swung around.

"Take no notice." Edgar's voice was calm and steady. "Bring the candles over here."

"I can't. There aren't any."

"Look in the kitchen then. I saw some candlesticks on the dresser."

David walked toward the doorway where the voice had come from. To his shame, he was feeling a little unsteady. He took a deep breath and went out into the long passage which led from the front door back to the kitchen. It was very cold, the draft from the door as bad as ever. The kitchen was a haven of warmth and brightness. He collected the two candlesticks from the dresser and, rummaging in the drawers, found two new blue candles. Putting them in place, he carried them back to the great hall.

Edgar frowned. "Were there no white ones? It's stupid of me. I should have brought them. I usually keep them in my case."

"They're the only ones I could find." David

471

put them reverently on either side of the cross. "What now?"

"I'm going to bless the house and cleanse it with holy water. Then I'm going to pray for the banishment of evil, and I'm going to celebrate Communion here at this table."

Sammy! Come and play! Sammy? Where are you?

The plaintive voice was very clear. The scuffle of feet on the stairs and the giggle as if someone was running away echoed across the room. "Take no notice," Edgar said calmly. He was lighting the two candles. "They are just what they seem. Two innocent mischievous children." He shook his head. "I conducted their funeral services. Both of them." He took a deep breath. "Sweet Jesus, bless this place. Look on us now and give us your strength to vanquish all evil from this house. Release and bless the souls of the children who have died in this house. Remove and cleanse the evil and the hatred which have trapped them here." He opened a leather case, which proved to contain a set of small bottles and silver-topped pots. "What Dot calls my traveling picnic kit," he said quietly. "Oil. Water. Wine. Salt and wafers."

There was a resounding crash upstairs. David looked up. His mouth had gone dry with fear. "Should we go and look?" he whispered.

Edgar shook his head. He had opened his prayer book. "Concentrate on the prayers. Stand here. Close beside me."

Somewhere a child had started crying. David

clutched at Edgar's sleeve. "We ought to go and look."

"We know there is no one there, man." Edgar's fingers had tightened on his prayer book convulsively. "Concentrate."

The candle flames were flickering wildly; as David watched, a splattering of blue wax fell across the table. "They should be white," he was muttering to himself. "The candles should be white." He found he was shivering convulsively.

Edgar frowned. He was having difficulty finding the right page. "Our Father," he began, "which art in Heaven. Hallowed be Thy name —"

Another crash, this time from directly overhead. In the hearth the ash was blowing about, a fine mist above the firedogs. With a puff of wind, a cloud blew out into the room, scattering across the floor to their feet. Edgar gave up trying to turn the fine India pages of his prayer book and put it down. His fear was making him angry. "Enough!" he suddenly bellowed. "Get thee hence! Out of this house, do you hear me? In the name of Jesus Christ Our Lord, leave this place. Now! Take your evildoings and your malice and your hatred out of this house and leave the people who live here in peace." He raised his hand and made the sign of the cross in the air. "Out!" Seizing his bottle of water, he tucked it under his arm. Taking one of his small pots, he struggled to remove the lid. "In the name of the Lord!" he cried through gritted teeth. The lid flew off and salt spilled all over the table. David stood back, shocked, tempted to dive forward and throw some over his shoulder, but Edgar had already scooped some up into his palm, and was putting it into the water, blessing it with the ancient words *Commixtio salis et aquae pariter fiat, in nomine Patris et Filii et Spiritus Sancti,* words that seemed to him more fitting for their purpose than the plain English he had been about to use.

Upstairs, the little boy was crying. Involuntarily, David took a step away from the table, unable to stop himself, his heart wrung by the misery of the sound. Edgar, without taking his eyes off the ritual he was performing, shot out a hand and grabbed David's jacket. "Don't move," he muttered. "Stay right here. There's nothing up there, I promise you. She's playing with us. We can defeat her. If only we believe hard enough."

He lifted up the cross. "Here. Carry this and follow me."

Slowly they processed around the room, Edgar in front, flicking the holy water into every corner, David behind clutching the cross. For all his fear, David could not help giving his own small prayer of gratitude that his headmaster could not see him at this moment, and unbelievably a small gurgle of laughter rose in his throat. Edgar stopped and turned. His face was white with anger. "You find this funny? After all we have discussed? After all you have heard here, you find this funny?" He was almost shouting with fury.

"No. I'm sorry." David bit his lip, holding the cross higher, in front of his face. "Put it down to hysteria. I'm not used to this sort of thing —"

"Thank God you are not!" Edgar stared at him for a long moment. "I just hope that our witch has not got to you as well. Perhaps it would be better if you waited outside."

"No." The thought that he might have been bewitched was so frightening, David felt the cold sweat drenching his shoulders. "No, Edgar, I'm sorry. Please. I'll help you." He glanced up at the beams of the high ceiling as they both heard clearly the sound of running feet. "Don't forget the king, Edgar. If the king is here too —"

"First things first," Edgar snapped. His hands had begun to shake. He tossed a shower of water into the dark corners beneath the gallery. "*Ab insidiis diaboli, libera nos, Domine. Ab ira, et odio, et omni, libera nos Domine!* This way." He turned toward the door. "*. . . ubicumque fuerit aspersa, per invocationem sancti nominis tui, omnis infestatio immundi spiritus abigator, terrorque venenosi serpentis procul pellatur . . .*"

"Mr. Tregarron? Are you there?" The loud voice echoing suddenly through the room stopped him dead. "Mr. Tregarron, are you all right?"

David closed his eyes. He wiped his face with the back of his arm. "It's Jimbo, Luke's mechanic," he whispered. His hands were shaking so much he had to clutch the cross against his chest.

"Mr. Tregarron?" The voice sounded less certain now.

"Keep quiet. He'll go away," Edgar commanded in a whisper.

"Mr. Tregarron? The back door was open."

475

The voice was closer suddenly. "I thought I'd better check."

"Speak to him." Edgar slumped forward, crossing his arms across his solar plexus, all the energy draining suddenly out of him. "Speak to him. Send him away."

David put the cross down on the table and made for the door. "Jim?" His voice was croaky. "Jim, it's all right. I'm here." He walked out into the kitchen, taking deep breaths, feeling as though he had been let out of prison. With a huge, body-shaking sigh, he leaned his arms on the kitchen table, his head in his hands.

"Are you sure you're all right, Mr. Tregarron?" Jimbo had been standing in the doorway. He moved forward, his face creased with concern. "You look white as a sheet, mate. What's happened?"

David forced himself upright. "Just a bit tired. Sorry, I didn't mean to give you a fright. I didn't realize I'd left the door open."

"No problem. As long as everything's OK." Jimbo hesitated. "There's nothing wrong through there, is there?"

David shook his head.

"I'll go on back to work then. I had to go into Ipswich this morning to collect some parts." He still hadn't moved. "Shall I put the kettle on for you? You look as though you could do with something hot."

David shook his head wearily. "No. Thanks, Jimbo. I'm fine. Perhaps I'll make some later." He forced himself to smile. "I'm going back to London today. I'll look in on you before I go and give you back the key."

He stood watching as the young man at last turned to go. As the door closed behind him, he had a tremendous urge to call him to stop, but somehow he resisted it.

He had to go back.

CHAPTER 33

"Luke, I have to visit the place my mother lived."

"Oh, Joss!" Luke sat up and stared at her. "We came here to leave all that behind."

"I can't leave it behind, Luke." She shook her head. "All I need to do is look. See where she stayed. I've got the address. I need to know she was happy here in Paris."

"And how will you know that?" He took a deep breath. "Joss, she's been dead for years. I don't suppose anyone is even going to remember her."

"They might." She clenched her fists. "It's not so long. Please, Luke. I'll go alone if I have to."

He sighed. "You know I won't let you do that."

She gave him a shaky smile. "Thank you."

"All right. I give in. Let's get something to eat, then we'll go and find it. Then, please, can we relax and enjoy ourselves again? For our last few days?"

She pushed back the bedclothes. "Of course. I promise."

Rue Aumont-Thiéville was in the seventeenth

Arrondissement. Their taxi driver dropped them off in a short street of ateliers. Looking up at the huge studio windows, Joss took a deep breath. "It was here. Here that she lived with Paul after she went to join him."

"Are you going to knock?"

She bit her lip. "Doesn't one look for the concièrge? Or don't they exist anymore? I seem to remember that they are supposed to know everything about every one of their tenants in Paris."

Luke grinned. "They're dragons. Direct descendants of the tricoteuses who sat at the foot of the guillotine knitting, counting heads as they fell into the basket!"

"You're trying to put me off."

"Not really. I know nothing will do that." He put his arm around her shoulders. "Go on. Ring the bell."

The young woman who opened the door to them looked nothing like a tricoteuse. She was smart, well made up, and spoke fluent English. "Monsieur Deauville? Yes, he still lives here, Madame."

Joss glanced at Luke, then she turned back to the young woman. "Perhaps you remember my — that is, his . . ." She floundered to a stop. It had suddenly dawned on her that she did not know if her mother had remarried or not. "Madame Deauville," she went on hastily. "She died about six years ago."

The young woman made a face. "Pardon, Madame. My mother was here then. I've only been here two years. All I can say is that there is no

Madame Deauville now." She shrugged. "Do you wish to go upstairs?"

Joss nodded. She glanced at Luke. "Do you want to come, or would you rather go for a walk or something?"

"Don't be silly." He stepped inside after her. "Of course I want to come."

The elevator was wrought iron, small, ornate, and terrifying. It carried them with unbelievable slowness up to the third floor, where they heaved back the gate and stepped out onto the bare scrubbed landing. It took several minutes for the door to be answered. Paul Deauville was, Joss guessed, in his eighties, tall, white-haired, astonishingly good looking, and full of charm. His smile was immediately welcoming. "Monsieur? Madame?" He looked from one to the other in inquiry.

Joss took a deep breath. "Monsieur Deauville? Do you speak English?"

His smile broadened. "Of course."

He was dressed in an open-necked shirt and heavy wool sweater. There were telltale paint stains on his sleeve.

"Monsieur, I am Laura's daughter." She stared at him anxiously, half expecting a rejection as a look of shock, then astonishment, and then at last delight played across his expressive features. "Jocelyn?"

He knew her name.

Her face relaxed into a smile of relief as she nodded. "Jocelyn," she confirmed.

"Oh, *ma chèrie!*" He put out his arms and pulled her to him, planting a kiss on each cheek. "At

480

last. Oh, how long we waited, Laura and I, for this moment." He drew back suddenly. "You knew — forgive me — you knew she was dead?"

Joss nodded.

He echoed her nod, then he seized her hand. "Please. Come in. Come in. This is your husband, no?" He released her to give Luke's hand an equally warm squeeze.

Joss nodded. "I am sorry to come without warning."

"That does not matter! What matters is that you come at last! Come in, come in. I will put on the coffee. No, we need something better than that. Something special to celebrate. Sit down. Sit down." He had ushered them into a huge studio room. The walls of the ground floor area were lined with paintings. There were two easels, both with canvases, standing near the vast window; behind them a small area served as the sitting room — three comfortable chairs covered in woolen throws, a coffee table, a television, and all around piles of books and papers. To one side of the studio an open plan staircase — almost a ladder — ran up to a gallery where presumably he had his bedroom. The old man had disappeared into the kitchen area. As Joss and Luke stood in front of one of the canvases, looking in delight at the riot of color in the painting, he reappeared with a tray carrying three glasses and a bottle of wine. "*Violà!* To drink a toast!" He put the tray down on a low table in front of the chairs. "Look, have you seen? The portraits of your mama? Here? And here?"

There were several of them. Huge, reflecting

his style of large solid blocks of color, pure emotion, warmth and vibrancy, and yet at the same time all managing to capture something of the delicacy of the woman they portrayed. Her hair — in two dark, streaked with white, in the last gray and white and wild, a Gypsy's hair. She was swathed in bright shawls, yet her skin had the fine luminous texture of the English aristocrat; her eyes remained wistful behind their teasing. Joss stood a long time in front of the last.

"I painted that after we knew she was ill." Paul came to stand beside her. "She was twenty years younger than me. It was very cruel that she should be taken so soon after we had found each other."

"Will you tell me about her?" Joss found there were tears in her eyes.

"Of course." He led her back to the chairs. "Come sit down. I will give you some wine, then I will tell you everything you want to know." He began to pour. "You have of course found Belheddon." He did not look up from the glasses.

She nodded. "That is how I knew how to find you." She took one from him. "Did you ever go there?"

He nodded, passing Luke his wine, and then sitting down himself, his long legs, encased in old denims, stretched out in front of him. "And are you pleased with your inheritance?" The question was posed cautiously as he took a sip of his wine.

Joss shrugged. "There are problems."

Paul nodded slowly. "There are always problems with old houses."

482

"Why?" Joss turned away from the picture and looked at him hard. "Why did she leave it to me when she was so afraid of it herself? Why, if she knew there was danger there? I don't understand."

Paul met her gaze for several seconds, then he put down his glass. With a shrug, he climbed awkwardly to his feet and went over to the huge window. The grayness of the afternoon had lightened a little and a few streaks of brightness illuminated the sky above the houses opposite. His back to her, he put his hands into the pockets of his jeans, his shoulders hunched. "She was in torment, Jocelyn. Torn this way and that. I had known her, I suppose, ten years. I met her a long time after your father died. She told me, of course, about your brothers and about you. She talked about you a lot." He was staring up, over the house roofs opposite, into the sky, as though his gaze could recall the past.

"I asked her to marry me then," he went on, "but she refused. She was a prisoner of that house." His voice took on a bitter tone. "She hated it. But also she loved it." There was another long silence. "You have asked yourself, of course, why she had you adopted?" Still he did not turn around.

Joss nodded. She found she couldn't answer.

He took her silence for assent. "I did not know her then, of course, but I can a little imagine her pain after your father died. She adored him all her life." He gave a self-deprecating smile. "I was only ever a poor second best for her. But even then I could not imagine how she could

483

give you, her last link with him, away to a stranger. Once or twice only, in all the time I knew her, she tried to explain a little to me, but that part of her life she guarded. I think" — he paused, choosing his words carefully — "I think she felt that if you stayed at Belheddon, you too would be harmed, as her sons had been harmed. The only reason that would make her give away the little *bébé* she loved was to save your life." He turned around at last with an expressive gesture of his hands. "Do not be angry with her, Jocelyn. She did it to save you. The act brought her only unhappiness."

"Then why —" Joss cleared her throat. It was hard to speak. "Why then did she leave the house to me?"

"I think it was the only way she could escape herself." He went back to his chair and sat down, running his hands through his thick white hair. "She found you, you know. I don't know how, but she found who had adopted you and somehow she kept an eye on you. I remember her saying" — he gave a wry smile — " 'The girl is being brought up very solidly. They are good people and they have no imagination.' I was very cross with her. I said, 'You mean you don't want your daughter to have imagination, the most precious thing in the world?' and she said 'No, I don't want her to have imagination. I want her to be down to earth. Solid. Happy. That way she will never look for her roots.' "

Joss bit her lip. She couldn't speak. It was Luke who turned to Paul. "You mean she never intended Joss to have the house?"

Paul shrugged. "She was a very complicated woman. I think she was trying to fool herself. If she left the house to Jocelyn, she would appease some spirit of the place which would then let her go. But when she made the will she made it sufficiently complicated, no?" He glanced at Joss again. "So that it was unlikely that she would inherit. It had to be Jocelyn's free choice. If she made that choice, then" — he lifted his hands helplessly — "she would have brought whatever fate brought to her upon herself. She was, if you like, being deliberately self-deluding."

"She said, in the letter she left me, that it was my father's wish that I inherit the house," Joss said slowly.

"Your father?" Paul looked shocked. "I find that very hard to believe. Your father hated the house, I understand. He begged and begged her to sell it, she told me."

"How did you make her leave, in the end?" Luke reached for the bottle of wine and poured himself a second glass.

"It was the will." He shrugged. "I don't know who persuaded her to leave the house to you, but as soon as she had done that it was as if the locks had been undone and suddenly she was free."

"I don't know why, but that thought leaves rather a nasty taste in my mouth," Luke said softly. He was watching Joss. "You know, the terms of her will forbid us to sell it for a set number of years."

Paul frowned. "But you don't have to live there."

485

There was a silence. He sighed. "It is perhaps already too late. The trap has closed. That is, of course, why you are here."

Joss sat down at last. Her face was pale and strained as she looked at him.

He found himself biting his lip. She was so like her mother — her mother as she had been when he first met her, before that last cruel illness had struck.

"Did she tell you about the ghosts?" she asked at last.

Paul's face grew wary. "The little boys upstairs? I did not believe her. It was the imaginings of a grieving woman."

"They weren't imaginings." Joss's voice was very quiet. "We've all heard them too." She looked at Luke, then back to Paul. "There is something else there. The devil himself."

Paul laughed. "*Le bon diable?* I don't think so. She would have told me that."

"She never told you about the tin man?"

"Tin man?" Paul shook his head.

"Or Katherine?"

He looked suddenly wary again. "Katherine who is buried in the little church?"

Joss nodded slowly.

"Yes. She told me of the sorrow that still haunts the house. She told me that like in a fairy story there needs to be a deliverance. To break the spell."

Joss stared at him, a sudden flash of hope in her eyes. "Did she tell you what that deliverance would have to be?"

He shook his head slowly. "She did not know,

486

Jocelyn. Otherwise she would have done it. Once, when she came to Paris for the weekend, we went to Montmartre, where I have many friends. That day we went to Sacré Coeur together. There she bought in the shop a cross. She asked the priest to bless it for her, and she wore it around her neck until she died. That day we lit a candle to bring peace to the children at Belheddon, and to Katrine" — he pronounced it the French way. "She was very superstitious, your mother, though she was so intelligent a woman. We quarreled about that." He gave a sudden mischievous smile. "We often quarreled. But there was much love between us."

"I'm glad she was happy here." Joss's eyes strayed back to the painting.

Paul followed her gaze. "The pictures of her will be yours one day. To take back to Belheddon. And" — he levered himself to his feet once more — "there are some things of hers here, which you should have. I will fetch them."

They watched as he climbed the stairs to the gallery. They heard the sound of drawers being pulled in and out, then he appeared once more, negotiating the ladderlike contraption without any difficulty in spite of his age. Under his arm he had wedged a small carved box. "Her pieces of jewelery. They should be yours." He pushed it at her.

Joss took the box with shaking hands and lifted the lid. Inside was a tangle of beads and pearls, two or three brooches, some rings. She looked down into the box, shaken by the emotion that had suddenly swept over her.

Paul was watching her. "Do not be sad, Jocelyn. She would not have wanted that."

"Is the cross here? The one she had specially blessed."

He shook his head. "She took that to her grave. With her wedding ring."

"You and she were married?" It was Luke who asked.

He nodded. "I could never persuade her at the beginning. We lived in sin for years." He grinned. "You are shocked?"

Joss shook her head. "Of course not."

"I think the people of Belheddon would have been. No matter. This is Paris. We lived *une vie bohème*. She liked that. It was part of the escape. We married in the end just before she died." He hesitated. "I can take you to see her grave if you wish? Tomorrow, perhaps? She is buried in a village outside Paris. Our real home, where I still go to paint in the summer. She loved it there. It was there that she died."

"I'd like that." Joss smiled. "You've been very kind."

He bent to hug her. "I wish she could have known you, Jocelyn. It would have given her so much pleasure. A pleasure she denied herself to save you." He sighed. "I hope the fact that you have gone to Belheddon has not made that sacrifice a vain one. It seems the fate of your family is very strong. The tie to the house is like a binding chain."

Luke frowned. "It is a beautiful house."

"I think that is its tragedy. Katrine died for it. And so many others."

They both stared at him. "You know something you haven't told us?"

He shook his head. "I know so little. Your mother would not talk about it once she came to Paris. The curse of the house goes back a long way. Yet it can be broken. She was so sure of that." He put his hands on Joss's shoulders. "You are like the daughter I never had. *Ma fille.* I like that. I want to help you. If you wish, perhaps you should go as she did to Sacré Coeur. Buy a crucifix. Have the blessing of a priest. Believe. Believe that God and Our Lady will protect you. They protected her. She said it was the prayers of Rome which reached out across the years as the prayers of her English church could not. She wanted Our Lady's blessing on Katrine."

"Codswollop!" Luke's muttered imprecation was clearly heard by both of them. Paul frowned at him. "You are not a believer. Nor am I. But for those who believe, the prayers work. Perhaps Katrine believes."

"Katherine has been dead for five hundred years," Joss said sharply.

"Your mother told me that she was a *sorcière,* a witch. She cannot rest without prayers."

"Oh, come on." Luke rammed his hands into his pockets.

"Is it not worth a try? Especially if one day you have children. Then perhaps you will understand why it is important — why they have to be protected."

"We have children!" Joss interrupted. "We have two little boys."

Paul stared at her. "*Mon Dieu* — forgive me.

489

I had not realized." He sat down abruptly. "That is why you are here, of course. Where are they?"

"In England. With their grandparents."

"Not at Belheddon?"

"No."

"That is good." He sighed. "Forgive me. I am tired. Tomorrow we will go out together. I will borrow a car. I will show you Laura's grave. Take her things. Go through them carefully. There are more at the house that you should have."

The interior of the Cathedral of Sacré Coeur was very dark. Luke looked through the door and gave a shudder. "Not my scene, Joss. You go on in. I'll wait here." He sat down on the steps, staring out across the panoramic view of Paris that was laid out in front of him. She glanced down at him and shrugged, then she stepped inside the huge domed church. The shop was packed with devotional aids — pictures, crosses and crucifixes, rosaries, statues. They lined the walls, crowded the counter, hung from the ceiling. Staring around, she wished she had asked Paul what kind of cross her mother had bought. It was silly. Silly to come here; superstitious, as he had said. And yet something in his words had struck a chord. Perhaps he was right. Perhaps it needed the trappings and the blessings of the Church of Rome to reach out to England's pre-Reformation past.

She chose a small silver crucifix and the least kitsch, most graceful little carved statue of the Virgin and carefully counted out her francs. Then she went in search of a priest. His blessing was perfunctory and in French, not Latin, which bothered her. She wanted to call him back, but already he had turned to others, and so, clutching her purchases, she wandered deeper into the church. For two francs she bought a candle and lit it from its neighbor, then she knelt before the blazing ranks of flame and gazed up at the statue of the Virgin and Child, strangely certain that this was the same spot where her mother had prayed.

At Belheddon, in the ice-cold darkness of the locked church, a new spray of white rosebuds lay on the stone step before the memorial plaque to Katherine de Vere.

CHAPTER 34

"Edgar?" David pushed open the door into the passage. "Edgar?"

He could hear someone laughing. It sounded like a woman. "Edgar? Where are you?" He stood in the doorway looking around the great hall. The cross and candles on the table had been knocked over. A pool of blue wax had spread across the dark oak and spilled onto the stone floor. "Edgar?" His voice sharpened. "Edgar, where are you? Are you all right?" He stepped into the room, his mouth dry with fear, and stared around. "Edgar?" His voice rose. The room was very silent — too silent. It was as if someone were listening to him. He took a huge gulp of breath, feeling his shoulders rise and holding them there, somewhere around his ears. "Edgar!" This time it wasn't so loud. Slowly he turned on his heel, staring into the dark corners of the room, looking at the chairs, the chests, his eyes going almost involuntarily to the dark shadows behind the curtains where someone — anyone — could hide.

There was no one there. He stepped closer to

the hearth and his eye was caught suddenly by something lying among the ashes. He stooped and picked it up. It was one of the small silver-lidded pots from Edgar's briefcase.

Spinning around, he strode toward the stairs and stood at the bottom looking up. "Edgar? Are you there?"

He put his hand on the newel post, clutching it tightly. "Edgar!"

The silence was unnerving. He glanced around, searching for a light switch. The well of the staircase was dark and he could see nothing beyond the bend where it turned out of sight. "Edgar?" Taking a deep breath, he put his foot on the bottom step.

The sound of laughter came from behind him this time. He spun around and ran back into the great hall. "Who's there? Who is it? Edgar, where are you? Answer me, for God's sake!"

It was a melodious laugh, attractive; husky, the laugh of a woman who once had known herself to be beautiful. He swallowed, clenching his fists inside his pockets as he stared around, fighting his panic. "What have you done with him?" he shouted suddenly. "What have you done with him, you bitch?"

Silence. Intense, pregnant, listening.

He whirled around. In two steps he was back in the hallway at the foot of the stairs. He threw open the study door and then the dining room door. There was no one in either room. Then his eye was caught by the cellar door. He frowned. The key was in the lock and the door was an inch or two open. "Edgar!" His voice sharpened.

Pushing the door open, he groped for the light switch.

Edgar was lying crumpled at the bottom of the steps. "Oh, Christ!" David ran down two at a time. The old man was alive. He could hear his forced noisy breathing, see the livid color of his face. "Edgar? What happened? Listen old chap, I'm going for help."

He scrambled back up the stairs and ran through toward the kitchen. It took only seconds to dial 999, then he threw open the door and ran out into the yard. "Jimbo?" Please God, let him still be here. "Jimbo? Quickly!"

Jimbo appeared at the door of the coach house, wiping oil off his hands onto a filthy old towel. "Problem?"

"Quickly. There's been an accident. I've called an ambulance. Come and help!"

He didn't wait to see if Jimbo was following. Turning back inside the house, he ran into the kitchen.

Jimbo was right behind him. "Did you ring the doctor? He's much closer than an ambulance."

"Can you do it? I don't know his number. Then come and help. In the cellar."

Grabbing a couple of coats from the rack as he passed, he ran back through the house and down the stairs. "Edgar? Edgar, can you hear me?" He didn't like to touch the man's head, which lay at an awkward angle. Resisting the urge to put something comfortable under it, he spread the two coats over him and gently touched his hand. "There's an ambulance on its way, and the doctor. Hang on in there. It's going to be all right." He saw a flicker beneath the old man's eyelids. He was trying to speak.

"No fool" — Edgar was gasping for breath — "like old fool. I thought I knew enough, thought I was strong enough. She's too good for me." He gave a rasping painful cough and David saw him wince with pain. "Don't stay here. Don't let them come back. Not yet. I must" — he took a deep harsh breath — "must talk to bishop."

"This cellar should be walled up." The doctor's voice above them made David jump. "Dear God, how many more people are going to fall down these stairs?" Bag in hand, he ran down lightly and knelt beside Edgar. "Well, Mr. Gower. I thought you had more sense! A man your age running up and down and playing hide and seek in the cellar!" His hands were running gently over Edgar's head and neck, then on down his body, checking his arms and legs. "The paramedics are not going to believe this, you know." He was frowning, but his voice was cheerful as he went on. "I suppose you were pushed by the ghost as well?" He raised an eyebrow as he turned to his bag and, opening it, drew out his stethoscope. "Here, let's make you a bit more comfortable. You haven't broken your neck as far as I can see. Tough old codgers, you clergymen!" He lifted Edgar's head and gently pulled some of the jacket under it to cushion it, then he glanced at David. "Do you want to run upstairs and keep a lookout for the ambulance? It should be here about now."

Jimbo was waiting in the kitchen. "What's happened?"

"You didn't think to come and look and perhaps help?" David rounded on him.

"You shouldn't have meddled." Jimbo backed away from him. "I'm not going through there. No way. Is he dead?"

"No, he's not dead. What do you mean, we shouldn't have meddled?"

"You were trying to exorcise him, weren't you. You were trying to chase him away from Belheddon. Well, you can't. There's dozens have tried and they've all failed. They've died or they've gone mad. I told Joss. I told her not to meddle, but she wouldn't listen. He won't hurt her. He never hurts women."

"It was a woman we were trying to exorcise. A witch." David thrust his hands deep into the pockets of his jeans. "She's at the root of all this trouble."

Jimbo stared at him. "What do you mean, a witch? It's Bael, the devil, old Nick. That's who lives here."

"Maybe. But it was a witch whom we were after. She's at the root of all this trouble." David shuddered. "Did you hear an engine? That must be the ambulance. I'll go and see."

In the silence broken only by the electronic bleeps in the ward, Edgar opened his eyes suddenly. He clutched David's sleeve. "You have to go back to the house. Collect all my stuff. Don't leave it there. You must not leave it there, do you understand?" Beside him, Dot, white with fear, was clutching his other hand.

David stared at him. "You want me to go back

to Belheddon?" He glanced involuntarily at the window. It was dark outside now.

"You have to." Edgar was breathing with difficulty, his chest heaving. Beside him a battery of monitors measured every step of his battle for life. Only his extreme agitation had forced the doctors in the intensive care unit to allow David in to stand now, helplessly, at his bedside. "Believe me, I wouldn't ask you to do it if it weren't important." His voice was very weak. "Don't stay. Don't do anything. Ignore everything else. Just collect the wine and the bread and the other things. They use them, you see. Use them for evil."

David nodded slowly. "I see."

"Please. You don't have to come back here. Keep them in your car. Just as long as I know they're not in the house." He was tiring. His face was draining of color as his eyes closed.

"Please." Dot took David's hand and led him away from the bed. "You'll be safe. Take this." She fumbled at her neck and produced a small gold cross. "Here. Let me put it on you." She reached up and fastened the chain around his neck, tucking the cross down out of sight under his shirt, then she smiled. "It'll keep you safe. Ring me from London and tell me you've done it. He won't rest till he knows." She turned back to the bed and David saw her lean over to plant a gentle kiss on the old man's forehead.

He opened his eyes and gave a faint smile. "She was too strong for me, Dot. My faith wasn't strong enough." David could just hear the agonized whisper. "I've failed."

"Edgar —" Dot bent closer to the bed. "Edgar, you haven't failed."

" 'Fraid so." The silence in the room as his fingers fell away, cold, beneath hers, was broken by the sudden strident alarm from the monitor by the bed as his heart slowed, faltered, and finally stopped.

As David drove slowly through the darkness away from the hospital sometime later, there were tears on his cheeks. The end had been so undignified, so panic-stricken, doctors and nurses pushing Dot out of the way, the electric paddles in a nurse's hands, and then the swinging door blocking everything from his view. He had offered to drive her home, but she had shaken her head. "Go. Do as he asked. Go back to Belheddon. Rescue the sacrament." Reluctantly, he had left her to wait for Edgar's brother, and set off into the dark consumed with misery and guilt.

And now as he drew closer to Belheddon he was growing more and more scared. He was not sure he would be able to enter the house.

He swung the car into the village and drove slowly down the row of small houses looking for the one where Jimbo lived. It was a pink half-timbered cottage two doors up from the post office. Drawing to a halt, he sat still for a moment staring out of the windshield, hoping that Jimbo would be out. Without the key he could not get into the Hall.

The lights were on in the cottage and he had a feeling that the strong smell of chips on the air came from behind its closed, brightly lit windows.

Mr. Cotting opened the door, which led straight into the small living room, dominated by a large television. Jimbo lay sprawled on the sofa, his feet over the arm, a can of lager in his hand. His gaze switched from the screen to David with an effort.

David gave him an unhappy grin. "It seems that I need the key to the Hall. Mr. Gower left some things there."

Jimbo's eyes widened. "You're going back there? Tonight?"

David nodded. "I don't suppose I could persuade you to come with me?"

"No way, mate." Jimbo stretched out even farther on the sofa and took another swig from his can. "Dad, get Mr. Tregarron a drink. I reckon he's going to need one. How is the old boy?"

David lowered himself gingerly onto a chair opposite the television. "I'm afraid he died."

"Died!" Jimbo echoed him in disbelief.

David nodded unhappily.

"Oh my Lor'." Jimbo sat up and swung his legs to the floor.

"Here." Fred Cotting handed David a can of lager. "Get that inside you. I reckon you need it."

"You can't go back in that house." Jimbo's face was pale beneath his tan. "You can't!"

"I've got to. I promised. Then I'm going on back to London."

"Pity young Jim's sister's not here," Fred Cotting observed slowly. He sat down on the edge of the table. "She'd go with you. She's never been afraid of that place. I tell you what, why

499

don't you get the vicar to go with you? That's his job, isn't it? To chase out evil."

"Mr. Wood doesn't believe in that sort of thing, Da," Jimbo pointed out uncomfortably. "Anyway, I told Mr. Tregarron it can't be done. Loads of people have tried to get rid of old Nick from the Hall. It's never worked. Never will."

David put down his can unopened and stood up. "I'm sorry, I don't think I want this after all. If you can give me the key . . ."

Jimbo climbed to his feet — a giant in the small room — and went over to the sideboard. He picked up the key and tossed it to David. "Bung it through the letter box on your way back, mate. Good luck."

David grimaced. "Thanks."

"If I were you, I'd go and get Mr. Wood anyway," Fred Cotting put in as he opened the door. He put his hand on David's arm. "You don't want to go up there on your own. Not now."

David nodded. He did not need to be reminded.

"Go on. The rectory is up there. On the left. Past the streetlight. You see it?" He had stepped outside onto the path in his slippers.

David nodded. "Thanks. Perhaps I will."

David watched as Jimbo's father went inside and closed the door, throwing the small front garden into darkness.

In his hand the back door key of Belheddon Hall felt heavy and very cold. He held it out, looking down at it, then he turned away from his car and began to walk swiftly up the road. They were right. It was the rector's job.

CHAPTER 35

From her window, Mary Sutton had seen the doctor's car and then the ambulance. For a long time after they had gone she stood staring across the green toward the Hall, then slowly she turned to her telephone and picked up the receiver. It rang for a long time unanswered and in the end she put it down. She walked through to her kitchen and there she pulled open the drawer in the table. Sorting through the kitchen knives and spoons, the ladles, the old flat grater, the used corks, the skewers and the peelers, she found what she was looking for at last. A key. A large old-fashioned key. The key to the front door of Belheddon Hall. It was cold in her hand and heavy. She held it for several minutes, deep in thought, then at last with a sigh she put it in the pocket of her skirt and went out into the hall. Taking down her winter coat and her scarf from the pegs, she pulled them on and let herself out of her front door.

The lock had rusted and the key was hard to turn, but at last she managed it, using both hands to force it around, and summoning every ounce of strength she had to push back the great oak door.

The atmosphere in the house was strange. She stood still, scenting the air like a dog. It was sulfurous, blood-stained, heavy with evil.

"Georgie, Sam?" Her voice quavered as she called. "Robert? Children, are you there?"

The answering silence was suddenly attentive, full of tension.

"Boys? It's Mary. Protect me, boys." Squaring her shoulders, she walked firmly toward the door into the great hall, a small determined figure in her ankle-length skirt and thick stockings. In the doorway, she reached up and clicked on the light, looking around.

So, they had tried another exorcism. Was that the priest they had taken away in the ambulance to die? She had no doubt he was dead. She could smell death, like a miasma over the room.

Walking across to the table, she stared at the cross, the candlesticks, the splashes of blue wax, and slowly she shook her head. The power was there in the holy things, if only they knew how to summon it; their God was almighty, it was His servants who were weak.

Once she might have taken the things herself — the bread and wine — and used them, not for evil exactly, never for evil, but to weave her own quiet spells, but not now. She had done with all that.

Glancing around, she listened carefully. The house was silent. They were watching to see what she would do next.

There was very little holy water left in the

flask. Picking it up, she dribbled it in a circle around the table and then stepped inside the circle — protective, powerful, as safe as a stone wall. Picking up the discarded briefcase, she quickly packed the cross, the candlesticks, the empty pots. The wafers and salt she put inside her clean handkerchief and tucked inside her pocket. The wine in one of the flasks she put under her coat, and the briefcase she slid under a coffer. Then she stood upright again.

"So, madam, you shall not have these to play with! You've done enough damage today, I think." Her voice was steady, ringing strongly through the room. "Leave the Grants alone. They know nothing of the past!"

Safe in her circle, she looked around, listening.

There was no reply. Shaking her head, she stepped out of the circle, leaving the holy water to dry upon the flags, and she walked slowly to the door.

Reaching for the light switch, she turned and glanced back into the room. Nothing had changed; there was no sound.

Locking the front door behind her, she switched on her small flashlight and began to walk swiftly across the gravel. Turning into the path that led to the church, she stopped once and glanced over her shoulder, listening, then she hurried on.

The key to the church was where it always had been, hidden near the porch. Inserting it into the lock, she pushed open the door and paused. It was ice cold inside and very black. She hesitated, then, reaching for the bundle in her handkerchief and the small flask, she stepped in and strode quickly up the aisle, her flashlight beam faintly lighting her footsteps.

On the rug between the choir stalls she paused. Perspiration had begun to stand out on her forehead. The handkerchief crumpled in her hand felt very hot.

With a last effort of will she almost ran the last few steps to the altar rails and stooped, looking for the latch to open the little gate, her fingers scrabbling among the intricate wooden carvings to reach the hidden bolt. She found it at last and tore it back; pushing the gate, she stepped up to the altar and put down the bread and wine in front of the cross. "There!" She was panting. "Safe! You can't touch it there, my lady!"

Turning, she shone her fading flashlight down the aisle in triumph.

At the far end she could see something moving between her and the door. She narrowed her eyes, peering through her thick glasses, and her throat constricted in fear.

Behind her was the God she had rejected in her youth. Was it too late to ask His help now? In front of her, the twisting spiral of light was growing larger. With a gasp of terror she plunged blindly down the chancel steps and ran into the side aisle, dodging behind the pillars, trying desperately to reach the door.

"Let me just get this straight." James Wood looked at David with a troubled frown between his eyes. "You and Edgar Gower went into the Hall with a view to performing an exorcism of the ghosts there?"

504

David nodded. He felt a small surge of irritation. "All I want is for you to come up with me and take charge of Edgar's kit. His holy water and stuff. He was worried that" — he hesitated — "that it might fall into the wrong hands."

"The hands of the ghosts, presumably." Wood tightened his lips. "Of course I'll come with you. Poor Edgar. I'm so very sorry." He glanced at David. "You mustn't blame yourself. It wasn't your fault, you know."

"No? I brought him here. If it wasn't for me —"

"Accidents happen. They are no one's fault. Edgar was always obsessed with that house; no one could have kept him away. And if he had heart trouble anyway —"

"They don't know that." David sighed.

"They are doing a post mortem, you say? I suppose they have to." Shaking his head sadly, James Wood reached up to the coatrack in his hall for a thick jacket and dragged it on, then he opened the drawer of a table by the front door and took out a serviceable-looking flashlight. "I will go over to see poor Dot. It must have been such a shock for her. Well, come on. We'll go over there now. I'll be back in twenty minutes, dear," he bellowed over his shoulder toward the kitchen from where David's nose had been picking up the wonderful smells of frying garlic and onions. Banging the door behind them, he set off on foot up the road.

"I've a car by the post office —" David protested.

"No need. It's only ten minutes' walk." Wood

505

was striding out in front of him, the beam of the flashlight playing across the frosty tarmac. "It will give us a chance to calm ourselves down."

David raised an eyebrow. There was no sign that James Wood was anything but calm. "You don't believe in ghosts, I think you said," he commented as they walked shoulder to shoulder across the green.

Wood gave a throaty chuckle. "Not when it comes to Belheddon Hall. I don't think I've ever come across such a case of mass hysteria. It's the house. Old, beautiful, full of history, probably a lack of modern bright lighting which floodlights the whole place at the flick of a switch and a tendency to be especially cold. I'm always being told about cold spots. People forget they are used to modern houses with central heating and double glazing. The slightest draft and they put it down to a malign spirit wafting across the room." He laughed quietly. "What has happened to Edgar is a dreadful, sad accident, David. You must not be taken in by all this ghost business. I know Edgar was much involved with it when the Duncans lived here. He encouraged them. Poor things, they had a very unhappy life, but in my view he was very, very wrong to take all this talk of ghosts seriously."

"I thought the church did take it seriously," David put in thoughtfully. "Edgar told me there was a special department within each diocese to deal with exorcism."

There was a moment's silence. "There are some very outdated aspects in the Church of England still. Not in my view healthy ones."

"I see." David raised an eyebrow. In front of them the entrance to the drive loomed out of the hedgerow and they turned into it. The shrubs were very black in the darkness, and the frost had set the gravel hard, cutting out the usual welcome crunching from beneath their feet as they made their way silently up to the front door.

"I've the key to the back," David whispered as they stood looking up at the house front. In the starlight they could see clearly the angles of the gables and the tall chimneys and the dark uncurtained windows. He shivered, remembering the blazing lights which had shone from every floor when he had driven away only twenty-four hours earlier.

Leading the way around the corner, he walked through the archway into the stable yard and paused, looking around. The doors of the coach houses were all locked fast. The courtyard was very silent. Groping in his pocket for the key, he walked slowly toward the back door.

The kitchen was still warm as they made their way in and turned on the lights. David glanced around, relieved to see that nothing appeared to have been moved. He gave James Wood a determined grin as the latter switched off his flashlight and rammed it into his jacket pocket. "This way. In the great hall."

Pushing open the door into the passage, he paused, listening. The house was very quiet. Resisting the urge to tiptoe, he strode down the passage to the Gothic oak door into the great hall and pushed it open, gratefully aware that Wood was very close behind him. Groping for the switch on the wall, he turned on the lights and looked around. The room looked normal. Stepping out onto the flagstones, he walked across to the oak refectory table and stared down. A pool of solid blue wax showed where the candles had stood and then been knocked over. Otherwise the table was bare. He turned around slowly. Edgar's briefcase had sat on a chair by the hearth; the bottles of wine and oil and water had been on the table. One small pot with a silver top, containing the salt for the exorcism, had been on the table, near the cross.

"I don't understand." He walked across to the hearth and poked around in the ashes with his foot. "It's all gone."

"What's gone?" Hands in pockets, James Wood was staring up at the portrait over the fireplace.

"Edgar's stuff. The cross. The candles. The sacrament." He ran his fingers over the cold wax on the table. "Here. See? This is where he was working. His case was here, on the chair." He turned around slowly, probing the shadows.

Wood frowned. "I'm sure there is a perfectly reasonable explanation. Young Jimbo Cotting, for instance. Do you think he cleared up after you had left for the hospital?"

David shook his head. "It was me who locked the door. He wouldn't come through here; he won't come into the house beyond the kitchen. I turned out the lights and locked up while they were loading poor Edgar into the ambulance, then I gave Jimbo the key and followed them in my car. He wouldn't have come back in, I'm sure of it. He's terrified of the place."

Wood pursed his lips. "It is possible you tidied up yourself? In the stress of the accident and everything, maybe you forgot you'd done it."

"No. Believe me, I'd have remembered." David could feel a small knot of anger and fear forming somewhere in the base of his stomach. "Perhaps we should search the place." He walked across to the hallway at the foot of the stairs. He had locked the cellar door, he remembered that clearly, and thrown the keys onto the desk in the study. Pushing open the door, he went in and stared down at the desk. The bunch of keys still lay where he had tossed them on the blotter, next to the neat pile of Joss's manuscript. Aware that Wood was watching him from the doorway, he turned around slowly, scanning the room for the battered black leather briefcase, but there was no sign of it.

"Shall we go upstairs?" He bit his lip.

Wood nodded. "We'd better have a good look around now we're here and make sure there have been no intruders. It's been known, you know. People follow ambulances and when the family rush off after them to the hospital, often not locking up properly in their panic, they nip into the house and clean it out." He shook his head. "It's a very sad, cynical world."

David scowled. "But in this case I did lock up."

"Of course." James Wood turned off the light and closed the door. He turned his attention to the cellar. "Should we check in there?"

"I suppose we should check everywhere." David picked up the keys. "Poor Edgar." Pushing open the door and clicking on the lights, he hesitated for a moment, then he led the way down the uneven steps and stood at the bottom looking around. "No sign of anything unusual down here."

They both listened for a moment in silence. "I wonder why he came down here?" James Wood was frowning as he stepped through into the farther cellar. "It does seem a rather odd thing to do." His voice echoed slightly as he moved out of sight.

David shrugged.

"Of course, one of the children died in here, didn't he." The disembodied voice drew farther away. "These cellars go on for miles. I'd no idea they were so big."

David frowned. "They're not that big! Mr. Wood? James?" In a sudden panic he sprinted toward the archway and peered through.

James was standing by the wine bins, peering into the darkened corner. "Someone has left some toys down here. What a shame, they'll get ruined in the damp. Look." He had picked up an old woven rush basket. In the harsh light of the electric bulb, they could clearly see the green mold growing on the handle. Inside were a half dozen or so of the same little wooden cars which David had seen earlier, and a rusty toy gun and beneath them a penknife and a red-painted yo-yo.

"I think they must have belonged to one of the boys who died," David said slowly. He reached out and touched the yo-yo with a finger. "They're not Tom's."

He shivered, unable to stop himself glancing

over his shoulder. "There's nothing else down here. Shall we go back up?" At least it was marginally less cold upstairs. All he wanted now was to get the hell out of here as soon as possible.

James nodded. He put down the basket. "So sad," he murmured. "So sad." He frowned. "What was that?"

"What?" David's nerves were raw. He spun around, listening.

"I thought I heard something. A voice."

"A woman laughing?" Swallowing, David faced the staircase.

"No." James looked confused. "I'm not sure. Probably the water pipes or something."

"Let's get out of here." David moved swiftly toward the stairs. "Come on. I don't like cellars."

"Nor I." With a rueful smile, James followed him. "I must confess I see your point about this house. The atmosphere leaves a lot to be desired when it's empty like this. But we mustn't be foolish. Our rational minds tell us there is nothing to fear."

Emerging on the landing, they stood for a moment looking toward the great hall. Reaching behind him, David turned off the cellar light and pulled the door closed. Locking it carefully, he withdrew the keys and went with them into the study. "Tell me, James, how does your rational mind cope with a belief in God if it rejects all other aspects of the supernatural?" he called over his shoulder. He was about to throw the keys down on the desk once more when his eye was caught by something lying on the manuscript of Joss's book. A dried flower. He was sure it hadn't been there before. Frowning, he dropped the keys and picked it up. A rose, an old dried rose, its petals, once white, now the color and texture of soft chamois leather. He stared at it thoughtfully, aware that the small hairs on the back of his forearms were stirring uncomfortably.

Roses. He dropped it and turned toward the door.

"James?"

There was no reply.

He took a deep breath. It couldn't happen again. Forcing himself to move slowly and calmly, he went through into the great hall and stopped dead. James was standing by the table staring down at it in disbelief, Edgar's briefcase open before him.

David went to stand beside the other man and looked down in silence. "They're empty," James said after a moment. He nodded toward the vessels. "All of them. The rest of it's here: the cross, the candlesticks. It was under the chest here. Someone must have hidden it all."

David shook his head. "There's no one else in the house, James."

"There must be." The rector sounded desperate. "There has to be some logical explanation. Children perhaps, children from the village. I remember Joss saying she thought there were children hiding in the house."

"There are." David was aware how bleak his voice sounded. "But not children from the village."

James looked at him in silence for a moment, then slowly he closed the lid of the case. Neither of them had noticed the faint outline on the flags where the salt water had dried in a perfect circle.

"What do you suppose has happened to the contents?" David asked soberly.

"Very desirable in some quarters. They use them for Satanic rites, witchcraft, that sort of thing." James's previous hearty tone had gone. It had been replaced with weary disillusion.

"So we were too late."

James nodded. "It looks like it." He gave a deep sigh. "The Grants are all away, you said?"

David nodded.

"Then there's no danger to the family in the immediate future." James stared around the room thoughtfully. "I can't feel anything, you know. Nothing at all. I wish I could, then I'd be more use in knowing how to deal with it."

David shook his head. "Just be thankful you can't feel anything! I don't think it can be very nice to be psychic. Not very nice at all."

He did not mention the rose. Waiting for James to pick up the case, he walked back to the wall to switch off the lights. There was someone up there in the gallery, watching, he was sure of it. He could even feel the suppressed triumph.

He did not look up. Walking back into the room, he hustled James out in front of him. The laughter he thought he could hear behind him was not that of a child. It was a woman's.

In the churchyard, Mary lay on her back in the long grass, staring up at the sky. One by one the stars had disappeared as the clouds rolled in from the sea and the sky was totally black

513

now. She closed her eyes, pleased the pain had gone away at last. Slowly her legs were growing numb.

Her shoe was still caught on the wrought iron curb around the old grave where she had tripped. In the dark she couldn't see the blood from her trapped foot seeping inexorably into the grass.

Somewhere in the distance she heard a door slam. "Here! I'm here!" she called, but her voice was barely more than a whisper and no one heard.

She should have known the evil was in the church now; she should have been able to feel it, realize that something had awakened it, but she was getting old. Too old. Too weak. She must warn Jocelyn. Slowly her eyes closed again and her head fell back onto the soft pillow of dead grass. Another short rest and she would try and move again, but suddenly she was so very tired.

"Georgie? Sam?" Her whisper was very faint. "Help me, boys. I need you."

CHAPTER 36

When Mat arrived in Oxford unannounced, hugging his parents and the children before giving her a brotherly kiss on the cheek, Lyn was as surprised and pleased as they were.

"You might have let us know, Matthew!" Elizabeth Grant feigned annoyance. "It's typical. You just arrive, assuming there will be room for you!"

"Of course there's room." He put his arms around his mother again and squeezed her hard. "There's oceans of room! I only knew yesterday that I could wangle five days in the south before starting on the new project, so I thought I'd grab the chance and I did. I didn't think I'd need to book."

"I'm afraid the boys and I are filling up the house a bit." Lyn felt suddenly shy as she smiled at the handsome, cheerful, carefree face.

"Nonsense." Elizabeth and Mat spoke at the same moment, and then both dissolved into laughter.

"There's room for all of you," Elizabeth went on firmly. "I was only teasing!"

It wasn't until the evening that Lyn found herself alone in the sitting room with Mat after the children had been put to bed. Mat poured her a sherry and sat down opposite her, his long legs loosely crossed at the ankle as he sipped at his own. He gave her an amiable grin. "So, how are Joss and Luke really?"

"Fine." She looked at him fiercely for a minute. "You never answered my letters."

"I know. I'm sorry." He seemed embarrassed. "I meant to. It's just — you know how things are."

"No. Supposing you tell me."

He looked distressed. Standing up, he put his glass down carefully and moved across the room to stand at the French doors looking down toward the bottom of the garden where the River Cherwell ran between banks of lush willow. "I live in Scotland, Lyn. I have a life up there."

"I see." She could not hide the bleakness in her voice. "How stupid of me to think you'd have time to write a few lines on a postcard!"

He swung around. "Please try and understand. You're a very attractive woman —"

"No." She stood up, slopping her sherry onto her skirt as she slammed the delicate cut glass down onto the coffee table. "Please don't make it worse." Her face was scarlet. "I have to go and check on the children, if you'll excuse me. Then I'll help your mother with the supper."

By the morning she had made up her mind.

"But Lyn, why don't you stay a bit longer, my dear! You know how much we love having the children." Elizabeth removed Tom's bib and helped him down from his breakfast chair.

516

"There, sweetheart, take a chocky out of Granny's tin and then go and play while Aunty Lyn and I have a talk."

Lyn gave a tight smile. "It's very nice of you, Mrs. Grant, but honestly, I'd rather have them in their own home. Their routine is getting badly unsettled by the break and it's time we got back. Tom was due to start playgroup for an hour or two this week." She watched Tom helping himself to a fistful of chocolate toffees.

"But this is so sudden and Luke was so insistent we look after you all, my dear. And it's been such fun." Elizabeth got up and went to the sink. "You know, I don't think you ought to go back without checking with them, I really don't." Squeezing a flannel out under the hot tap, she went in pursuit of her grandson before he managed to spread the mess on his fingers to her gingham tablecloth.

Lyn hid a scowl. "It has been fun here," she said as sincerely as she could. "But I think Luke and Joss would want him to go to the playgroup. There is such a waiting list. We were very lucky to get him in."

Elizabeth looked up. Then she shrugged unhappily. "I hope it's nothing to do with Matthew's coming." She glanced at Lyn shrewdly and noted the sudden defensive look in her eyes. She sighed. Wretched boy! Another heart broken. She shook her head, too tactful to say any more. "Well, you're in charge of the little ones, I suppose. Perhaps you're right," she added after a minute. She looked down at the revolting cloth in her hand and gave a rueful laugh. "Yes, perhaps you are right. Short visits, and often — that's always supposed to be the best, isn't it? But do try and ring Luke and Joss, my dear. They left the hotel number. Just check it's all right to go back, won't you?"

When Lyn turned the mini under the arch into the courtyard, a light rain was falling from a leaden sky. She glanced at the open garages; obviously, Jimbo was around somewhere, but to her relief she couldn't see him. She was not comfortable in his company. Each time she had seen him when Luke was not around he had leered at her suggestively, and the awful thing was she did find him and his strange eyes extremely attractive.

Pulling Luke's keys from her pocket, she climbed out of the car. Unstrapping Tom, she lifted him out, then she turned to Ned. "Come on, baby. Let's have you. It'll soon be time for your lunch and I'll bet the house is freezing cold. We'll have to put the fire on in your bedroom before you can go upstairs." His harness was awkward to undo. Swearing to herself, she pulled at the small square buckles and at last managed to extricate him from the backseat. Standing upright, the child in her arms, she turned around to lift out the cat basket — Kit and Kat were anxiously squeaking for their release after their long journey — then she looked around for Tom.

"Tom! Tom, where are you?" He had vanished. "Tom?" She turned around crossly, flicking the rain out of her eyes. "Come on, you're getting wet." The little brat had obviously made a beeline for the open carriage house door. Damn. The last thing she wanted to do was have a long conversation with Jimbo. "Tom, come here quickly. I want to get lunch."

She could hear him giggling. "Tom! Where are you hiding, you horror?" His footsteps rang out behind her, running over the cobbles. She spun around, Ned in her arms. "Tom!"

"You're back then." Jimbo had appeared in the doorway to the garage, a spanner in his hand. He was dressed as always in filthy oily overalls, his unkempt hair knotted back on his neck with an elastic band. He ran his eye up and down her as though she were wearing a skimpy bikini instead of an old pair of jeans and a bright blue anorak. She could feel herself growing hot in spite of the icy rain trickling down her neck.

"As you see. Is Tom in there?"

"Tom?" He stared around his feet as though the child might be hiding behind his legs. "No, I don't think so."

"Can you look, please? In the garage. I want to get him inside. The rain is getting worse." She was trying to shelter Ned with the flap of her anorak.

Jimbo ducked out of sight. There was a transistor radio playing softly somewhere inside, Lyn realized suddenly. To her surprise this time it appeared to be playing some sort of classical music. She took a step closer. "Is he there?"

"No, he's not here. I didn't think he was. I'd have seen him. The little monkey gave you the slip, did he?"

"He did." Lyn tightened her lips.

"Tell you what. You take the baby inside and I'll look for him." Jimbo stopped in his tracks, a frown slowly spreading across his face. "Does Joss know you've brought them back?"

"I'm going to ring them tonight. I tried their hotel last night but they were out." She hesitated. "I can't think where Tom's got to."

"I don't think you ought to have brought them back, you know." Jimbo rubbed the back of his neck with an oily hand. "They shouldn't be in the house."

"Oh for goodness sake, not you as well!" Lyn spun around and began walking quickly toward the back door. She was not about to tell him that it was Joss herself who had hurt the children and imagined all the stories about the house. If anyone was going to explain anything to him, it would have to be Luke. "Please, Jimbo, find him quickly. He's going to get so wet out here in the rain."

Still looking around her for him, she juggled the baby over her shoulder and fished in her pocket for the keys. The back door swung open onto a house that was surprisingly warm. She paused thoughtfully, then she went on into the kitchen. Sure enough the range, although nearly out, had been stoked in the last twenty-four hours. She had done it enough times herself to know exactly how long it would have lasted. There were two glasses on the kitchen table, and Luke's whiskey bottle, nearly empty, together with a wooden toy car.

Setting Ned down in the chair, she propped him up against the cushions and began to pull off his waterproof jacket and trousers. His small bouncy chair was where they had left it behind the rocking horse in the corner. Strapping him in near the range, she gave him a gentle shove to make it swing, then she turned back to the door.

"Jimbo, who's been in here? Was it you?"

For a moment she couldn't see him, then she caught sight of a movement in the bushes in the far corner of the yard. "Is he there? Oh, thank God!"

Jimbo had appeared carrying the small boy. Tom was crying.

"What is it? What's happened?" Grabbing him from Jimbo, Lyn turned toward the kitchen. With a slight hesitation Jimbo followed her and stood in the doorway watching as she tried to console the boy.

"You shouldn't have brought him back."

"Why not?" She turned on him furiously. "Look, you've frightened him."

"It wasn't me frightened him." Jimbo set his mouth in a tight line.

"What did then?"

"You'd best ask him, hadn't you." He sniffed loudly. "And no, it wasn't me sitting in here drinking when I should have been working, so there's no need to think it. Mr. Tregarron was up here with the Reverend Gower. There was an accident. The reverend's dead. He had a heart attack, I heard."

Lyn stared at him in horror. "When was this?"

"Night before last."

"And where's Mr. Tregarron now?"

"Back to London. He wouldn't have liked you bringing the boys back."

"No, I bet he wouldn't." Lyn scowled. "OK Jimbo, thanks. I'd better get these two fed and let them have a rest. They've had a tiring journey." For a moment she thought he wasn't going to go.

He hesitated just too long on the threshold and then with a shrug he turned away. No need to tell her yet about poor Mary. She'd been dead for hours when they found her, and no one knew even now what she'd been doing in the church in the dark. She'd left the door open when she left, and had fallen among the old graves under the yews.

"You call me if you need me," he shouted over his shoulder as he ran down the steps. "But if I were you, I'd spend the night with Mrs. Goodyear. Don't let the boys stay under this roof at night."

Lyn stared after him for a moment, then she turned to Tom, scolding, as she pulled off his jacket. He had spotted the car on the table and stood on tiptoe to reach up and get it. "That's Georgie's toy," he said conversationally as she straightened his jumper and reached it over for him before she turned toward the kitchen range. "Tom play with Georgie's car."

"We must ring your parents later, Luke." Joss was sitting with him at the huge scrubbed table in the farmhouse which had been her mother's last home. They had eaten a wonderful meal, cooked by Paul, washed down with a rough, thick

522

country wine, and they were both feeling sleepy and more rested than they had for a long time.

"I am glad that I persuaded you to leave your hotel and come here to stay." He was spooning thick coffee grounds into the *cafetière*. "You both look better already." He gave his slow, charming smile. "Of course, you may ring whomever you like. I wish you had the children with you." He shook his head. "How Laura would have loved to know that she had grandchildren. Now, while you drink your coffee, I shall bring for you Laura's things." He hesitated. "I do not want you to be sad, Jocelyn. Are you sure you want these things?"

She was peeling an apple with a small fruit knife. "I would love to have them, Paul." She smiled wistfully. "It sounds strange when I already have so much that was my mother's at Belheddon, but none of it seems personal. It consists of all the stuff she didn't want, the things she was prepared to abandon. Apart from a workbasket and the things in her desk, there is nothing that was close to her."

He frowned. "What is a workbasket?"

"Sewing."

"Ah, I see." He let out a guffaw of laughter. "She hated sewing. Not even a button. I did all the buttons! I'm surprised she didn't put it in the garbage!"

"So." Joss shrugged her shoulders and raised her hands in an unconscious imitation of his wonderful Gallic gestures. "What did she love?"

"She loved books. She read and read. She loved poetry. She loved art. That was of course how

523

we met. But there were things she hated. Strange things." He shook his head. "She hated flowers, especially roses —"

"Roses?" Joss tensed.

"Roses." He did not notice the sharpening of her tone. "She detested roses. She said the *greniers* — the attics — at Belheddon always smelled of roses. I could not understand why she disliked them so much. Roses are beautiful things; their smell is" — he searched visibly for a word and found it with a kiss of his fingertips — *"incroyable."*

Joss glanced at Luke. "I can understand. The roses at Belheddon are not like other people's roses." She gave a small sad smile. "Poor mother."

The men left her with the suitcase full of letters and books and the leather box full of more of Laura's jewelery, planning to walk across the fields and down to the river. Settling down alone on the hearth rug in front of a gentle, sweet-smelling fire of apple logs, Joss sat for a long time gazing into the flames, hugging her legs, her chin resting on her knees. She felt closer to her mother here than she had at any time at Belheddon. It was a nice feeling, warm, protective. Safe.

It was almost with reluctance that at last she reached into the box and began to sort through the papers. There were loads of letters — all from strangers — none of special interest, though all showed how much her mother was loved — and several demonstrated how she was missed by friends back in England. None, however, came from the village of Belheddon, she noticed, remembering how Mary Sutton had complained that Laura had never written; no one mentioned the life she had abandoned in East Anglia.

At the bottom of the box she found two notebooks she did recognize. The same make that Laura had used for her diaries and commonplace books at home. They were full of closely written notes. The same mixture as before. Poems, interesting snippets, and diary entries. She settled herself more comfortably, leaning back against one of the chairs and pulling a cushion down behind her head as she started to read.

I had a dream last night about the old days. I woke in a cold sweat and lay there shaking, praying I had not awakened Paul. Then I wished I had. I snuggled against him for comfort, but he did not stir. Bless him, he needs his sleep. An earthquake would not awaken him.

And two days later:

The dream came again. He is looking for me. I could see him searching the house, slowly, unhappily. He is lost and lonely. Dear sweet God, am I never to be free of this? I thought of speaking to Monsieur le curé, but I don't want to breathe His name aloud out here. This is too special a place and surely he can't reach me anymore. Not in France!

Joss looked up for a moment. So *He* — *it* — had a name. She read on. At the beginning of the second book came a revelation:

I wonder whether I should write to John Corn-
ish and ask him to tear up the will; to leave
the house straight to charity. How would anyone
at Belheddon know what I had done? Here he
can only reach me in my dreams and I cannot
tolerate the thought of Jocelyn learning of her
good fortune and going in all innocence into the
trap. There will be no danger to her, of course.
He will love her. But should she ever have chil-
dren. What then? If only I could talk to Paul,
but I want nothing to spoil our relationship, not
even the mention of the name . . .

Joss put the book down, tears in her eyes. She
shivered. So her mother had known only too well
the nature of the dangers at Belheddon and had
felt guilty enough after all, about leaving the house
to her, to have thought of changing the will. She
sighed. But if she had done that, there would
have been no story, no family, no home, once
Luke's business had folded, no cars, no money.
She frowned, brushing away the tears. There was
so much that was wonderful at Belheddon.

Surely — surely there must be a way of re-
moving the danger. She sighed. At least the children were safe. There was no possibility of them
going back to Belheddon until the problems had
been resolved.

She picked up the diary again, turning almost
fearfully to the last pages.

The pain grows worse each day. Soon I shall
not be able to hide it from Paul and I shall
have to stop my writing. I must burn this and

all the rest before I grow too weak or silly to do it.

Joss paused. So, she had never meant anyone to read all this. For a moment she felt guilty, but she read on.

One of my fears is that he — Edward — will be waiting for me when I die. But how can he if he is earthbound? Will Philip be there, and my boys? Or are they too trapped at Belheddon?

So, she and David had been right. It was Edward. Edward IV of England, and inadvertently she had named her younger son after him! Shuddering, Joss skipped on. There were several more pages of closely written script, the writing growing more and more illegible as the days passed. Then came the last page.

So. I am accepted into the Catholic church and Paul and I are married at last. I have done all I can for the safety of my soul.

There was a trail of ink across the page as though her hand were too tired to hold the pen properly anymore, then the writing resumed.

I was so sure she could not cross water.
Katherine
my nemesis . . .

That was all. Joss rested the book on her knee

and stared into the flames.

Katherine:

The name that echoed through her head and through the history of the house. *I was so sure she could not cross water.* What did that mean? That she had come to France? Followed Laura here?

What was the significance of crossing water? Witches couldn't cross water; wasn't that a part of the tradition? But it was Katherine's mother who was the witch. And why should Katherine come here? What was Laura to her?

Her head was throbbing. She rested it wearily on her knees as the book slid to the floor and lay facedown on the carpet. She could hear the ticking of the long case clock in the hall, slow, hypnotic, reassuring. In the hearth, the logs burned with occasional quiet hiss, throwing a wonderful fragrant warmth around her. Closing her eyes, she rested her head back against the cushions.

Come back to me, Katherine, love of my life and my destiny . . .

The cry wrenched her back from sleep with a leap of fear. It had been too loud, too desperate.

It was a dream, nothing more. A nightmare sparked off by reading the diaries. She picked up the book and clutched it against her chest. Poor Laura. Did she have any peace at all before she died? She had died here, in this house, Paul had said, attended by a full-time nurse over the last few days. The end had been quiet, he said,

528

although she had said she wanted no more drugs. He had been sitting with her, her hand in his, and she had smiled at him, perfectly lucid, before closing her eyes for the last time. If she had cried out the names of any strangers, he had not mentioned it.

Trying to shake off her melancholy, she drew the small leather jewel box toward her and opened the latch on the flap which fastened it. Inside, cushioned in faded blue velvet, lay several very beautiful pieces — a string of pearls, some lapis beads, several brooches, and half a dozen rings.

It was growing dark when Paul and Luke returned, hearty, glowing with cold, and eager, they had already laughingly agreed, for an English cup of tea. Standing in the doorway, Paul looked down at Joss near the fire. He could hardly see her in the dusk of the room. "*Ma chère* Jocelyn, I'm sorry. Were you asleep?"

For a moment she closed her eyes, trying to compose herself, then with a smile she scrambled to her feet. "No. Only dreaming and perhaps a little sad."

"Ah. Perhaps we should have given you longer to look at your treasures." He came over and put his arm around her, giving her shoulder a squeeze. "Laura would not have wanted you to be sad, Jocelyn. She was happy in France."

"Was she?" Joss hadn't meant it to come out that way — as an accusation. "Are you sure? Are you sure she didn't bring her demons with her?" She brushed her eyes with the back of her hand.

"Demons?" he echoed.

529

She gestured at the notebook on the carpet. "Did you read her diaries?"

For a moment he looked shocked, then slowly he sat down. "Jocelyn, it may surprise you to know that I never did. Laura asked me to burn them, and I meant to. I put all her things in that box to take them outside to the garden and put them on the fire, but I couldn't bear to do it. In the end I put the whole box away — perhaps in a strange way to wait for you to make the decision if you ever came." He shrugged. "I don't know. But for whatever reason the things were there for you. But they were not mine to read."

"But you were her husband."

"Yes." He gave a grave smile.

Joss looked up at him. "You were only married at the very end."

He nodded. "So, she wrote about that."

"And that she had converted to Catholicism."

Sighing, he leaned back in the chair and stared up at the ceiling. Behind him, Joss was conscious of Luke standing silently by the window. No one had turned on the lights and the only illumination came from the dying fire and the slight tinge of pale light still showing in the sky out of the window. "I am not a religious man. I did not encourage her in this — either the marriage or the lessons with the *curé* — this came from inside her. I asked her to marry me of course, when she came to France, but she did not want it and here no one minded — no one asked. We were both free — I think as I told you that perhaps she enjoyed the — how you call — naughtiness of it? She had been for so long a respectable

530

lady in England." He gave a huge warm smile, his eyes focusing on a distant memory. "Then at the end, when she became ill, I think she became a little afraid." He frowned. "Do not misunderstand. She was very brave, your mother. So brave. When the pain came she did not complain ever. But there was something — something out there" — he gestured toward the sky outside the window — "something which had always haunted her, the thing she had fought with her visit to Sacré Coeur. For a while it was held at bay. She did not think of it. Then one day, I came home and found her sitting by the fire in the dark, much as you were doing just now. And she was crying and she told me that the ghosts had followed her to France. That first they had come in her dreams, and that now she thought they were growing stronger."

"No." Luke stepped forward suddenly. "I'm sorry, Paul, but I think we've had enough of these ghosts. They were the reason we came to France in the first place."

Paul turned in his seat. "Put on the lights, my friend. Pull the curtains. Let us see what we are doing." He turned back to Joss. "Do you wish to talk of this now?"

She nodded. "Luke. It's important. Paul, I have to know. Did she say who was haunting her?"

"The ghost of her lover."

Joss stared at him, completely shocked. "Her lover?"

"That is what she said."

"She had a lover!"

"Why not. She was a beautiful woman."

531

"But I thought —" She shook her head as though trying to dislodge her thoughts. "I thought that it was a ghost. A real ghost. From the past."

He smiled again. "All ghosts are from the past, Jocelyn."

Her thoughts were whirling. "Did she mention anyone else to you? Anyone else who came here? A woman called Katherine."

He nodded. "At the end. It upset her very much. I do not know how she came in — the nurse said she had opened the door to no one, but somehow she came to see Laura."

"Did you see her?"

"*Non.*"

"Who was she, do you know?"

"She had been this man's lover too. And he had left her, that much I understood. She was very bitter that Laura had stolen him. I was so angry when Laura told me. Not about the lover, although she had never told me about him either" — he shrugged gallantly — "but this woman was, apparently, young and beautiful, and my Laura was so ravaged by the disease. It was an obscenity for this Katherine to come here. It was only a day or so later that your mother died."

Katherine.

The word seemed to fill the silence in the room.

Luke came and sat down near Joss. "That's a terrible story. What happened to her? Did she ever come back?"

Paul shrugged. "No. If she had, she would have regretted it. All my rage and misery and grief was directed at that woman. To come to a dying woman and taunt her with her own beauty. Laura kept talking about her beautiful, long dark hair. And then she brought some roses. The roses which Laura hated most in the whole world."

"White roses," Joss whispered.

"*Exactement!* White roses. I threw them from the window. It was as if she knew, Laura said, that it would kill her to bring them here."

"How did she know where Laura was?" Joss was still frowning, trying to rearrange her thoughts.

Paul shrugged once more. "Who knows? She probably hired a detective. I do not make a secret of my home. I have this house for thirty years. Everyone knows me. We had nothing to hide."

There were several seconds of silence, then Luke cleared his throat. "Why don't I go and put on the kettle."

When he returned with a tray and three mugs of tea and a saucer full of lemon slices for Paul, they were both still sitting there, staring at the fire, each preoccupied with their own thoughts.

"Were there two Katherines then?" Joss said at last. "The Katherine who died in 1482, whose presence fills the house at home; and now this other. I never thought — I never ever guessed, that mother had a lover."

Paul got up to throw a log onto the fire. "She had me!"

"I know." Joss smiled fondly. "But that was different. One expects everything to do with the French to be decadent and shocking —" She was teasing now. "The thought that mother had a lover — an English lover — at Belheddon —

that is somehow wrong."

Paul clicked his teeth. "You English are not logical. Not at all. Ever."

"I know."

"Your father died thirty years ago, Jocelyn. Would you expect your mother to be without love for so long? Surely you would not have condemned her to that."

Joss shook her head. "No. Of course I wouldn't. No one should have to live without love." She held out her hand toward Luke, who came and took it. He put his arm around her.

"It is all a little bewildering for us, Paul," he said slowly. "We have been imagining the house full of ghosts from the past — the distant past — and now it seems that they come as well from the living present."

"But not the children," Joss whispered. "The children came from the past."

"That house is not good for children," Paul said thoughtfully. "You should be careful. Laura was full of superstition about it. Coincidence is strange. It attracts more coincidence. The expectation of people is liable to be fulfilled. Once the expectation changes, then slowly the mood will change and the coincidences will no longer be there."

"You sound very wise."

He let out a crack of laughter. "That is probably the only good thing about being as old as me. Age gives a spurious sense of experience and wisdom. Now" — with a groan he levered himself to his feet — "I shall stop being pompous and I shall go and look for a bottle of wine while you ring *grand'mère* and check that your babies are well. When you have done that we can all relax and talk of what we shall do tomorrow."

Luke waited until Paul had left the room before he spoke. "What an incredibly nice man. Your mother was so lucky to have found him."

"Wasn't she." Joss curled up on the sofa, hugging a cushion. "I'm so confused, Luke."

"But happier, I hope."

"I think so." As he reached for the phone and began to dial, she rubbed her eyes wearily.

Katherine.

A medieval Katherine with long wild hair and flowing gowns. And a modern Katherine. A Katherine in high heels with soignée artfully tumbled hair and red lipstick, a Katherine who could fly to Orly just as they had, not on a broomstick but on a plane. Were they different women or the same? She would never know now.

Katherine.

The echo in her head would not go away; it was an echo from the past, an echo that was tinged with laughter . . .

Luke had, she realized, put down the phone. He looked thoughtful. "Lyn took the boys back to Belheddon yesterday," he said slowly.

Joss went white. "Why?"

He took a deep breath. "Mum says she was getting more and more resentful and possessive; she didn't want any help or advice and con-

535

tradicted everything they tried to do." He raised an eyebrow.

Joss scowled. "That sounds familiar. The stupid stupid girl! How dare she! Luke, what are we going to do?"

"Ring her, presumably. No —" He raised his hand. "Let me. You'll rush in and make things worse."

"She can't stay there, Luke. She's got to take them out of the house. Tell her to go to Janet. She won't mind —"

"Let me speak to her first." He was dialing, lifting the receiver to his ear.

Katherine.

The echo in her ears was louder, the laughter wilder; a medieval Katherine and a modern Katherine. Two women with the same eyes, the same red lips, the same wild hair, two women out for revenge.

Scrambling to her feet, Joss went to stand beside Luke. She could hear the phone ringing on and on. No one answered.

Behind them Paul appeared with a small tray. He stood for a moment in the doorway, then he put down the tray. "What is wrong? Can't you get through?"

"Lyn has taken the boys back to Belheddon." Joss was biting her lip hard. "There's no reply."

Paul frowned. "Is there a neighbor you can ring? I am sure there is no need to worry." He put his arm around Joss's shoulders.

"Janet. Ring Janet." Joss dug Luke in the ribs.

536

"OK. OK. Wait." He put the receiver down and picked it up again.

In Janet's house, too, the phone rang on and on, unanswered.

CHAPTER 37

Cuddled up on the end of Lyn's bed, Kat stood up. Staring with huge eyes toward the half-open door, she arched her back and spat in terror. In a fraction of a second she had leaped from the bed and disappeared through the door and down the stairs in a blur of yellow, black, and white fur.

Lyn woke very suddenly and lay staring at the ceiling, her heart thudding beneath her ribs. She listened hard, focusing on the doorway. Had one of the children stirred? She had left all the doors between them open a little so that if one of them cried she would wake up.

The house was very silent. Her gaze went to the window. She had left a crack open between the curtains, and beyond them she could see the sky, bright with moonlight. There must be a heavy frost out there; there didn't appear to be a breath of wind. For several moments longer she lay still, then, reluctantly, she pushed her feet out of the warm bed and reached for her dressing gown.

She had left the light on. Padding across the

landing, she went through Joss and Luke's empty room. The curtains there were open and moonlight flooded across the floor. Standing still for a moment, she stared around the room, half expecting to see something out of place. But there was nothing wrong that she could see. Pulling her belt a little tighter around her waist, she tiptoed through toward Tom's room. He was asleep, his thumb in his mouth, having kicked off all his bedclothes. He seemed warm enough, though, his small face pink and relaxed in the light of the night-light near him. Pulling his covers up, Lyn tucked them in, careful not to disturb him, then she turned toward Ned's room.

The crib was empty.

She stared at it for several seconds, her stomach tying itself in knots, then she flew back across to Tom's room.

"Tom? Tom, wake up! Tom, what have you done with your brother?" Oh please God, let him be all right. She was shaking like a leaf. "Tom, wake up!"

The little boy opened his eyes slowly and stared up at her sleepily, his eyes blank.

"Tom!"

There was no recognition in his gaze.

"Tom, wake up!" She shook him. "Where's Ned?"

He was looking at her vacantly, his body awake but his mind still lost in some dream far away. "Oh, please God, let him be all right!" She couldn't hear the baby crying. If he was cold or hungry he would cry as loudly as he could, unless — She did not let herself pursue that thought. "Tom, darling, I want you to wake up and help me." She took the little boy's shoulders and pulled him into the sitting position. "Can you hear me, sweetheart? I need you to help me."

He was beginning to move at last. Puzzled, he blinked several times and at last the thumb went back into his mouth. She smiled at him, trying to keep her voice gentle. "Now. Were you playing with little Ned?"

Tom nodded.

"Do you know where he is now?"

The little boy shook his head.

"Try and think, Tom. Where were you both playing? It's important. Ned is cold and frightened all by himself. He wants us to go and find him."

"Tom show Lyn." He scrambled to his feet.

Lifting him out of the crib, she put him down on the floor and pulled on his small pale blue dressing gown. "That's it. Now slippers." Her hands were shaking so much she was finding it difficult to dress him. "Now, Tom, show me where he is."

Tom took her hand and skipped confidently out into his parents' bedroom. From there he led the way across to the landing and on up the attic stairs. Lyn was trembling. It was bitterly cold up there. No heating relieved the iciness as they walked through into the first attic.

"What were you doing up here, Tom?" she asked as he led the way across the floor toward the door in the far wall. "It's dark and cold."

"The moon." He gestured toward the window. "Georgie wants us to play in the moon."

Lyn swallowed. Opening the door, she peered

into the darkness of the passage and then at the doors opening off it. Moonlight flooded across the dusty floorboards. "Where's Ned, darling? Show me quickly."

Tom seemed less confident now. He hung back. "Don't like it."

"I know. It's cold. But Ned is cold too. Let's fetch him and then we can all go back downstairs to the warm."

Still unwilling to move, Tom pointed ahead of them. "He's there."

"There? In the next attic?" She ran toward the door, leaving Tom standing in the middle of the room. He had begun to cry.

The door was locked. "Oh, no. Please God, this can't be happening. It can't." She spun around. "Tom, where's the key?"

He shook his head, tears running down his cheeks.

"Darling, please, try and remember. We have to have the key. Poor Ned is very cold. We must find him quickly."

"It's Georgie's key."

Lyn took a deep breath. "Georgie is imaginary, Tom. He's not really there. He can't have a key. Tom has got the key. Where is it?" Her voice was beginning to shake.

"Georgie put it on the door." He pointed above the doorway. She stared up at the pale, worm-eaten beams which framed the room, then she reached up, feeling on the dry, splintered wood. A heavy iron key, dislodged by her groping fingers, fell down with a clatter and lay at her feet. Grabbing it, she tried it in the lock. It was very stiff, but at last it turned and she managed to force the door open. There was what seemed a cruelly small bundle of blankets lying on the floor in the far corner.

"Ned?" Icy with terror, she ran toward it and fell on her knees. For a moment she thought he was dead. He lay quite still in her arms, his eyes shut, then as she clutched him against her they fluttered open and he stared at her. For several moments he did not move, then at last he gave a big smile of recognition.

"Oh, thank God! Thank God! Thank God!" She was crying now in earnest.

Behind her Tom crept into the room and came over to her. His hand clutched at her dressing gown. "Is Ned happy now?"

"Yes, darling. Ned is happy now. Come on, let's go downstairs and get warm."

She took them both down to the kitchen. Warming milk on the stove, she was thinking very hard. Of course, he must have fetched a chair to put the key so high, but why? Why should the little boy want to get rid of his brother? She glanced at Tom, who was sitting half asleep on the rocking chair, cuddling Kit. Ned, in his bouncy chair, was watching her alertly, obviously pleased with the idea of a warm nighttime drink — something he had finally relinquished as a regular activity weeks before. Of course hostility was common in elder children when their siblings arrived, very common, it wasn't really surprising. It was only odd that Tom had shown no sign of it before.

As if conscious of her gaze, Tom looked at

her suddenly. He gave her a sleepy smile. "Georgie likes Ned," he said slowly.

"Everything OK?" Jimbo was standing in the doorway next morning watching as she cooked breakfast.

"Fine. Why shouldn't it be?" Astonishingly, she felt pleased to see him. She took two pieces of toast from the toaster and put them in the rack. "Would you like some coffee?"

He hesitated, then slowly nodded. "All right then. Thanks."

"Sit down." Lyn spread the pieces of toast and cut them into fingers. "Is something wrong?" He was still standing by the door.

"No. No, I suppose not. Thanks."

He moved into the room awkwardly, half shy, half nervous, and inserted himself without pulling it out onto a chair that was drawn up close to the table.

Lyn smiled to herself. Putting a large cup of coffee down in front of him, she turned back to the dresser. "Do you want some toast now you're here?"

"Might as well. Thanks."

"Help yourself to milk and sugar." She paused. "Jimbo, what is it? I'm not going to bite you."

He blushed scarlet. "I know that. It's just . . . it's just I reckon I don't like this house, that's all. It don't feel right. I don't know how you could stay here by yourself."

"There's nothing to be afraid of here." She sat down with her own cup. "Nothing at all. It's a lovely house."

543

"Look at what happened to Reverend Gower."

"A heart attack can happen to anyone."

"I suppose so." He shook his head and shrugged. "I reckon it had something to do with this house an' all. You heard when Joss and Luke are coming back?"

Lyn shook her head. "There's no hurry. They need the break. There's nothing wrong in the workshop, is there?"

"No. That's all fine. You'll be staying on here on your own then, until they get back?"

Lyn nodded. "Try and look a bit more pleased about it."

He gave a tight little laugh. "I'm very pleased. I don't like being up here, even outside, on my own. I was just thinking about those kids." He gestured toward Tom with his head. "I don't like to think of them up here. Things happen to kids in this house."

"Oh, please. Not that again." Lyn stopped. The night before, after giving them their drinks, she had put the boys back to bed. Then she had switched on the baby alarm in Ned's room and, threading the wire under the door, had put the speaker in her own. She had not liked locking the door on the baby, but the key was not going to leave her person. She had threaded it on a piece of ribbon and hung it around her own neck. The rest of the night had been peaceful, but this morning — she chewed her lip again at the memory — this morning when she let herself into the room to the contented sound of Ned's gurgling away to himself in his crib, she had found him playing with a small wooden elephant that she did not remember ever having seen before.

"Something wrong?" Ever alert, Jimbo had noticed her sudden silence.

She shook her head.

"Right." He plainly wasn't going to press her. Standing up, he drained his mug. "I'd best be getting on."

"What about your toast?"

"I'll take it with me, if that's all right." He scraped some honey onto it and turned toward the door, stopping at the last moment to turn back to her for a second. "You sure you're all right?"

"I told you!"

"Yes. Right."

She stood silently for several seconds after he had gone, then she shrugged and shook her head.

Tom looked up at her for a moment and stopped chewing. He wondered why Aunty Lyn hadn't noticed the woman standing behind her; it was the woman who had carried Ned up to the attic and then beckoned him to follow. She hadn't seen the tin man last night either. He took another solemn bite out of his toast finger. If she wasn't frightened, he supposed it must be all right.

"You don't usually come home dinnertime. What's the matter, boy?" Jimbo's father was reading the *Mirror* at the kitchen table amid a litter of take-away containers from the night before.

"I want to talk to Nat. You got her number?"

"You leave your sister alone, Jim. She doesn't need you ringing her at work."

"She said I could anytime. And this is important. They've got problems up at the Hall, and I reckon she should come over and speak to them."

"Oh, no. Now you keep your nose out of all that. If I think you mean what I think you mean —"

"Dad. Listen. It's bad. Those kids are in danger. That Lyn doesn't have a clue. She wouldn't see a tractor if it drove through her kitchen wall and plowed up her breakfast dishes. With Luke and Joss away, it's up to me."

"Luke and Joss, is it." His father put on a la-di-da voice. "They say you could call them that?"

" 'Course. Shut up, Dad. Just tell me where the number is." Jimbo was riffling through the pile of old newspapers and notes on the kitchen counter beside the phone.

"Up there. Pinned on the wall."

"Right." His face grim, Jimbo began to dial.

"Nat, that you? Can you talk? It's important." He glared at his father, who was lounging back in his chair, listening. "Listen, I reckon you need to come back here and talk to the Grants up at the Hall. Things are bad there again."

He listened intently for a few seconds. "Yes. Joss has seen him, and the little boy. Reverend Gower came back to try and do something and he ended up dead. It's only a matter of time before someone else gets killed. I reckon you're the only one who can help."

He scowled at his father, who was shaking his head, looking up at the ceiling. "Yes. Joss will listen to you. She's really nice. Luke doesn't believe what's in front of his nose, and that Lyn who looks after the kids is as thick as two planks. It's up to you. Reckon you can come home this weekend? Great!" He beamed at the phone. "See you then."

"Your sister's got better things to do than come back here and interfere with things that don't concern her."

"No she ain't. She's pleased to help. You should be proud of her, Dad, not ashamed."

"I'm not ashamed."

"You are. And you called her a witch. That's stupid. And sexist." Jim grinned. "Even I know that. Now, what you got for dinner? I'm starving."

Janet had seen Lyn walking toward the village with the children in the double buggy as she was making her way up to the church to do the flowers. She frowned. She hadn't realized they were back. Lyn looked very tired, and little Tom, she could see from the car as she drove past waving, was fast asleep. Neither of them saw her. Intent on her own thoughts, Lyn was pushing the buggy across the village green, her head down, her steps weary, plodding in the direction of the village shop. She could catch them there after she had checked the church and topped up the vases with water.

Janet hesitated near the church door, gazing across the quiet churchyard to the spot where they had found Mary Sutton's body. The village was still shocked at the tragedy, and whispers were flying from door to door about what she had been doing out there in the dark and cold alone. The rector had rung Roy, who was one of the churchwardens, about what they had found in the church — the bread and wine on the altar, almost certainly that used in the exorcism at the Hall — and there had been an emergency meeting at the rectory. Roy did not tell her what they had discussed, but it seemed there would be no funeral in the church. Mary had always said that she wished to be cremated and her ashes scattered in the sea.

Letting herself into the shadowy nave, Janet groped for the light switches and made her way toward the vestry. The church was looking good; Michaelmas daisies lasted well, and there were quantities of them in the chancel and in front of the pulpit. She picked up the heavy brass water jug and began to tour each arrangement. In front of the small brass plaque to Katherine, she stopped. Someone had left a bunch of white roses on the ground in front of it. She stared down at it thoughtfully. The church was open for visitors during the day. Anyone could have done it — so why did she feel suddenly so wary. She eyed the flowers, then slowly she backed away.

Between one moment and the next the church had become uncomfortable; there was a strange feeling of hostility where usually she felt nothing but an all-encompassing peace and security. Hastily, with a glance over her shoulder, she retraced her steps to the vestry and set the jug on its shelf. Coming out, she pulled the door shut and made her accustomed small bow to the altar before walking quickly back down the aisle toward the door at the rear of the church. Four pews from the end she stopped. There was something between her and the door. She blinked. It was a trick of the light, a patch of sunlight thrown unexpectedly through the south windows out of the gloom of the morning onto the old flagstones. It looked like a mist, a slowly spinning mist. She caught hold of the pew end near her and shook her head, disoriented and slightly dizzy. It was moving almost imperceptibly away from the door across the back of the church toward the font, then as she watched it stopped, seemed to hesitate, and then changed direction. It was moving east now, up the center of the aisle toward her.

She took a step backward and then another, her legs shaking so much they would barely support her. The church seemed very empty, the lights high on the roof beams directed up into the vaulted ceiling, the chancel still in comparative darkness where she hadn't switched on the lights. She glanced over her shoulder toward the altar and then turned and ran, skipping around the front of the pews and into the side aisle. The spinning mist seemed to hesitate, then it moved on toward the chancel steps. Janet ran on tiptoe down the small side chapel, dodged around the pillar, and reached the door.

Grabbing the ring, she tried to open it. For a moment in her panic she thought it was locked, wrestling with it desperately, then at last the latch clicked up and she hauled the heavy door open, throwing herself out into the porch. Slamming the door behind her, she ran out into the churchyard, taking deep breaths of the cold air.

There was no sunshine. The sky was heavy with cloud. She glanced over her shoulder, almost expecting to see the door opening, but the porch was still; the door remained closed. Head down, walking as quickly as she could, she hurried down the path to her car and climbed in. Slamming down the locks, she tried with shaking hand to insert the key in the ignition. After a couple of attempts she managed it and turned it on, revving the engine before shooting the car out onto the road.

Lyn was choosing some cold meats from the delicatessen counter when Janet walked into the shop. She glanced up as the door banged shut and smiled. "Tom says he's hungry enough to eat that horse you gave him."

"That hungry, eh?" Janet ruffled Tom's hair. Her hand was shaking and she found she was shivering violently. Behind the counter, Sally Fairchild glanced up from the meat slicer. "You look peaky, Janet. Something wrong?" She was peeling the ham from the blade onto her plastic-gloved palm with a rhythmic hissing sound that had Tom mesmerized.

Janet shook her head. "I was up in the church. The door banged. Gave me a fright, that's all."

Sally stopped slicing and gave her a long appraising look. "Since when did a door banging make you shake like a leaf?"

Janet shrugged. "Nerves. Probably too much coffee this morning." She gave an unconvincing laugh.

"You're getting like Joss." Lyn did not make the remark sound like a compliment. "You'll be seeing ghosts around every corner next." She turned back to her purchases. "That's plenty, Sal, thanks. And some sausages, please. A pound will do."

"Where is Joss?" Janet tried to steady herself with an effort.

"Still in Paris as far as I know."

"Are you up at the house alone?"

The question sounded too urgent.

Lyn frowned. "Of course. Why not?"

"No reason." Janet shrugged. "I just thought — Lyn, you will be careful, won't you?"

Lyn turned to face her. "Listen. There is nothing wrong with that house now that Joss isn't there. Do you understand me? Nothing goes wrong. Nothing sinister happens —" She broke off suddenly, remembering her panic of the night before.

Sally glanced up from the bag into which she was inserting Lyn's purchases. She caught Janet's eye.

Janet shrugged. "OK. I'm sorry. Just remember I'm here if you need me." She turned toward the door.

"Janet, wait." Lyn fumbled in her purse for some money. "Look, that was rude of me. But there isn't anything wrong."

"Good." Janet stood for a moment, her hands wedged in her pockets, looking into Lyn's eyes. Then she turned to leave. "Just remember where I am if you get fed up with your own company."

Sally was ringing up Lyn's purchases on the till. She stopped as soon as the door had shut behind Janet. "She looked really ragged."

Lyn nodded. "I wonder what happened up there."

"Something strange, I'll be bound. Maybe old Mary is haunting the place already!" She gave an ostentatious shiver. "You are sure you are all right up there, my dear? Nothing would make most of the locals sleep alone in that house, you know, never mind with small children."

"So I keep being told." Lyn packed the shopping into her haversack. "Thanks, Sally. I'll probably be back tomorrow."

The buggy seemed heavier on the way back, or perhaps it was that she was tired. Lyn regretted for a moment that she hadn't begged a lift from Janet, then she remembered why. Janet would have lectured and hectored her and tried to put on the pressure to bring the boys to stay at the farm, when all Lyn wanted was to have them to herself while she had the chance. Plodding on, she glanced up at the sky. The clouds were becoming heavier and more threatening; she would be lucky if it didn't rain before she got home. She glanced down at her charges. Warmly wrapped and tucked beneath their blankets, they were sound asleep.

The first raindrops were beginning to fall as she reached the gate and began the last haul up the drive.

The house seemed very dark as she came around the corner. Puffing along behind the buggy, forcing the wheels through the muddy gravel, she glanced up at the rain-streaked windows. There was a face at the attic window above the front door. She stopped and stared. Was Joss home?

Squinting, she shook the ice-cold drops of sleet off her eyelashes, trying to make out who it was for several seconds longer, then she headed for the back of the house and the kitchen. The courtyard was empty. Jimbo appeared to have closed up and gone — for lunch, she supposed. There were no other cars there. She frowned. Who on earth was it then at the window? Groping in her pocket with ice-cold fingers for the key, she pushed the door open and bent to lift Tom out. "Come on, sausage. You know I can't pick you both up. You'll have to run inside for Aunty Lyn and open the kitchen door. Shall we try and do it without waking the tornado?" That was their private name for Ned.

Tom giggled and pushed himself out of the buggy, rushing ahead of her into the kitchen. Turning, she bumped the buggy up the back steps and maneuvered it past the coats and into the kitchen before she stopped to unbutton her own jacket. "Tom? Come and take your coat off."

There was silence.

"Oh, Tom, not again. Come on." She sighed, turning to hang up her coat and shake and fold the damp blankets onto the rail in front of the stove to dry. "Tom? Come on, then you can help me get lunch."

The door into the hall was open. With a glance at Ned, who was still asleep, Lyn left him in the buggy and ran into the corridor and through into the great hall. "Tom? Come on. Where are you?" She stopped, staring at the fireplace. A fire was burning in the grate. She could see the logs, neatly heaped into a pyramid, the blown ash swept up, the room warm and filled with the sweet rich smell of burning oak.

"Joss? Luke? When did you get back?" She went to the study door and peered around it. "Where's the car? I didn't see it."

The study was deserted, the curtains still half drawn as she had left them that morning.

"Joss? Luke? Where are you?" Lyn stood for a minute at the bottom of the stairs. Then she began to climb.

CHAPTER 38

Luke neatened all the small empty pots and containers and lined up the knives and forks on the tray in front of him with precision and pushed it to one side. He glanced at Joss. "Not long now. We'll be landing in about fifteen minutes I should think." The flight attendants were trundling their carts along the plane, collecting all the rubbish. He looked down at Joss's meal. She had barely touched anything. "They'll be all right. Lyn's just been out, that's all."

"Out late at night, with two small children? Out again first thing in the morning?" She shook her head in despair. "We should have rung the police, Luke. Supposing something's happened to them."

"Nothing's happened to them, Joss." He gave a deep sigh. "Look, we'll try and phone again from the air terminal, and if we can't get through to Lyn we'll try Janet again. There's always the chance of course that they've gone off on a spree together. Don't forget, they're not expecting us yet." He reached for her tray and passed it with his own to the flight attendant. "Come on. Cheer up. We don't want to undo all the good the rest has done you."

"I know." She nodded wearily. "I did enjoy it. I did like Paul."

She fell silent. Paul had arranged the flights — getting them on the plane at short notice by pulling one or two strings with someone he knew — and he had insisted on driving them back to Orly. There had been tears in his eyes as well as Joss's when they finally embraced at the check-in. "Come and see us," she had whispered. "If it doesn't make you unhappy to come there without her, come and see us."

"Of course." He kissed her on both cheeks. "And you will come back to stay with me in the summer and you will bring your little boys with you."

There had been a moment's silence as they had both thought the unthinkable, and he squeezed her shoulders again. "They will be all right," he said, watching as Luke pushed their passports over the counter. "You will see. They will be just fine."

In the phone booth in the high airy terminal building at Stansted, Joss stood listening to the line ringing. There was no reply. She glanced at her watch. The boys should be resting by now after their lunch. With a glance at Luke who was standing only three feet away watching their luggage, she dialed Janet. This time there was an answer.

A few minutes later she hung up. When she turned to face Luke she was smiling. "Janet saw them all in the shop this morning. She says they're fine. The phone must be out of order or I've rung each time when Lyn has been out. She saw them on their way home too."

"Good." Luke stooped to swing their cases up and he began to walk toward the doors. "Then perhaps you can stop worrying while we find the car and sort ourselves out." He was heading toward the bus, which would take them out to the distant car park. Outside the huge ever-circling door, he stopped and waited for her. "Joss. You're going to be sensible from now on; no overdoing it. No arguing with Lyn. No worrying about ghosts and noises and silliness where there is no need for it. Remember, you've got to see that doctor again."

Joss stared at him. "I haven't been making any of it up, Luke. Why do you think we've come stampeding back like this! For goodness sake. Paul believed me. He knew. He had seen my mother go through it —"

"Your mother was being persecuted by a real woman, Joss. Not a ghost. A real flesh-and-blood woman." He swung the cases onto the bus and they found some seats. "Her Katherine wasn't a ghost."

"Wasn't she?" Joss seemed to be looking right through him. "We'll see."

Pulling the car up in the courtyard next to Lyn's mini, Janet peered through the windshield at the house.

For a moment she didn't move, then, almost reluctantly, she opened the door and climbed out.

The back door of the house was unlocked. After

a couple of knocks, she pushed it open and walked through the lobby into the kitchen. It was empty. The buggy stood near the window, and the neatly folded blankets were hanging on the rail in front of the range. She touched them; they were completely dry and warm. There was no sign of anything cooking. In the corner the rocking horse stood abandoned, its rein hanging to the floor. She frowned. For a moment she had thought it was rocking gently by itself as though pushed by an unseen hand. She stared at it. It was her imagination, of course. It had to be. Walking to the door, she peered through.

"Lyn? Where are you?"

Her voice echoed in the silence.

"Lyn? It's Janet. Are you there?"

She took a few steps into the great hall and looked around. The place was in shadow, the remains of a fire smoldering in the hearth. Although the room was quite warm, she found she was shivering as she walked through toward the study. It was empty, so she went back and peered up the staircase. "Lyn?" she called softly. If the boys were asleep she didn't want to wake them. "Lyn, where are you?"

Tiptoeing up, she paused on the landing outside Lyn's room. The door was shut and she tapped on it gently. "Lyn? Can I come in?"

There was no answer. She hesitated a moment, not liking to open it in case Lyn was asleep, then she took her courage in both hands and pushed it. The room was empty and somehow very bare. There was no sign that Lyn had been there recently at all.

She was on her way to the boys' bedrooms when she heard a faint knocking in the distance. She stopped, listening. There it was again — a distinct hammering sound from somewhere upstairs. She eyed the ceiling suspiciously, then she turned and went out to the stairs again.

The attic was very cold. Nervously, she peered into the first room. It was furnished as a spare bedroom, but there was no sign of anyone there. Beyond it the rest of the top floor was empty — a long string of low-ceilinged rooms leading out of each other the length of the house. "Lyn?" she shouted. "Are you up here?" The sound of her voice was somehow shocking in the intense silence. It was as she was standing listening for a response that she heard the knocking once again, louder this time, and more frenzied. "Lyn? Are you there?" Ducking through the door, she made her way into the next room. That too was empty, dusty and smelling of cold and damp. "Lyn, where are you?"

The door at the farthest end of the line of attic rooms was closed. The banging was coming from behind it. "Lyn, is that you?" Janet put her ear to the wood paneling. "Lyn?" She put her hand on the latch and rattled it. The door appeared to be locked.

"Let me out. For God's sake let me out!" Lyn's voice from behind the door was completely hysterical. "I've been here for hours. Are the boys all right?"

Janet grimaced. "I haven't seen the boys. Hold on. I'll try and find the key." She looked around frantically. The room in which she was standing was empty. There was nowhere a key could be hidden.

"Feel on the beam over the door," Lyn instructed, her voice muffled by the thickness of the wood. "That's where it was last time."

Janet looked up. Cautiously, she put her hand above her head and ran her fingers over the studs and cross beams which made the partition wall. It was several seconds before she connected with cold metal. "Here it is. Found it!" She grabbed it and inserted it into the large keyhole.

A second later the door swung open. Lyn was white-faced, her hair disheveled, her clothes filthy. "Thank God you came. I was afraid I'd be there forever."

"Who locked you in?" Janet was running after her back toward the stairs.

"Tom. It must have been. The little devil."

"It can't have been. That beam was far too high for Tom."

"He must have fetched a chair or something. Believe me, Janet, he's done it before." Lyn brushed the tears out of her eyes with the back of her hand. "For pity's sake, hurry. There's no knowing what he may have done."

She hurtled down the staircase and through toward his bedroom. It was empty. "Tom? Tom where are you? Don't hide from me." She pushed open the door to Ned's little bedroom. That too was empty.

"Oh, God!" It was a sob. "Janet, where is he?"

Janet bit her lip. "Where were they when you last saw them? Tom presumably upstairs and Ned? Where was Ned?"

"Ned should be in his buggy in the kitchen."

Janet shook her head. "No, I've just come from there. The buggy's empty."

"He was still fast asleep, so I left him. He was strapped in. There was no danger. It was only for a minute." Lyn burst into tears again. "Oh, God!" She wiped her face with her sleeve. "Tom ran away and hid and I heard noises up there in the attic. Giggling. Running about. It was Tom. It had to be, so I ran up to find him. He's not allowed to play up there on his own, and anyway I wanted to get lunch." She sniffed. "I looked everywhere for him. I could hear him. He was hiding somewhere up there. When I was in that far attic the door banged and I heard the key turn. Then there was complete silence. I begged him. I promised him all sorts of things if he would open it, but there was total silence. No more running about, no more giggles. I knelt down to look through the keyhole at once — did you see how big it was? — I could see the whole attic. He wasn't there, Janet. Nowhere. And there was no chair. I'd have heard if he'd dragged a chair cross the floor. He's only a little boy. He couldn't have lifted it by himself."

Janet put her arm around her shoulders. "Try and keep calm, Lyn. We've got to work this out. We must search the house again, carefully. You know how children love hiding. Tom has probably hidden himself somewhere and he's having a good laugh."

"With Ned?" It was a whisper.

Janet shrugged. "I expect he's tucked Ned up somewhere and left him; he's too young to play

561

with properly." Her voice died away. After a second's silence, she went on. "We know he's not in the attic. Let's search this floor, then we'll go on down. We must be systematic."

They were. They searched each room in turn, looking under beds, behind curtains, and in cupboards, then, certain neither child was there, they went down to the study.

"No sign." Janet had even looked in the drawers of the desk.

"The cellar," Lyn whispered. "We must check the cellar."

The door was locked and there was no sign of the key.

"They can't be down there." Janet was eyeing the door dubiously.

"They might be. I'll fetch the key." Lyn disappeared for a moment and then reappeared with it in her hand. She inserted it into the lock with a shaking hand and pushed open the door.

The cellar was in darkness. "There's no one here." Janet's voice echoed slightly as she reached past Lyn and switched on the lights. "It doesn't look as if anyone has been here for weeks. Do you want us to go down to look?"

Lyn nodded. "We have to look everywhere." She was feeling very sick.

"OK." After a moment's hesitation, Janet led the way down the steps.

At the bottom they both stopped and listened. "He's not down here," Lyn whispered. "He can't be."

"We'd better look." Janet was feeling distinctly uneasy. "Where is his favorite hiding place? Does he have one?"

"He does seem to like the attic. I've never known him to come down here. He's not allowed to. It's always kept locked, and the key was where it's supposed to be — so how could he be down here?"

Janet shrugged. "We had to check. After what happened to Edgar."

Lyn stared at her. "But that was a heart attack."

"I know. But why was he down here? No one seems to know."

They stood for a moment looking around, then Lyn walked through and stood in the second cellar. There was no sign of anything and nowhere to hide. Closing her eyes with a deep sigh of relief, she turned. "We'd better go on looking upstairs."

The great hall, dining room, morning room, passages, pantries and sculleries behind the kitchen — each one was subjected to a careful and thorough search. When they were once more in the kitchen Janet reached for her jacket. "Come on. We're going to have to look outside. I wonder if Jim is back yet. He can give us a hand."

But the courtyard was empty, the garages and coach houses all padlocked. "At least we know they can't be there." Lyn rattled one of the locks. She was feeling more and more afraid.

The gardens were bleak, the November light failing as they let themselves through the gate onto the lawn. "We've got to check the lake." Lyn's hands were shaking. "Oh, Janet, why? What was Tom thinking of?" Suddenly she was crying again.

"We don't know anything's wrong." Janet put her arm around her shoulders and gave her a quick hug. "Come on. It's a childish prank, that's all. I'm sure they're perfectly safe." Her voice lacked conviction.

Walking down the lawn toward the still water of the lake, both women were silent. After a few steps Lyn broke into a run. On the bank she stared around, scanning the reeds and lilies. A moorhen broke cover near her and paddled furiously toward the far bank with a sharp cry of distress, and a heron, which had been feeding on the island in the center of the water, lumbered awkwardly into the air, croaking with indignation.

"I can't see anything." Lyn dashed the tears out of her eyes as Janet caught up with her, panting.

"Nor can I. You go that way and I'll go this way. I'll meet you around the other side. That way we can be sure." She squeezed Lyn's arm and set off, her shoes squelching in the damp muddy grass. The air felt very cold and she shivered as she hurried on, her eyes scanning the water, dreading the thought that she might actually see something there, but the lake and its surroundings were empty of any signs of the small boy or the baby. When she caught up with Lyn she was smiling. "Thank God they're not here. I couldn't have borne it. Where else can we look?"

Lyn stared around desperately. "Tom's only little. He can't have got far. Not on his own." She bit her lip. "You don't think — you don't think they've been taken away?"

"Who on earth by?" Janet shook her head. "They were in the house. You'd have known if there was someone else there."

"Someone locked me in, Janet."

They stared at each other for a moment. "I think we'd better call the police," Lyn said at last. "Let's go back to the house."

As they walked they both scanned the garden for any signs. "You know he could just be hiding — in a hedge or a bush or something. We should be calling." Janet stopped and, turning around, cupped her hands around her mouth. "Tom! Tom Tom, where are you?"

"Tom!" Lyn echoed. She ran toward the shrubbery at the edge of the lawn. "Tom Tom! Come on. It's lunchtime."

By the time they had worked their way around to the front of the house they were both exhausted, hoarse with shouting and filthy from peering into the muddy places under bushes and trees.

"It's no good. It will have to be the police. The woods go for miles. We can't search them on our own." Lyn was white as a sheet.

"No." Janet eased her frozen hands into her pockets. "No, you're right. We'd better go in and phone."

They walked across the gravel in front of the house, and ducked through the arch into the courtyard. Luke's car was parked by the back door.

"Oh, no." Lyn stopped. She had gone white. "What am I going to tell them?"

"The truth, love. Come on. The sooner we've done that, the sooner we can call the police."

Janet put her arm around Lyn's shoulders again.

Together they went into the back hall and pushed open the kitchen door.

Luke and Joss were standing by the table laughing. Tom was between them, holding Joss's hand. In the other he was clutching a model of the Eiffel Tower.

"Tom?" Lyn's cry made them all turn around. "Tom, where have you been? Where's Ned?"

"Lyn! Janet! What on earth is the matter?" Joss stared at them in horror. "Ned's here. Asleep. In the buggy. What's wrong? Why are you both so wet?"

Lyn walked slowly around the table and stood in front of the buggy for a full minute staring down at the sleeping baby, then slowly she knelt down and began to undo the harness which held him safely in, the harness which had clips far too stiff for Tom's small fingers to undo. Around him was tucked one of the soft blankets which she remembered hanging on the front of the range.

She felt it carefully. It was bone dry. Tears running down her cheeks, she stared up at Joss, who had come to stand behind her.

"What happened, Lyn?" Joss was frowning.

"I thought I'd lost them." Lifting Ned out, Lyn kissed the top of his head. Climbing to her feet, she pushed him into Joss's arms. "I thought we'd lost them. I thought . . . I thought . . ." Sitting down at the table, she put her head in her arms and burst into sobs.

Luke frowned at Joss. "It looks as though it's a good thing we came back. Hey, old thing, come on. Cheer up. Everyone is all right." He patted Lyn's head awkwardly, then he looked at Janet. "You both look as though you'd been dragged through a hedge backward. Do you mind telling me exactly what's been going on here?"

"Wait. First let me ask Tom something." Janet knelt down before the little boy and gave him a hug. "OK, sausage. I want you to tell Aunty Janet where you and Ned were hiding." She gave him an encouraging smile. "You were hiding, weren't you."

Tom nodded vigorously.

"So. Where were you? Aunty Lyn and I looked and looked and we couldn't find you."

"We were playing with Georgie."

"Now, why don't I find that surprising," Janet said softly. She raised her hand sharply to forestall Joss's cry of alarm. "So, where do you go to play with Georgie, Tom?"

"Upstairs."

"Right upstairs? In the attic?"

He nodded.

"And was it you that locked Aunty Lyn in the attic?"

He stared at her for a moment. "That was Georgie."

"I see. You knew that was naughty of him, didn't you."

Tom looked shamefaced. He peeked at Lyn and then buried his face in Janet's sweater. She looked up at Joss over the little boy's head. "Please, bring them back to me. Don't keep them here."

"Janet —"

Luke's protest was cut short by Lyn. "Please,

Luke. Until we've sorted out what happened."

"But you don't believe in all this rubbish about ghosts!" Luke stared at her.

"I don't know what I believe anymore. I think we should all go to Janet's. If she'll have us. Just till we find out what's happening."

"I'd love to have you all, Luke."

Suddenly he caved in. "OK. You girls go, and the kids. But I'm staying here."

"No. Remember what Paul said."

"Joss, I am not afraid of a jumble of legends and stories. I live here. My job is here. I like this house and I'm not afraid of it." He gave a sober smile. "Honestly. I'll be all right. You two take Tom and Ned to Janet's because I know you won't get a wink of sleep unless you do, but then tomorrow we're going to have to work something out. We can't go on like this."

In the end they persuaded him to come back to the farm for supper at least, but later, after they had all eaten, and checked on the children, asleep and safe upstairs in the long low-ceilinged bedroom, Luke eventually got up and stretched his arms above his head. Lyn had gone to bed half an hour before. "I don't know about you, Joss, but I'm feeling a bit jet-lagged." He grinned at his own joke. "I think I'm off home now."

"No." Joss clutched at his hand. "Stay here. Just tonight."

He shook his head. "Joss, my love. I must go back. I am not going to be chased out of our own house. That is ridiculous. And tomorrow we've got to find a way of reassuring you and Lyn." He turned to Janet and gave her a kiss on the cheek. "Thanks for a wonderful meal. You look after them and keep the hysteria levels down, OK? I think perhaps what we'll do is get the family to rally around. The christening contingent. Your mum and dad, Lyn, and my mum and dad and perhaps Mat as well. And David and anyone else who wants to come. We'll have a pre-Christmas wassail." He grinned. "No ghost would dare show its face in a house that full, would it?" He gave Joss a hug. "Now, no more worry, OK? And remember, if Janet doesn't mind, you promised you'd ring Paul and tell him everything was all right."

In a moment he was gone. Janet sighed. "Men. They won't be told. Isn't he scared at all?"

Joss shook her head sadly. "I think he's as scared as hell. He just won't admit it. Not even to himself."

Paul was reassuring. "He'll be all right, Jocelyn. He is strong, your husband. But if you want more reinforcement, call me and I will come too." She could hear his laughter and his affection through the phone.

"Bless you, Paul, I will." When she had hung up, she turned to Janet, who had picked up her needlepoint and was working by the light of a lamp near the fire. "Can I ring David? I want to find out what happened here when he came."

"Of course." Janet bit off a thread. "Get him up here as well."

"I don't think I can. It's term time still." She pulled the phone down off the table and sat in front of the fire near Janet with the instrument on her knee.

David was marking a pile of essays on the Education Act. Nemesis, he thought ruefully as he sat staring at them, listening to a soft background Sibelius. He was far from displeased when the phone rang even though it was after eleven.

"David? It's Joss."

"Joss?" His heart leaped at the sound of her voice. "Where are you? Are you home?"

"The boys and I are with Janet."

"Thank God you're not in that house. I suppose you heard what happened."

"Some." She was conscious of Janet staring at her. "Can you tell me exactly what happened?"

It was several minutes before she spoke again.

"Can you come, David? Can you come, so we can talk?"

He hesitated. His flat was warm and comfortable and above all safe. Staring down at the pile of essays, he was tempted to say no, but the edge of panic in Joss's voice had reached him. Her dumbo husband still did not seem to have caught on about what was happening. She needed someone who understood.

"OK. I'm free after fifth period tomorrow. I'll come up then." There was a moment's silence as he mentally questioned his own sanity. "Can you stay away till I come?"

"No, David. Of course I can't stay away."

"Then keep the children away and you be careful. Please."

She sat for a long time after she had rung off, staring into the flames, aware that Janet had put

570

down her embroidery and was watching her carefully.

She looked up at last. "So, supposing you tell me what really happened this afternoon. You and Lyn seemed determined to keep it quiet."

"We didn't want to frighten you."

"So, frighten me now they're safe." She turned a speculative gaze on Janet.

It did not take long to tell the story.

Joss turned back to the fire. She did not want Janet to see her fear.

"It can't have been Tom," Janet repeated. "He couldn't have reached the key and he couldn't undo the baby harness in the buggy."

"But you don't think it was a real person."

"Jimbo?" Janet shrugged. "I gather he has a key, but somehow I doubt it. Who else is there?" She began to fold her work away into her sewing basket. "I'll tell you one thing, Joss. I wish Luke hadn't gone back there, I really do."

CHAPTER 39

Luke turned off the kitchen light and made his way slowly toward the stairs. In the great hall he stopped and stared around. The room was still warm, though the fire had long ago died, and it smelled nice — wood smoke and flowers and old lavender polish. He stood savoring the moment, his hand on the light switch. It was good to be home again, though he had enjoyed the trip to France; he had liked Paul enormously, as had Joss, and he hoped to see him again. Sighing, he turned off the switch and began to climb the stairs.

Flicking on their bedroom light, he was pulling off his jacket when he noticed the bed. He stared for a minute, hardly able to believe his eyes, then slowly he walked across to it and bent down to run his hand over it. It was covered in white rose petals. His mouth fell open. They were ice cold, like snowflakes, scattered thickly over the whole area of the crewelwork cover.

Lyn or Janet? A practical joke — and not a very kind one — aimed at Joss. Angrily, he swept them off the bed, watching as they scattered all over the floor.

In the corner of the room, in the far shadows, the slumbering silence stirred and one of the shadows detached itself and moved a little closer to the bed.

Luke was pulling the cover back, shaking it and folding it onto the chair in the corner. He turned, surveying the floor, and decided it was too late to bother with sweeping it. Time enough for that tomorrow before Joss came home. Hauling his sweater up over his head, he walked through into the bathroom and began to run the hot water.

Whistling to himself under his breath, he peered at his reflection in the mirror as he reached for the toothpaste, noting the bags under his eyes with a scowl, then he stopped what he was doing suddenly and held his breath; he was listening, he realized, straining his ears above the sound of running water. Impatiently, he turned off the tap, wrenching at it as the water flow continued for a few seconds. Then came the drips plopping seemingly unstoppably into the bath with the sound of stones rattling in a dustbin and then at last silence. Tiptoeing to the door, he turned the handle soundlessly and eased it open, peering out into the hallway. The house was silent.

Reaching for his dressing gown, he pulled it on, belting it over his jeans, and took a step out onto the landing. Cautiously, he peered over the banisters and down into the stairwell. He wasn't sure now what he had heard, but he could feel rather than hear that there was something — or someone — there.

"Joss?" It was a whisper. "Joss?" He tried

louder. The silence seemed to deepen. He wished he had some kind of a weapon at hand. Looking around desperately, he spotted the pewter candlestick on the coffer between the doors to the bedrooms. Stealthily, he crossed over and, taking out the candle, he hefted the heavy lump of metal into his hand before turning once more to the stairs.

"Joss? Who's there?" His voice was stronger this time. "Come on, I can hear you."

It wasn't true; the silence was so intense it was almost tangible.

"Joss?" He put a foot on the first step down. "Joss? Lyn?"

He was halfway down the stairs when he heard a movement behind him. Spinning around, he looked up onto the landing, peering through the turned wooden posts of the banisters, and caught sight of something as it fled into his bedroom. Not Kit or Kat. A woman.

"Joss? That is you, isn't it? Come on. Stop playing the fool. I nearly hit you with the candlestick." Two at a time, he retraced his steps and pushed open the door.

She was lying on the bed under the covers — an indistinct shape in the dim light of the bedside lamp. He smiled, relief flooding through him. "My God, you had me going there; I thought it must be your ghost." Putting down the candlestick, he walked across to the bed. "Joss? Come on. No need to hide." Reaching down, he pulled back the covers.

There was no one there.

"Joss?" His voice slid up the register. "Joss,

for Christ's sake, stop messing about."

He peered behind the hangings and then stooped to look under the bed.

"Joss, where are you?" Spinning around, he peered into every corner of the room. "Joss!" The palms of his hands were sweating. "That's enough. You've had your little joke." He backed away from the bed toward the door. With one last glance over his shoulder, he turned and fled down the stairs.

In the kitchen he threw himself into the chair at the head of the table and put his head in his hands. What in God's name was the matter with him? He was going neurotic; he was going mad. He rubbed his face with his hands and for a moment he sat still, just staring at the door, half expecting someone to appear through it at any moment.

It was several seconds before he stood up again and went to the stove. Pulling open the door to the firebox, he peered in. The coals were glowing nicely and for a minute he stood, his hands outstretched to the warmth. There was no way he was going back to Janet's! He was not going to be chased out of the house by the girls' having a joke on him, or by anything else.

He frowned for a moment, not wanting to think about what else it might be. Joss's terror and Paul's very real warning hovered for a moment at the corners of his mind, but he pushed them back angrily. This was complete nonsense. He had allowed them to get to him, that's all. And it wasn't going to go on. He was going to stay in the house and that was that.

For a moment he was tempted to retrace his steps to the great hall, stand up and make an announcement to that effect to any ghosts or spirits or demons who might be lurking, but he thought better of it. A good night's sleep — or at least what was left of the night — he looked at his watch and realized suddenly that it was well after one — was a more sensible plan of action, and in the morning the others would be back.

Sitting at the kitchen table, a mug of hot chocolate in front of him, he cupped his hands around the comforting warmth of the pottery and sat staring blankly in front of him, aware that his eyes were closing. Slowly his head began to nod. Once or twice he jerked it up and resolved to stand up and go back upstairs, but each time he leaned back, sipped the chocolate, and decided to wait a few more minutes by the warmth of the stove.

He was awakened by the phone ringing. Staring around, confused, he found he was still in the kitchen and it was — he peered at the wall clock — nearly seven o'clock. Outside it was still pitch dark. Fumbling for the phone, he picked up the receiver.

"Mr. Grant?" The voice was unfamiliar. A woman with a soft local accent.

He grunted assent, running stiff fingers through his hair. The inside of his mouth felt like old moldy felt.

"Mr. Grant, I'm Natalie Cotting. Jim's sister."

"Jim?" For a moment Luke was confused. "Oh, Jimbo."

There was an amused snort from the other end of the line. "Jimbo. Right. Did he tell you he'd been on to me?"

"No. He didn't. Did you want to speak to him?"

"No. No. I'm sorry to ring so early, but I've been thinking and I reckon I should come over today if I can get the day off. Is your wife there, Mr. Grant?"

"Joss? No." He was shaking his head, confused. "She spent the night with a neighbor."

"Ah." There was a moment's silence. "And your children. They're with her, right?"

"Yes."

"Good." The relief at the other end of the line was palpable.

"Look —" Luke took a deep breath, trying to clear his mind. "I'm sorry. Perhaps I'm being obtuse. You want to speak to Joss, right?"

"Right." He could hear the amusement in her voice. "If I set off now, I should be with you in an hour and a half, or thereabouts. Can you tell Jim — that is, Jimbo" — she snorted once more — "that I'm coming, please. And tell Mrs. Grant to stay away until I get there, OK?"

"What do you mean, stay away —" Luke was indignant. "Hello? Are you still there?" He knew she wasn't. He had heard the click as she hung up.

Washed and shaved and in a fresh shirt, he felt a new man. It was only as he walked through into the bedroom and rummaged in the chest of drawers for a thick sweater that he noticed the bed. Staring, he walked toward it and stood looking down. It was neatly made, the covers

577

in place, not a dent or wrinkle anywhere, and around it the floor was spotless. There was no sign anywhere of a single white petal.

Jimbo arrived at eight-thirty as usual. He was unlocking the carriage house when Luke walked out of the back door and joined him, looking down at the shining chassis on the blocks before them. "Nearly finished." Jimbo's voice was filled with pride. "I got a lot done while you were away."

"You did indeed." Luke glanced at him. "Jimbo, your sister rang this morning. She said to tell you she was coming over."

"Nat? She's coming? That's good." Jimbo avoided his eyes. "I thought she should talk to Joss."

"So she said. May I ask what about?"

Jim took a deep breath. "Ghosts. She knows a lot about ghosts. She can talk to them. They never frighten her."

"And they frighten you?" Luke's hands were rammed down in his jeans' pockets. He felt less confident than he had before.

"I'll say. No way will I go into that house." Jimbo smiled sheepishly. "I never liked it, and now —" His voice trailed away.

"And you think Joss and the children are in danger."

"Not Joss. No. Joss has never been in danger." Jimbo shifted his feet uncomfortably. Then he glanced up. "I think you should watch it, though." He shrugged, embarrassed. "Not keen on men, the ghosts in this house. Look at what happened to the Reverend Gower."

"He had a heart attack, Jimbo. It could have happened anywhere."

"It didn't though, did it. It happened here." Jimbo turned to the workbench and reached for a spanner. "That Lyn, she's over at the Goodyears' too, is she?" he asked casually.

"Yes," Luke nodded. "They're all over there."

"That's good." Jimbo turned back, the spanner in his hand. "You just think what happened to old Mr. Duncan, and his two boys. I thought Nat should know Joss says it's all happening again."

"So, how can Nat — Natalie — help?"

Jimbo shrugged his shoulders. "She always said she could. When she was little. No one would listen to her then, of course. But now — well, she knows about these things. She's a psychic, you see."

"Oh." Luke raised an eyebrow. "I see."

He wasn't at all sure what he was expecting a psychic to look like — shawls, beads and big hooped earrings, at least, certainly not the neat young woman in a business suit who turned in under the archway some forty minutes later, driving a Golf GTi.

"Sorry." She reached out to shake Luke's hand. "I couldn't leave at once after all. I had to look in at the office first. Is Joss here?"

Luke shook his head. "My wife is still over at the Goodyears' with the children."

"Good." Natalie glanced over her shoulder at the house. "May I go in and wander around? There's no need for you to come in too."

Luke hesitated.

"That's a bit rich, Nat. He doesn't know you're not a burglar," Jimbo put in. "He doesn't know you from Adam."

Luke laughed. "I'll take a risk. Yes, please, go on in."

He stood and watched as she walked over the cobbles toward the back door, noting absentmindedly that she had extremely good legs beneath her short executive skirt.

"What sort of job does she do, Jim?" he asked as he turned back to the workbench.

"She works in a solicitor's office." Jim grinned at him over an oily carburetor. "She inherited all the brains of the family. None left for me." He sniffed good-naturedly. "Can't think where she got them from. Not my dad, bless him, that's for sure."

"Are you going over to the house later?" Lyn had finished clearing away the children's breakfast and returned Janet's kitchen to a pristine neatness. She glanced over at Joss, who was sitting at the table over a cup of coffee. "You haven't eaten anything, you know. You must have something."

Joss shook her head. "I'm feeling a bit queasy, to tell you the truth. I'll get something later. This will do. I thought I'd go and have a chat with Luke a bit later, yes. If you don't mind keeping the boys here." She smiled fondly at Tom, who was playing on the mat with the brother of Kit and Kat, who was still firmly resident at the farm.

"Have you rung Luke?"

Joss shook her head. "I've been trying not to since five o'clock this morning. I'm sure he's OK."

Lyn raised an eyebrow. "Sure he is." She scrutinized Joss for a moment. "You are looking lousy. Why not go back to bed for a bit. Janet won't mind. As soon as she comes in from her hens or wherever she is, she suggested she and I take the boys shopping. Tom would enjoy it and Ned can come in his pram. It'll give you the chance to rest."

I've been resting. For days. Joss could feel the words hovering on her lips, but she didn't say them. She did feel lousy, and she would like nothing more than to go back to bed, but she had to go over to the house. She had to talk to Luke. And above all she did not want the boys there. Not ever again.

She waited until they had gone before letting herself out of the back door and walking swiftly across the garden toward the orchard. The morning was dull and cold; occasional showers of drips cascaded from the bare branches of the tall old apple trees as she walked past, and above through the network of twigs she could see the rain waiting in the bellying clouds. Shivering, she walked more quickly, feeling the wet grass and mud slippery beneath her shoes as she turned out of the orchard and across the footpath. In the distance she could see the roofs of Belheddon Hall huddling in the mist on the crest of the ridge.

The garden seemed very silent as she let herself in by the gate and walked slowly around the lake. A duck was paddling on the far side, dipping its beak from time to time into the weed, and she stood for a moment, staring at the pattern of rings spreading out from it across the water.

The shutters in the study were still closed. She could see the blank windows from here. Standing still, she studied the house and surreptitiously her hand went up to the crucifix on the chain around her neck.

No one saw her approach. Leaving a trail of darker footprints in the wet grass, she stepped onto the terrace, shivering with cold, and walked toward the windows. Peering into the great hall, she could see the room in the dim morning light. There was no fire, and on the table she could see a vase of dead flowers, petals scattered around on the dusty surface. Her scalp was tingling and she rammed her fingers down into her pockets. They were ordinary flowers. Chrysanthemums and autumn daisies, but why had Lyn left them to die?

With heavy steps, she walked around toward the gate into the courtyard and stopped. The coach house doors were open and the lights were on, brilliant strips of fluorescent tubing, and she could hear the cheerful banging of a hammer on metal. Someone — Jimbo — was whistling.

It was like looking at a stage from a darkened auditorium; a world that was separate and unreal was displayed before her — a world of noise and bright lights and happiness and laughter while she, on the outside, peering through the bars of the gate, was in some strange limbo where time stood still and shadows lurked in the darkness.

There was a tightness in her chest, and in her

pockets the palms of her hands were beginning to sweat. Quietly she unlatched the gate and pushed it open. Passing the garage without announcing herself, she let herself into the kitchen and stopped in astonishment. A stranger was standing near the kitchen table.

"Joss?" The young woman held out her hand. "I'm Natalie Cotting, Jim's sister. I've come to help."

CHAPTER 40

"This was always one of the centers of activity."
They were standing in the great hall in front
of the fireplace. "Here and the large bedroom
upstairs." Natalie stood for a long moment in
complete silence, her eyes on the floor a few inches
in front of her feet. Joss watched her, standing
a yard or so from her. She could feel a tight
knot of tension somewhere below her ribs. It was
interfering with her breathing.

Slowly Natalie nodded. Without saying a word,
she moved toward the staircase, where she
stopped for a moment. "There never used to be
any trouble in the study. Is it still happy in there?"

Joss nodded.

"Good. Let's go upstairs then."

They toured the house slowly, room by room,
then found themselves back once more in the
kitchen. There too Natalie stood in silence, her
head bowed until at last she looked up and caught
Joss's eye. "Sorry. You must think I'm loopy."

Joss smiled. "No. Tell me what you've been
doing."

"Just having a feel around." Natalie slipped

into the chair at the head of the table and leaned forward earnestly, her chin cupped in her hands. She looked as if she were about to address a board of directors. "I used to come here a lot when I was little. I would play with the boys, Georgie and Sam. Georgie died about ten years before I was born and Sam I think about ten years before that. They must have been your brothers, I suppose?" She waited for Joss's nod. "Of course, they didn't know each other in life, but where they are now, in whatever dimension it is, they are a pair of tearaways." She smiled affectionately.

"My son Tom talks about them. He's found some of their toys. And —" Joss hesitated — "I've heard them calling to each other."

Natalie nodded. "Monkeys. There are other children here too, of course — the boys who have been lost. There's Robert. He was your mum's brother. And little John. He's only a wee thing of about three, with golden curls and big blue eyes."

Joss gasped. "You can see them?"

Natalie nodded. "Inside my head. Not always. Not today. I'm not seeing today." She frowned. "There's a lot of other things here today. Unpleasant things." She clenched her fists. "People have been meddling. The Reverend Gower — Jim told me. He always made things worse because he didn't understand what he was dealing with here. Exorcism works when the priests understand. So many don't. Often they are dealing with people — people like you and me, not demons. Other times they are dealing with evil far worse than they can conceive, and their faith in what they are doing lets them down. They aren't strong enough."

"And what are we dealing with here?" whispered Joss. Her eyes were fixed on Natalie's.

"I'm not sure yet. When I came as a child, I was always welcome. I could talk to Sam and George and Robert. But they're not here. They're hiding. There's something else." She stood up, her movements restless and quick. Looking out of the window, she shook her head. "There's too much here now. It's confused. I'm going to need some time. Let's go back to the great hall."

A few minutes later, standing in front of the fireplace, she shook her head again. "I can feel so much anger and so much pain." She put her hands to her temples. "It's filling my head. I can't sort out the voices."

Joss shivered. There was something in her own head as well — an echo, nothing more; an echo she couldn't quite hear.

Katherine.

It was the name from the shadows.

"Katherine," she whispered. "Is she a part of this?"

Natalie frowned. She half raised a hand to silence Joss, still listening hard to something Joss could not hear.

Katherine my love. You were meant to be mine forever.
Katherine! Where are you?

586

Natalie was nodding. "Katherine is part of the grief. His mourning is trapped in every stone and timber and tile of this house."

"Whose mourning?" Joss whispered. "Is it the king?"

Natalie's eyes focused sharply. "So you know? You've seen him?"

Joss shrugged helplessly. The shutter had suddenly come down in her mind again, the black wall she could not penetrate. "I think so. Yes. My little boy calls him the tin man because of his armor."

Natalie gave a small puzzled smile and nodded. "It is odd, isn't it, to wear armor in his lover's house."

"That's what I thought. But he's an angry, bitter man. Why else should he kill?"

"Ssh." Natalie lifted her hand sharply. "Perhaps we can get him to speak to us. But not now." She shook her head. "Let's go outside. Do you mind?"

There was no sign of Jimbo or Luke in the coach house as they walked out and into the garden, Natalie wearing a pair of Lyn's boots and an old jacket of Joss's over her smart office clothes.

Once on the grass she shook her neat, glossy hair out in the wind and took a couple of small childish skips across the grass.

"Sorry. The atmosphere in there was so oppressive I couldn't think straight. I could feel them listening all around me. Better to talk out here and decide what to do in private, as it were."

"Tom and Ned are in danger, aren't they."
Joss was walking beside her slowly, her hands in her pockets as they headed toward the lake.

"I think if the past history of this place is anything to go by, you must assume so, yes."

"But why? Why does he hurt the boys?" She paused for a moment, then she looked up. "Did you mean it? Can you get him to speak to us?"

Natalie shrugged. "I can try." She sighed. "I wish I wasn't feeling so tired. I feel as though I'm being drained."

They had reached the lake. She stood staring down into the water. "You know, I said in there I couldn't sort out the voices. There were more than I expected. Not the children's voices, not the lost boys or the men who have died. Other voices, powerful voices."

"Men's voices or women's?" Joss was watching a moorhen scurrying back and forth between the water lily leaves.

"That's the strange thing. I'm not sure. I can hear snatches of words — powerful words, but I can't make them out. It's like fiddling with the dial on a radio. One flashes backward and forward through the stations — some are loud, some faint, and there is lots of static — then occasionally — just occasionally — one finds a station where one can understand the language and the reception is good and for a while one can tune in, then something happens — perhaps the wind changes or the antennae in my head move slightly and it's gone and I can't find it again."

There was a long silence. Joss was shivering.

"You can hear them, but can they hear you?"

"Why do you think I came out here?"

"You think they're trapped within the walls of the house, that they can't travel?"

Natalie shrugged. "I don't know." She gave a grimace. "But I feel safer out here."

Joss pulled up the collar of her jacket. "Luke and I have just returned from France. We went over there to see Paul Deauville, my mother's second husband. He gave me her last diaries. She mentioned Edward by name. She said she dreamed that he was looking everywhere for her here. He couldn't reach her in France. Then she made a strange entry: she said, 'I was so sure she could not cross water.'"

"She?"

"What kind of person can't cross water? A vampire? A dead person?"

"A witch?" Natalie's voice was very thoughtful.

"Margaret de Vere was accused of witchcraft, accused of trying to kill the king," Joss went on slowly. "She was Katherine's mother; Katherine, who we think was the king's lover. Here." The moorhen took flight suddenly. Flapping its wings wildly, it ran across the top of the lilies until it was airborne and dived out of sight behind the hedge. "While we were in France I found out that Katherine — a Katherine no one except my mother saw — visited her when she was dying. She took my mother white roses. Paul says that a Katherine had been the mistress of the man who became my mother's lover here at Belheddon, and that her rage and jealousy were so great she hunted my mother down across the water."

589

She was staring sightlessly down at the slowly spreading ripples beneath a wind-spun leaf. "I'm trying to work this out, and it makes no sense. Are we saying that King Edward of England, a man who had been dead for five hundred years, was my mother's lover?" She looked up and held Natalie's gaze. "That is what we're saying, aren't we? But it can't be. It can't."

"They were both lonely, Joss. Your father had died. And he, Edward, had lost his Katherine."

"But he was dead!" Joss was revolted.

"He's an earthbound spirit who still has earthly emotions," Natalie said gently. "He still feels anger and fear and bitterness — those are the things that I suspect anchor him here — but perhaps he also feels loneliness and even love. We don't understand these things, Joss, so we must use our intuition. It's all we have."

Joss was staring down at the water again. A memory had surfaced out of nowhere: the cellar, a face, a pair of arms . . .

"Joss? Joss, what is it? What's wrong?" Natalie's arm was around her shoulders. "Joss, you're white as a sheet. Come on, it's cold out here. We ought to go in."

"No." Joss shook her off. She was trying to think, to remember, to grasp at a sliding mirage, a chimera at the edge of her mind, but already it had gone and the wall was once more firmly back in place, leaving nothing but the sour aftertaste of blinding panic.

Natalie was watching her carefully. She could see the fear and the revulsion like a cloak around the other woman and suddenly she began to understand. "Dear God," she whispered. "He's made love to you too."

"No!" Joss shook her head violently. "No, of course he hasn't. How could he? That's disgusting. It's not possible! No!" She was growing increasingly agitated. Running a few steps along the bank, she stopped. Under the warm layers of jacket and sweater and shirt her skin was ice cold and she could feel crawling shivers of disgust. Another memory flashed before her. Eyes. Blue, warm eyes, close to her face, and a swirl of soft dark velvet, then they were gone again and she was standing by the lake with Natalie under the lowering November clouds.

There was another long silence, then, "Are you all right?" Natalie said softly. She had followed her and her eyes met Joss's sympathetically.

Joss gave a weak smile. "Let's go back in."

"All right. If that's what you want." Natalie hesitated. "I could try and speak to him on my own, but" — she paused — "it would be better if you were with me. You belong to the house, you see. You're part of it all."

Joss nodded. Walking slowly back up the lawn, she stared at the house in front of her. It looked strangely blank, the study windows shuttered, her bedroom curtains only half open, the glass deadened and unreflective beneath the heavy sky. "David Tregarron is coming up sometime this afternoon," she said at last. "He's a friend of ours — Ned's godfather. He was with Edgar Gower when he had his heart attack. He's been studying the history of the house. He's the one who found out about Margaret de Vere."

Natalie stopped dead. "Does he see?"

Joss shook her head. "Not that I know of. He loves the history and romance of it all. And the mystery, of course."

"Of course." It was said somewhat dryly.

"I asked him to come so I could find out what really happened that night with Edgar and also because he believes it all. Unlike my husband, who questions my sanity. He believes Margaret de Vere really was a witch. Not a poor silly misguided old woman, but an educated clever practitioner of some kind of black magic. There's a brass to her in the floor of the church here, did you know?"

Natalie stopped in her tracks. "A brass? In the church?"

"Under that old rug in the chancel."

"She can't be buried there. It must be just a monument."

"Why not? Why can't she be buried here?"

"Not if she was a witch."

"Of course not." Joss hesitated. "Do you want to come and see the brass?"

"Now?"

"Why not." Joss gestured toward the church. She shuddered. It would at least put off for a while the need to go back inside the house.

A few cold drops of rain were beginning to fall as Joss grasped the iron ring to lift the latch and pushed open the door. The church was very dark. Behind her, Natalie hesitated. "Wait, I'll switch on the lights." Joss moved ahead, and a few seconds later the lights in the nave and the chancel came on, illuminating the vaulted roof.

"It's over here. See?" Joss was standing near the rug. "Natalie?" Natalie was still hesitating in the doorway. "What's wrong?" She stooped to lift the corner of the rug.

"Don't touch it!" Natalie called sharply. Slowly she stepped away from the door and began walking up the aisle between the pews. She could feel the thick miasma of hatred coming from the spot where Joss was standing. It was like a tangible object in the center of the floor.

By the time she was beside her she could feel the sweat standing out on the palms of her hands. "Whoever buried her here did so against the wishes of the church, and with her they buried the tools of her trade," she whispered. "They must have been very powerful or very influential to have managed to do that."

"They were a powerful family," Joss murmured back. "In with the king."

"Indeed," Natalie replied grimly. She hooked her foot under the corner of the rug and nudged it backward, exposing a little of the beautiful filigree metalwork in the stone. "I don't remember ever seeing this before, ever feeling anything before. Something has woken the evil up."

Joss grimaced. She gave a small shudder. "There's another brass over there — a tiny one let into the wall, to her daughter, Katherine."

Natalie glanced at her. She too shivered. The church was cold.

"Margaret was accused of bewitching the king to win him for Katherine, but then she died. Natalie?" Her voice sharpened suddenly. "What's that? It smells like smoke."

"It is smoke." Natalie was staring down the church toward the door through which they had just come in. A column of smoke, wispy, smelling of autumn bonfires, was slowly revolving in the back of the church.

Joss caught her arm. "What is it?" she whispered.

Natalie gave Joss a small push. "I don't think we're going to wait to debate about it. Let's get out of here."

"We need to turn off the lights —"

"Forget the lights! Come on, quickly." She dragged Joss down toward the side aisle as the column of smoke began to move toward them. In thirty seconds they were out, pulling the door shut with a crash.

"What was it?" Joss was panting as they made their way swiftly up the path. She was feeling sick with fear.

"Some kind of energy. Black energy."

"It wasn't a person?"

"No, it wasn't a person."

Joss stopped, clutching her side. "I'm sorry, I've got a stitch. I can't go on. Are we safe here? I thought churches were safe, sacred places, Natalie!"

"They are usually, but this one was desecrated by the burial of someone who practiced the black arts, right in front of the altar. Who knows what it might have done to the church?" Natalie took a deep breath, more unnerved than she liked to admit even to herself. "As I said, I've never felt anything before here, but then" — she gave a tight smile — "I never came here much. Something has happened here recently —" She paused. "Mary Sutton. Jim told me she died here. Maybe it was her. Maybe it was you coming back to the Hall with small children; there haven't been any children here in years. I don't know." She shook her head. "There used to be stories about the church — there was a booklet, my mum had it. Maybe I'll ask her. I think we should go back to the house."

"But the house —"

"I know." Natalie gave a grim laugh. "The house is frightening too. But at least I know what I'm dealing with there."

"I hope you're right." Joss had doubled up, trying to ease the pain in her side, overcome by a wave of dizziness.

Natalie did not appear to have noticed. She was frowning back at the church. "Joss, did you see where that energy came from?"

"Near the door."

"It started in front of Katherine's brass."

Katherine.

The word reverberated in the silence.

This time they both heard it.

"Is she buried near that brass or is it just a memorial?"

Joss shrugged. Slowly she straightened. She leaned back against the old chestnut tree near the gate and took deep slow breaths, trying to calm the lurching in her stomach. Nearby, the grave of her father lay in deep shadow. Beyond it she could just see the small white crosses which showed her where Georgie and Sam were buried.

Almost without realizing it, Joss reached out for Natalie's hand. "I'm scared," she whispered. "Terribly scared."

CHAPTER 41

David was standing in the courtyard with Luke when they emerged from the path. He kissed Joss and shook hands with Natalie and led the way into the kitchen. Jimbo, after giving his sister a perfunctory slap on the back, preferred to stay with the car he was working on.

"I found someone to look after the boys for me this afternoon so I could get away." David was carrying his holdall and an armful of books and papers, which he dropped onto the kitchen table. "Lots more about Belheddon and the families that lived here and the De Veres and Edward IV and Richard III." Neither he nor Luke appeared to have noticed the women's white faces or their silence.

Acutely aware that her hands were shaking, Joss reached for the books, staring curiously, in spite of herself, at the top one.

"It was dreadful — the accident. Quite dreadful. I still feel so guilty." David met Joss's eye at last. "I should never have rung him, never have let him come here. I'm so sorry."

"It wasn't your fault, David." Joss reached out

and took his hand. "You mustn't blame yourself."

His fingers closed over hers and for a moment he felt he was drowning in her gaze. Beautiful, bewitching woman. Abruptly he remembered where he was and let go of her hand. Luke hadn't noticed. He was talking to Natalie.

He glanced at the newcomer again. She was a very attractive woman, he noticed, and smartly dressed now that she had taken off that horrendous old jacket. He wondered how she fit in.

As if she had heard his question, she fixed her large gray eyes on his. "You are asking yourself what I am doing here. Let me introduce myself. Visiting psychic, medium, nutter, and, according to my father, witch." She smiled in, he thought, an extremely sane fashion. "I'm here to try to help." She glanced at Joss and gave her a reassuring nod. Neither of them, for the moment, was going to mention what had happened in the church.

"That's good to hear." David smiled back. His nervousness about returning to the house had gone. It was all right, here in the warm kitchen, with three other people in broad daylight. He looked at Luke. "The boys are staying with the Goodyears, you say? Don't let them come back until this is sorted out."

Luke tightened his lips. "I think that has already been agreed. So, what are you going to do? I take it that you have come to help too." His gaze rested on David's face for a few seconds longer than was necessary. Then he looked from David to Natalie and back.

David shrugged. "I leave it up to the expert."

Natalie grimaced. "Who is, at the moment, a little at a loss." She pushed back her chair and stood up. "Can I suggest you wait in here? Make some coffee or something and let me go for a wander around on my own. There are things I need to understand."

They watched in silence as she let herself out of the kitchen and listened as the sound of her heels on the flags in the hall died away.

"Brave lady," David commented quietly. "Especially in view of some of the things I've read in here. One interesting snippet of history. Katherine's child, whether he was the son of her husband or of the king, survived the birth that killed her. He lived until 1500, and although he was only eighteen when he died, he had time to marry and father a daughter, a daughter named for his mother, Katherine." He patted his pile of books. "Otherwise these are more to do with witchcraft and magic. They were into some really sophisticated evil in those days."

"Do you think Natalie's really a witch?" Luke raised an eyebrow. "Not quite my image of what a witch should be. I can see her commuting on the seven-forty to the City far more easily than I could see her dancing naked around a bonfire with a broomstick!"

"Sounds to me, old boy, as if you're guilty of some fairly serious stereotyping, if not chauvinistic and politically incorrect something or other there!" David put in amiably. He winked at Joss. "What do you think? Can she sort it all out?"

Joss shrugged. "I hope so for all our sakes."

"I'm going to see what she's up to." Luke headed for the door.

"Luke! No!" Joss called.

"Let him go for a minute, Joss." David caught Joss's hand. "A word quickly, while we're on our own." His tone was serious.

She raised an eyebrow. "What is it?"

"Joss, I wanted to tell you. I've decided to leave Dame Felicia's at the end of next year." It sounded so easy, so matter-of-fact. She would never guess the sadness behind those words, the loneliness. "I've accepted a post, teaching in Paris." He forced a grin. "A complete change is always good, as you know. After all, my research fellowship with Belheddon Enterprises will be over soon. When we know all there is to know, then what will I do with my spare time?"

"David —"

"No, Joss. My mind is made up. Don't worry. I won't lose touch. After all, I have to keep an eye on my godson. And you'll be coming to Paris more often too now you've discovered Paul." He grimaced. "Pastures new, Joss. Always a good idea." He held her eye for a moment, then looked away. Did she, he wondered, even suspect how fond he had become of her? He hoped not.

"We'll miss you, David." Her voice was very quiet.

He nodded, unable to trust himself to speak for a moment. "Well, you'll see plenty of me before I leave, I promise. I'm not going for months yet." He gave her hand a squeeze. "And now, back to the fray. Let's call old Luke back before our witch spots him and turns him into a toad!"

In the great hall Natalie was standing in front of the fireplace once again. She could feel it clearly now. The power which was surging around her — uncontrolled, random power — coming up from beneath the cold flags. She frowned, holding out her hands, palms down, allowing herself to sense its origin. There was something there, deep beneath the ground.

Frowning with concentration, she moved slowly across the floor toward the hall and the staircase and put her hand on the door to the cellar. It was locked. She shook the handle. Before, the feelings from the cellar had been negative, unhappy but gentle. The grief which had surrounded the small crumpled body of a little boy had permeated the walls, but that had disappeared. Even through the door she could feel something else.

Making up her mind, she turned on her heel and marched back to the kitchen. "I need the key to the cellar, please."

"The cellar," Joss echoed. "Again?"

"Please. There's something down there. No —" she raised a hand as Joss stood up — "please, stay in here. All of you. Just tell me where the key is."

With it in her hand at last, she stood for a minute in the middle of the study, taking slow deep breaths, feeling herself centered and strong, surrounding herself with an armor of light. Pushing the small niggling core of fear which was worming its way into her stomach firmly to one side, she moved resolutely back to the cellar door and put the key into the lock.

A blast of cold air rose from the damp darkness. Switching on the lights, she stepped through the door, onto the top step.

And began to walk down.

At the bottom of the stairs she stood still, every sense alert. She was not seeing the wine racks, or the dust, or the festooned pipes and electric cables which the twentieth century had introduced. Her eyes were focused on medieval vaulting, and in the farthest corner of the cellar, beneath the great hall, the shadows cast by long-dead candles.

Silently she stepped closer. She could feel it more strongly now: a feral, sweat-sharp scent of danger and excitement.

Joss shivered. "I can't stand it anymore. I've got to go and see what she's doing."

"She's told you not to, Joss." Luke shook his head. He was uncomfortably tense, every nerve in his body stretched.

"I have to. This is my house, Luke. I have to be there." She said it gently without challenge, but both he and David heard the steel in the tone.

"Be careful, Joss."

Her smile was absentminded. "I will."

She paused at the top of the cellar stairs and looked down. The lights were on but the first cellar was empty.

Biting back a shout to Natalie, she carefully and silently began to descend the stairs into the cold, holding her breath as she strained her ears for any sound. The silence was intense, solid.

At the bottom of the stairs she waited a moment, looking around. "Natalie?" The call under her breath was barely more than a whisper. "Where are you?"

There was no reply.

Cautiously she stepped toward the archway which led into the second cellar. Natalie was standing near the far wall, staring at the stone. She appeared to be listening intently.

Silently Joss stepped up beside her. Natalie gave no indication that she knew she was there. Her eyes were focused on the wall, her hands out in front of her, fingers spread as if searching for something she could not see.

"It's here," she murmured. "The focus. Can you feel it?"

Joss stepped a little closer to her. She could feel every nerve and muscle in her body clenched.

"What is it?" she breathed.

"I don't know." Natalie was shaking her head. "There's a lot of energy underground here. I think a dowser might tell you there was an underground river or spring or perhaps just earth energy. But it's been tapped. Someone has used it, and they've used it wrongly."

Joss swallowed hard. She could feel her skin prickling. "Can you do anything?"

"I'm not sure yet." Natalie took a step closer to the wall and rested her hands on the cold stones and as Joss watched her she ran her fingers down the wall, almost to the floor.

"It's behind here. Whatever it is." She turned to Joss. "I think we need to look. I'm sorry, but we've got to do it."

"You mean we have to take the wall down?"

Natalie nodded. "Not all of it. I think it's here. I can feel it through the stone." Her hand was pressed for a moment on one of the roughly shaped blocks. Griping the edges as best she could with her nails, she gave a tug but nothing happened.

"It's been cemented in. Look." Joss leaned over her shoulder and pointed at the crumbling mortar.

Natalie nodded. "We need a crowbar."

"I'll go and fetch the others." Joss hesitated. "Do you want to come with me? Don't wait down here."

Natalie gave a grim smile. "Don't worry. I'm all right. Just fetch something to lever this out with and bring your friend David down. Not Luke. Not at the moment. Not till we know what we're dealing with."

Joss stared at her, then she nodded. Without a word she retraced her steps up into the hall. Staring at the dead flowers on the oak table, she shuddered violently and almost without realizing it her fingers went to the small cross at her throat.

"No, I can't stand it. I'm not staying away!" Luke had found a crowbar in the coach house. "For God's sake, Joss! If it's dangerous do you think I'd let you go down there? Either I come or neither of us goes."

"You could stay here with me, Luke." Jimbo was wiping his hands on an oily rag. "If Nat says you shouldn't be there, you shouldn't be. She knows what she's talking about."

"I'm sure she does, but it's my house and what goes on in it is my business."

"It might be woman's business, Luke." Jimbo shifted uncomfortably.

"Then they wouldn't want David." Luke hefted the crowbar into one hand and brought the handle down with a smack onto the palm of the other. "You come or stay, whichever you like, but I'm going down there now."

David and Joss exchanged glances and Joss gave a rueful shrug. "OK. Come on. Let's see what Natalie says."

Natalie was standing where Joss had left her when they trooped silently back down the stairs. She didn't look around. "Joss, you wear a crucifix. Give it to Luke. Put it around his neck."

The other three looked at one another. Natalie had not taken her eyes off the wall; the cross was hidden beneath Joss's clothes. As far as Joss knew, Natalie had not seen it at any time since she had arrived. Reaching up obediently, she unclasped the chain. To her surprise Luke made no fuss when she put it around his neck and she thought she knew why; the atmosphere in the cellar had thickened perceptibly.

Without a word, David took the crowbar out of Luke's hand and stepped forward. "What do you want me to do?" he whispered.

"Here. I think it's here." Natalie pointed. "See if you can loosen this stone."

Cautiously, David inserted the end of the crowbar. "It's old lime mortar. Look. It's very soft." He wiggled it back and forth, pushing the wedge-shaped point farther in. "There. It's coming. Everything is so crumbly down here." Panting with exertion, he gave one last push and levered the stone out. It fell with a loud crash onto the flags.

There was a long silence as, putting down the crowbar, David felt in his pocket for the flashlight he had picked up from the dresser as they left the kitchen. He shone it into the cavity. "There's quite a hole in here."

"You'd better give it to me." Natalie's voice was husky. She could feel waves of emotion coming out of the wall at her, sour malevolent tides of anger and hatred and spite as, reluctantly, she took the flashlight from David's hand. She glanced at the others. "You all all right?"

They could all feel it to some degree, she could see, even Luke. Joss's face was gray and drawn with pain.

Stepping forward, she shone the flashlight into the hole.

At first she thought there was nothing there, then as her hand steadied the shaking beam she slowly began to make out the shapes in the cavity behind the wall. It was far smaller than she had expected, perhaps three feet by two. No room for the body or bodies she had half expected to find immured there. With an inward sigh of relief, she shone the light around the dark space again and only then did she notice, lying among the rubble in what was little more than a hidden cupboard, the small wrapped package.

"That's it." She was talking to herself, although she spoke out loud. "That's where the energy is coming from."

Her skin crawling with revulsion, she reached

into the hole and picked the packet up with her fingertips.

"What is it?" Joss breathed. They were all staring down at the object on Natalie's palm. It was about three inches long, perhaps a little less wide, covered in dust and cobwebs and crumbs of mortar.

"It's wrapped in some kind of material," David said slowly. He reached out to touch it, then changed his mind and drew back. He looked at Natalie's face. "What is it?"

Slowly she shook her head.

"We have to look." It was Luke. He took a deep breath. "Do you want me to open it?"

"No." Natalie shook her head again. "I think we need to be very careful with this." She could feel the power in it, the weight, the cold. With a shudder, she had to restrain herself from hurling it as far away from her as she could. "I think we should take it upstairs — outside —" She had begun to feel sick. Her fear and distaste were gripping her with a violence she couldn't control. Her hand was beginning to shake.

"Natalie —"

"Out of my way." Gritting her teeth, she closed her fingers over the object in her hand and headed for the stairs. She had to get outside. Now. Quickly. Before the evil closed over them all.

607

CHAPTER 42

"Ego te baptiso —"

She stopped suddenly and held her breath, the only sound in the darkened church the beating of her own heart. Above her head the sanctuary lamp flickered wildly and she heard the squeak of the chains on which it hung.

"Ego te baptiso in nomine Patris, et Filii, et Spiritus Sancti —" she started again.

"Edward —" Her fingers traced the sign of the cross over the little wax figure in her hand.

"Edward of York, king of England —"

She smiled, stroking the doll's head with its little roughly shaped crown of wire. Her fingertip moved down across its shoulders, down the chest, and rested for a moment at the top of its legs, where a small lump depicted its manhood.

Setting the doll down on the altar, she reached into the tasseled purse hanging at her girdle for a second doll as crude as the first, meant, from the small swellings on its chest, to be a woman.

"I baptize thee Katherine . . ."

Katherine!

The name reverberated through the shadows of the church.

"And now," she breathed, "I bring you together, together here in the house of your God!"

Holding both figures up before the crucifix high above the altar, she smiled and slowly she pressed them together, feeling the beeswax grow soft in the heat of her hand. The sweet stickiness of honey was all around her as she bound the two little dolls face to face with a scarlet thread of silk.

"In the name of God, I pronounce you man and wife." She smiled. "Not in the porch but here before the altar of God, and now the act of union will be sanctified by the holy Mass itself."

She glanced over her shoulder, uncertain of the shadows, never sure that eyes weren't watching, that the priest might not be there, somewhere behind the carved screen.

Lifting the embroidered altar cloth in an act which was somehow as indecent as the act she had perpetrated on the dolls, she tucked them out of sight and then with a smile she let the cloth fall. Soon the priest would come to celebrate the Mass and the union of the dolls, sanctified by his act, would be complete. Indissoluble for all eternity.

She wiped her hands on the heavy brocade of her skirts and stepped away from the altar.

Only then did she smile.

Edward and Katherine.

Nothing now could keep them apart and nothing could prevent Katherine from conceiving a child.

Nothing.

"Bring it out here. Put it on the table." They were outside on the terrace in the wind and rain, standing around the gray, lichen-encrusted garden table.

Joss put her hand on Natalie's shoulder. "Are you OK?"

Natalie nodded. She felt better now they were outside; the oppression and the anger were less. The rain was growing heavier and she raised her face to it, feeling it fresh and clean, sweeping back across her face and into her hair. Taking a deep breath, she laid her hand on the table palm up and opened her fingers.

"Wait, I'll put up the umbrella." Luke had grabbed it as they went out.

"No." Natalie shook her head. "Let it get wet."

The wrapping was silk — old and gray and fragmented, disintegrating beneath her fingers in the rain. As she cautiously peeled it back, they stared down at what lay within.

Two pale sausage-shaped objects, pressed close together, with fragments of nearly black thread around the middle, lay before them on the wet table.

"What is it?" Joss breathed.

"I think you'll find it's what are they." Natalie stood back, looking down as the rain battered down on the object on the table.

"It's wax." David had bent close. "Two wax dolls." He glanced up at Natalie. "They're witch dolls!"

She nodded. "I think so."

"Shit." He shook his head. "The real thing.

610

Who do you suppose they're supposed to be?"

Natalie shrugged. "Look at that one's head."

"A crown?" He glanced at Joss. "It's Edward, isn't it, King Edward." He reached out.

"Don't touch," Natalie cried sharply. "Whoever made those dolls was evil. Those dolls spelled disaster: disaster for the two people concerned, disaster for their child and their descendants, and disaster for this house!"

The rain was growing heavier. Standing around the table, the four looked down at the pathetic little figures of melded wax as a pool of rainwater formed around them on the gray oak, soaking the wood until it turned black.

"Their child?" Joss echoed. She looked up from the dolls. The rain was plastering her hair around her face. "You think they had a child?"

Natalie nodded.

"He was called Edward," David put in. "I found it in the records. The house was inherited by Edward de Vere after the death of Katherine's father in 1496. She had no brothers, and no other more distant relations who would fit. Her husband, as far as we can tell, was called Richard and his inheritance went to his brother, so my guess is that Edward de Vere was the son of Edward IV — the pregnancy that the marriage to Richard was designed to conceal."

Natalie was watching Joss's face. "That boy was your ancestor, Joss. The last man to inherit Belheddon."

"And he died at eighteen, as soon as he had a daughter." David's voice was awestruck.

They were all staring down at the table. Joss's

611

face had drained of color.

"I think we're looking at the beginning of the curse." Natalie studied the dolls sadly.

"So, what do we do with them?" Joss's voice was husky.

Natalie shook her head.

"Do we separate them?"

"I don't know. I don't *know.*" Natalie turned away in anguish and looked up at the sky, feeling the rain on her face. "We have to help them; we have to release them. Both Edward and the girl."

The girl.

Katherine.

They were all watching her. Natalie could feel their eyes first on her shoulder blades, then on the poor misshapen dolls, and then back to her again. She had set herself up as some sort of expert and they were relying on her to save them, to save Joss's two children and to save Luke.

The rain was running down her face, dripping off her short hair into her collar. It was cold and clean and fresh.

She couldn't do it. Not on her own. She couldn't fight Margaret's spell by herself.

Slowly she turned. They were still watching her, the two men uncertain, David understanding the implications of what they were dealing with and a little afraid; Luke self-mocking, practical, still not letting himself believe that the small two-headed lump of wax on the table could threaten the lives of his two sons, even his own.

And why did it threaten them? It was a love charm, one of the commonest objects a witch

612

was asked to produce, a piece of childlike sympathetic magic, meant to bring a man and a woman together. So why did it give off such evil vibes? And why did it threaten Joss, or the women of the house; the women who were wooed by a king?

No one said anything; they were all watching her, waiting for her to tell them what to do.

And suddenly she knew.

"Joss —" Her hands had gone clammy. "How strong are you?"

Joss looked away, first into the distance toward the lake and then down at the figures on the table. Her face was white and very strained but her eyes, when she raised them at last to Natalie's face, were steady. "Strong enough."

Natalie nodded. "Luke, I want you and David to go away. Right away from the house. Go to the little boys and stay with them. We'll tell you when you can come back."

"I'm not leaving Joss." Luke caught his wife's hand.

"Please, Luke, I'm not asking lightly." Natalie glanced at David, sensing an ally.

He picked up the cue. "Come on, old chap. I have a feeling this is women's work."

Natalie's face relaxed into a smile. "That's exactly what it is."

"I'll be all right, Luke." Joss stepped closer to him and, reaching up, kissed him on the cheek. "Please, go with David." He wrapped his arms around her and for a moment they clung together, then reluctantly she pushed him away. "Go on."

"You're sure?"

"I'm sure."

She and Natalie stood where they were in the rain and watched as the two men walked slowly back to the gate. As David pushed it open, Luke looked back. Joss raised a hand and blew him a kiss, then she turned away. When seconds later she glanced back, the two men had gone.

Natalie was watching absentmindedly. The illusion of reality was slipping away, withdrawing to the periphery of her vision, as she reached down toward her intuition. "Are you ready?" She frowned. "This is going to be hard." She hesitated. "Joss, you do know you're pregnant."

Joss stared at her. "Don't be silly; I can't be."

Natalie nodded. "It's because you are carrying a little girl that we can do this, and it's because it's a girl that we have to do it soon." She took Joss's hands in her own wet cold ones. "In a minute we're going into the church with these" — she nodded toward the dolls — "and we're going to separate them."

"What about that stuff we saw in there?" Joss's mind was spinning, beating against the blackness, grappling with Natalie's certainty. "I'm not pregnant, you know. I can't be. Luke and I — well, we took precautions. It's too soon after Ned. We didn't want any more children —"

Natalie frowned. "Just for now believe me, please. We have to be together in this, Joss. David was right, this is women's work and there are some things that women know."

She hesitated, wondering how she could explain.

"The spell was cast by someone who knew what they were doing. It worked. These two people" — she gestured at the wax dolls — "were tied together by magic" — she smiled uncertainly, used to people's raised eyebrows when she used the word — "magic that was powerful, a force of nature, harnessed and directed so well that it lasted beyond death for the people who were tied together."

"Edward and Katherine," Joss murmured.

"Edward and Katherine."

"But what went wrong? Why are they so angry? Why are they hurting people? Was that part of Margaret's intention?"

Natalie shrugged. "They're trapped here. Perhaps that is all the reason they need. Perhaps there is more. Perhaps the king is still searching for her. Perhaps he's lost her somehow; perhaps he wants something else." She glanced at Joss. "A human lover."

Joss shook her head vehemently, her mind trapped, cannoning against the black wall inside her head, refusing to focus, but Natalie nodded. "Face it. You have to face the truth."

"There isn't any truth to face. All he's done to us —" She paused. The cellar. The eyes. The arms, drawing her against him. Black velvet and then nakedness. "No." She shook her head again. "No, all he has done, perhaps, is bring me roses." She shuddered. The black wall was back in place. There was a long pause. She could feel Natalie's eyes on her face and resolutely she refused to meet them.

Eventually Natalie spoke. "Well," she cleared her throat. "Come on. We'd better get on with it." She fished a blue scarf out of her pocket — silk, Joss noticed — and carefully picked up

615

the dolls and wrapped them in it, then she walked toward the gate.

The lights were still on in the church. Standing just inside the door, they paused. Resolutely, Joss shut it behind them. The sound of the heavy latch dropping echoed around them and then it died away. She held her breath and stood watching as slowly Natalie began to walk up the aisle toward the altar. After a few steps she stopped. "Joss? Come with me."

Joss stepped down the two steps onto the stone floor and forced herself to move. Her legs were trembling violently and it was all she could do to follow.

"Pull back the rug." Natalie was standing to one side of it, between the choir stalls.

Reluctantly, Joss did as she was bid. Before them on the floor the brass glinted in the lights which were tucked out of sight behind the roof beams. An eerie cold seemed to radiate up from the ornate figure depicted before them. "See." Natalie pointed with her toe. She was speaking very softly. "The symbols of her art are there. The cross is upside down. You don't realize it until you realize which way up she is. And are those cabalistic signs? We'd have to look them up."

"She really was a magician — a real witch, then, not just a poor old woman playing at magic," Joss murmured.

"Oh, yes. She was a real witch all right. And I guess she was a very clever one. She may have been under suspicion, but she was never caught at it. How else would she have been buried here?"

"The king trusted her —"

"I don't think so." Natalie was unwrapping the blue silk scarf. Her hands, Joss noticed, were trembling violently. "He was wearing armor, remember?"

Not always. Sometimes he wore velvet.

The cold was growing more intense.

"Do you know what to do?" Joss said softly. Her eyes were riveted to the tiny wax figures as the silk fell to the floor.

"I'm going to bless them, then I'm going to separate them, then I'm going to melt them —"

"No!" Joss clutched at Natalie's arm. "No, you mustn't do that."

"Why?" Natalie's gray eyes were fixed on hers.

"Help them. You've got to help them, not destroy them. They've suffered enough already."

"He has killed, Joss."

"I know. I know he has. But only because he's trapped here. Please — the evil is Margaret's, you said. Don't destroy them. We have to find a way of helping them."

They were both looking down at the dolls in Natalie's hands. "Supposing he kills again?"

"We can stop him. There must be a way. He wasn't evil."

Eyes. Blue. Desperate eyes, staring into hers. Arms around her. Ice-cold lips on hers —

"Joss! Joss are you all right?"

Katherine.

The wall in her head was crumbling.

He thought she was Katherine! He hadn't even

seen *her*. It was Katherine he had held, Katherine he had kissed; to Katherine he brought the roses. Her mother, her grandmother — how many other women in the house had he pursued, believing they were his Katherine? She was shivering violently too now. "Don't separate them." She held out her hand. "Leave them together."

Natalie put the figures in her palm.

Silently Joss bent and picked up the scarf. Carefully she wrapped the two dolls up once again.

"They don't belong in here," she said quietly. "No."

"Can we remove the hold she has over them?" Joss nodded down at the floor.

"We can try." Natalie stood for a moment deep in thought. "The rituals of the church can't reach her. We need to speak to her in a language she understands. Play her at her own game."

"Witchcraft?" Joss shook her head.

"I prefer to call it sympathetic magic. We have to cut the ties that bind her to them and to this place. We need something to tie and something to cut."

"In the vestry." Joss hesitated, looking down at the blue silk package in her hands, then she put it down on a pew. "I'll have to look."

The door was unlocked. Switching on the light, she stared around. The flower arranging materials were stacked more or less to one side near a small sink, the church paraphernalia to the other near the locked cupboards where James Wood kept books and vessels and the unconsecrated wine and bread. Her hands still stiff with cold, she groped across the flower shelves, moving vases

618

and blocks of oasis, jugs, and flower wire. Picking up a coil of the fine wire, she considered it, then looked around for the snips. They were there, among the scrabble of old dusters and dried fir cones, part of a long-gone Christmas display.

"Here." She handed the wire to Natalie. "Will this do?"

Natalie fumbled for the end of the wire. "My hands are so cold —"

"I know. It's only here, near the grave. The rest of the church is bearable."

Natalie glanced at her. "There's an energy drain. She's using the heat in some way. Here." She nipped off a couple of yards of wire. "Wind this end around the dolls. I'm going to try and hook this end into the brass somehow." She knelt down, the end of the fine wire between her fingers. "It's worn so flat. For five hundred years people have been walking over her."

"It doesn't seem to have done her any harm!" Joss commented tartly. The wire was fiddly, hard to twist. "There, I think that will hold."

"Good. Put them down here, on the step, while I try to fix this."

"Natalie!" Turning from putting the dolls down, Joss had glanced at the back of the church. "Look!"

The strange mist was there again, level with the back pews; it was thinner this time, less distinct, but the shape was clear.

"She's going to manifest!" Natalie breathed. "Oh, Jesus Christ!"

"What do we do?" Joss groped at her throat for the little crucifix and realized with a lurch

619

of terror that it was still where she herself had put it, around Luke's neck.

"Stand firm. Visualize a solid wall of light between us and her. Remember, she can't hurt you," Natalie went on urgently under her breath. She dropped to her knees again, frantically jabbing at the brass with the fine end of the wire, trying to hook it into the figure.

She could hear Joss's breath rasping harshly in the back of her throat. "Shall I pick them up?"

"Yes. Carefully. Don't pull the wire." Natalie's voice was hoarse.

Joss picked the figures up and stood, her back to the altar, her hand out in front of her. The image was stronger now. They could make out the shape of the woman clearly, her long dress standing out stiffly from the hips, some kind of a headdress over her hair.

"Stop!" Natalie's voice was surprisingly strong suddenly. "You are in the house of God! Stop now, while you have time."

The figure didn't hesitate. It was coming closer, seeming to drift toward them without quite touching the ground.

"Margaret de Vere, in the name of Jesus Christ, I command you to stop!" Natalie raised her hand.

"She can't hear you," Joss whispered. The woman's face was slowly becoming visible. It registered no expression at all. "What do we do?" Her voice slid up into a cry of fear.

"She must be able to hear us — or at least she can sense us. Why else is she here?" Natalie jabbed at the brass frantically. "Stick, damn it.

Stick in, will you!"

The figure was drifting closer, with every moment becoming clearer to the eye. They could see the heavy embroidery on her gown now — the jeweled girdle, the detail of her headdress with its floating veil, and above all her face. It was a strong face with heavy features, the mouth a hard narrow line, the skin almost colorless, the eyes open, the color of the winter sea, unseeing and expressionless.

"We've summoned her presence by interfering," Natalie murmured. "Somehow we have to stop her!" She pushed the wire frantically, bending it almost double with the force of her gesture and with a slight click the hook caught under a rough edge of the ornate headdress of the figure on the ground.

"Done it!" She scrambled to her feet, the snips in her hand.

"Margaret de Vere, you have been guilty of sorcery in this holy place. You have made images of your king and of your daughter, and because of your evil spells they cannot rest in peace. This wire which holds you all together I am now going to cut. Your influence will be over. Your time on this earth is finished. Go from this place and find peace and light away from Belheddon. Go!"

She put the snips to the wire and pressed the handles together as hard as she could.

No! No! Nooo!

The scream that filled the church came from neither woman, nor from the shadowy figure

621

standing before them. It came from the air, from the echoes, from the ground beneath their feet.

Natalie hesitated, the wire slipping out of the blades.

"Go on! Cut it!" Joss called. "Quickly. Now!"

Using both hands, Natalie managed to jam the wire back between the stumpy steel blades and chopped as hard as she could. This time the ends parted. The longer piece sprang free and coiled itself down onto the brass, while the shorter end snapped back around Joss's hand and the wax figures in it. Her eyes hadn't left the figure before them. It was barely ten feet from them now, still moving. "It hasn't worked," she gasped. "Natalie, it hasn't worked."

She was getting closer. Joss could feel the cold so intense now that the air seemed scarcely breathable.

"Natalie!" Her voice had risen to a scream. Pressing herself back against the pew out of the way, she felt and saw the woman pass within three feet of her, drift on over the top of the brass, up the chancel steps, through the altar itself, and out through the east wall of the church.

"Dear God." Joss looked down at the figures in her hands. She had clutched them so tightly they had grown soft in her fingers. "Has she gone?"

"She's gone." Natalie sat down in a pew. She was white with shock.

"Did you do it?" Joss was staring at the wax dolls.

"I don't know." Natalie bent over and put her head on her hands as if she were praying. "I don't know."

For a moment they both sat there too shocked to move, then Joss straightened. "Let's go back to the house."

Natalie looked up. "What do you want to do with the dolls?"

"I think we should bury them together. Come on, let's go." Joss kicked the rug back across the brass. "I'll turn out the lights. I don't want to stay here."

Both still very afraid, they left the church, closing the door behind them. The dolls, once more wrapped in the silk scarf, were clutched in Joss's hand. "Let's get back in the house. I'm too cold to think. We'll need to find a spade."

Hurrying to avoid the heavy rain, they threaded their way down the path and into the back door of the house. Joss put the scarf down on the kitchen table. They could both smell the heavy honey of the wax. "What about the boys? Georgie and Sammy. Have they gone?"

Natalie threw herself down in a chair. She was exhausted. "I don't know."

"Suddenly you don't know much."

"I'm sorry, Joss."

Joss was rubbing her hands hard on the front of her coat. "No, it's me who should be sorry. You're helping me and I'm not being grateful." She looked at the bundle of blue silk. "Poor things. I hope they're free." Biting her lip, she was silent for a moment. "There's only one way to find out. I'll go upstairs."

"I'll come with you."

"No." Joss hesitated. "No. This is something I have to do on my own, Natalie. Just be here, if I call, OK?" She shook her head. "I've never called him — summoned him, I mean. But I think if he were still there he might come." The blue eyes had been gentle, full of love.

"And so would Georgie and Sam, Joss. They always come when they're called."

The two women looked at each other grimly. Joss put the dolls gently into the dresser drawer. "Just for a while. Until we can bury them." She took a deep breath, visibly steadying herself, then she smiled at Natalie. "Wish me luck."

CHAPTER 43

At the bottom of the stairs she stopped, her hand on the newel post, and looked up. The landing was always in deep shadow. On even the sunniest day the light never penetrated there. Listening carefully, she put her foot on the bottom step.

"Edward!" she called in a low voice. It came out croakily, barely audible. Edward, sire, your grace . . . your majesty? How did one address a king who had been dead for five hundred years?

Her fists clenched, she began slowly to climb the stairs, one step at a time, her eyes and ears straining into the emptiness.

"Are you there? Georgie? Sammy?"

She reached the top and looked around. The landing was deserted, the door into her and Luke's bedroom ajar. She moved toward it carefully, consciously avoiding the creaky board near the coffer chest with its pewter candlestick.

"Is there anyone there? Georgie? Sammy?" She could deal with them, her own brothers, little boys.

Her hand outstretched, she pushed open the bedroom door and looked in. The curtains were half drawn and the room was almost dark. Outside, the rain streamed down the windowpanes, slamming every now and again against the glass with extra force.

She loved this room. It was beautiful, gracious, redolent with history, and yet cosy. She could see Tom's discarded teddy in the corner, an old jumper of Luke's still inside out on the floor where he had dropped it. She smiled affectionately.

Moving toward the bed, she rested a hand on one of the bedposts. The black oak, turned and carved, was warm beneath her fingers and she stroked it gently. "Was it here? Did you lie together here?" She spoke out loud without looking around. "She's gone, my lord. No one else can take her place, not here. You and she belong together in another world."

Her hand dropped from the bedpost and slowly she moved up the side of the bed, trailing her fingers on the crewelwork cover. "I'm going to bury the effigies Margaret made of you both in the rose garden down beyond the lake." She smiled ruefully. "I'll find a white rose, a rose of York, to put there so you can rest in peace."

She jumped at a sudden clatter in the corner of the room near the back window. The draft had stirred the curtain, which had knocked a small wooden car onto the floor. Walking over to it, she stooped and picked it up. "Georgie? Sammy? Is this yours?"

There was no answer.

Slowly she turned around. The palms of her

626

hands were wet, the small hairs on the back of her neck were tingling. Something in the room had changed.

He was standing near the front window.

Joss held her breath. Her stomach turned over with fear. He was tall, very tall, and as she moved closer she could see the graying hair, the anguished narrow eyes, the strong chin, the broad shoulders shrouded by a dark cloak, and beneath it again the plate armor of a man who feared assassination in this house, the house of his mistress.

He was coming closer. Suddenly she was terrified; she had called him, but now she could not control him. "Please," she murmured. "Please . . . No!" Again she could smell the roses.

He was coming closer still.

"I'm not Katherine," she whispered desperately. "Please, listen to me. I'm not Katherine. Katherine has gone. She's not here anymore. Please, please, don't hurt me. Don't hurt my children or Luke — please —"

She took a step backward and felt the bed immovable behind her.

"Please. We've cut the link. Your love was cursed. It was evil. Margaret made it happen. She tied you together and to this house with her magic, but we've released you; you can go. Please —" She held her hand in front of her face. "Please. Go."

He had stopped moving. For several seconds he seemed to be watching her, then slowly he lifted his arm toward her. She shrank back with a whimper, but the bed stopped her as his fingers

627

brushed her cheek. It was like the touch of cold wet leaves.

Katherine.

His lips hadn't moved but she heard the name inside her head.

"I'm not Katherine," she sobbed. She retreated further, bending backward away from him across the bed. "Please, I'm not Katherine!"

Katherine.

She had ordered them to send for him.

Lying in the high bed as the contractions tore her apart, she asked, then she begged, then she screamed for him.

It was her mother who told them to wait, who forbade them to go.

As her seventeen-year-old daughter's belly had swollen with the king's child, Margaret had smiled and nodded and watched. The girl's revulsion and panic were nothing out of the ordinary. After her milksop husband had been removed — so easy a task, she blew him out like a candle — it was a matter of time only before she would grow used to her kingly lover, a man whose early stunning good looks had turned to corpulence in middle age; the man who, once so attractive he could have had any woman in England, was now enslaved by her — so enslaved that he would grant his little mistress's mother anything she asked.

As she stood looking down at the bed where

628

two frightened midwives were sponging her daughter's sweat-stained face, she smiled again and firmly shook her head.

Though he was only a few miles away, he could not be summoned yet. He mustn't see Katherine looking like this. She was ugly, she stank, she screamed and tore at the bedclothes, shouting obscenities which might have suited a London tavern but which sounded bestial from the lips of a gently born girl of seventeen.

Let the child be born — the daughter, the precious pretty treasure who would captivate and hold her father's affections, then he could come. Then he could shower Katherine, cleansed and rested and smelling of sweet flower waters and perfumes, with gold and jewels and fine silks, and bring his child ivory rattles and coral beads.

Katherine!

"No!" Joss flung herself away from him across the bed, bunched her knees and threw herself onto the floor. With the bed between them she faced him, panting. "I am not Katherine! Can't you see that? Katherine's dead! You're dead!" She was sobbing desperately. "Please. The link is cut. Margaret's spell is broken; it's all over; you are free of her at last. Don't you see? It's finished!"

He hadn't moved any closer to the bed. He stood for a long time looking at, or perhaps through, her, then slowly he put his hand to his waist and she realized for the first time that beneath the long shadowy cloak he was wearing a sword. He drew it without a sound.

629

"No." She gasped. "For Christ's sake, no! Haven't you heard me? Please —" She retreated backward away from the bed toward the windows which overlooked the garden, moving carefully step by step, her stomach knotted with terror. "Please —"

"So, does the great king, the son of York, terrorize women with a sword?" Natalie's voice from the door was harsh with fear. "Are you going to kill her? Are you going to put your sword to the throat of a woman who is carrying a child? Your child!"

She ignored Joss's gasp. "Put away your sword. You have no enemies here anymore. You have no place here. This is not your time!"

Joss staggered backward against the wall, her arms crossed across her breasts, and suddenly her legs wouldn't support her anymore. With a sob she found herself sliding to her knees.

Natalie stepped into the room. "Put up your sword. You cannot hurt her. She is nothing to you, don't you see? Nothing. She is from a different world. Let her go. Let her and her family live in peace. You have to leave Belheddon. The time has come. It's time to go."

The sword point wavered, then slowly it began to fall. Joss watched mesmerized. It looked very real. She could see the glimmer of the steel as his hand dropped to his side.

Katherine.

"Katherine is waiting for you," Natalie's voice was gentle suddenly. "Let your child live. I'll take care of her."

They were watching the man's face. The pain and anger etched into every line of it were clearly visible, as was the velvet-trimmed neck of his shirt beneath the breastplate and the cords which held the cloak in place.

"Let him go, Joss," Natalie murmured. "Release him."

"What do you mean?" Joss was watching him, mesmerized.

He was holding out his hands to her, the heavy ruby ring on his forefinger catching the light dully.

"Give him your blessing and your love —"

"My love!" Joss recoiled.

"It will help him to leave. Send him away in love and peace."

"What about the people he killed?" In spite of herself, she raised her eyes to his. The anger in his gaze had gone but the pain was still there.

"They will be released as well. Love is the healer, Joss. Love and forgiveness. You are the spokeswoman, the one who has to do it for all the women — your mother, and your grandmother, and her mother, and all the women through the generations who have lived in this house."

"And what about the men? What about the children who have died?"

He was shaking his head slowly back and forth.

Katherine.

"You cannot speak for them. They must speak for themselves. If we fill the house with love we can help them do it."

Katherine.

Joss shook her head. She could feel it like an intense pressure inside her eardrums, the name of the woman he had loved: Katherine.

"What is it?" Suddenly she was talking to him again. "What are you telling me?"

The room was growing darker, the rattle of rain on the window was louder, and for a moment she felt her attention shift. There was an almost imperceptible movement of tension in the room and he had gone.

For a moment she stood gazing at the place where he had been standing, then she spun around. Natalie was only a few feet from her now and for a moment they stared at each other.

"What happened?" Joss sat down on the bed. She was shaking violently.

Natalie shook her head. "Something happened out there in the world he inhabits. The energy discharged itself in some way." She hauled herself up onto the bed beside Joss and sat with her head in her hands. "We so nearly did it. We had reached him — or, at least, you had. He was listening."

"He was trying to tell us something —" Joss broke off. From upstairs came the sound of children laughing.

"No. Oh no, I can't bear it."

Natalie took her hand. "At least they're happy, Joss."

Joss shook her head. Sliding off the bed, she

ran to the door. "Georgie? Sammy? Where are you?" With the last vestiges of strength she possessed, she ran up the stairs and threw open the door of the first empty attic room. "Where are you?" There were tears pouring down her cheeks.

The room was very cold. In the silence she could hear the rain on the windows. "Georgie? Sammy?"

Behind her Natalie stopped in the doorway.

A gust of wind buffeted the end gable of the roof and in the distance they both heard suddenly the sound of a child singing far away in the distance.

tum tum te tum te tum tum tum

Joss rubbed her nose on her sleeve, staring around helplessly — the sound was so distant, lost in the wind.

tum tum te tum te tum tum tum

She took a step into the room. It was empty — bare, dusty boards, the old shabby wallpaper, a damp place on the ceiling where the water had begun to seep in.

tum tum te tum te Kath-er-ine

She could hear it more clearly now, from beyond the door. With hands stiff with cold, she fought the latch to pull it open. The sounds were louder now. More clear.

It was my Lad-y Kath-er-ine

The chant echoed across the next attic above the howling of the wind.

It was my Lad-y Kath-er-ine
It was my Lady Katherine

Joss moved slowly toward the sound. It was coming from the end attic.

The melancholy little refrain echoed in her ears as she fumbled for the key and pushed open the door. As it creaked back, the words were cut off abruptly.

She stared around.

"Where are you?" she cried. She could hardly see for her tears.

"Joss." Natalie had come up behind her softly. "Let's go back downstairs."

"No." She shook her head violently. "No, I have to see them! Where are they?"

"They're not here, Joss —"

"They are. They're singing about Katherine. Can't you hear them?"

"Yes, I can hear them." Natalie put her arm around Joss's shoulders. "Come on down. If they want to tell us something they will."

Joss let out a sob. She had not stopped

trembling. "I can't cope with this."

"Yes, you can. You're doing fine. Come on down, out of the cold, and we'll talk about it." Firmly, she turned Joss around and half led, half pushed her down the passage toward the stairs.

It was my Lady Katherine

The little song, masked by the wind and rain, echoed in the distance as they reached the stairs.

Natalie squeezed Joss's arm. "Don't take any notice. They'll come if they want to." Leading her back into the bedroom, she went over to the bedside table and turned on the lamp. In the sudden light she could see Joss's face puffy with grief and tears.

Joss wrapped her arms around herself. "You said I was carrying his child," she whispered. "You said it was his daughter —"

"I was speaking metaphorically, Joss." Natalie kept her voice calm.

"It's Luke's. I remembered. We made love in the bathroom. That's when it must have happened —"

"Of course it did."

"It can't be his." She gestured at the empty air near the bed where Edward had stood. "That's not possible. It's not. That's obscene!"

"Joss, I said metaphorically —"

"You are saying he made love to me in the cellar —" Joss rushed on, not heeding her interruption. "He put his arms around me and he kissed me and he held me. I think I must have

635

fainted — I don't remember what happened next."

His eyes. She could remember his eyes, close to hers, full of love and compassion, the black velvet, then the touch of his hands, warm, commanding . . .

"He could have done anything —"

"Joss, calm down. He couldn't have done anything. He has no body; no real body."

"Supposing he did the same to my mother. Supposing he raped my mother!" She was rushing on now, her thoughts out of control. "Supposing —"

Forgive me, Jocelyn, but I can no longer fight your father's wishes. I have no strength left. I am leaving Belheddon, with all its blessings and its curses, but he will only let me escape if I give in. He wants Belheddon to be yours and I have to obey. If you read this letter then he will have got his way.

"Supposing he's my father!" She stared at Natalie, numb with shock.

"No, Joss. Don't even think it —"

"The women of this house. Laura, Lydia, Mary Sarah — all of them! He made love to all of them!" She sat down abruptly, her arms wrapped tightly around herself. "My mother knew. That's why she tried to send me away. She tried to break the spell! To save me! But she couldn't. He wouldn't let her!"

"The spell was very powerful, Joss. A real spell." Natalie knelt in front of her and took her cold hands in her own warm ones. Her voice was very gentle. "But we're going to break it. It's half done already. Then Belheddon will be a safe, happy, place again." She smiled. "I promise. We can do it. You can do it."

"The others couldn't." It was a whisper. Her lips were cracked and dry.

"The others didn't know how to. We do. The time is right and you aren't alone as your poor mother was. You can do it, Joss." Natalie's large gray eyes were fixed unblinkingly on Joss's. "You can."

"How?"

"We have to call him back." Natalie was trying to will some of her own strength into the woman sitting in front of her. "We have to call him back and release him so he never wants to come back."

Joss bit her lip. "He's buried at Windsor. In St. George's Chapel. I looked it up," she said slowly.

"His body may be," Natalie said firmly. "And when this is over you can go and see his tomb if you want to, but his spirit is at Belheddon Hall." She stood up and walked across to the window. Rain was slanting across the garden, pitting the lake, soaking the grass. It was almost dark. As she watched, she saw a faint flicker on the horizon.

"There's a storm coming." She turned. "Joss, we have to summon Katherine."

"Call him! In the name of Christ and the Virgin, bring him here!"

637

Her mouth was too dry; the words she was screaming were barely audible.

"Let him see what he has done to me!"

"Hush, sweeting, save your strength!"

The old woman who had been her own nurse wiped her face again with the piece of linen wrung out in rose water, soothing the sweat-soaked hair off her face with a gentle hand. She looked up at Margaret. "You should send for him, my lady. Now."

The message conveyed in the direct gaze was clear. Send now or it will be too late. Your daughter is dying.

Margaret half closed her eyes and looked away. The spell was a powerful one. It had worked well. It would not fail her now. The king was in thrall; the daughter who would hold him long after the child's mother had lost her attraction was nearly born.

*She smiled and walked across to the sideboard. Pouring a cup of wine, she sipped a little herself, then turned back to the bed. "Here, child. Drink this. It will give you strength." Raising Katherine's head a little, she held the cup to her lips, then dabbed them gently with a fine linen napkin. "There. Rest now." She bent low, putting her lips to her daughter's ear. "Remember your mother's art. You have my strength and my power, and through me, the power that lies sleeping in the ground beneath this place. With it you can do **anything**."*

The last word was a hiss of triumph as her daughter caught her hand and, convulsed with new waves of pain, began to scream again.

638

"How do we call her?" Joss was staring at the floor. She shook her head slightly, trying to rid it of the noises — the voices, echoing in her ears just beyond her hearing.

"We could try her name."

"In here?"

"Why not. I suspect this has always been the main bedroom. They could have made love here. Perhaps even in this very bed."

They both stared at it in silence.

"I don't think I can go through with this." Joss rubbed her eyes wearily.

"Yes, you can. I promise." Natalie came and knelt in front of her again. "Think of your two little boys. You can do it for them."

Joss took a deep breath. She looked up as the lightning flickered at the window again. "Yes, I can do it for them."

There was a veil of red across her eyes. Beneath her hips the red soaked into sheets and mattresses and dripped into the thick-strewn herbs. Behind the red there was darkness.

Power.

Summon the power.

Remember the words she had heard her mother cry in the black candleless undercroft of the hall, the cry that would summon the powers of darkness from the very bowels of the earth.

Shrinking back from the woman in the bed who only seconds before had been her child, the old nurse stared into the shadows of the room. The whole household was there, watching in terror.

"You," she caught the sleeve of the steward as he was slipping with the other men from the room, "call the priest and then ride for the king. Don't stop for anything or he will be too late."

"But the Lady Margaret said —" The man's face was pasty with horror at what he had heard and seen.

"This is not the time to obey the Lady Margaret. Lady Katherine's wishes rule this house now."

He nodded and, with a final glance at the bed, he slipped from the room.

For a while she drifted in and out of consciousness, then, slowly, her body began to tense preparing for its last convulsive effort to rid itself of the burden that was killing it.

Her eyes flew open and she grabbed at the hands of the woman who still dared to come near her.

Behind them the priest, his hand outstretched to form the holy cross, had begun to murmur the words designed to bring her peace.

"Per istam sanctam unctionem indulgeat tibi Dominus quidquid deliquisti —"

"Stop!" she screamed. "If God cannot help me, the devil will. The devil conjured by my mother to oversee my daughter's birth."

She half sat up, galvanized by one last burst of energy.

"Go! Go priest! I don't need you. If I die I will be buried in the devil's earth! Go!" Her voice had risen to a shriek.

"Lie back, my lady, lie back. The little one is nearly here."

The midwives had long gone, it was her own old nurse who pushed her back on the pillows, who reached amid the bloodied sheets and who at last held up the limp, half dead baby.

"It is a boy, my lady," she whispered. "A little boy."

"No!" Margaret pushed her aside. "It can't be a boy!"

"It is, my lady, a sweeting boy."

The nurse busied herself with towels from the rail by the fire, rubbing the small cold body back to life. Behind her, Katherine lay inert, her own life pouring from her.

"See, my love, see your baby." The nurse wrapped the child tightly in a blanket and tried to push it into Katherine's arms.

She opened her eyes. "No," she whispered. "No! No —"

The last word was a scream.

"I curse the man who got that child on me! I curse all men. I curse my son. He took my life from me. I curse that baby — the devil's child — and I curse my mother for her sorcery."

The hot tears trickled down her cheeks.

"I wanted to live!

"I wanted to live. Forever!"

It was my Lad-y Kath-er-ine!

The childish treble sounded in the room suddenly.

It was my Lad-y Kath-er-ine!

"Georgie!" Joss stood up. She took a deep

641

breath. "Georgie, I want to see you!"

He was a dark-haired boy, sturdy, with a scattering of small freckles over his nose. Standing near the door, he seemed very small, an uncertain shadow among deeper shadows. He grinned at Joss and she found herself grinning back.

"Do you and Sammy want to go to heaven, Georgie? To be with our mother?" She found she could speak quite steadily now.

He didn't seem to hear her. He was staring past her at the window. "It was my Lady Katherine!" he sang again, his voice more husky this time.

"Shall we call her, Georgie? Shall we call the Lady Katherine here?" she asked, but he had gone.

A flicker of lightning showed at the window, followed by a low rumble of thunder and the lights flickered.

"I'm afraid."

"So am I. So was Georgie. That song. He was trying to warn us."

"Of what? That we had got it wrong? Is it Katherine who is the killer?" Joss was still standing by the bed. She stared down at the crewelwork cover as though she could find the answer stitched into the faded wools.

"I don't think she's buried in the church, Joss. I don't think she can be buried in consecrated ground."

"Not here. You don't mean she's somewhere here?"

They stared at each other in silence. It was Joss who spoke at last. "She's under the cellar, isn't she. Oh God, what are we going to do?"

"We're going to summon her."

"Down there? In the cellar?" Joss took a deep breath. "Yes, that's the best place. I don't want her here. Oh God, Nattie, what are we going to do?"

"Come on." Natalie took her hand. "Let's get it over."

"Will Edward come down there? We need him. Katherine is the one who has killed. He never hurt anyone. He never hurt Tom or Ned, or not intentionally. He carried them. He hid them. He hid them from her." Joss's face was white with strain.

"You don't know that, Joss. We must be careful. That's all. Careful of everyone and everything."

Her jaw set, Natalie led the way to the staircase. Lying on the top step was a white rose.

Joss stopped and picked it up. She stared around the shadowy landing.

"Help us," she whispered. "Help us help her."

It was my Lady Katherine!
It was my Lady Katherine!

The high voice was barely audible now, echoing down from somewhere in the attic.

She took a deep breath and, still holding the rose, she began to walk down the stairs.

CHAPTER 44

"We can't wait here, David. We've got to go back." Luke was staring out of the window in Janet's kitchen. Janet and Lyn were making sandwiches, spreading strawberry jam on thick slices of homemade bread. "What the hell do we know about that woman? For all we know she's a complete fraud. Or worse."

David didn't bother to ask what he meant by worse. He was feeling very uncomfortable. Out there in the rain on the terrace at the Hall he had been carried away by Natalie's calm. He had believed that this was something almost mystically female, something from which men were excluded, something mysterious and movable and watery, like moonlight on the lake, something borne of thousands of years of female secrets, but now he wondered. If Margaret de Vere was a practiced sorceress — not just a witch with her herbs and her healings and her wax dolls to help with her spells and curses — what if she were more powerful than that?

Janet put down her knife. "If Lyn is willing to look after the children, I'll come with you."

They all looked at Lyn, who shrugged. "I don't mind. I'd rather stay here anyway." She glanced at David and sighed. She had admired him so much when she first met him; he was such an attractive man — but now. At least Luke had had more sense than to believe all this. David had proved himself in the long run as neurotic as Joss!

She watched from the window as they all climbed into Janet's car, then she turned back to Tom, who was cheerfully eating jam sandwiches, sitting in the old oak carver at the end of the table, his legs stuck straight out in front of him.

He looked up at her and gave her a jammy grin. "The tin man is cross," he said conversationally.

"Oh, Tom, I wish we could forget about the tin man," she said as she pulled her cup of tea, long cold, toward her. "Your mummy thinks he's real, whereas we both know you made him up, don't we. The tin man on the yellow brick road, looking for his heart."

Behind them Ned let out a gurgle of delight. He abandoned the brightly colored bunch of plastic keys he had been playing with on the hearth rug and reached for the white flower that had appeared on the floor in front of him. One by one he began to pull at the petals. Tom was watching. "Ned's made a mess," he said to Lyn.

She glanced around and let out a cry of dismay. Falling on her knees, she took the flower away from him and stared down at it. It was cold and wet, every petal perfect and unblemished. For a moment she stared down at it in her hands, then, gathering up the scattered petals, she threw it in the bin with a shudder. Behind her Ned began to cry.

The house was in darkness. Pushing open the back door, they peered into the kitchen. Luke groped for the light switch, clicking it up and down. Nothing happened.

"There must have been another power cut." He groped his way in toward the dresser. "There's a flashlight here somewhere." He couldn't find it, and as he scrabbled for matches and candles Janet went back outside for the flashlight she kept in the glove compartment of the Audi. On the doorstep she took a deep breath of the cold evening air. The atmosphere in the house had been poisonous.

None of them spoke as she handed the flashlight to David. Pushing open the kitchen door, he peered out into the passage. He looked back at Luke and gave a faint grin. "Householder first?"

Luke nodded. He was beginning to feel very uncomfortable. "Fair enough. Give me the flashlight." He pushed past him and led the way into the great hall. They stood still as Luke shone the beam around the room, up into the empty gallery, toward the fireplace, across the table and on toward the door in the far wall.

"Where are they?" Janet's voice was tremulous.

"They must be upstairs." Luke headed in that direction, closely followed by the others.

"Why are all the lights out?" Janet whispered. "I don't like it."

"Neither do I." David sounded very grim. He stopped, as Luke headed up the stairs, staring at the cellar door. The key was in the lock. He frowned. "Luke," he called softly. His voice contained enough urgency for Luke to stop. He shone the flashlight back down the stairs.

"The cellar." David pointed.

"They're down there?" Luke could feel his stomach churning uncomfortably. "We'd better look." He stepped forward and put his hand on the key. It was unlocked. Pushing the door slowly open, he peered down into the darkness. There was no sound at all.

Jimbo was parked near the main gate in his old Cortina when he saw Luke and David drive back into the house. He had been sitting there, smoking, for some time, his fingers drumming on the wheel, torn between fear and curiosity as he thought of his sister alone in the house with Joss. Tossing the stub of the cigarette out of the car window, he leaned forward and watched the taillights of the Citroën disappear among the laurels. There had been three people in the car. It was Mrs. Goodyear in the back, he was fairly sure. So Lyn was alone with the kids over at the farm. He sat for a minute deep in thought, feeling the chill of the evening air on his face from the open car window. At last he came to a decision. Winding up the window he reached for the ignition key and gunned the engine into life. There was no harm in checking that Lyn was all right — her and the boys. If she was there on her own, maybe she could do with some company. She wasn't that bad, Lyn, when he came to think about it. In fact, he grinned sheepishly to himself as he changed gear and pulled out into the lane, he could quite fancy her, if he thought about it.

On the road behind him his cigarette butt flared for a minute on the wet tarmac and then went out with a hiss.

Joss and Natalie were standing near the hole in the wall where they had found the wax figures when the lights went out.

Clinging together, they stared around in the darkness, their eyes and ears straining against a thick impenetrable blackness which seemed to wrap itself around them.

"The flashlight," Natalie whispered. "Where's the flashlight?"

"I don't know."

"Matches?"

"No."

"Shit!" She put an experimental hand out in front of her, half expecting to meet something or someone, but the darkness was empty.

"Has she done it on purpose?" Joss moved closer to her companion.

"I don't know. What we need to do is get out of here, mend the fuse, or get a flashlight and candles or a floodlight or something and then come back." She took a cautious step backward, one hand linked to Joss's, one held out in front as she slowly turned back to where she thought the arch through to the first cellar was.

Joss followed her. "It's this way. It must be.

We left the door open at the top of the stairs. There'll be some sort of light."

The movement of air behind them was so slight Joss thought she had imagined it. She stopped, her fingers digging into Natalie's arm, the hairs on the back of her neck prickling.

Natalie stopped too. Neither of them said anything; they were both listening hard.

Slowly Joss turned around. In the far corner of the cellar she could see something moving against the blackness. Her throat tightened; she could hardly breathe.

"Be strong," Natalie murmured. "We have to win."

Joss was very conscious of the huge old house above them empty, listening as they were to the silence. Panic swept over her, drenching her in cold sweat. For a moment she was sure that her legs were going to collapse under her, then she felt the steady pressure of Natalie's hand on her arm. "Deep breaths. Arm yourself with the light — visualize it all around you, light the cellar with it," she whispered. "Don't let her see you're afraid."

Her?

She could see it too now: the faintest outline of a woman's shape glowing like dim phosphorescence against the wall —

It was my Lady Kath-er-ine

The words echoed faintly in the back of her skull, a child's song, the song of a little boy, lost in the shadows of time.

"Katherine?" She found her voice suddenly. "Katherine, you have to leave this house. You have done enough here. Enough people have paid for your pain. Don't let it go on."

She waited, half hoping for an answer in the silence.

"You need to move on into the light, into happiness," she went on. Her voice had begun to shake.

"We can help you, Katherine," Natalie put in. Her words were clear and strong. "We're not here to banish you to hell. We can help give you strength to move on. Please, let us help you." Her eyes were closed; inside her head she could see her clearly, not a mad witch but a girl, scarcely more than a child, crazed with pain and grief, cheated of life by the greed and ambition of the mother she hated, killed by the child she never wanted.

"Don't hurt any more children, Katherine. They are not to blame," she went on softly. "Their fear and agony can't help you — it adds to your own. Please let us give you our blessings. Let our love and strength help you."

She took a cautious step nearer the corner of the cellar, her eyes still closed. It was Joss who was watching. The glowing outline of the figure had grown stronger. It had a shape now, clearly a slim, not very tall girl.

"Are you buried down here, Katherine? Is this where you lie?" Natalie had dropped Joss's hand and held her own out toward the spot where she sensed the girl was standing. "Shall we move you? Would you like to be buried outside in the garden somewhere? Or in the churchyard?"

They both felt the frisson, the cold shiver in the air.

"In the garden here, then. Under the sun and in the moonlight," Natalie went on. "We can do that for you, Katherine. Just show us where they buried you."

There was a long breathless silence. It is not going to work, thought Joss. She is not going to tell us. The atmosphere was stifling. There seemed to be no air in the cellar. It had been growing steadily colder, but now she felt a wave of heat roll over her. She put her hand to the collar of her sweater and ran her finger around under it, feeling her perspiration like ice.

"Where is it, Katherine?" Natalie went on. "You must give us a sign. You must show us what you want."

It was my Lady Kath-er-ine

Georgie's voice reached Joss's ears very faintly.

It was my Lady Kath-er-ine

Something dropped in the silence. It rattled on the ground like a pebble. The noise came again, then nothing more.

In the corner of the cellar the light slowly faded; in seconds it was gone.

Neither of them moved. Joss put her hand out to Natalie. "Has she gone?" she whispered at last.

"She's gone."

Natalie spun around; behind them they could

suddenly hear the sound of voices. The squeak of the cellar door opening was followed by a flash of flashlight.

"Joss? Natalie?" It was Luke's voice.

With the help of a flashlight they found Katherine's sign, unmistakable on the cellar floor. A scattering of small bricks and stones lay in the shape of an equal-armed cross on one of the old flagstones in the corner. They stood in a ring looking down at it.

"What do we do?" Luke was holding the flashlight, focusing the beam steadily on it. His skepticism had dissolved.

"We have to keep our promise. We have to dig her up and rebury her in the garden." Joss was very firm.

"What about coroners and things?"

"What about them?" She put her hands on his shoulders. "Luke, this is Belheddon's business. No one else's. Katherine belongs here. She doesn't want to be buried in the church or in the churchyard. She wants to be buried in the garden. Quietly. With our blessing and love."

"This is the woman who murdered your brothers, Joss."

"I know." Joss took a deep breath, trying to steady her voice. "She's so unhappy, Luke. She's lost. I don't believe she was really evil. She was in too much pain to know what she was doing. I think we can help her — and make Belheddon safe for children. Our children."

He shrugged. "OK. Let's go for it. I'll get a pick."

They mended the fuses first and it was in a cellar full of light that they met again, half an hour later with pickax and shovel.

"You realize this whole thing could be a waste of time." Luke gazed around them. He was feeling stronger now that the cellar was lit. "We are digging on a flash of intuition and the word of a ghost, who might or might not be imaginary."

Joss smiled tolerantly. "We're never really going to convince you, are we. Just dig."

"OK." He shrugged. Lifting the ax, he inserted the point under the edge of the flag and began to try to lever it up.

Taking turns with the ax, David and Luke finally managed to lift four flags, then they stood back exhausted. Janet had at some point left the cellar where Joss and Natalie stood, eyes riveted to the floor, and reappeared with a jug of Lyn's homemade lemonade and some glasses.

"Come on, rest for a moment," she said, setting the tray on the ground. They stood in a circle, looking down as they drank, staring at the sandy earth, aware of the acute silence around them.

It was Luke who put down his glass first. He had barely touched his drink. "Come on. Let's get it over." He picked up the spade and drove it into the soil.

"Gently, Luke. We don't know if there's a coffin." Joss put her hand on his shoulder. He straightened and looked at her for a moment, then he nodded.

"Right. Gently does it."

An hour later they had found nothing. A hole

653

about three feet deep and as much across opened at their feet.

"There's nothing here." Luke put down the spade and reached for his glass.

"There is. I'm sorry, Luke, but you have to go on."

"It could be six feet down, I suppose." David looked exhausted. There was a smear of earth across his face.

"Perhaps you could ask her, Natalie?" Janet was sitting on an old wine crate. "See if we're on the right track."

Natalie stepped forward. "Katherine?" she called. "Katherine, you see. We're trying to help you, but we must know, is this the right place?"

They all waited in silence. Joss was staring at the cavity in the wall where they had found the wax figures. Natalie's eyes were fixed on the hole where the spade stood alone, shoved into the soil as Luke stood back to pick up his drink.

"She's got tired and gone off to bed. And I think that's what I'm going to do as well."

"No. No, wait. Let's try for just a while longer, please." Joss dropped to her haunches and picked up the trowel. She dug it into the earth and heard the small chink of metal. The sound electrified the others. They turned. Luke moved closer and knelt beside her. "What is it?"

"Here." Joss lifted the trowel full of soil and ran it through her fingers. Left lying in her palm was a small gold ring.

Joss took a deep breath. "It's her message."

Luke nodded. He caught her eye and gave a rueful, private smile. He dug more carefully this time, inserting the spade almost gently, transferring the lifted earth to the steadily growing pile on the floor behind them.

They found the body at about a meter depth. There was no coffin; there were no clothes; no flesh now, just the bones, lying on a floor of earth much harder than the soft friable soil which had lain on top of them. Using the trowel, Luke lifted away as much of the earth as he could without touching the bones and they stood looking down at the skeleton before them. There were two other rings on the finger bones and a gold chain around the neck, an earth-encrusted enameled pendant lying among the narrow, fragile ribs.

It was my Lady Katherine

Joss knelt down. Her eyes had filled with tears. "Poor girl. She was so small."

"How are we going to move her?" David put his hand on her shoulder.

She shrugged. The face she raised to him and Luke was white and strained. "First we must dig the new grave."

"Tonight?"

Joss nodded. "Tonight. While it's dark. Then the sun can warm her in the morning."

Natalie offered to stay with the bones; it seemed somehow indecent to leave them alone now that they were exposed. The others went out into the garden with flashlights. Joss had already chosen the spot in her mind. It was perfect: out beyond the lake, where the wild roses tangled over the old pergola and the sundial registered the passing of the hours.

They dug the hole in the old rose bed, the earth soft and cold under the clogging November mist which had closed over the garden as the wind dropped and the rain petered away.

Joss emptied the carved cedar box from the study of its piles of old sheet music. She lined it with her own fringed scarf of rough wild silk and then on her knees lifted the skull from the earth as the others watched. The rest of the bones she picked from the soil and put them reverently into the box and with them the rings and chain and pendant, then last of all the wax dolls, still wrapped in their blue scarf from the dresser drawer, then she closed the lid at last.

Luke picked up the box and carried it slowly up the stairs.

The garden was dank and cold as they walked after him across the wet grass and under the pergola to the little grave. Puffing, he set the box down beside it. "Are you going to say something?"

Joss stood staring down. "I don't know what to say. I don't think she wants our prayers."

"She wants peace, Joss. Peace and forgiveness," Natalie murmured quietly. "Then all the other spirits here can rest too; the lost boys from all the centuries and their fathers, the poor men she cursed and hounded to their deaths in her pain and hatred."

"And the king." Joss met her eye. "What about the king?"

"I think you'll find he's already gone, Joss. You were very special to him, remember." She smiled. She would never, Joss knew, reveal what they had talked about with Edward of England, the son of York, who, had he been a man, would have fathered Joss's unborn child and who might have been her father, and her mother's father, and her grandmother's father before that, and who was, with Katherine de Vere, her ancestor by blood and true descent.

"I wish the moon was out." Joss looked down into the blackness of the hole.

"It will be, look." Janet had been the only one looking up at the sky. Behind the mist the full moon was a wraith high above the wrack. As they watched it found a gap in the drifting cloud and for a moment shone down into the garden.

David and Luke between them lowered the box into the ground and Joss and then Natalie each threw down a handful of soil. For a minute they waited as the moonlight ran light fingers over the carved wood, then as the mist returned like a veil across the garden David lifted the spade. As the first shovelful of earth poured down into the grave, they all saw the spray of white roses as the darkness returned.

It was my Lady Katherine

Muffled in the mist the voice seemed to drift across the lake.

It was my Lady Katherine
It was my Lady Katherine

Each time the voice was farther away.

They looked at each other.

"I shall miss them." Joss smiled.

Natalie shook her head. "Rascals," she said. "Let them join their mum. The only children at Belheddon should be real children."

"It's done, Joss." David had patted down the last of the earth with the back of the spade. "Are you going to put something here to mark it?"

Joss shook her head slowly. "I don't know. Perhaps." She gave a deep sigh. "I just can't believe that it's really over. That there's no more danger."

"There's no more danger," Natalie said firmly. She took Joss's cold hand. "Come on. It's time to go in. Leave Katherine to her moonlight."

Slowly they made their way back across the grass. On the terrace Joss stopped and looked back. The garden was silent.

The echoes were gone.

The Daily Telegraph
17th July 1995

*To Luke and Jocelyn Grant a daughter
(Alice Laura Katherine), sister for
Tom and Ned.*

The Sunday Times
September 1995

Son of the Sword
by Jocelyn Grant-Hibberds, £14.99

*An accomplished first novel written with wit
and pace, set largely in the author's own house
during the years of the Wars of the Roses.
Richard Mortimer and Ann de Vere tread a
heady tightrope of romance, adventure, and
near disaster which culminates in an extraordinarily satisfactory ending, leaving the reader
clinging to the edge of his chair. Highly rec-
ommended. I shall look forward to seeing more
from this author.*

AUTHOR'S NOTE

Belheddon does not exist. Nor did this branch of the De Vere family. King Edward IV had many mistresses during his lifetime. The names of the last two are unknown, and the story of Katherine de Vere, woven through this tale, is entirely fictional. Accusations of witchcraft and sorcery were made at Edward's court against both his queen and other highborn women around him, but whether these were merely political propaganda or substantiated in truth is for the reader to decide for himself or herself.

As always, so many people have provided me with help and information in the research of this book. I should particularly like to thank James Maitland of Lay & Wheeler in Colchester for his suggestions on the contents of the Belheddon cellar (any spelling mistakes in the wine names are my fault entirely), Janet Hanlon for her assistance, and Carole Blake for her attempts at keeping my characters' drinking habits within bounds! Also Rachel Hore for her editorial advice during what must have been the hottest days in East Anglia since the reign of Edward IV! I should also like to thank my son Adrian for his help with research, and Peter Shepherd, Dr. Robert Brownell, and my son Jonathan for their help in sorting out my computer crash, computer crises, and computer panic! I think I prefer to use a quill pen!

We hope you have enjoyed this Large Print book. Other G.K. Hall & Co. or Chivers Press Large Print books are available at your library or directly from the publishers.

For more information about current and upcoming titles, please call or write, without obligation, to:

G.K. Hall & Co.
P.O. Box 159
Thorndike, Maine 04986
USA
Tel. (800) 223-2336

OR

Chivers Press Limited
Windsor Bridge Road
Bath BA2 3AX
England
Tel. (0225) 335336

All our Large Print titles are designed for easy reading, and all our books are made to last.